D0585274

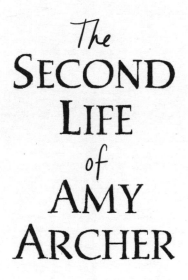

The
SECOND
LIFE
of
AMY
ARCHER

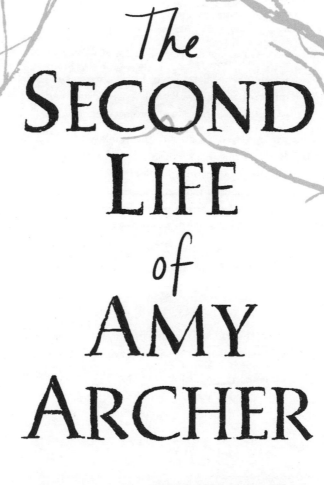

The
SECOND
LIFE
of
AMY
ARCHER

R.S. PATEMAN

First published in Great Britain in 2013 by Orion Books,
an imprint of The Orion Publishing Group Ltd
Orion House, 5 Upper Saint Martin's Lane
London WC2H 9EA

An Hachette Livre UK Company

1 3 5 7 9 10 8 6 4 2

Copyright © R.S. Pateman 2013

The moral right of R.S. Pateman to be identified as the author
of this work has been asserted in accordance with
the Copyright, Designs and Patents Act of 1988.

All rights reserved. No part of this publication may be
reproduced, stored in a retrieval system, or transmitted
in any form or by any means, electronic, mechanical,
photocopying, recording, or otherwise, without the
prior permission of both the copyright owner and
the above publisher of this book.

All the characters in this book, except for those already
in the public domain, are fictitious, and any resemblance
to actual persons living or dead is purely coincidental.

Photo of Durning Library © John Hoyland

A CIP catalogue record for this book is
available from the British Library.

ISBN (Hardback) 978 1 4091 2853 3
ISBN (Trade Paperback) 978 1 4091 2856 4
ISBN (Ebook) 978 1 4091 2855 7

Typeset by Deltatype Ltd, Birkenhead, Merseyside

Printed in Great Britain by Clays Ltd, St Ives plc

The Orion Publishing Group's policy is to use papers
that are natural, renewable and recyclable products and
made from wood grown in sustainable forests. The logging
and manufacturing processes are expected to conform to the
environmental regulations of the country of origin.

www.orionbooks.co.uk

For Mum, Sue and Ellie

&

Elsie P
who said it would be so

I

Sometimes I see her in the roundabout's blur. Hear a giggle in the squeak of the slide. But she's not really there, of course. Nor are the slide or the swings.

The council have ripped out the rickety see-saw and roundabout and replaced them with more modern playground equipment: a bucket swing, gyroscope, fountain and sand pit, traversed by platforms and zip wires. For safe but adventurous play.

They've moved the site of the playground too, shunting it to the other side of the park so it's close to the café. Parents now chat and drink cappuccinos as their children dangle, dig and spin.

But I have been robbed of the last place Amy was ever seen.

The old playground, the one Amy knew and loved, has been swallowed by smooth tarmac and marked out as courts for umpteen different ball sports. Lines and circles criss-cross the tarmac, like a dropped geometry set.

No one seems to know what the courts are for; I've never seen them being used. Not for sports, anyway. Today is no different.

Beneath a buckled, net-less hoop, a gang of boys smoke,

their heads bowed over mobile phones. They look up as I get closer to the fence. I grip the bouquet in my hand tighter. The cellophane rustles.

I avoid the boys' stares as I bend down to lean the flowers against the glossy blue railings. They're new too, straighter than the previous ones. Stronger too, I hope, capable of keeping children in.

I take off my gloves and adjust the card on the flowers. *For my darling girl. Forgive me. Love always, Mum xxx.*

I clasp my hands together and dip my head. My words are misted by the chilled air, little puffs of prayer that evaporate into nothing, just as Amy did.

I stand up, using the railings for support, and pull my gloves on. I wonder if the park staff will clear the flowers away tomorrow morning, like they did last year. Maybe they won't even last that long.

The bouquets I've seen attached to lampposts, marking the scene of fatal road accidents, remain until the stems are withered and the cellophane around them is shredded and grey. They are as much road safety warnings as acts of remembrance. My bouquet is no different, although the danger it warns of is stealthier than a speeding car and trickier for parents to explain.

At the end of the path I stop and look back. If I'd been here to turn around and look, ten years ago today, keeping watch, like a mother should . . .

One of the gang gives a sarcastic wave. The others laugh and mutter. The flowers will probably be kicked around before I'm even out of the park, or lobbed through the basketball hoops, the petals making the tarmac's geometry even more hectic.

Cold bites at my face. Frost ghosts the branches of the plane trees and makes a glistening web of the nets on the tennis courts. The clock on St Mark's church chimes ten.

I have an hour before my appointment, enough time for a coffee – but not in the park's café. I can't bear to walk past the playground, let alone sit in earshot of the children's squeals and squabbles. The scrapes and grazes, the tears and hugs that heal. That is intolerable even on an ordinary day, and today is no ordinary day.

I pull my coat up around my neck and walk towards the park gates.

The receptionist looks up as I open the door. She must be new; I haven't seen her before. Her smile is quick and efficient.

'Can I help?'

'Beth Archer,' I say, unbuttoning my coat. 'I have an appointment at eleven.'

Her eyes drop to the diary on her desk. Ragged finger-nails drag down the list of handwritten names.

'Ah, yes. Eleven o'clock with Ian Poynton.' She smiles again. 'He's our new boy.'

'Yes,' I say. 'I know.'

I've been dubious about seeing Ian. The picture on the website shows a boyish face framed by a schoolboy hair-cut. He looks too young to be qualified to do anything, let alone speak with the dead.

My doubts over his credentials feed a creeping scepticism that has dogged my annual visit over the last few years. I've shut it out because I want to believe Amy will come through to me. But I also want my hope in psychics to be proved right as much as I want – *need* – Brian's cynicism to be wrong.

I made my husband come with me the very first time I went, soon after Amy first went missing.

'If not for my sake, then for Amy's,' I said. 'She's your daughter too.'

He sat outside the room, huffing and puffing, tapping his foot on the floor, muttering about it all being a waste of time, a con. He was no better once we got inside, and refused to shake the hand of the tiny, white-haired old woman who ushered us into the room.

She introduced herself as Edna Hussey and asked us to close our hands in silent prayer as she summoned her spirit guide, Akara. Brian snorted but loosely linked his fingers.

'I'm not getting anything. Except a sense of resistance,' Edna said.

She screwed her eyes up in concentration and fiddled with the hearing aid in her left ear. Brian suggested that she change the battery. When she failed to deliver anything conclusive, he sneered that she should change the frequency too.

'That will get it working as efficiently as my bullshit detector,' he said, and walked out.

I muttered a quick apology and hurried after him. But

4

I made another appointment for the following week. And the month after that. Every month, in fact, for a year.

'If psychics had loyalty cards, you'd have enough air miles to fly around the world,' Brian would say. 'I wonder if their air miles can only be redeemed for astral flying?'

He said it was just holding me back, preventing me from moving on. My counsellor took the same line.

But I can't give up on Amy, not altogether. I let her down once before and she paid with her life, although of course her body has yet to be found. I'm not going to let her down again. If she tries to reach me from the other side, I have to be there.

If there is any one day when Amy's voice is more likely to be heard, it would be the anniversary of her disappearance, so I promised Brian I would cut back my visits and only go once a year.

'It's still one time too many,' he said. 'Just when you're starting to heal, you pick at the scab and open the wound again. I never had you down as a masochist.'

'I never had you down as a sadist.'

'*I'm* not hurting you, Beth.'

'You are if you don't let me go.'

I didn't need his permission. I could have gone without him even knowing. But the secrecy would only have made it feel grubby and sordid – as if I was doing something to be ashamed of. And I needed Brian to accept that it was part of my grieving process, even if he couldn't approve of it. My annual appointment was a grudging compromise that ate away at our marriage. One of them, anyway.

Over the years I've seen a succession of psychics. The pudgy man whose body odour soured the small room; a flint-eyed Scot who wore the same blouse and skirt whatever the weather; a former miner, breathless from nicotine and coal dust. Each of them gave me something: vague exhortations to go to America, a warning about my back or needing an eye test, jokes about doing too much housework. All of which had a kernel of truth, or seemed to have, at some point.

But none of them made contact with Amy.

'They haven't even got the decency to lie,' Brian said, as he tapped at his laptop on the kitchen table. 'Well, lie even more than they already are about being psychic.' He shook his head. 'They must know who you are and why you're there. All they need to do is say Amy's fine and is watching over you and sends her love. But they can't even do that. Or won't.' He sniggered. 'Fortune. Teller. They're well named. Counting cash doesn't have quite the same ring.'

'It's *because* they don't lie that I keep going back,' I said. 'You're right, they could easily tell me what I want to hear, build a reputation on it, but they don't. Why?'

'You tell me.'

'Integrity.'

Brian chuckled.

'From a psychic? Don't make me laugh.' He stood up and kissed me in the centre of my forehead, where my 'third eye' should be. 'Beth, the only thing they see coming is you. But as you seem to think it helps . . .'

6

It did. And it still does, although I don't know why. Whatever it is, I keep going back, a compulsive gambler who needs one more throw of the dice that might, *just might*, be the one that wins the jackpot.

Even though my faith is dwindling, I hope Ian succeeds. According to his biography on the website, his approach is modern and fresh. Maybe that's what Amy needs.

Let her be here today. Let her speak. Help me hear her.

The receptionist tells me to wait outside room twelve.

'It's just up the stairs,' she says, 'just—'

'Thank you. I know the way.'

She gives another quick smile and I turn and climb the stairs. Other people don't come back as often as I do, I think. Maybe they don't hear what they want either and have got wise to the ruse quicker than I have.

The white paint of the narrow corridor is scuffed by shoe and elbow marks – mostly mine, probably – and the thinning carpet is grubby. The chairs outside each of the rooms are empty, the doors closed.

A sign outside room twelve says there's a sitting in progress and asks not to be interrupted. Another sign instructs passers-by to be quiet.

The door opens and a young woman steps out, eyes bright and energised. She loops a scarf around her neck and tucks a strand of hair behind her ear.

'Thanks again,' she says over her shoulder, and closes the door. 'He said to give him a few minutes before you go in.'

I nod.

'He's very good,' she whispers. 'He got that I was preg-nant right away. A boy, he said.'

She screws her face up in delight. I do my best to smile my congratulations.

My eyes drop to her belly. It is flat, inscrutable. It could have just been a lucky guess, but guess or not, he's got it right. The fact of it anyway; the detail has yet to be proved.

The woman walks away, her step light. I envy her certainty, her confidence that what she's heard is true. I resent the fact that she's been told something meaningful at all.

The door opens quickly, startling me.

'Sorry!' he says. 'Didn't mean to make you jump. Come on in.'

He stands back to let me pass. He's shorter than I thought he'd be, but his eyes are as blue as they were in his picture – a glacial blue, one eye set slightly higher than the other, refracting his gaze. If any eyes can see into heaven, his can.

'I'm Ian, the newbie,' he says, sitting down at a small table and waving me towards a chair on the other side. 'Have you been here before?'

I nod.

'So you know how this works? About—'

'There are no guarantees. I know.'

My tone sounds defeated, even to me. It must sound suspicious to him, as if I'm daring him to prove that he can really do it. And I suppose I am.

Somewhere inside me I sense the shadow of doubt

darken. It isn't personal; it is not *his* clairvoyance I doubt as such, but the possibility of communion with the dead, full stop.

I twitch with irritation, angry at Brian, at Ian, at my own circumspection. Angry that, even now, I'm still hoping I'm wrong.

Ian pulls his chair in closer. His face is flawless, its skin smooth and waxy; only the faintest of lines appear when he smiles. He reminds me of a choirboy; even his voice is suitably musical. I reach into my handbag and take out my portable cassette recorder.

Ian smiles.

'I haven't seen one of those for a while,' he says. 'Most people use the digital recorders now.'

I feel old and out of touch. Vulnerable.

He leans towards me. 'Are you all set?'

I nod, and he takes my hand.

His approach isn't new, just more direct. Who's Arthur? Who's thinking of getting a new car? Why am I being shown a bunch of heather? I sense he's fishing and I have no answers to fit neatly on his hook.

'Will you take it anyway?' he says, after I give each question a shrug. Even his catchphrase is more direct than the psychics I've seen before. They just say 'I'll leave it with you', or 'Maybe its meaning will come to you later.' Ian demands a response, my participation, as though he needs the reassurance. Each time he asks if I will take it, I answer with a shrug.

He coughs and closes his eyes. His breathing is deep

9

and deliberate. Then he changes tack and talks of darkness lifting, of escaping quicksand, of problems bursting like bubbles, all delivered in a gentle, chiming tone.

He sees a 'For Sale' sign, alerts me to an important turning point in the spring but doesn't specify what it is or which year, and nags me to take more supplements to help with my apparently feeble joints.

I stop listening, nod when his tone implies I should respond and sneak a look at my watch. When he asks if I have any particular questions or issues I want help with, I say no, like I always do. He is here to interpret, not for me to prompt. He must lead for me to believe.

'Was that all right?' he asks when our thirty minutes are up. 'Helpful?'

'Thank you,' I say, switching off the cassette recorder and slipping it back into my bag.

He opens the door, smiles, says he hopes to maybe see me again. As I pass, he puts a hand on my shoulder. His head is tilted to one side and he's staring at a corner of the ceiling in a strange, unfocused way.

'She's close,' he says. 'The little girl. Close.'

The ground seems to buckle beneath me. I've waited so long for something – anything – that I could link to Amy. Now it's here I'm flushed with surprise and relief; I feel vindicated in my persistence, glad that I haven't let Amy down once again. But there is something else too: fear.

Before, I was scared she wouldn't come through to me. Now, I'm afraid of what she might say, of learning the truth.

I put my hand against the door for support.

'Who?' I say breathlessly.

He screws his eyes up, tilts his head the other way, tuning in.

'I'm being shown an E,' he says. 'No, wait ... There are two of them. A capital E and a small one.' He nods and opens his eyes. 'Sorry. It's gone. Eleanor? Elizabeth? Ellie, maybe? Will you take it anyway?'

He looks anxious, as if he needs to get something right, not for my sake, but for his.

Only he's got it wrong. If he'd given me an A instead of an E, I'd have taken it and insisted we continue the reading. But he hasn't even got one letter right. Disappointment snuffs out my flickering faith.

The smile from the receptionist is snide and knowing. As I close the door behind me, I know I will never come back here again.

Outside, the air is brittle cold. I breathe it in deeply, feel giddy from its chill and purge.

At home, there's a message from Jill on the answerphone, reminding me of her New Year's 'gathering' later on.

'Nothing fancy,' she says. 'Just a few friends, some bits from M and S and a couple of bottles of bubbly. I know you prefer to stay in. I understand why. But, well, if you fancy a change – a break – you're more than welcome.'

I delete the message. I cannot face a party, informal or otherwise. I have my own New Year's Eve ritual: flowers at the playground, a sitting with a psychic, a bout of furious housework and sobs so loud they drown out the midnight booms and bangs from the celebrations along the Thames. Doing anything else is unthinkable to me and disrespectful to Amy.

I pick up the phone and dial Brian's number, my call yet another part of my vigil. He answers within three rings.

'Beth,' he says. 'I thought it would be you.'

His intonation is flat and matter-of-fact. Joyless. I am one of his New Year's Eve chores. Like taking out the rubbish. 'How's things?'

'I'm . . .' I bite back the tears.

'Oh Beth, please.'

'Ten years, Brian, ten years.'

'I know. I haven't forgotten.'

'I didn't say you had.'

There's a pause, as if he's counting up to ten, cutting me some slack. In the background I can hear pop music and girlish laughter. His new family, excited and ready to see in yet another new year.

'Sounds like you're having a party,' I say sulkily.

'No. It's just the girls mucking about in front of MTV.'

The girls. Not just one daughter, but two. Stepdaughters anyway. Amy's replacements. I grip the phone tight. I shouldn't resent them, but I do.

Instead of dedicating a bench to Amy's memory in the park like we'd agreed, Brian bought a session in a recording studio. The girls' school choir made a CD of show tunes and classic pop, including a song by her favourite group, the Spice Girls.

'It's better than a bench,' he said. 'Amy would have loved it.'

The dedication to her in the CD booklet was lost beneath the name of the choir and the list of its members, his daughters at the top. The Spice Girls' track wasn't even one of Amy's favourites and felt more like an instruction from Brian: *Stop*.

'I'd better go,' I say. 'Happy New Year.'

I hang up before he can meet my sarcasm with some stinging comment of his own.

I go into the kitchen, switch on Radio 4 and pull on my rubber gloves. Armed with bottles of bleach and polish and swathes of sponges and cloths, I set about each room. It's a big house, more room than the three of us needed really, so definitely too big for just one. But I won't move. It keeps me close to Amy. My memories of her are as integral to the structure as the walls and ceilings.

After the divorce Brian thought I'd sell up. A handsome red-brick Victorian villa overlooking the park, just five minutes' walk from the tube and within striking distance of several good private schools – I could downsize to something more manageable, with fewer memories.

'It's the memories I want,' I said.

'You can take them with you wherever you go. Amy will always be with you.'

'And I'll be here for her.'

If – by the most unlikely, fluky of chances – Amy *is* still alive, I must make it easy for her to find me, should she care to look. So there will be no 'For Sale' sign outside my door, despite the psychic's prediction that there would be.

I spray and rub and buff until my arm aches and my brow is damp. The house smells of scented chemicals, a heady fog of lemon, lavender and pine; the Hoover adds a dusky base note of warm dust and rubber.

I sit for a moment in Amy's room, although there is no physical trace of her here. It is not a shrine; Brian saw to that. He cleared out her stuff a year after she vanished so we could begin to be free of her and find room for something else – each other maybe.

I watched as he carried out boxes and bags, weeping fitfully at Tracy Beaker books, Spice Girls posters, a tangled Slinky. I'd rescued a few favourites – her battered panda with the missing eye, the grubby Bagpuss, the bendy Postman Pat she hid so her friends wouldn't call her a baby – but the rest was swept away in an apocalyptic rush.

I made Brian promise he'd take it to charity shops in Streatham or Greenwich – anywhere but locally so we wouldn't have to see somebody else with our daughter's toys or clothes. He said that the Sue Ryder shop in Lewisham had been glad of the haul, but soon afterwards I saw a little girl in our local Tesco wearing Hello Kitty jeans with frayed hems, just like Amy's. The purple Puffa jacket looked familiar too.

I've had Amy's room decorated several times since then, and the curtains and bed linen have been replaced, but no one has ever slept in there. No one ever will. I never have guests, and there are several other bedrooms to choose from even if I did.

I wipe the mirror on the back of the door, where Amy used to watch herself pretending to be Baby Spice. All blonde and dreamy, blue-eyed and white-smiled. I see her in my reflection, although my mouth is set firm, my eyes flat and haunted by dark rings and crow's feet. My blonde hair is infused with grey, like mist in a cornfield, but lacks the elegance I've seen in other women of fifty-plus. But that discrepancy is nothing in comparison to the growing gap in my resemblance to Amy. Even my reflection is dissolving.

I put the cleaning materials back in the cupboard, rinse the rubber gloves and hang them over the side of the pristine butler sink. When I open the front door to put the rubbish bags in the wheelie bin, the sky is already dark and busy with premature fireworks. A Roman candle sends up intermittent puffs of colour; each one is announced by a soft pop of gunpowder, but reaches only a few feet into the air before flickering out – like my prayers to Amy and my calls for her to come back to me.

I shut the door, wash my hands and unwrap the tissue paper from around the creamy beeswax candle I bought from Borough Market. A match rasps against the box; the flame heats the spike of the iron candle-holder, which slides easily into the base of the candle. I carry it, unlit, into the front room and place it on the mantelpiece, next to the photo of Amy. It was taken in Zante, the year before she disappeared. She's brown as a Caramac, her smile fresh as surf. Behind her, the glint of sunlit water and the dazzle of white sand. Her cupped hands cradle a huge dead jellyfish, its translucent blubber like a melted crystal ball.

I light the candle; shadows jump around the photo. Tears prick my eyes as I kiss the tip of my finger and press it to the glass of the picture frame.

I draw the curtains, then switch on the hi-fi. The CD I was listening to earlier is still in the player. The Spice Girls' Greatest Hits. I press '4' on the remote control, then the repeat button, and sit down facing Amy's picture, watching the candlelight dance on her sun-kissed face.

Mama.

Halfway through the fourth play, there's a knock on the door.

I turn the music down, hoping that whoever it is will go away. I want to be left to my vigil. But the knock comes again. Louder. The letter box rattles.

'Mrs Archer? Are you there?'

It's a woman's voice; not one I recognise and with an accent I can't quite place. I mute the music, then wish I hadn't, as it tells whoever it is that I'm in.

'Mrs Archer. Please. It's important.'

I stand up and peer through the curtains. I jump back. The woman's got her nose pressed to the window right in front of me. I gasp and let the curtain drop.

'Sorry!' she says. 'I didn't mean to scare you.'

'Go away,' I say loudly so that she can hear me through the glass. I hope she hears my insistence too.

'But I need to talk to you.'

'If it's about swapping electricity suppliers, I'm not interested. I'm busy.'

'That's not why I'm here,' she says quickly, her voice getting louder. 'Please. It's important. It's about Amy.'

'I've got nothing to say to the papers.'

'I'm not from the papers.'

'If you're the police, then show me your badge.'

'I'm not the police either.'

'So who are you? What do you want?'

'My name's Libby Lawrence. I really need to talk to you.' She sounds anxious and impatient. 'Face to face. Without a pane of glass between us. I've come a long way. Please. This isn't something you'd want shouted through a window or a letter box.'

I pull the curtain back. Deep auburn hair frames a pale-skinned face. Her eyes are a hectic blue. They hold mine and soften with the smile on her lips as I open the window.

'Well?'

'It's Amy,' she says. 'Mrs Archer, I know where she is.'

For years I've dreamed of someone bringing news of Amy. I've dreaded it too in equal measure. Hope or heartbreak on my doorstep. The police with news of a body. Journalists chasing gossip. Ghouls come to gawp or commiserate. Sometimes I used to think the knock might be from Amy herself.

My heart thumps.

This could be the moment I've waited for. All the questions of the last ten years finally finding an answer. It might be the chance to hold my daughter once again, feel her real and solid in my arms, the beat of her heart against mine. Or the opportunity to lay her to rest, for us both to begin to find some peace.

All that agony of not knowing is suddenly swamped by fear of what I might discover. I want to know; I don't want to know. What this woman has to say could break me once and for all. I'm caught in a whirlpool of hope and horror and have nothing to cling to but myself – and that might not be enough. I fight for air, sink beneath waves of pain and sorrow, then crest the surface on a surge of hope and expectation.

I run to the front door. My trembling fingers fumble with the latch and pull the door ajar.

She's taller than she looked from the window and her face is made paler by the sliver of light falling through the doorway. Her smile falters. When she tries to speak, no words come. They desert me too. I take a deep breath. My question comes out in a desperate whisper.

'Where's my daughter?'

Libby swallows and bites her lip.

'It's a long story. You might want to sit down.'

Slowly I stand back and open the front door. The cold follows her into the hallway. She takes off her gloves and holds out her right hand. Her grip is brief but I can feel every bone in her fingers. I pull my hand away.

'I know this can't be easy,' she says. 'Believe me, it's not easy for me either.'

'Just tell me what you know,' I plead. 'Please.'

She shrugs and takes a breath.

'This is going to sound very odd. You'll think I'm mad – if you don't already.'

She takes my hand again. Once more I take it back.

'I know where Amy is.' Her voice is firm. Her tone final.

'So you've said. But . . . if her body had been found, they'd have sent the police round to tell me.'

'I haven't found her body.'

I lean against the wall, eyes closed, and pinch the bridge of my nose. I can barely find the breath or the courage to say out loud what I think she's telling me.

'I . . . don't understand. Do you mean . . .?' My head swims with impossible promise.

Libby nods imperceptibly.

'That's right, Mrs Archer. Amy is alive.'

2

I remember the sudden rush of darkness, the sense of Libby's arms around me, the moth-soft flutter of her hands about my face. I hear the thud of her foot as she kicks the door shut, her quick breaths as she manoeuvres me along the hallway and into the give of the sofa.

When I come round, she's standing in front of the fireplace, gazing at the photo of Amy. She picks it up and smiles.

'Put that down,' I say.

Libby turns and puts the picture back on the mantelpiece. I struggle to sit up and she raises her hand, like a policeman stopping traffic.

'Stay where you are for a while. Just in case. Can I get you some water?'

She's out of the room and into the kitchen before I can answer. I hear cupboards being opened and closed, the rattle of glasses and the splash of a running tap.

'Here you go.'

She helps me sit up and puts the glass in my hands. The water is tepid and tastes metallic.

'Are you okay?' Libby says, sweeping hair from my face. I flinch and she takes her hand away.

'Sorry.' She stands up and moves to the window. 'I've been agonising about how to tell you about Amy for some time . . . I wasn't sure if I could bring myself to tell you at all.' She screws her eyes up and sighs. 'But she insisted. She's been so . . . unhappy. Angry. I couldn't sit back and watch her suffer any longer . . . Mind you, what happens once I've told you could be even more painful. For me anyway.' She bites her lip. 'Well, it's done now. For better or worse. Sorry if it came out too bluntly, but . . . there's only one way to say it really.'

'It's what you said that matters, not how you said it.' I sip some water, fix my eyes on hers. 'Amy is alive? Are you sure?'

She nods and takes the glass from me.

I sink back into the sofa. All the pain of the last decade swarms around me. My disbelief that my daughter had vanished. The growing certainty of it. The endless what ifs and recriminations. The wish that I'd done things differently that day. The justifications for letting Amy go out.

Most painful of all is the aching regret for all the things I didn't say, all the things we'd never had the chance to do together. All the anger and resentment. The grief.

But the shock has blocked my tears and I blink, dry-eyed.

'But . . . but how?' I put my head in my hands. It feels heavy with questions. 'Where's she been? What happened to her? Why didn't she get in touch? Where is she now?'

'One thing at a time, eh? For my sake, as much as yours.' Libby's body tenses and her eyes drop to the floor.

'*Your* sake?'

She swallows hard. Bony fingers clench and flex.

'All this affects me too,' she says flatly.

'*I'm* her mother,' I say, indignation making me sit up on the sofa. 'You're just the messenger.'

Libby's eyes flash with anger. She takes a breath as if to spit out some words but changes her mind.

'Tell me,' I say, leaning forward.

She runs her fingers through her hair.

'Look, what I have to tell you isn't an easy thing to understand.' She sighs. 'It will change everything. For all of us.'

She looks back at the photo of Amy on the mantelpiece.

I deliberately chose a picture as far removed as possible from the 'official' one used by the police in their appeal to the public for information. Her smile in that one was more studied, self-conscious, the single plait of blonde hair lustrous against the green of her school uniform jumper, the knot in her tie a neat 'V'. It appeared in the papers and over the shoulders of newsreaders, on posters in supermarkets. It is seared into the nation's consciousness, a benchmark for careless motherhood, a warning to children everywhere. It is no longer just a picture of my little girl.

Just thinking of it sets off the memories. Our pleas for her to get in touch, the assurances that she wasn't in any trouble. After a week with no news, a doppelgänger in pink tracksuit bottoms, headband and tiger print fleece ghosted Amy's last known movements for the press and television cameras.

Increasingly concerned, the police said. Someone knows where she is. No piece of information is too small. The tears on my face flickered in the strobe of press conference cameras as a blank-looking Brian held my hand. Amy's face stared out from the enlarged photo, her features pixelated, as if in the first stage of decay.

'You need to see this,' Libby says.

She reaches slowly into her coat pocket, like a magician pulling a rabbit from a hat, and takes out a pink photo album. She flicks it open and thumbs through the clear plastic sleeves inside.

'Here,' she says, passing it to me with a slow reluctance, as if she might never get it back.

It's a picture of a girl with startling blue eyes and a hesitant smile, her thick blonde ponytail throttled by a leopardskin band. Skinny arms dangle by her sides, the pink hoodie hot against the tight white leggings.

I feel my blood drain away. A flash of recognition. Of recollection. Of *what was*.

'Where did you get this?' My voice is hushed, almost reverential.

'I took it. At a friend's barbecue in Manchester.' She turns the photo over and points at the date written on the bottom in black block capitals: July 2009.

My hand is shaking as I bring the photo closer to my face.

'But this girl's not even a teenager! Amy would have been twenty this year.' I look up. Anger and disappointment choke me. 'I don't know who this is, but I'm telling you now, it is *not* my daughter.'

'It's Amy, I swear. If you'll just let me explain—'

'No! I don't know who you are or what you want, but you're sick. Depraved. What have I done to you, to anyone, to deserve this? Get out of here.' I throw the picture at her and stand up. 'Now! Or I'll call the police.'

I'm surprised at my own strength as I push her out of the room, along the hallway and through the front door. I slam it behind her, lock it and sink to the floor racked by hard, dry sobs.

Libby bangs on the door.

'But you've got to listen,' she whines. 'Please. She's here. Right along the street. I'll get her. Mrs Archer! Don't lose your daughter all over again.'

I hear her footsteps run along the garden path, the squeak of the gate.

'Esme! Esme!' she calls. 'Come here, quickly. Esme!'

I freeze behind the door, swallow a choke.

A capital 'E' and a small one, Ian had said. *Ellie, maybe?*

He'd said she was close, too. *The little girl. Close.* And here she is, Esme, right at my door.

Whoever she is, I have to see her, not just because of some as yet unexplained connection to Amy, but because her name – her presence – is the only prediction I've ever had from a psychic that has come true. I stand up, unlock and open the door.

Libby stands on the street side of my gate, flanked by the tall yew hedge on either side of it. She's waving to someone, calling them on.

I hear footsteps on the other side of the hedge, then

some words I can't quite make out. Libby moves to the left, vanishes behind the hedge. A girl steps into view from the right.

She's as tall as Amy was, but any other telltale signs are lost beneath her shiny silver Puffa coat. Her silhouette glows in the yellow street light; the headlamps from a passing car cast a ghostly nimbus. Her shadow flits across the garden and vanishes.

I put my hand against the wall, will my heart not to burst, try not to succumb to the shock, the impossible, illogical hope that this is Amy finally come home. She stands motionless at the gate, her face lost in the hood of her coat. Libby says something to her and she turns her head. Her profile is indistinct, misted by white puffs of breath.

Breath. She's breathing. Alive.

'Amy?'

The name falters from my mouth. She walks towards me, slowly, my heartbeat louder with her every step, louder still as she lifts her hands to pull back her hood.

I'm too scared to look. Scared of what I might see. Scared of what I might not.

The hood slips back.

Her hair is loose. Long and blonde. It falls around her face like a veil. She scrapes it back and her sweetly pink lips push into a tentative smile. The blue of her eyes is a shade or two short of azure, their expression vaguely sad and enquiring, yet alive and excited.

'Hello, Mum,' she says.

I catch my breath. Feel confusion creep across my face like a stain. It isn't Amy. Not exactly. But, but . . .

There *is* something familiar about her. Something altered, like when a deep tan would make a stranger of Amy, or when illness pinched her features, shifting their symmetry off kilter.

The similarity is unsettling, slowly overwhelming me until my legs give under its weight. I sink to my knees, see my hand reaching out towards her, wanting to touch her to prove that she's real, but scared my touch might make her vanish, like a toddler bursting a bubble.

I'm powerless to resist as the girl runs towards me and presses her cheek against mine. I catch a rush of almonds about her, sweet and heady. I breathe in her scent, feel the firmness of her body against mine.

Amy. My Amy. She's solid. Real. Here.

Her proximity winds me. Instinct flutters, tentative but thrilling. I want to fight it – *she can't be Amy, isn't Amy* – and yet, and yet . . .

Libby walks down the path towards us. Her expression is hard to fathom. Relief. Regret. Sympathy. Jealousy.

'We need to talk,' she says, her tone half conciliatory, half begrudging.

I start to nod, then catch myself. This is ridiculous. Impossible. Capable of finally tipping me over into the madness I've fought off for so long. This girl is too young to be Amy, and my desperate wish for her to be my daughter is not enough to make it so. An illusionist's trick only works if the stooge is halfway to believing in the first place, so they see what the trickster wants them to see. As much as I want this girl to be Amy, I know that she can't be; logic ruptures my dream.

'No.'

I push the girl away from me. She looks up, her startling blue eyes wet, her gaze reproachful.

'Get away from me!' I hiss. 'You are *not* my daughter.'

'But Mum . . .'

How I have longed to be called Mum again. To have that label. That connection. But not like this, from the mouth of a stranger. The word sounds ugly and false, taunting. They sound beguiling and intoxicating too.

'Don't you dare call me that,' I say.

But now I've heard it once, I ache to hear it again.

'Mrs Archer, please,' Libby pleads, placing a hand on the girl's shoulder. 'She's just a child. She's been through so much to get to this point. So have I. Please . . . go easy on her. I'm begging you . . . one mother to another.'

I blink.

'She's . . . she's *your* daughter?' I say.

Libby nods and blots her tears with a coat sleeve.

'Please, if you'll just listen—'

'No,' I say, throwing my hands up. 'You said yourself she's your daughter. She can't be mine too. How could she be? And anyway, she's too young.'

'She's the same age as Amy.'

'As Amy *was*. Or has she been in a time warp? Overlooked by the last ten years?' Sarcasm drips from me.

'You're closer to the truth than you think,' Libby says.

27

'Get out!'

I nudge the girl away and she stumbles down the door-step and on to the ground.

'Mum!' she wails. 'Don't send me away. I *am* Amy. I'm your little girl. The one who did this. Remember?' She scrambles to a corner of the doorstep and points to a scratched mosaic tile. 'See?'

Her finger traces two faint and shaky letters etched into the tile: AA.

'Amy Archer,' she says. Her finger glides to the monogram on the neighbouring tile. 'DB. Dana Bishop. My best friend! You slapped us both on the legs for doing this.'

I gasp, unable to speak, my heart rushing.

The girl stands up, pushes past me and peers into the hallway. Her face lights up with recognition.

'That statue on the shelf,' she says. 'The little boy with the fishing rod. Dad got that for you for Christmas. Only he broke it one day when you were out so we dashed to Oxford Street to get another. They only had one left. Dad said it was a second. I laughed and said it was our second one too, but that's not what he meant. You look. It's got some colour missing on its back heel. Dad said you'd never notice the difference, and you didn't.'

I step inside and pick up the figurine. My hands are shaking. I'm half hoping the heel isn't discoloured but appalled and excited by the hope that it is. I hesitate to turn it round. The phlegm colour is consistent – apart from a splodge of white on the left heel.

It could have been like that from the start; I never really

looked that closely, never really liked it. Even so, I need both hands to put it safely back on the shelf.

'I . . . I don't understand,' I say. 'It's just . . .'

'What?' Libby says, stepping into the hallway. 'Coincidence? It would be easier for all of us if it was. But there's more to it than just a lucky guess.'

'That's exactly what it is,' I say, nodding my head for emphasis.

'No it isn't!' the girl says, tears brimming in her eyes. 'I promise. I wouldn't lie to you. You always told me it was wrong to lie, didn't you? And I never did. You've got to believe me, Mum.'

'I told you not to call me that,' I say, forcing my eyes from her tear-streaked face. I always hated to see Amy crying, and this girl's tears look and sound like hers. It's all I can do to stop myself putting my arms around her and telling her it will all be all right.

'Even someone good at lucky guesses runs out of luck at some point,' Libby says, shifting her weight so that she is standing firm and upright. 'Esme won't.'

'Ask me something, Mum,' the girl says. 'Anything you like. I bet I get it right.'

'This isn't a game!'

'I know. And I'm not playing. Honest.'

Libby tilts her head to one side, as if daring me to take the challenge but hoping that I won't. I close my eyes, pinch the bridge of my nose. Playing along will bring this nonsense to an end and they will have to leave me to my vigil for Amy. The *real* Amy.

'All right. What was my husband's nickname for me?'

'Which one?' the girl says, without hesitation.

Her nonchalance rocks me as much as her knowing I had two nicknames. Brian would call me Pookie when he was drunk, wanted sex or to get his own way, but most of the time he called me Dabs. It was meant to be light-hearted, but it had a quiet criticism. Dabs. Fingerprints. Shorthand for stop interfering and leave me alone.

I'm so surprised she knows there were two names, it barely registers when she gives them both correctly.

'Another lucky guess?' Libby says, her eyebrows raised as if daring me not to believe what I've heard.

The girl gives a relieved smile and nods towards me.

'Next question,' she says.

'How did Amy break her leg?'

Again there is no hesitation in her answer, no trace of doubt in her voice.

'I didn't. But I broke my *arm* when me and Dana were climbing the trees behind the tennis courts in the park. I fell. Dana ran home to get you.'

Her eyes shine. At first I think it is defiance, but there's something else too: a plea to be accepted.

I bite my lip, bend down and look into her eyes. They are the same colour and shape as Amy's; speaking eyes, I always called them. Now they are even more eloquent, shaded by a nuance I do not understand and have to struggle to resist.

'What happened to you?' I say.

'*You?*' Libby says. 'Does that mean you believe her?'

I ignore her, keep my eyes on the girl and repeat my question. Frowns cloud her face.

'I . . . can't remember exactly,' she says. 'But I think I must have died.'

Her words rip into me. Although she isn't Amy – *she can't be* – hearing my worst suspicions confirmed by a mouth that looks so much like Amy's is too much for me to bear. I'm torn between holding her to me and pushing her away.

'I'm sorry. I don't believe in ghosts.'

'Esme's not a ghost as such,' Libby says, putting her arm around the girl's shoulders. 'She's Amy. Reincarnated.'

The clock in the hall strikes midnight.

Balls of sparks and embers burst through the sky, exploding with a roar that makes the ground shake. Light and darkness chase each other across the sky, into the park. The spindly fingers of the bare-boned trees stretch into the light until they are lost in the blackness once more.

In the hinterland of shadows I catch heart-stopping flashes of Amy. In between, I see Esme's face looking up at me, wide-eyed, beseeching, happy.

I feel her rush past me and into the hall. I'm too shaken to stop her as she darts into the front room for a few seconds, then reappears, bolting up the stairs.

'I want to see my room!' she squeals.

Libby steps into the hall, slams the door behind her and runs after Esme.

'Esme! Please,' she calls. 'You promised. We've got to do this slowly.'

But Esme doesn't stop. She turns right at the top of the stairs without hesitation, making straight for Amy's room. I hear a door open; a yelp of delight is quickly followed by a grunt of disappointment.

I stand blinking and immobile in the hallway, resting my hand against the wall for support. Confusion swarms and I struggle to catch my breath. Esme shouts down the stairs.

'You changed my room! It's like I never lived here.'

I push myself away from the wall, gulp in air and climb the stairs as quickly as I can.

'Please. Stay out of there, I beg you.'

Libby is standing at the bedroom door, as if scared of intruding. I squeeze past her and see Esme lying face down on the bed, one hand punching the pillow, the other throttling the threadbare Bagpuss. The drawers in the chest are open and the wardrobe doors ajar.

My indignation at seeing Amy's room being violated is fused with the shock of a living, breathing blonde girl lying on her bed. The combination roots me to the spot.

'Everything's gone!' Esme sobs into the duvet. 'Where are my posters? My CDs? All my clothes? You've painted the room. I don't even like beige.' She looks up. 'It's like you couldn't wait to get rid of any sign of me.'

'Esme, please,' Libby says. 'I'm sure it wasn't like that. Let's all calm down, eh?'

Esme turns over and sits up, her face scrunched by tears and anger.

'How could you do it, Mum?'

I sense Libby wincing as much as I do.

'I ... didn't know,' I say in a whisper. 'I couldn't keep ...'

I can barely believe I'm trying to explain myself, but her outrage is just an echo of mine when Brian cleared the room. Guilt makes me flounder.

'At least you kept this,' Esme says. She sweeps Bagpuss into her arms and smothers it with kisses. 'You got me this when I had chickenpox.'

She's right. I find myself nodding, mouth open but mute. Esme scoots along the bed and rests her back against the wall, cradling the toy on her knees. I see Amy – sick, vulnerable, in need of my care – and shudder.

'I hated chickenpox,' Esme says. 'Not because they were scratchy but because they were spots. I wanted stripes. Like Bagpuss.'

She's right again. Her accuracy rocks me on my heels. She can't possibly remember these details and yet they fall from her lips so easily. How can she know these seemingly trivial but incredibly personal things? Her knowledge is shocking, terrifying and too, too precise. I'm as scared of who Esme is as much as I am scared of who she might be. It's impossible, ludicrous, but ...

'Let's go downstairs, shall we?' Libby says, taking my arm. 'It might be easier for all of us if we talk there.'

Esme leads the way into the front room and sits down on an armchair, Bagpuss clutched to her chest. Her eyes dart around the room, greedy and inquisitive, as if doing a 'spot the difference' puzzle. Most of it has changed – the decor, carpet and sofa – but her eyes seem to rest on the things that have stayed the same: the worn patina of the coffee table, the pewter figure of a Georgian flower seller, the broad sweep of the windows, the glossy black fire grate.

What holds her attention, though, is the photo of Amy on the mantelpiece. She smiles.

'I loved it in Zante,' she says. 'Except for the jellyfish. And the sea urchins. Dad had to pee on my foot to stop it stinging.' She shudders at the thought and frowns. 'Where is Dad?'

'He's ... we're not ...' I shake my head. Brian is not *her* father. Unlike her, I don't have to explain anything. My tone hardens. 'So you know all about the little things, but not about my husband and me? I don't understand. Surely your ... supernatural powers ...'

I reach for the sofa with my hand and slowly lower myself into it, not taking my eyes from Esme.

'I don't think it works like that,' Libby says, taking off her scarf and unzipping her coat. 'Not that I'm an expert on reincarnation, of course. But I have done some reading around it since Esme convinced me who she really is.' She coughs drily. 'I think I knew even before she was born that she was different. But I didn't know why ... not for definite. Not until a few months ago.' She coughs again. 'It wasn't easy. It still isn't. Took a while to sink in. It will be the same for you.'

'Yes, I suppose it will. I mean ...'

Libby puts her coat and scarf on the back of the sofa and sits down next to me.

'Look, I know this is hard,' she says. 'Believe me, I've been there.'

'*Believe you?* I . . . How can I? Reincarnation? It's impossible.'

'There are millions of Buddhists who'd say differently. They build their whole lives around their belief in it.'

'Maybe faith makes fools of us all.'

I sound like Brian when he scorned my trust in psychics. But psychic powers at least seem possible; science hasn't explained away strange phenomena, not entirely. It hasn't proved them either. In between there is room for manoeuvre. For interpretation. Hope.

There is nothing to prove the possibility of reincarnation. But there is nothing to debunk the idea either. Not conclusively. Not as far as I know, anyway.

The subject cropped up at a dinner party I went to years before Amy was born. Someone said that reincarnation was impossible because if everyone who'd ever lived on the planet was able to come back, there wouldn't be enough room for them all. Someone else suggested they took it in turns. The notion of a great celestial waiting room brought hoots of derision.

Esme spots the box of the CD I was playing when Libby first knocked at my door.

'Yay! The Spice Girls!' She stands up and grabs it. 'Can I listen to it?'

'Not now, love,' Libby says. 'Me and Beth need to talk.'

'I'll take it up to my room, then.'

'No,' I say. 'I want you to stay out of there.'

Esme grimaces like Amy used to when she couldn't get her own way, a mix of petulance, 'poor me' and resignation.

Then, the flash of guile, a gift for negotiation that Brian said marked her out as a future politician.

'Can I listen on those headphones, then?' she says, nodding at the set tucked into a gap in the bookcase.

At least it means I can keep an eye on her and she won't be able to interrupt. For the next hour she sits in a chair, miming the words, twitching with suppressed dance moves. Like Amy used to. I shut the thought out and keep my head turned away from her while Libby tries to explain what all this is about.

'The Spice Girls were Amy's favourite too, weren't they?' she says, wriggling further back into the sofa.

'Yes, but that's not unusual. It doesn't prove anything.'

'No, but it *is* unusual for a young girl today to like the Spice Girls rather than, say, Lady Gaga – although she likes her too.' Libby sighs. 'They were all about girl power. Which is what this is all about, I suppose, one way or the other. Girls, our girls. And power – inexplicable, unearthly power.'

She says she was never aware of it before, but looking back, its faint pulse was there from the start. From the moment Esme was conceived.

'I was only sixteen. Or about to be. When I was a kid, I used to hate having my birthday on New Year's Day. Everyone was always partied out and suffering from the night before. It was so quiet. Dead. Boring. But that changed the older I got. Suddenly the parties on New Year's Eve were all for me.'

Never more so than in 1999, it seems, when the last day of the old millennium put her on the brink of a notable rite of passage. At the stroke of midnight she would become – officially – more adult than child, and rowdy crowds around the entire world would celebrate it with her.

A group of her school friends were spending New Year in Edinburgh, and she'd nagged her parents into letting her go too.

'We dumped our bags in a dreary bed and breakfast near Leith and spent the rest of the day crawling from bar to bar. I was well gone by the time we got to Princes Street. People all around us just kept passing bottles along. Vodka, champagne, cider. You name it, I had it. My head was fizzing. The boy beside me was dead generous. The schnapps in his bottle burned as it slid down my throat.'

She can't recall the boy's name, only that his eyes were bright, his skin pinked by cold, his voice and laughter warm.

'I was pretty smitten, but I was so pissed, everyone looked good. I felt good too – until the booze and the heat and the press of the crowd caught up with me. I had to get out.'

The boy took her by the hand and led her clear of the crowds. They ended up back in his hotel room overlooking the castle and the melee on Princes Street.

'I'd sobered up a bit by then. The Edinburgh air is as effective at clearing heads as its whisky is at clouding them.

Me and schnapps boy ended up in bed.' She leans towards me, hands on knees, frowning.

'It was my first time, but I'd been on the pill for a while, just in case. *And* he had a condom too. I used to think we were just unlucky. Now I know nothing could have stopped me getting pregnant. Despite our precautions, the odds were stacked against us.'

She took a deep breath and went on.

'We made love as the countdown to midnight began. Outside, the cheers and whistles grew. The crowd chanted. Ten, nine, eight . . . Then, boom!'

The room flickered blue and white, caught in a schism between light and dark. The sky exploded with techni-coloured shrapnel.

Libby was unaware that inside her, a subtler, quieter explosive had detonated, its echoes and aftershocks palpable and permanent.

Listening to her account of Millennium Eve makes my own memories of it roll.

I have played that night back in my head so frequently it is worn and faded, like an old film. The memories jump and push, rush in and over each other until I can no longer tell where one ends and the next begins. Sometimes I wonder if a detail I feel certain of actually happened at all, while others I'm sure I've imagined seem horribly real.

I remember watching the new millennium creep around the world on the television. As grass-skirted natives in Vanuatu played salutes on sea conches, I remember the crack and fizz of an ice cube dropped into my cheeky gin and tonic. The tang of a salted pretzel on my tongue.

I remember the irritation in Brian's voice when I rang him at work to remind him he was only working a half-day.

'And please don't forget to pick up some champagne,' I say. 'We can't show up at your biggest client's party empty-handed.'

'I haven't forgotten,' he says, tutting. 'I can follow simple instructions, you know.'

'Right. You won't leave it too late, will you? The traffic's going to be mad, what with all the diversions around Parliament and along the river.'

'We're nearly done,' he says tersely. 'I'll be back in plenty of time. It's only Putney, for God's sake.'

'No, it's Richmond. Why don't these things ever stay in your head?'

I remember the clock on the kitchen wall showing ten past one. I remember running through my checklist of things I still had to do: finish cleaning the house, put the laundry away, bath, do my hair and make-up, sew a button back on to my party dress, iron Brian's shirt, cook a light supper of tuna steaks, basil and tomato, wrap the luxury chocolates I'd bought from Borough Market to give to the party hostess. I remember thinking it was just as well Amy had a sleepover at Dana's, as I didn't have time to worry about getting her tea or watching over her to make sure she ate it.

I remember I used my teeth to sever the thread securing the button to my dress. That the 'snap' resonated in my head and the needle pricked my palm. I remember it was half past two, the time I'd agreed with Dana's parents that one of them would pick Amy and Dana up from the playground and take them home for the sleepover.

I remember the pewter light of dusk through the window as I cleaned the bathroom, in readiness for my long, bubbly soak. I remember rubbing the bath's ledge vigorously, the way I caught the pumice stone and sent it flying, the spider's-web crack in the bathroom mirror. I remember lying in the bath and thinking it was just as well I wasn't superstitious, as I could do without seven years' bad luck. That I could get a new mirror in the January sales.

I remember the bang of early fireworks, the moment-ary glare in a rapidly darkening sky. I remember my anger growing like a sting from a nettle, as Brian still wasn't home.

I remember the phone ringing at four fifteen and my sharp tone as I answered it with 'What's the excuse this time, Brian?' I remember the awkward pause before the voice at the other end of the line said that it was Mrs Bishop and asked if Amy was still coming to the sleepover.

'She's not there?' I said.

'No. Dana says they had a row, so I reckoned maybe Amy weren't coming no more.'

'You didn't pick her up?'

'There weren't no need. Dana came home and said Amy was gonna go home too. God knows what the row was about, but right now, Dana says she never wants to see Amy again.'

I wonder if those words, tossed out in temper, haunt the Bishops as much as they still haunt me.

I remember the sudden shock of the cold as I went out into the street to see if Amy was coming. I remember a passer-by with a bottle and a party hat smiling and wishing me happy New Year. That I barely mumbled the same thing to him.

I remember the black void beyond the open park gates, my fear of what might lie in the bushes I would have to pass to get to the playground. I remember thinking that Amy might be scared too. I remember my calls across the park being lost in the bangs and whizzes of fireworks and the celebratory blasts on car horns.

I remember coming home to get a torch from the kitchen drawer and picking up the phone instead. The call being diverted to Brian's voicemail reassured me he was on his way home on the tube. Or ignoring me as he downed a pint with his colleagues in a pub.

I remember my phone calls to Amy's other friends, working through the names like a teacher at registration, ticking them off in my head. I remember their parents, their assurances that Amy would turn up, to give her a little bit longer, that kids always lose track of the time.

I remember my finger hovering over the '9' on the phone's handset, scarcely believing I was considering pressing it three times. I remember thinking it was futile. That I was overreacting, wasting police time. She'll turn up the instant I call them, I thought, and tut at me for being such a stress-head.

People all over the world were watching the clock, but no one watched it as closely as me. Time was leaden. Laden with a desperate dread. I remember the pop of boiled-dry pans, the acrid smoke. Telling myself not to worry or panic about Amy, that there was a perfectly reasonable explanation. I remember wishing I could imagine what that might be.

I remember the thud of my heart at the sound of a key in the lock, how disappointed I was to see Brian, how his beery breath filled the hall.

'Don't look at me like that,' he snapped. 'So I've had a few drinks. Big deal. It's New Year's Eve, for fuck's sake. The turn of the century. Of the *millennium*. And anyway, we're getting a cab to the party.'

I remember him glaring at me as tears welled in my eyes.

'Now what?' His face froze. 'Oh shit! The champagne. I'll go and get it now.' He turned and fumbled with the door latch. 'Christ, Beth, it's really not worth getting worked up about. It's only champagne.'

'It's Amy,' I said. 'She's not come home.'

'She's at Dana's, isn't she?'

I remember being struck that he'd at least managed to remember that part of the arrangement. How the thought triggered my tears. I remember how strange it was to be in his arms again, the clamminess of his cheek, the stench of residual smoke.

He said to take it easy, give her a bit longer. I remember I found his calmness comforting, was reassured when he said he'd go out and look for her. The hero I once thought he was, back and fighting my corner.

'I'll come too,' I said.

'No, stay here in case she comes home.'

I remember going from room to room like I'd done in the games of hide and seek she loved so much as a toddler. I called her name from the bedroom windows, bit back tears when I got no reply.

I remember that Brian seemed to be gone for hours, but that was probably just time playing tricks, that night when every second lumbered with a heavy significance.

I remember how I ran downstairs when I heard him come home, his ghastly pallor, the fear dancing in his eyes, the way his voice didn't sound like his.

'I think we'd better call the police.'

I remember how small the phone looked in his hand, how reassuringly inconsequential. How until he spoke into it we were unknown to the police. That once he'd put it down the world felt darker.

I remember the sibilant hiss of the police radios, the way the policemen dropped their heads to talk into them. They nodded understandingly when I struggled to picture what Amy was wearing, and told me to take my time.

I remember them asking if there was anyone else she might be with, anywhere else she might go, if everything had been okay at home. I remember I didn't look up when I assured them everything was fine.

I remember disbelief seeping through me as I went through the photo albums to find them a decent picture. A recent one, they said, close up, head and shoulders only, if possible. I remember thinking that none of it was actually happening, and thumbed the pages without really looking at them until Brian took over and pulled out her most recent school picture.

'She looks like a bright girl,' one of the policemen said.

'That's right,' Brian said, 'not the sort that would get herself into any trouble.'

'Try not to worry,' the policemen said as they put their caps on in the hallway.

I remember that midnight struck as they opened the door. I remember the cacophony of fireworks on the river, like the earth folding in upon itself. I remember my terror, willing the noise to stop. And when it did, I remember that the silence was worse.

At that precise moment, according to Libby's explanation, time rocked and rolled on the cusp between now and then, shaking out the spirits of the last thousand years, making room for those to come. Amy and Esme were caught in the churn.

That was the moment when they snagged on each other, when Amy's soul was wrapped up in Esme's body. When the essence of Esme was fused with the spirit of Amy.

When two became one.

By the time Libby finishes, we're both crying, not for each other but for our different memories of the evening that changed our lives so completely. She stands up, wiping her eyes, and says she can't take any more right now and can't imagine I can either. Everything is muffled and distant, as if I'm in a separate room.

I don't want them to stay but I don't want them to go either. I have too many questions, too many doubts, none of which they can answer satisfactorily or soothe. It's just a fabulous story in its truest sense, dreamt up by some warped individual with a taste for the macabre and a daughter with a striking resemblance to mine.

Esme hijacked in the womb by Amy! It's laughable. Beyond ridiculous. Beyond belief. And yet I can't discount it as completely as I'd like to. Esme's physical resemblance to Amy could just be coincidental, but her knowledge of the minutiae of Amy's life is too exact to be random or accidental.

And my heart. *My heart.* The way it skips and sinks whenever I look at Esme. Her expressions, her smile, the way she danced to the Spice Girls, the light in her eyes. I recognise them all and each of them tugs at instincts I thought I'd forgotten.

Libby is right. We all need some time to gather our thoughts, although I doubt there is enough time in eternity for me to collect all mine and put together an answer that spells anything other than madness.

When Libby writes her mobile number on a pad, her hand moves in slow motion.

'We go back to Manchester in a few days,' she says. I don't actually hear the words, just see them on her lips. 'It's up to you what happens next.'

She mimes to Esme to stand up and take off the headphones. Esme is reluctant to let go of Bagpuss, but Libby takes it from her hands and drops it on the sofa. Esme's lip trembles as she turns and waves goodbye, not with her whole hand, from side to side, but palm up, moving just the top half of her fingers, like Amy used to. My own hand moves slowly towards my mouth. I wonder if she thinks I am waving back instead of just trying to hold in a gasp. I wonder if I am too.

After they've gone, I fizz with restless energy. I ricochet from room to room, plunging in like I'm looking for something, certain that it's there, only to find that it isn't. That I can't even remember what it was I was looking for. All I see is disorder and dust, squashed sofa cushions, things not where they should be.

I pummel cushions, adjust the position of Amy's photo, think about putting Bagpuss in the washing machine. The dusters and polishes come out again.

When we first got together, Brian found it endearing that I'd try and solve any problem or upset by reaching for the contents of the cleaning cupboard. The balm of scented aerosol sprays was better and cheaper than hard drugs or alcohol, he used to say. But his amusement turned to bemusement and irritation at living in a chemical fog and being afraid to leave anything slightly out of place.

'It's obsessive,' he said. 'A bit of dirt never hurt anyone. The reverse actually. We need it to maintain a good immune system.'

I didn't care and took no notice. Vigorous dusting and washing blunts the angst, releases endorphins and keeps the house spotless – if only for a while.

In the front room, I pick up the wireless headphones Esme was wearing. When I go to turn them off, I notice the switch is already in the off position. For a moment I think she must have turned them off herself when she got up to go. Then I notice the display on the hi-fi system; the CD was paused just thirty seconds into track one. For all her twitchy dance moves, lip-synching and head dips, Esme was listening to every word Libby and I said.

I feel foolish, vulnerable, violated. But her deception has backfired; whatever her ploy has gained her, it has undermined what little trust I had in her. Amy would never have been so sneaky.

I move over to the table where I keep my computer and jolt it into life with an accidental touch of my hand against the mouse. I sit for a moment to catch my breath, entranced by the glow of the computer screen.

I shuffle papers and pens, dig my fingers into slabs of Blu-Tack. Sweep the lot into the bin when I hear voices outside. I run to the door, put my ear against it. There's no one there. Not this time. The panic subsides and I tiptoe away from the door. Reach for the banisters.

I sit halfway up the stairs for what seems like hours. It's where I spent much of the first two years of Amy's disappearance. I forced myself to get up each morning but my resolve evaporated before I'd even made it halfway down. I would sit in limbo, head propped against the banisters, lost in an awful blankness, colourless and constant, like a concrete tomb. I could see nothing, no way forward, no way out.

47

Now that solid, static nothingness begins to undulate like mist in the wind. I want to believe that Amy has returned, and tease myself with the chance of a second bite at a future that never happened. Possibilities tingle. Hope surges. But there is something else too: a creeping fear, insinuating doubt, and in between them, madness.

I've been close before. Like that time in Tesco when I saw the little girl in what I thought were Amy's clothes. I shouldn't have tried to take her hand. Didn't even know that I had. Her screams brought her mum running. And the security staff. They only let me off when one of them recognised me. Their pity was as hard to take as the mother's accusations. She looked at me in the same way I imagined every mother in the country would: reproachful, disgusted, appalled at my lack of care and attention towards my own daughter.

Public sympathy was on my side when news of Amy's disappearance first broke, but as time went on and she still wasn't found, sympathy turned to accusation. What was I doing letting her go to the park on her own when it would soon be getting dark? Were preparations for a party really more important than my only child's safety? Everyone else could see it might be asking for trouble; why hadn't I?

The press insinuations went beyond saying I was responsible for Amy's disappearance; they claimed I was directly involved in it. Their speculations were discussed at length on Mumsnet and news websites, despite police assurances that there was no evidence to implicate me. Even so, I was vilified as a monster and as big a danger to children as whoever had taken Amy.

The few friends I had – former work colleagues and mothers from Amy's school mostly – had their doubts too. I could see it in their eyes when they dropped by. Their questions about the events of that night had the unmistakable twang of accusation and disbelief.

I shut them out and refused to take calls or answer the door. It wasn't long before they stopped calling or emailing me altogether. I was glad they did. I was free to grieve without worrying if I was doing it properly or convincingly. I no longer had to watch them leave my house knowing they were going back to their own children, safely tucked up at home.

But my solitude gave fantasy room to roam. I began to think that wishing for something long and hard enough would make it happen. Or if I pretended nothing was wrong, nothing would be.

That's how I came to be found in Mothercare with the nappies and baby powder that somehow got into my handbag. And why I turned up at Heathrow for a flight to Disneyland Paris with a ticket in Amy's name but no child by my side. I even insisted that the airline page Amy Archer, even though I could tell the staff recognised my daughter's name. But I didn't know they'd called the police at the same time. Amy's name echoed in the departure hall long after the flight had gone and Brian had collected me from the airport's medical centre.

I've heard voices too. Voices that weren't there. Amy.

Laughing. Singing. And other voices, saying I'm bad. Mad. Need help. Brian's voice maybe, or my shrink's, or the public's. Maybe it's God.

I wouldn't know. I can't tell anything any more. Black might just as well be white. Day night. Esme Amy.

3

I notice it a few hours later, as I'm coming down the stairs. A white envelope on the doormat. It wasn't there earlier – I'm sure of it – but my head was full of Amy and Esme and I only had eyes for dirt.

I put the dusters and polish on the table in the hall and pick up the envelope. The front is blank and there is no postage stamp or postmark. Junk mail, I think, even on New Year's Eve. New Year's *Day*, rather.

I'm about to throw it away unopened, but I notice the seal is still sticky, not with glue but with spit. I tear open the envelope and take out the sheets of white paper covered in typewritten text. I assume it's a letter, but there's no address or salutation at the top. Only a title.

My legs give way as my mind slowly takes in what it is. Who it's from.

I read in a rush at first, just to get it over with, but have to keep going back to make sure I've really understood what it says. I reach out to the banister for support and lower myself on to the stairs, my eyes fixed on the page, heart racing, breathless.

I hold the pages closer and start to read once more.

THE HISTORY OF ESME LAWRENCE IN FIVE OBJECTS

The Sign Of Gemini

Gemini is the star sign of people born in June. Their element is the air and they have two sides, like twins. But they're not identical. More like opposites. Like good and evil, hot and cold, yes and no. Gemini minds bounce around from one thing to another. They change their minds like the wind. People say they are two-faced.

They are ruled by Mercury, who is the messenger of the gods. Mercury can move around the sun faster than any other planet. That's why Geminis talk and think quickly.

Their birth flower is the rose. They are beautiful to look at and have a lovely smell but they're also dead prickly. In Victorian times, flowers had a special code. Each flower had a different meaning and so did its colour. My favourite colour is pink.

A pink rose means 'believe me'.

The Gemini birthstone is the agate. They come from volcanoes. It is a hard stone so it can't be damaged by acid. It gets really shiny when it's polished.

I am not a Gemini.

But I should be.

Guinea Pig

When I lived in London, I had a guinea pig
called Moon. She was a birthday present when I
was seven. My other mum and dad bought her for
me but it must have been Dad's idea.

He used to take me out on Sunday mornings
to give Mum a rest and the chance to read the
papers. On the way home I'd have a strawberry
milkshake and biscuits in the café in Dulwich
Park. The best bit was stopping at a big pet
shop on the way home so I could look at the
animals.

Dad liked the snakes and lizards best. He
always hoped to be there when it was feeding
time as he wanted to watch the snakes eat the
mice. I always prayed that we'd missed it. But
really Dad was only teasing. The man in the
shop told me they didn't feed the snakes and
lizards during shop times as they weren't a
zoo.

I liked the guinea pigs as they were cute
and cuddly. I moaned at Mum and Dad about
getting one for ages. Mum said I'd never
clean it out and she'd end up doing it, but I
promised I'd do it every week. I even said she
could take my pocket money if I didn't.

Dana wanted a guinea pig too. She was my
best friend from school. She lived in a flat

on the Brandon Estate. The flats didn't have
gardens so she couldn't have a guinea pig. All
she had was a hamster. They're boring as they
only come out at night.

Dad said he could get Dana a guinea pig too
and she could keep it in our garden. But I
heard Mum tell him that would mean Dana coming
round every day to feed it.

I don't think Mum liked Dana as much as me
and Dad did. I felt sorry for Dana, so when
she came to my house to play I'd let her hold
Moon. That's how we found out Moon was a boy.
His willy was like a strawberry Tic Tac. Dana
never picked him up again.

Mrs Doubtfire

I watched this last Christmas Eve. It's a bit
of a silly film as the man doesn't look like
a real old lady at all. He's even bigger than
our postman who's really, really fat. When
the lift isn't working he dumps the letters
in the lobby and people have to sort them out
themselves.

Mum lost a new credit card because someone
took it from the pile. They went out to the
Trafford Centre and bought lots of things with
it. Like a big TV and clothes from Diesel. The
people at the bank wanted to take the things

away because she couldn't pay for them – even though she'd never even bought them. I could hear her crying at night when I was in bed.

Mum is really sad sometimes. She pretends not to be, but I can tell. It's because she's on her own, I think. I do the washing-up, peel the vegetables and keep my room tidy, but she needs more help. Sometimes she says she's not a good mum. But she is. She's the best. Every bit as good as my other one.

If I had a dad, it would be easier for her. But I haven't. I've never met him. Mum only met him once too.

Things were easier with Mrs Doubtfire around. She was funny and kind and made everything all right. Made a family of three happy and whole.

Even though it's a bit of a silly film, it made me cry. Mum too. I told her everything would be fine. But there are no more Mrs Doubtfires. Lightning doesn't strike twice.

Ice Blast

I made Mum go on this when we went to Blackpool. It was scarier than the Big One. That's just a roller coaster. The only exciting part of the Big One was the first bit. It climbs the steep hill and then drops straight down in one go. But after that it's just little dips and turns. Everyone else screamed all the way through, but I didn't. I didn't even blink. Mum said I was fearless.

The Ice Blast showed she was wrong.

I was really, really scared as soon as the red safety harness clamped me into my seat. I'd been strapped in on the Big One. That was okay. No different from being in a car. This time I was being shot up, in a sort of rocket. The harness held me like a fist. It was so tight I couldn't breathe. I tried to wriggle free and told Mum I wanted to get off. She just laughed and said she was getting her own back. I was screaming before the ride even started.

I flew up in the sky so fast I thought God had reached down and grabbed me. The people on the ground were just dots. They got smaller and smaller. My ears popped and my stomach did a loop the loop. My heart felt like it stopped.

I went higher and higher, up through the clouds, into space. It was cold and dark. Not even any stars. I could see the earth below me and tried to tip my head forward so gravity would pull me down.

But I kept going up and up. Faster and faster. Higher than planets and stars. My face felt heavy, like it was melting. I kept shouting, 'Take me back! Take me back!'

Something soft and white fell all around me.
I thought I was in an angel's wings at first,
but then it felt more like being in a bubble.
I floated down again, really slowly, back
through space and clouds.

When I landed, the world looked different.
It felt all brand new and strange.

My heart was beating again – fast and loud
enough for two.

Pois

One of my favourite games was juggling.

I won a set of three red leather juggling
balls in a raffle at my old school. I was
pretty bad at it at first. I couldn't catch two
balls but I soon got the hang of it and in no
time I could juggle three.

None of the other girls could do it so I'd
show them during playtime. Some of them got
really good at it but Dana never did. She'd
throw the first ball too high to give her more
time, and wait too long to launch the second.
The balls went everywhere and she'd cry and
sulk. But she kept at it just so she could be
with me. She got better. Bit by bit.

One day Miss Pratt showed us pois. They're
like balls on a string that Maoris use in
their dancing. Miss Pratt was a Maori. She had

the same light coffee-coloured skin as Rishna Patel, only Miss Pratt had a funny accent. We did a project on New Zealand and learnt all about Captain Cook, sheep farming, kiwis and Maori culture.

Miss Pratt taught us the haka and a stick dance which was like playing a pat-a-cake hand game, only with sticks instead of hands. Dana didn't like it very much as she kept dropping the sticks.

She was better with the pois as you didn't have to catch them. Miss Pratt showed us how to make them. We pushed a long, thick needle through an old tennis ball, threaded a piece of string through it and tied a knot at the end.

We'd have a poi in each hand and move our wrists to make the balls swing in wide circles. When the whole class did it together, we looked like a wind farm. Miss Pratt showed us how to transfer both balls into one hand, then back again. Even Dana could do it. It was like having two worlds in your hands, spinning next to one another but with a blurry gap in between.

I made the pois turn so quickly they didn't look like they were moving at all. They just seemed to hang in the air on their own. All frozen. When that happened, I felt safe and peaceful.

Miss Pratt taught us a folk song that went with the pois.

> *Pokarekare ana*
> *Nga wai o Waiapu*
> *Whiti atu koe hine*
> *Marino ana e.*
> *E hine e hoki mai ra*
> *Ka mate ahau I te*
> *Aroha e.*

I loved the tune and the strange words but I didn't know what they meant. Miss Pratt said it was a love song.

> *They are agitated*
> *The waters of Waiapu,*
> *But when you cross over, girl,*
> *They will be calm.*
> *Oh girl return to me,*
> *I could die of love for you.*

The words fitted the action of the pois perfectly. Two worlds chasing one another, trying to get together. The call to come back. The promise of peace and love.

There's a note at the bottom of the paper, written in blue biro.

My teacher only gave me a D for my project as she said it was meant to be an autobiography, not a made-up story. I told her it was all true. She marked me down to an E for lying.

I wasn't.

My hands are shaking as I put the pages down, my mind blank with confusion. All I'm sure of is that Libby must have pushed it through the letter box soon after she left. She might even have written it herself for all I know, although the handwriting at the bottom could easily be a child's. Did she dictate the footnote to Esme as a final flourish of authenticity?

The question of which of them wrote it troubles me less than what it contains. It's a mishmash of two lives, a composite. Every detail about Amy is correct. How could either Libby or Esme know about the guinea pig, the name of Amy's teacher, the Sunday morning walks in Dulwich Park? Even *I'd* forgotten about the Maori folk song.

Their knowledge of Dana's name is easier to explain, as it appeared in all the press reports. But the rest of it? It just isn't possible that she could know these things. Unless.

Unless.

No. There's no way that Esme is telling the truth and she really *is* Amy. There has to be an answer. A logical, watertight explanation. There has to be.

I only wish I could think what it might be.

4

When I wake up, I'm on Amy's bed. I shift to avoid an uncomfortable lump digging into my back, reach down and pull out Bagpuss.

He's warm and squashed and his once cute expression now seems more astonished. Incredulous that I might believe Esme's story – or shocked that I might not.

I squeeze him hard and press him against my face. He smells of synthetic fibres and dust. I wonder if he recognised Amy's touch in Esme's fingers. I wonder if I do too. The thought of it makes me tremble.

I turn over and Esme's essay flutters to the floor. It's creased from where I've lain on it, the corners of the pages curled and grubby from my anxious, fumbling fingers. I've lost count of the number of times I read it, studying every line and word until I saw only shapes that made no sense but teased and thrilled me, like a code that could be deciphered but had defied me by the time sleep overwhelmed me.

I dreamt of guinea pigs, shooting stars, a leering Bagpuss and decomposing dolls – all seen through a mist of bubble-gum pink and police-light blue. Amy danced around with a hairbrush microphone, then morphed into Esme, who grew into Libby, her hands stretched out as she asked me what I wanted.

I want my daughter back. I want to feel her arms around me. I want to hear her laugh again. Not in my head; in my house. In my life. Real. I want to have flour fights with her as we bake cupcakes on a wet Saturday afternoon. I want to see her flawless limbs glide through her dance school routine. I want to iron her Brownie uniform, ferry her to sugar-fuelled parties, bicker with Brian over the necessary equipment for pupils at Alleyn's secondary school and for him to make up with me with a kiss and that puppy-dog expression I never could resist. I want to feel the power of the love between us once more, instead of the slap of rows and painful silences.

I want to warn Amy off cigarettes and alcohol, buy her first bra, scold her for not getting on with her homework, for her choice of boyfriends, for staying out late and throwing impromptu parties when Brian and I are away.

I want to gloat over her A-level results, help pack a trunk for Oxbridge, jostle for a good graduation photo, console her after failed job applications, pay the deposit on her first home, stem pre-wedding jitters and coo at baby's first scan. And then I want to do it all again with *her* children.

I want all this to happen. And it can. Most of it, anyway. Brian's second wife Fiona makes any reunion impossible, but a reconciliation, a return to the understanding and familiarity we used to have, would at least be something. With Amy's life to share once again, maybe the miracles wouldn't end there.

It is all possible. It could be mine. If I let myself believe.

A rush of adrenalin forces me to get up and run down the stairs. I take my mobile from the hall table, dial and wait. It rings out before the answerphone message tells me that the Spiritualist Association is closed until the second of January.

'Damn!'

I wait and leave a message.

'This is Beth Archer. I need to see Ian Poynton again. Please ring me back with his first available appointment. Or let me have his number so I can call him? Please? It's urgent.'

I need clarity. Ian Poynton might be able to help. His prediction came true – and quickly. Any delay now is more than I can stand, so I hurry to the computer on the desk in the living room. It's old and slow and it clanks and whirs as it gradually lumbers into life. I pray that for once it won't crash as I trawl the internet for a way to contact Ian.

There's no number for him on the Spiritualist Association site, but he does have his own one-page website – a photo, brief blurb and a telephone number. I pick up my phone and dial. It's answered on the fifth ring, barely more than a grunt.

'Is that Ian? Ian Poynton?'

'Yes.' He sounds croaky.

'Oh, thank God. You've got to help me.'

'Who is this?' He sounds wary and suspicious, as if I'm a crank caller. Maybe I am.

'It's Mrs Archer. Beth Archer. You did a reading for me earlier today? At the Spiritualist Association?'

He coughs.

'*Yesterday*, you mean.'

'Oh, yes,' I say quietly. A quick glance at my wristwatch tells me it's five twenty-five. 'I suppose I do. I'm sorry. But ... it's urgent. I just had to ... I ...'

'Mrs Archer?'

'I shouldn't have called.'

'I'm awake now,' he says, his sigh failing to disguise his irritation. 'Well, truth be told, I've not been to bed yet. Just as well New Year's Eve only comes around once a year.' A yawn stretches through his voice. 'You sound upset.'

I nod, even though he can't see me.

'Something you told me yesterday came true.'

'Well, forgive me if this sounds like bragging,' he says, 'but it's not unusual for what the spirits tell me to actually happen.'

'It is for me.' I put my hand to my forehead and hold it there as if trying to hang on to my sanity.

'Then I appreciate you ringing to thank me, but ... couldn't it have waited?' The irritation in his voice has been replaced by exasperation.

'That's not why I'm calling,' I say quickly. 'I need you to do another reading. Now, if possible. Please?'

'Now?'

'If you wouldn't mind.' I straighten my back in readiness.

'I'm sorry. I can't.'

'Oh?' My back slumps. 'Why not?'

'The only spirits in my head right now are Johnny Walker and Smirnoff. And anyway, I don't do readings over the telephone. Some psychics do, but it's never really worked for me – or my clients.'

'Please. You've got to. I'm desperate.' My grip on the handset grows tighter.

'I can tell. And that's not a good state of mind to have a reading in.' His suddenly businesslike tone rankles with me. 'I think it would be best if you made an appointment to see me at the Association. I'm there the week after next. I'm away on holiday until then.'

'But you've got to understand! I really can't wait that long. Please. I'm begging you! I'll pay you whatever you want.' The handset is slippy with sweat.

'It's not that, Mrs Archer,' he says firmly. 'It's just—'

'I need you, Ian. You can't turn your back on people who need your gift.'

He sighs and says that he'll try, even if it is against his better judgement. He stresses that there's no guarantee it will work.

'It might help if you hold something,' he says. 'A picture or a watch. That sort of thing. But don't tell me what it is. In fact, don't say anything at all.'

A few moments later I've turned on the phone's loudspeaker and have Bagpuss and Amy's photo in one hand and Esme's essay in the other. A study of judgement when I have no judgement at all.

I screw my eyes up tight and hold my breath, willing him to tell me something conclusive.

'I'm sorry,' he says after a few minutes. 'It's just as I expected. There's nothing. Just blackness and silence.'

I lean closer to the phone.

'Give it a bit longer. Please.'

I stare at Amy's picture, hoping to project it on to Ian's third eye, but once again he says that nothing's coming through. I curl into myself to muffle my frustrated sobs.

'I think we'd better call it a day,' he says, stifling another yawn.

'Wait. Do you ...' I sit up and catch my breath before I can continue. I'm scared of what he'll say, what it will mean for me, where it will lead. 'Do you believe in reincarnation?' The words come out in a rush. They sound to me like a dare.

'Reincarnation?' His intonation gives away his surprise. There's a moment's pause, and then he continues. 'Well, I've read some impressive recollections of past lives. And seen some of my peers do regression sessions with amazing results. So, yes, I do believe in reincarnation.'

'Regression sessions?' My eyes widen.

'Where people recall past lives under hypnosis.'

'That's it!' Bagpuss and the essay fall from my hands as I stand up quickly, but my grip is firm on Amy's photo. Hope and tears choke my voice. 'That's what I need. That will sort everything out.'

'You sound ... overwrought, Mrs Archer,' he says. 'If you're thinking of trying regression therapy, it's probably best to steer clear until you're more yourself. It can be a tricky business at the best of times.'

But I'm too excited to be stalled by his reasoning.

'Can I make an appointment? Right away?'

'Like I said, I'm going on holiday. And anyway I don't do regression work. I've not had the training.' He sighs. 'I really have to go now. I need some sleep. You can send me a cheque care of the Association.'

I hang up and wipe the tears from my eyes with my sleeve. I don't know what I expected from him, but that doesn't stop me feeling disappointed. Anything would have been better than silence. Even the tiniest hint from the other side could have tipped the balance either way, but the silent void leaves me teetering on the brink.

I put Amy's picture back on the mantelpiece. Her smile no longer seems so sweet and carefree. I place Bagpuss on the sofa. Beaded eyes bore into me. The words from Esme's essay seem to slide off the page as I drop it on the table. I grab my coat from the rack in the hallway and run out of the front door.

My footsteps are metronomic, quick and even, then hurried and frantic. I don't even know where I'm going. I stop and catch my breath, look around to see if anyone is watching. To see where I am. What I might be doing. But there's no one around. The entire city has been put to sleep by the spell of New Year's Day.

Yet I think I hear footsteps.

I run down the street. As I get closer to the river, I pick my way through empty champagne bottles, beer cans, burger boxes and soggy fronds of party streamers. I walk down roads I never knew existed before, turn right or left when my feet decide I should. All that matters is to keep moving.

In Borough High Street I sidestep an unruly conga.

'Happy New Year!' one of them shouts.

I put my hand against the wall and feel my way along it, not daring to look at the revellers.

'Christ, state of her.'

'Whatever she had last night, I want some right now!'

Their laughter rips through me. I run on, finally emerging at the entrance to Borough Market.

It's deserted, the stalls shut up, candy-striped canvas awnings curled under the dark railway arches. The ground is littered with empty bottles and cans, the mess made festive by sparkly confetti and a battered plastic trumpet. The smell of beer and urine mixes with the residual scent from a thousand years of market trading: sawdust, rotting vegetables, blood. It is the smell of something enduring colliding with the transient. Of celebration and decay.

The bells of Southwark Cathedral strike eight. The peals thunder in my head. I run on, magnetised by the promise of sanctuary. Of salvation. Truth.

I dash round the corner, praying the cathedral will be open. The beige and grey edifice thrusts into the lightening sky, as if trying to get God's attention. The heavy wooden doors are ajar. They creak as I yank them open and burst through the inner door, startling a woman in an overall dusting the pews.

'Oh, you gave me a fright!' she says, smiling at me nervously.

Her eyes flick either side of me, as if checking her escape route should she need one. I try and catch my breath, tuck some loose hair behind my ears. Smile as best I can.

'Is it okay to come in?' I whisper.

'We're getting ready for a thanksgiving service later on.' Her tone is clipped, officious, as if I'm being intrusive and impertinent.

'Please,' I say, my hands stretched out towards her. 'I just need to sit down. Think. Pray.'

'Yes,' the woman says slowly. 'I think you might.' She shakes out her duster and sneezes. 'Well, if you don't mind the vacuum cleaner ... God's house is always open, as they say.'

She plugs in a Hoover and pushes it around the base of the font. I walk down the nave's central aisle, the gaze of the stained-glass saints subdued by grimy light. My head bows under their scrutiny. Jesus looks disdainful.

I tiptoe towards the altar, but a woman buffing the railings with a duster reroutes me along a pew to my left, outside a small chapel. The sign on the door explains that it is the Harvard Chapel, reserved for private prayer and quiet meditation.

I step inside and sit down on a chair at the back, glad of the support provided by an adjacent pillar. I rub my temples, will the Hoover to stop. A moment later it docs.

The chapel is so perfectly still and hushed that I think I can hear the altar candles melting. I stare into the arch of the window until its colours run and swamp the stiff little figures kneeling at the feet of a smug-looking Jesus.

An inscription explains that the original window was destroyed in the Blitz. Staff and alumni from Harvard University raised money for a replacement in honour of the university's founder, who was baptised in the cathedral. Fate stretched across a vast, untamed ocean to distant worlds, reached through time to repair and replace. To heal. Maybe God has done the same by sending Amy back wrapped up in Esme. Perhaps He has finally heard my prayers and considered my penance spent.

A sudden surge of sunlight makes the window glow, a red panel in the middle burning brightest. *Veritas*, it says. Truth.

My heart throbs. I pray for guidance as hard and as long as I prayed for Amy's safe return. Bitter tears burn my face.

'Help me,' I sob. 'Please, help me.'

I sense a movement to my right and my gaze jerks away from the window. A young man in a grey shirt and white dog collar stands at the door, his face soft with concern.

'Sorry,' he says, stepping into the chapel. 'Is everything okay?'

'I'm fine,' I say, and dab my eyes with my coat sleeve.

'If you'd like to talk . . .'

'No,' I say quickly, forcing a smile to try and soften my reproach. 'But thank you.'

He takes out a box of votive candles from a small cupboard and lights one with a match. The candle flame is dull and tentative, then grows longer and brighter.

The young cleric replaces the box in the cupboard and smiles.

'Right,' he says. 'I'll leave you in peace.'

If only it was that simple.

'Wait,' I say. 'Please.'

My gaze drops to the seat beside me and he accepts my invitation.

'How can I help?'

I bite my lip.

'You're going to think I'm a mad, desperate woman, and God knows, maybe I am, but . . .'

I shake my head.

'Go on,' he says gently.

I can barely bring myself to look him in the eye as I ask him if he believes that reincarnation is possible.

He raises his eyebrows.

'I'll admit I wasn't expecting something like *that*.' His smile seems more receptive than amused or mocking. 'But it's not such a daft question. Not at all, in fact.' The chair squeaks as he shifts in his seat. 'You see, I suppose anything is possible, maybe even reincarnation . . .'

'But?'

'But I don't think it's likely.'

My heart sinks.

'Is that logic or belief?' I say, although I'm not sure if it makes any difference either way.

'Both. It undermines the basics of the faith.' He puts a hand on his heart. 'Of *my* faith. But there are millions of practising Christians who see it differently. Ours is a broad church in every sense — so there's room for people to have beliefs that others might regard as silly or abhorrent.'

I swallow and nod.

'Why do you ask?' he says, cocking his head to one side.

'No reason,' I say quickly. 'Not really. Just all this talk of the new year. You know how it goes. New beginnings. Endings. *Dreams.* Everyone questioning and analysing everything.'

'It is a bit unsettling, isn't it? Exciting too, though. Hopeful.' He puts his hand on mine. 'At the end of the day, we all find the comfort of faith in something – whether it's Buddhism, Christianity or Man United. Believing in something is better than believing in nothing at all. It's what feels right and true to you that matters.'

'But how can we be certain that what we feel is right?' Desperation has crept back into my voice.

'Well, we all have doubts, of course,' he says with a slow shrug.

'Even you?'

He stands up and smiles.

'You'd be surprised.' He taps his dog collar. 'This doesn't immunise me from little wobbles. And I wouldn't want it to either. It's God who steers me back to my faith each time – and knowing that makes it stronger.'

As he walks past the candle, the flame bends and sputters. Smoke hangs in the air like a thin grey ghost.

'You see,' he says. 'Even the Light of God needs to be rebooted once in a while.'

He lights the candle again and leaves.

Above the door there's a red flag, with the syllables of a single word embroidered in golden thread.

I look away quickly and stare at the relit candle instead. Its strong, steady flame mesmerises me. I've missed the clear bright light of hope and the heady warmth of love and want to feel the glow of both again. Esme may be my last chance. *If* I can allow myself to believe her.

Her resemblance to Amy is striking. Her recall of events uncanny. Her accuracy baffling. None of the details she told me were reported in the media, other than Amy's love of the Spice Girls, and that was hardly unique for a ten-year-old girl at that time. Esme said every word with an unwavering certainty, without a hint of hesitation. It was too accomplished and assured to be a performance, especially by someone so young.

I tear my gaze from the candle and look up. The stones and arches of the ceiling are linked together like the fingers of a hand in prayer. One of the stones boasts a gilt hexagon, its blood-red centre traced by gold letters.

VER

IT

AS

I get up to leave and stop at the chapel door. I look at the flag above me, the stone in the ceiling, the glowing window panel.

Veritas. Times three.

A trio of affirmations.

A trinity of truth.

The echo of my footsteps chases me along the aisle towards the cathedral doors and out into Borough High Street. When I stop to catch my breath, I feel I'm being watched and look around nervously.

The empty frames in an optician's window stare at me. An advert for bifocals tells me I can see things differently. I feel madness twitch, like a spider in a corner. I take deep, slow breaths, just as Dr Morgan taught me.

It was Brian's idea for me to go and see a psychiatrist, a last-ditch attempt to get me to move on. We'd started out having joint sessions with a bereavement counsellor in a stuffy little room at our local clinic. It didn't take long for Brian to point the finger at me, just like the press had.

At first he told me to ignore their allegations, said they had to find a scapegoat somewhere seeing as the police hadn't identified a culprit. I was a good mother, he told me, but his eyes said something different. Something dark and doubtful.

It was my fault Amy had gone. Me who wasn't looking, who wasn't even there, keeping watch. Who let her go off, crossing a road, to play on her own, keen to get her out from under my feet.

His litany of accusations brought my rote responses. The park gates were just fifty metres from the house, the road wasn't busy, her friend was in the playground, she was ten years old, sensible, bright. She was being picked up by a responsible adult. How was I to know her friend would run off and leave her?

And why was I busy that night anyway? Because I was getting us *both* organised for a party that was important to him and his business. And where was he? At work, on a pitch for a bloody toilet-roll campaign that could have waited for a day or two. Except maybe it wasn't the pitch deadline that was so pressing, but some doe-eyed colleague eager to make her name. *Neither of us was looking.*

The counsellor flapped and floundered, suggesting that we try separate sessions. Brian pulled out altogether.

'Beth, all we do is go round in circles,' he said, clenching his fists. '*Painful* circles. I need to work through this on my own. In my own way. Maybe you should try it too.'

'I can't. It helps to talk to someone about it. I wish that could be you, but . . .'

I continued with the counsellor for a while, but when my state of mind showed no improvement, Brian suggested I try a psychiatrist instead. I resented the subtle criticism that it was all my problem, but I knew I needed help.

And Dr Morgan *did* help, initially at least.

In a tranquil study overlooking the lush, tidy garden of his Dulwich home, he listened attentively to my memories of Amy and absorbed my anger and anguish like water in a sponge. But when he tried to move me on, to look at my past and my relationship with Brian, I resisted.

'None of that is relevant to Amy's death!' I said, hands out, incredulous that he couldn't see my point.

'But it *is* relevant to how you lead your life without her,' he said, nodding his head for emphasis.

'I have no life without her.'

'You can do,' he said, linking his fingers together. '*If* you want to.'

He maintained that the trauma of Amy's death was all the more profound because she was the only part of my life that had been working.

'You gave up your career in advertising to bring her up. You lost the status it gave you, the independence. Your sense of place in the world. Without her, there is nothing but your marriage.' He gave a little shrug. 'Maybe that isn't enough?'

It wasn't. It never had been. Never could have been. Not with me as one half of the equation.

Brian and I had been thrown together by departmental reorganisation in a mediocre advertising agency. I was surprised and relieved not to be given my P45 and even more surprised to be hooked up with the agency's hotshot.

Instead of working in the office, he dragged me out to a nearby café. Our relationship played out against a backdrop fugged by steam and cigarettes and burnt toast. Everything smouldered, passion included.

Sitting in a booth with flaky leather seats and a chipped Formica table, he spouted one catchy ad line after another. I was merely a secretary, taking dictation, dressing his ideas up to create ads that worked. Ads that won awards.

He made me look better than I was and my gratitude fired my love. His love for me was rooted in my easy acquiescence – something that faltered once Amy arrived and shifted my priorities.

What I saw as dedicated parenting, he saw as dogmatic control. I wanted the best for Amy and did all I could to make sure she got it. He wanted the same but thought she'd be happier getting there as a free spirit. Liberal, he called it. I called it lazy and dangerous. Disagreement and resentment seethed.

'My marriage isn't the problem,' I assured Dr Morgan.

'It's part of it. Work on that and maybe you can fix the rest.' He made it sound so simple.

'It won't bring Amy back,' I said, my teeth clenched.

'I'm sorry to say that nothing will. But if you and your husband start loving one another as deeply and as readily as you blame one another, you might, one day, start a new family.'

'I can't replace Amy!' The thought of it caved me in, made me feel traitorous and flighty.

'It's not about replacing Amy,' Dr Morgan said firmly. 'It's about finding you.'

I didn't go back. A few months later my marriage collapsed under the weight of Brian's affair with a colleague.

'Fiona's not to blame,' Brian said. 'It's you and your morbid obsession.'

'It's not an obsession!'

'No? What would you call it then?'

'Love.'

I don't have to wonder what he and Dr Morgan would make of me claiming that Amy had returned. They'd say I was deluded. Neurotic. Mad.

Maybe I am.

I press my head against the glass of the optician's window. Its chill is soothing. My gaze rests on a sign for eye tests.

What are you missing?

Beneath it is a display of Clear View contact lenses.

Look to your future.

I lean my head against the shop window once more. The cathedral clock chimes the half-hour. I think of the message in the Harvard Chapel.

Veritas.

I hear the clergyman telling me I will know in my heart what I should believe. I see Amy's initials scratched in the doorstep tile. The glint of her hair. I feel Esme's tresses soft and warm beneath my hand. The kick of recognition, of hope for a future. The flare of a decision.

I take my phone from my coat pocket. My text to Libby is written and sent in a flash.

I believe.

5

I keep my phone in my hand the whole way home. I expect Libby to get in touch as soon as she receives my message, picturing the pair of them waiting in their hotel room, desperate to hear from me. But the phone is stubbornly silent.

Part of me wishes I'd been silent too. I wonder if I've been rash in sending my text message when I did – in sending *that* text message at all.

I believe.

Ever since I pressed send, my mind's been churning, fluctuating between belief and disbelief and back again.

I saw *Veritas* in the cathedral as God prompting me to believe and the adverts in the optician's window as code that backed Him up. But what if God is still playing games with me? He let Amy be taken and refused to give her back to me despite my pleas and prayers. Maybe this is just another spiteful twist to make me suffer more.

I can't deny I want to be wrong. I want Esme to be Amy. But I know that wanting something, wishing for it until it hurts, is no foundation for belief. I need proof, but I can see no way of getting it that will settle the matter beyond any doubt.

Even if Esme was to tell me where Amy's body is, how could I trust it to be true? Would the police really take the word of a ten-year-old girl and start digging where she said they should? And if they did and they found Amy's body, Libby would have some difficult questions to answer. It's in their interests *not* to tell me where Amy's body is – even if they know.

I shall have to find proof, one way or the other, that Esme is who she says she is. I shall have to listen to both my heart *and* my head – and I'm not certain either can be trusted.

It strikes me that maybe Libby hasn't responded to my message because she doesn't trust me. She's sure to ask me why I now believe their story, and I have nothing to answer her with. Not yet. Nothing concrete. Nothing but hope and wishes, and that might not be enough for her, or for me.

There is a more logical reason for their silence, I realise. They could still be asleep, though I doubt either of them could have slept at all. Maybe they're having breakfast and don't want to make such an important call in a hotel restaurant. Perhaps the battery is dead or Libby's out of credit.

Then the phone rings.

'Hello?'

'Beth! Happy New Year to you.'

'Jill,' I say, hoping my disappointment doesn't show in my voice. 'Happy New Year to you too.'

'You're up and about early. I've just tried you at home.'

'I needed to get out for some fresh air.' I pull my coat collar around my neck, as much to hide my lie as to keep out the cold.

'I could do with some of that myself,' she says. 'Bloody champagne! Only had a couple of glasses, but at my age . . .' Her voice lowers with concern. 'Were you okay last night? I couldn't stop thinking about you but didn't want to ring. I know you don't like to be disturbed.'

Disturbed. If only she knew. But she can't. Not yet. Maybe not ever. She would never believe Esme's story, but she wouldn't be surprised that I did. My belief has not had time to set firm, and might collapse under the weight of her scorn.

Jill has been resolute in her friendship ever since Amy went missing. I didn't know her when Amy was alive – not really – although our paths did cross twice a day, every day, outside the school.

Clad in her dayglo-yellow coat and cap, Jill would halt the traffic with her lollipop sign. The steely stare she gave the drivers would soften as she turned towards the children and waved them across to safety. She had a cheery word for every parent, a smile for every child and was inundated with cards and chocolates at the end of every term.

I avoided the school after Amy disappeared and made sure I didn't go out anywhere until all the mums had finished the school run. It was awkward trying to chat normally when their own children, Amy's classmates, were by their side, reminding us of the gap where Amy should be.

Swimming, tap-dancing, Brownies and birthday parties had been the oxygen for my friendship with the parents, the time at the gates the lungs. Without them, the relationships withered, before dying abruptly in the wake of the press allegations against me.

But Jill would drop by on her way home from her shift, make us some tea and listen without complaint as I wept and wailed. She didn't believe I was to blame for Amy's disappearance and thought that those who did only pointed the finger at me to detract from their sense of guilt when they'd been too busy for their own children.

'It's not really about you, Beth, however much it looks that way,' she used to say. 'It's about them. You're living their nightmare and it's easier to ignore your own demons if they have somebody else's face.'

Her support was unerring and unconditional. I feared she'd soon tire of me and drift away, but she was constant, continuing to call in on me even when arthritis forced her to retire.

'I can't get out of the way of the cars quickly enough any more,' she said. 'And the cold stays in my bones for the rest of the day. But it gives us more time to do things, doesn't it?'

She sounded like Dr Morgan. He was always trying to get me to get out and do things. Trips to the cinema, museums and theatre would distract me, he said, and joining a painting or poetry group would give me the space to express myself and meet new people. But sideshows had no answers for me.

Jill took a slightly different tack.

'I got involved with the Friends of Durning Library after Arthur died,' she told me. 'I'm not saying him keeling over with a heart attack watching cricket at the Oval compares in any way with what you've been through with Amy, but losing him was still painful. The Friends helped fill the gap. It might help you too.'

'I don't think I'm ready yet,' I said, shaking my head. 'Maybe later.'

She smiled.

'I am an incorrigible busybody, which makes me an ideal Friend, capital F, but something of a nuisance as a friend, small f. I won't give up on you, Beth. I promise you, the best way to get over losing someone is other people. The *right* people. Not to take their place, but to remind you what living feels like.'

Her persistence was gentle and polite, but relentless. Eventually I succumbed, becoming part of a crack troop of volunteers organising jumble sales, making sandwiches and cakes for special events and rallying support whenever council cutbacks loomed.

One voluntary group quickly led to others. I became a Friend of St Anselm's Church, a local charity training people in horticulture, the Kennington Gardens Society and the Imperial War Museum. But even Jill drew the line at trying to persuade me to join the Friends of Kennington Park.

The groups I belong to are usually the same set of people wearing a different badge and swapping one issue or interest for another. The members are invariably older than me and less judgemental than my peers. Perhaps it's because they're near the end of their lives, closer to God, and want to show the forgiveness they hope they'll get from Him.

Whatever the reason for their acceptance of me, their sage sympathy and understanding gives me room and licence to brood. So instead of showing me a way out of my grief, Jill has inadvertently nurtured a warm, moist culture where thoughts and memories of Amy multiply like bacteria.

Lately she's been saying that I need some friends that don't come with a subscription fee, newsletter and annual general meeting. Friends of my own age, with interests to match.

I've shared so much with Jill, I'm bursting to tell her about Esme. About the possibility that Amy is back. But I can't. It's like when I thought I was pregnant with Amy and didn't tell anyone, not even Brian, not until I was sure. And even then I made him keep it secret, until after the first scan showed everything was going well.

There is no scan this time, no proof of anything. I will have to wait. In the meantime, the least I can do is spare Jill from fretting over me.

'Don't worry about me, Jill,' I say as I walk down the street. 'I'm fine. In fact, I feel quite optimistic about this year.'

There's a pause.

'Yes,' she says, 'you *do* sound quite ... bright and

breezy. Maybe the tenth anniversary will turn out to be a real turning point for you.'

'I think you could be right.'

'No more looking back?' It sounds like an instruction as much as a question.

'No need,' I say with a confidence I don't really feel.

'Excellent. I'll drop in later. Swap resolutions over coffee. I'll bring some leftover mince pies.'

Panic bites. It's too soon. I'll be tempted to tell her even if she doesn't guess that something has changed fundamentally – although not even Jill would be able to guess what that something might be.

'I won't be back for a while,' I say.

It's a lie, as I'm already turning in to my street and feeling in my pocket for my house keys. It's the first of many lies I will have to tell to keep the truth at bay. I promise Jill I'll call her later and hang up. I shut the front door behind me and lock it, unsure who it is I'm trying to keep out.

The statue on the shelf in the hall catches my eye. The memory of Esme's explanation for the missing spot of colour on its heel makes me shiver. I take it in my hand, weighing it up, as if testing for the truth, then place it on the cabinet in the front room. A moment later I move it to the mantelpiece, to the left of Amy's photograph. The arrangement looks unbalanced. I move the statue to the right.

Bagpuss smiles from the sofa. Esme's essay winks from the table. I pick them up and slowly climb the stairs to Amy's room. The duvet and pillows are crumpled, the curtains closed. I set about making the bed, then strip it, placing the linen in the laundry basket.

I'm tantalised by the realisation that one day, Amy might just sleep in that bed again. The thought gathers momentum. She'll want a new duvet cover, something more suitable for a ten-year-old girl. Pink probably.

And what about clothes? The latest must-have trainers, fancy party frocks, sensible winter coats, swimsuits, scarves and school uniforms. I throw open the wardrobe doors, tug out every drawer. They are dark and musty – empty. Full of promise yet somehow stuffed with doubt.

I try to fight the tease in the prospect of buying her things, but it's no good; my desire outruns my logic. She'll want games, books, toys and gadgets with headphones and screens. I owe her a decade of birthday and Christmas presents, holidays, treats and trips to the panto and cinema. I can bake cakes again, complete with candles and icing. I can forgo my ready meals for one in favour of vats of carbonara sauce and whole slow-roasted chickens. I'll have someone to pull the wishbone with, someone at the other end of my festive cracker. *Two* people. Libby will be around too.

My fantasy is stopped in its tracks, each thought and image of my new future colliding with the one preceding it. My mind is carnage, logic mangled and twisted with hope.

I throw open the window, take deep breaths of the cold, murky air. The park's turf is scrappy and the pathways are uneven.

I fall back on to the bed and massage my temples. The shrill ring of my phone makes me wince.

'Mrs Archer? It's Libby.'

She's whispering, and there's a humming noise in the background.

I sit up quickly, suddenly alert and watchful. Expectant and hopeful.

'Libby. At last! Where are you? What's that noise?'

'It's the extractor fan in the bathroom.'

'Why are you whispering?' I say. 'Speak up, I can barely hear you.' I flick my hair away and push the handset closer to my ear.

'Esme's asleep,' Libby says, her voice still a whisper. 'She had a bad night. Last night took a lot out of her. Me too.'

'Oh no. Is she all right?' A frown rucks my forehead.

I'm surprised at my concern for a child I don't really know, much less trust, but I can't deny my feelings for a girl who might yet be mine. The old instincts are still there.

'Under the circumstances, yes, I suppose she is,' Libby says. She sounds distant, deflated – bored even.

'I have to see her. Forget the hotel. Come and stay here for the rest of your visit. There's plenty of room.'

'Mrs Archer—'

'*Beth*, please.'

'Beth.' She says my name as if the word doesn't quite fit in her mouth. 'You've got to slow down. Think of Esme. Where *she's* at. What she's feeling. We have to tread carefully.'

'But I have to see her.' My tone was meant to be pleading, but it came out more like a demand.

There's a pause before Libby answers.

'You will,' she says. 'This afternoon. But I don't think we should come to your house again. Not yet. It might be too much for her. Besides, we need to talk. Just the two of us.'

'You can't stop me seeing her,' I say, scraping the hair back from my face and getting up off the bed.

'Actually, I can. I *am* still her mother.'

'I am too.' The certainty in my claim startles me.

'You wouldn't show up on any DNA test,' Libby says tersely. 'It's my blood in her veins. My name on her birth certificate under the heading of "mother".'

I didn't have to fight for custody of Amy – there was no one for me and Brian to argue over. If there had been, though, I would have won. But that's not the case this time; I can't afford to antagonise Libby, but I can't let go of any claim I might make to Amy either.

'But if you didn't want me to be part of her life, why did you turn up last night?' I say.

Libby pauses again, as if she's wondering the same thing.

'Because it's what Esme wanted,' she says. 'Because I thought it might help her.'

'Even if it didn't help you.'

'Exactly. Mothers have to be selfless.'

She sounds triumphant, like she's played a trump card or pulled rank on me. Reminding me that I'm out of practice. A has-been. Anger bristles.

She tells me to meet her at the Tower of London at two o'clock.

'They've set up a skating rink in the moat. You'll get to see Esme and the two of us will have the chance to talk.'

I find Libby sitting at a table alongside the ice rink. She looks tired and worried; the tight-fitting bobble-less hat on her head deepens the furrows in her brow. Her eyes are sunken but I can tell she's been crying.

She stiffens when she sees me approaching, then shudders and rubs her arms, masking her discomfort by blaming the weather.

'It's freezing,' she says.

'We could always go back to my place for tea and crumpets by the fire?'

Libby shakes her head and points to the ice rink.

'You don't have one of those in your back garden, though.' She squints as she watches the skaters. 'Esme needs a bit of fun. And we need her distracted.'

People in brightly coloured hats and gloves glide by, preceded by puffs of white breath. Others shuffle around close to the edge, wobbling and lunging for the perimeter wall. The powdery artificial ice muffles the slice of the blades and amplifies the thud of tumbling bodies.

'I can't see her,' I say, shielding my eyes with my hand.

'At the far end. Just coming up to do the turn.'

I spot Esme's silver Puffa coat flashing through the crowd, her hair trailing behind her. She moves with steady, sweeping strides, shortening them to weave in and out of the people in front of her, missing them by millimetres, then pushing out again confidently.

'She always was a good skater,' I say. 'You should see her on roller blades.'

'I have,' Libby says flatly, then gives an almost imperceptible shake of her head.

I wave as Esme glides towards us, her cheeks pink. She is panting, spent breath streaming like ectoplasm. She smiles and picks up speed.

'Mum!'

The word is like a slap in the face bringing me round after a fainting fit. Restoring me to the consciousness of motherhood once again. When she called me Mum the night before, it felt cruel and inappropriate. Now it feels more familiar and comfortable, although that could still prove to be as transient as the misted air that accompanies the word from Esme's mouth.

I move closer to the barrier. Esme swerves wide then swings in again, her skates cutting into the ice, kicking up a wake of white powder. It sprays behind her like stardust. The thud of her boots against the barrier echoes the thump of my heart.

She reaches over the barrier and throws her arms around me. Instinct makes me do the same, albeit slowly, like when I'd told Amy off as a toddler and have to gradually displace my disapproval with a comforting, reassuring hug.

But once she's in my arms I find I can't let go. I bury my face in her hair, breathe in her warm and clammy citrus-scented skin. Her coat is bulky with padding and I keep squeezing until I can feel her body beneath it, until I'm certain she is real.

'I can't breathe!' she says, and tries to pull away from me.

'Beth,' Libby says. 'Stop. She doesn't like it.'

'Nonsense. What child doesn't like being cuddled?'

But Esme's elbows flail and her shoulders buck until she shakes me off. She totters back, off balance, and for a moment I think she'll fall, but she recovers and shoots off back into the crowd.

'I *told* you,' Libby says with a gloating smile. 'She doesn't like being hugged for too long. Not any more. Not like she used to. There was a time when I couldn't hug her long or tight enough.' Libby huddles into her own arms. 'I miss that.'

'She's at that funny age, I suppose.'

It feels good to swap clichés about children with a mother again.

'If you say so,' Libby says doubtfully, and jerks her head at the seat alongside her. 'We'd better get started. Her session only lasts half an hour and I'm not laying out for another one, even if I could afford it. But half an hour should be enough anyway, after the night Esme had.' She gives a little laugh. 'It will be enough for me too.'

'What about me?' I say as I sit down next to her.

'This isn't just about you, Beth. In some ways, you're the least important of the three of us.'

Her words smack of the accusations levelled at me by

the press; of my family of three, Amy and Brian were more deserving of sympathy and consideration than I was. In the hierarchy of hurt, I was a distant third.

'But I'm Amy's mother,' I say, conscious that such a statement would have brought howls of derision from the press.

'Right,' Libby says, nodding her head. 'You're *Amy's mother*. For as long as you *choose* to be. If you have second thoughts – and you could – it will crucify Esme. I'm the one who'll have to pick up the pieces. It's been hard enough holding her together up to this point. I have no choice – as *Esme's mother*. You do.'

'You make it sound like it's not been easy for me.'

Libby snorts.

'We haven't even started yet,' she says. 'Have you any idea how tricky all this is going to be? How painful? It'll be brutal. Maybe even downright bloody dangerous for Esme. She's just a kid. You've got to remember that.'

'How could I ever forget it?' I pull my coat tighter around me. 'And I promise I'm not going to walk away either. I couldn't bear losing Amy twice.'

Libby shrugs.

'I hope you're right,' she says.

'Well, if you're worried I'll let her down,' I say, 'why bring her to my doorstep in the first place?'

Libby lifts her head and stares at the sky. Her eyes are brimming.

'Because my sweet, precious little girl was turning into somebody I didn't recognise. Instead of hugs and bubbles at bathtime, instead of giggles in front of the telly with fish-finger sandwiches, instead of a healthy, clever and hard-working schoolgirl ...' she wipes her eyes, 'I got an anxious little madam who tells me – and everyone else – about her *other* mother who loves her more than I do. A kid who gets all weepy during her lessons for no good reason, who spends playtimes kicking a wall until her toes are bruised and bleeding, who has terrifying, violent fits – after which she tells me stuff that makes no sense and then moans at me for not believing her.'

She takes a tissue from her pocket and blows her nose.

'And through all this,' she continues, 'I still get glimpses of the daughter I once had. One who *does* eat ravioli and who likes Lady Gaga. Who helps me out with the hoovering and washing-up and lets me snuggle up during *Corrie*.'

Her eyes snap to mine.

'*That's* why I brought her down here,' she says. 'To try and make sense of everything and hopefully find some kind of happiness.'

I nod slowly, think of taking her hand, but pull back, certain she'll spurn it.

'I'm sorry,' I say. 'I had no idea. I mean, how could I?'

'No, well you will from now on. First-hand. Because all the confusion, all the agony you've no doubt been through since last night, all that is only the beginning. You have to know what you're signing up for before I tell her you believe her.'

I blink, uncertain if I've heard her correctly.

'You mean, she doesn't know yet?'

'That's right.'

The hand I was going to offer her only a moment ago is now clenched in a fist. How dare she not tell her? But then, I think, she is only doing what she feels is best for her child. What I would do if our roles were reversed. Besides, maybe it's better Esme doesn't think I believe her, given that I'm not sure I do.

'I don't want to get her hopes up until I know you really understand what's involved,' Libby says firmly. 'Like I said, you can choose to walk away. I don't have that luxury.' She leans towards me. 'It took me a while to even begin to get my head around this. You've done it in less than a day – apparently. How can you be so sure it's not just wishful thinking?'

I can't help laughing.

'I wouldn't wish for *this*.'

'Really? Isn't it a second chance?' Libby says. 'A painful and unlikely one, I admit, but better than no chance at all, surely?'

I shake my head.

'No, not if it doesn't feel right. You know, right here,' I say. My hand hovers over my heart but doesn't touch my chest. 'I may not have been a mother for a long time, but the instincts have never left me.'

Libby leans back and blows a stream of iced breath into the air.

'So what's changed?' she says.

'You want *me* to tell *you*?'

'No. I want you to *convince* me.'

94

I toss my head back angrily.

'This is ridiculous,' I snap.

'That's what you said last night. So, like I said, what's changed?'

I'm indignant that she wants to hear my reasons, but can understand why she does. And saying them out loud to her might also make me more certain of them.

I push my hair back from my face and sit up straight.

'It's her memories,' I say. 'The details she knows. All of them are spot on, yet none of them were in the press reports.'

'I know,' Libby says. 'I checked.'

'But it's not just that she knows them. It's her certainty. Not a flicker of doubt. No trace of a lie. She couldn't have made it all up.'

Libby raises her eyebrows.

'And that's all it took to convince you?'

'There's what Ian said too, of course,' I say, laying my hands on the table.

'Ian?'

'A psychic.' I feel my cheeks flush, as if I'm confessing to something embarrassing. 'He told me a little girl was close. A girl whose name began with an E. He suggested various names, Ellie being one of them. A few hours later *Esme* was at my door.'

'Could just have been a fluke,' Libby says. 'And he didn't say anything about Amy, did he? Only Esme – and even then he got her name wrong.'

'But don't you see? It's not the detail that matters. Not

this time. It's the fact that he got anything at all.'

Libby shrugs.

'Sorry,' she says. 'I'm not with you.'

I shuffle closer to her.

'I've been going to psychics for years,' I say, 'and none of them even came close to reaching Amy on the other side. Now I know why.'

Libby frowns.

'Sorry,' she says. 'I still don't get it.'

'Don't you see? Amy wasn't there to hear him because she never actually made it to the spirit world.'

'Aah,' Libby says, nodding slowly. 'I suppose that makes sense — even if I'm not much of a believer in all that sort of stuff myself. That's why it took me such a long time to see what was really going on with Esme.'

'What about God? Do you believe in him?'

'God?'

'Yes. He pointed me towards the truth.'

Libby's eyebrows shoot up in surprise.

'I wouldn't have had you down for one of the God squad. Not after what you've been through.'

'I don't go to church, if that's what you mean,' I say. 'But I did the Sunday school thing and went to a church school. That sort of drip-feeding leaves its mark — however much you might rebel against it later, whatever tragedies life throws your way.'

I look away from Libby, grind the heel of one shoe into the frozen turf.

Esme glides across the ice. The Tower's battlements

shine like bleached bone. I shudder and rub my gloved hands together.

'So, have I convinced you? Do I pass the test?'

'It's not like that, Beth.'

'Yes it is,' I say, patting her hand. 'But I understand.' I clear my throat. 'What was it that first made you think Esme was different?'

Libby looks me directly in the eye.

'It was about a year ago, I suppose,' she says. 'It was little things at first. Like her saying she missed hearing the bells of Big Ben from her bedroom. I thought she meant the bongs on *News at Ten*.' She twirls a strand of hair around a finger. 'Esme spoke about London so much her teachers thought we'd lived here, when she'd never even been. And on Saturday mornings she used to wonder why *Live and Kicking* wasn't on TV. I watched that when *I* was a girl. She was only a year old when it went off the air.'

I remember Amy entering the programme's talent show. She and Dana and three other girls were going to sing a Spice Girls song. They didn't even get asked to audition. A few weeks later Amy sneered and snarked at another group of girls doing the same song.

'Then,' Libby says, 'she kept talking about friends and teachers from school – only none of them were actually *at* her school.'

'Most kids have imaginary friends.'

'Which is why I didn't think anything of it at first. But other mums said their kids made them lay a place for the invisible friend at the table. Esme never did. Her "friend"

Dana was real to her and had a house and table of her own. The other kids soon forgot their made-up friends. Esme's stories got more vivid. Then the fits started.'

'Yes,' I say, trying not to sound too suspicious. 'I wanted to come back to that. Amy wasn't epileptic, you see.'

Libby holds her hands out.

'I don't think Esme is either,' she says. 'The doctors do, but I don't agree. I think they're brought on when Amy is stretching in Esme's body. Flashbacks. That sort of thing.'

My heart is thumping hard, pushing out the question I've most needed an answer to during the last ten years. The one that's given me more sleepless nights than any other, the one that drove my darkest nightmares whenever I did manage to get to sleep.

I try to speak but my mouth is too dry to shape the words. I swallow and try again.

'Has she . . . ever said anything about what happened to Amy? I mean . . . where her body is?'

My heart breaks once more as soon as the words leave my mouth. I can barely breathe as I wait for Libby's answer.

'No,' she says. 'Not yet.'

I'm caught between disappointment and relief; knowing might be just as painful as not knowing.

'And you mustn't quiz her about it,' Libby says. 'Okay?'

'But I—'

'Yes, I know you need to know, but we can't force it out of her. These fits are . . .' She screws her face up in anguish. 'They're horrible to see. She's so scared when she comes round, dazed and trembling. She looks so . . .

bloody vulnerable. All I want to do is hold her and tell it will be all right, but she won't let me and we both know it won't be all right in the end.'

She jabs a finger at me.

'Whatever horrors she sees during these fits will come out in their own time,' she says. 'I almost don't want it to happen. But it *has* to if Esme is ever to move through it. You've got to promise not to put pressure on her.'

'But wouldn't it be better to get it over with?'

'No. Not for her. Or for me. It's not easy hearing my daughter talk about things we've never done. Places we've never been.' She looks off into the distance. 'She's becoming a total stranger to me. After each fit there's a bit more of Amy and a little bit less of Esme. I don't know which is worse. Losing your daughter, like that,' she says, snapping her fingers, 'or watching her disappear bit by bit.'

I take her hand and squeeze it. She looks up and smiles weakly.

'Promise me you won't interrogate her, Beth, or I won't let you near her again.'

I swallow hard and nod. It's not the moment to suggest past-life regression therapy. But it will come. Soon. She'll see the sense of it when I do.

'I promise,' I say.

The music from the loudspeakers fades. The announcement that the session will finish in five minutes sends the skaters into a frenzy. Some slither to the exit; most skate faster and more freely as the space on the ice increases.

'There's one more thing,' Libby says, standing up.

'I don't want her getting even more confused than she already is. So you have to call her Esme — at least for the moment. It'll be easier all round and spare us any awkward questions. Agreed?'

I say yes; it's too early for me to even think about calling her anything but Esme anyway.

Esme sweeps around in smooth loops, hair streaming behind her, silver jacket glinting. An orbiting star. When the music stops and the stewards herd people to the exit, her transition from the ice to the rubber matting is elegant and effortless.

As she walks towards us, wobbling on the blades, I see Amy as a toddler, teetering in my high-heeled shoes.

'Hello, Esme,' I say. 'You looked pretty cool out there.'

Her face has a sheen of sweat and is flushed pink.

'Go get your shoes, love,' Libby says. 'We'll wait here.'

'How about a drink?' I say, pointing to a stall swathed in ribbons of fruit-scented steam. 'You must be thirsty after all that dashing about?'

Esme nods.

'Oooh, yes please!'

It's good to see she has Amy's enthusiasm and manners.

'Do you like Ribena?' I ask. Amy did.

Esme says she does and totters off to reclaim her shoes from the collection point. Libby and I walk to the drinks stall and wait for her there. I get us both a glass of mulled wine, but Libby doesn't touch hers.

'I need a clear head,' she says, and puts the Styrofoam cup back on the counter. 'You do too.'

I sip from my cup; the hot ruby liquid burns the roof of my mouth. I blow on it to cool it down, take another sip. And another. By the time Esme gets back, I've finished mine and most of Libby's. I pass Esme the Ribena and she rips the straw from the carton and stabs at the seal on the top.

'Thank you,' she says, before sucking on the straw. The carton warps and buckles. She smacks her lips as she finishes and squeezes the carton flat.

'Does you being here mean you believe who I am?' she says.

I'm about to speak, but Libby gets in first.

'Why don't you put the carton in that bin over there, love? Then we'll go for a walk.'

'All of us?'

'All of us,' I say.

Esme smiles and runs towards the bin. A few metres away she stops, takes aim and launches the carton. It sails through the air and lands in the bin, dead centre.

'Bullseye!' she shouts, and runs back, slipping in be-tween me and Libby. Her hand slides into mine like a key into a well-used lock.

We cross Tower Bridge, find our way down to the path along the river, where we're swept along in the tide of families out for a stroll. The thrill of belonging once again brings a rash of goosebumps. I try to ignore that it's Libby on the other side of Esme, and imagine it's Brian there instead. Esme tugs on my hand.

'Why didn't Dad come too?' she says. 'I really want to see him.'

I feel my cheek twitch.

'You will,' I say. 'Later.'

'He's meeting us?' Esme gives a little skip.

'Not today, no.'

'Is he at home?'

'Probably, Esme,' I say slowly. 'But not my home. You see, we don't live together any more.'

Esme stops abruptly.

'Is that because of me?' she asks.

I swallow hard.

'No, not really. I think we just stopped loving one another.'

Esme squeezes my hand.

'That's really sad,' she says. 'You did love him, though, didn't you?'

Her need for reassurance brings a lump to my throat.

'Yes, of course,' I say. 'Very much so.'

'Even though you argued?'

'It's . . . difficult to explain. Sometimes that's just how things go.'

'But—'

'That's enough,' Libby says, pulling Esme on.

'He does still love *me*, though,' Esme says. 'Doesn't he?'

'Oh, yes. He never stopped loving *you*.'

And I suppose he didn't. He just found it easier to forget her than I did. And he'll find it much harder to accept that Amy has returned than I have, too. He'll be cynical, sarcastic, brutal. I have to protect her from Brian for as long as I can.

I pull my neck further into my coat and pick up the pace. Westminster Bridge divides the glowering sky from the grey of the Thames. Boats and buoys bob in the incoming tide and gulls hang on the breeze.

The crowds thicken as we get closer to the bars and restaurants at the South Bank Centre. I'm struck by the number of young girls with blonde hair wearing pink coats, hats or leggings, as alike as mannequins on a conveyor belt. Like the girl whose hand is in mine. She could be any of them. And her parents could be any of those passing by. I fight the thought. I like the prospect of belonging once more.

We pass under a bridge, its gloomy shade made darker by the twinkle of spinning lights at the far end. Old-fashioned organ music grows louder as we get closer.

'Look! A carousel!' Esme pulls away from us and runs ahead. 'Can I go on it? Please?'

'Of course.' I start rummaging in my bag for my purse.

'I don't think it's a good idea,' Libby says to me under her breath.

'Oh, it's hardly a roller coaster,' I say. 'Just a bit of fun. Exactly what you said she needed.'

'Fun that could trigger a fit,' Libby says. 'It's not fair, Beth. You can't induce these flashbacks just because it suits you.'

The accusation stops me dead.

'How can you possibly believe that I would want to hurt her?' I say.

Libby doesn't answer.

'Look, Libby,' I say, starting to walk on, 'if you're so worried about her going round in circles, what exactly was she doing at the ice rink? She was going a lot faster than this merry-go-round does and she did it for longer, too. She's fine now, isn't she?'

Libby nods.

'Well then,' I say, taking some money from my purse and snapping it shut. 'And she'll be fine after a go on this. I promise you.'

Libby shrugs.

'Okay,' she says. 'But only if you go with her and keep an eye on her.'

'Come on!' Esme yells from the ticket booth. 'Or I'll miss the next ride.'

She claps her hands when she realises I'm going on too. She leaps up the steps to the rows of horses, runs her hands over their glossy painted manes and checks the names written in fancy lettering on the saddles.

'Tinkerbell!' she squeals, and climbs on, pointing for me to get on the one next to hers. 'What's yours called?'

'Misty.'

'Perfect!'

The carousel begins to turn, the horses rise and fall. As we pass, Libby's face is anxious and watchful. Esme waves and leans back, her hair matching the colour of her palomino's tail.

'Hold on tight,' I tell her.

We pick up speed and the peaks and dips of the undulations get higher and lower. The onrush of cold air muffles the drone of the organ music and makes my eyes water. Lights flash, blurring into a haze of watery white. I grip the handle on the horse's neck tighter, suddenly queasy. I turn to Esme to see if she is okay. She's laughing, whipping her horse with her hand.

'I'm going to beat you!' she shouts. She kicks her heels to spur her horse on and turns to me. Her smile has gone and her expression is serious; the joyful light in her eyes has the glint of mischief. 'You'll never catch me!'

It might just be gravity or the pitch of my horse, but her mouth seems off kilter, as if she's smirking. Libby has the same look when the ride ends and Esme has to help me down from my horse.

'So much for you looking after Esme,' she says.

'I didn't need looking after!' Esme says. 'It's only a merry-go-round.' She points at me and laughs. 'You look like you've seen a ghost. You'd be no good on proper, fast rides.'

'No, I don't suppose I would.' I lean against the railings overlooking the river. The murky water swells into small, grease-slicked waves, then recedes. My stomach does the same.

'What about the London Eye?' Esme says, pointing further along the riverbank. 'That looks great.'

'No, I don't think I could go on that,' I say. 'Not right now.'

'I think you've had enough for one day too, love,' Libby says. 'Maybe tomorrow, eh?'

Esme beams at me.

'Will you come on it with me?' she says.

The thought of it makes bile burn in my throat and mouth.

'Why not?' I try to smile. The effort makes me nauseous.

Libby winks at Esme.

6

I'm queasy for the rest of the day and stretch out on the sofa, fighting a headache. When I close my eyes, I feel giddy. Snatches of sleep go by in a blur of fairground lights, laughter, Esme's lopsided smile.

I wake up squinting: an echo of Libby's wink. The room begins to spin once more. I'm orbited by Bagpuss, Esme's essay, Amy's photo, the statue with the colour missing from its heel. Discordant fairground organ music plays in my head.

I force myself to my feet and up the stairs. Amy's bed is stripped bare, cold to the touch. I shiver and retreat to my own bedroom. Still the organ music plays. I get up and shut the bedroom door.

Libby rings first thing in the morning.

'I've told Esme you believe her. She guessed as much after the way you behaved yesterday.'

Part of me feels guilty for leading her on; I am not totally convinced she's Amy after all. But another part of me feels guilty because I might be letting Amy down, by not believing what she says and looking the other way.

'How is she?' I say. 'No fits or tantrums?' My question is driven by worry as much as curiosity.

'The happiest I've seen her in ages.' Libby sounds defeated, resentful. 'She's raring to go. *Dying* to see you.' She sucks in her breath. 'Sorry, Beth. That was . . . clumsy of me.' She doesn't sound sorry.

My head thumps.

'I'm glad she's looking forward to seeing me.' There's a reluctance in me that I can't explain but manage to ignore. 'You'll come here then? For some lunch?'

'Esme's set her heart on the London Eye.' There's a challenge in her voice, daring me to go, daring me to say no.

My stomach kicks.

'Oh, okay then,' I say. 'I'll just wait for you at the bottom.'

'No. She wants us all to go together. Like a real family, she said.'

'Libby, I'm not sure I can cope with going round in circles again. Especially way up over the river. Maybe Esme can't either.'

'She was fine after the merry-go-round.'

'I wasn't.'

'No.' I think I hear a smile in her voice. 'But the Eye goes a lot slower than that did. You'll both be fine.'

I agree to meet them at noon at the London Eye.

A long shower invigorates me. I dress quickly, keen to see Esme but desperate to avoid a whirl on the London Eye. The thought of it puts me off having breakfast, but I brew some strong coffee, hot and black.

When the phone rings again, I pray that it's Libby with a change of plan.

'Mrs Archer?'

I don't recognise the voice, and for a moment I think it might be a journalist who's somehow got hold of the story of Amy's return.

'Yes,' I say warily.

'It's Sandra. The receptionist at the Spiritualist Association in Belgrave Square?' She says it like a question, as if she's not sure.

'Oh, hello,' I say hesitantly.

'I know,' Sandra says, laughing. 'Makes a change for us to be ringing you, doesn't it?'

'Yes. Is something wrong?'

'No, not at all. It's just that we've had an email from Ian. Ian Poynton? He's away on holiday but he said you called him before he went? Asking for a phone reading?'

'That's right, yes.' My hand flies to my head. 'Oh, the cheque! Sorry, it completely slipped my mind.'

'That's not why I'm ringing, although now you've mentioned it . . .'

'Of course. I'll get it off today.' I frown and shift the phone into my other hand. 'What is it Ian wanted, then? Can I speak to him?'

'I'm afraid not, no. Like I said, he's on holiday. America. But he has sent an email that he's asked us to forward to you, only we don't have your email address.'

Once I've given it to her, I hang up and run into the front room to switch the computer on. It's a blueberry iMac, a gift from the staff at the ad agency when I left to have Amy.

Funky and curvy. Just like you, the card said.

Shows how well they knew me, how they struggled to find something to say. I was never funky. The same could be said for iMacs now. It's clumsy and cumbersome. Slow. It has to think about sending emails and often crashes when it does. I only use it for designing posters for jumble sales, talks at the library, flower shows and charity auctions. Clunky, out-of-date software makes the little wheel spin while the computer thinks about every command.

I avoid using the internet, not because of the time it takes to load the pages, but because of what I might see there once it does. I stumbled across *that* picture of Amy once. On a feature about missing children on the BBC news home page. She was a poster girl, recognised all over the country. Shorthand for lost. I didn't need to open the page to know I'd be condemned as a careless mother in the comments section.

I thump the side of the computer as it growls into life. As usual, my email inbox is full of spam and messages from Jill.

Friends of Durning Library AGM
FW: FW: Beware. Fake twenty-pound notes in Kennington
Appeal for blankets for Vauxhall City Farm animals
Leaky tap in church hall
Lunch?

There is nothing from Ian. I thump the computer again. A moment later his email appears in the inbox.

FW: Will You Take It?

My heart is in my throat. This email could be the proof I need to underpin my belief or prevent me from making a mistake. There is sweat on my brow and the now familiar push of nausea.

Dear Sandra

Please forward this to Mrs Beth Archer. She called for a reading over the phone during the New Year break. Nothing came through then, but earlier today I got something here in New York. I couldn't call her – she needs to *see* this. And anyway, I don't have her number any more – it's been wiped automatically from my phone.

Thanks. See you at the end of the week.

Ian

Dear Mrs Archer

Apologies for sending this email via the Association, but I don't have an email address for you. I hope that *they* do, or can get one, as I think you need to see the picture I've attached.

As you know, I've got my doubts about telephone readings. Ditto for email readings – more so even. But I'm going ahead for two reasons:

a) you sounded like you really needed help

b) the connection I got when I saw this on the wall of a second-hand shop in New York earlier was so strong I felt like I'd been electrocuted. Which is appropriate given what's in the picture.

A bit of background: I collect superhero comics and inevitably end up in flea markets and shops full of old books, CDs and general tat – very kitsch usually. This is as well. It's odd, too. Took my breath away really – and not just because of the strength of the connection I got from it.

I don't know what it was you were calling me about, so I don't know the significance of the picture or its meaning – if any. All I know is that it was meant for you. I saw your face as clearly as if a light had suddenly been switched on.

I hope it helps.

Regards

Ian Poynton

My hands are shaking so much I can barely move the mouse or click on the attachment.

The computer shudders and stalls. The picture opens slowly, bit by bit, from top to bottom, like creeping damp.

A flat, grainy grey surface.

A head, moulded in a cream-coloured plastic.

A head with a centre parting. Long hair.

Jesus's head.

His neck and upper body. In a tunic.

His arms. Reaching down. Either side of an oblong panel.

At the top of the panel, words.

HONOR THY FATHER AND MOTHER.

A little boy on the left-hand side of the panel.

A little girl on the right.

In between them the stub of an old-fashioned light switch.

In the off position.

Sticking up.

Sticking out.

Erect.

Oh God!

I recoil from the screen as if I've been punched. Blood rushes to my head as I stand up too quickly; bile burns in the pit of my stomach. I am clammy, unsteady, forced to sit back at the desk. I can't look at the screen but I can't turn away from it either. When I close my eyes, I still see the image, as if it's seared on to my eyelids.

What sick kind of imagination could conceive such a thing? Even if it's meant to be tongue in cheek, it's grotesque, inappropriate, *wrong*. Anyone could see that. And if it *was* made with all sincerity, surely even the most devout of Christians, however innocent, would feel some consternation? See the knowing, salacious hand of the devil?

My shock gives way to the horrible realisation that Ian felt it was connected with me. It was a strong connection too; like an electric shock, he said. A connection so powerful it had compelled him to interrupt his holiday and ignore his own misgivings about 'remote' readings.

The real horror is that he's right. It's Amy's fate cast in plastic and stuck on the wall for everyone to see. There were never any leads to prove it — no body with the telltale signs; it was just assumed that Amy had been abducted by a paedophile.

My heartbeat quickens. The picture is a clue to her killer's identity. It must have been a vicar! The vicar assigned to Amy's school. Or someone closely involved with the church. The thought overwhelms me. My skin chills, seeps cold sweat.

I pick up the phone and dial Jill's number.

'Beth!' she says. 'I was just about to ring you. I won—'

'Who was the vicar at Amy's school when she disappeared?'

Jill hesitates.

'What?' she says.

'The vicar!' Impatience is making me shout. 'Who was he? Did you know him? Is he still there?'

'I can't remem . . .' She clears her throat. 'Beth, what's wrong? What's happened?'

'The psychic. He told me . . .' I grip the handset tighter.

'Oh Beth, no. Not again,' Jill says, more disappointed than sympathetic. 'I thought you'd decided to move on.'

'I can't. It's the vicar! He did it. I just know it.'

'How, Beth? How do you know?'

'It's right in front of me. Right here. Written on the wall. Nailed to it.' I close my eyes. '*Screwed.*'

'Beth, you're not making any sense,' she says. 'I want you to stay where you are. I'm coming over. And don't call anyone else. You can't just go accusing people willy-nilly.'

She's gone before I can tell her not to bother. She won't listen to me. Won't believe me even if she does.

The vicar's name used to be displayed on the sign outside the school. It might still be there.

The church nearest the school is St Peter's, just off Walworth Road. I'm out of the door in a flash, and follow the route Amy and I used to take when we walked to school. The route I've avoided for the last ten years.

Amy enjoyed school. On her first day, I was more nervous than she was. We both counted off the days on the calendar, but for different reasons. She was excited and pestered me to go shopping for the school uniform. It was all I could do to keep her out of it before term started. For me, each day brought the end of an era closer. My little girl was growing up and I had to let her go. The days of making up feeding bottles and changing dirty nappies were long gone. So were the afternoons spent feeding the ducks in Brockwell Park, making collages with autumn leaves and baking cornflake cakes.

I felt jealous of all the time Amy would spend with her teachers and anxious about the influence they'd have, the experiences I wouldn't be there to share or moderate.

The hug I gave her at the school gates was hungry, lingering. I could feel her waiting for it to end, ready to spring free like a Slinky. She didn't look back as she ran to join the children lining up in front of a teacher with a clipboard.

The girl behind her was whimpering, her wet cheeks shiny as she tried to see her mother in the crowd at the school gates. I almost wished Amy had done the same. The teacher knelt down and said something to the girl, then called Amy back. Amy took the girl's hand and led her in.

A stitch stabs at my ribs as I get closer to the school. Memories stab even harder. The gates are closed. The sign has changed. So has the name of the head teacher. There is no mention of a vicar. The gates clang and rattle as I kick them.

I'm running in the direction of the church when a car pulls up alongside me.

'Beth, where are you going?' Jill calls through the window.

'St Peter's,' I say, gasping for breath.

Jill drives on a short way, stops the car and gets out. She stands a few feet in front of me, arms stretched out to block my way. Like Jesus on the cross. She's not a big woman, rather slight in fact, so I could get past her quite easily. But her presence stops me in my tracks. Her green eyes, usually so soft with sympathy, are reproachful, and the thin-lipped mouth that has imparted wisdom and the kindest of kisses is set firm.

'Let's go home, Beth,' she says, stepping closer to me. 'Now. You can tell me all about it.'

'No. I can't.'

She grips my arm firmly.

'I want to help you,' she says, 'but I can't unless I know how, can I?'

A car stuck behind Jill's beeps its horn. Jill nods at the driver and steers me towards her car.

'In you get,' she says, opening the door on the passenger's side.

'Are you taking me to St Peter's?'

'Not right now, Beth,' she says, clearing a newspaper from the seat. 'Maybe later. Once I know what's been going on.'

The pressure of her hand on my arm grows stronger as she ushers me into the car. It smells of mints and petrol. She shuts the door behind me, then trots round to the driver's side.

'Thank God I brought the car,' she says, as she pulls away. 'I wouldn't normally bother, but I wanted to get here quickly.' She looks at me and shakes her head. Her wave of white hair doesn't move.

When we get back to the house, she helps me along the path.

'You left your front door wide open too, Beth,' she tuts. 'Let's hope you've not been burgled. That would really put the tin hat on things.'

She hesitates at the door, listening, then takes me into the front room and lowers me on to the sofa.

'I'll just get you some water.'

'No,' I say. 'I'm fine.'

'Tea, then. Hot and sweet.'

'No, really, Jill. I'm fine.'

She sits beside me and takes my hand.

'Now, why don't you tell me all about it?' She looks around the room. 'You said something about writing on the wall. I can't see anything. I hope you're not hallucinating again.'

'No . . .'

'I should call the doctor,' she says. 'Have you been getting enough sleep?'

I sit up.

'I didn't imagine it,' I say indignantly. 'It's real.'

'Where, Beth?' she says, looking around the room again. 'Where is it? Show me.'

'On the computer.'

I go to stand up, but Jill puts her hand on my shoulder and stands up herself. She walks over to the computer, slowly, as if it might bite her. She pushes her glasses up her nose and leans closer to the screen.

'Oh my God,' she says, turning towards me. 'Where on earth did you get this?'

'Ian – the psychic – sent it to me.'

'Then I don't know who's sicker,' she says firmly. 'Whoever dreamt this revolting thing up. The damned psychic for sending it to you. Or you for believing it's got anything to do with Amy.'

'But it has! Ian knows things about her.'

'He knows things about *you*, more like.' Her face softens. '*Everyone* does, Beth. The press saw to that . . . picking over details about you and your family life and holding them up for everyone in the country to see and sit in judgement on. It's easy for these so-called mediums to exploit you; I can't understand why you can't see that! Why you keep hurting yourself.' She turns the computer off by pulling the plug from the wall socket. 'This . . . Ian wants reporting to the police.'

'No. It's not just that picture. He's told me other stuff too. I don't want to frighten him off.'

I regret saying it as soon as the words have left my mouth. In defending myself I've exposed myself to further attack.

'Why?' Jill says, adjusting her glasses. 'What else has he told you?'

I look away from her. I can't tell her about Esme and Libby.

'There's no point,' I say. 'You won't believe it.'

'No, I certainly won't.' Jill sits down next to me. 'Look, that picture, the things you say he's told you, it's all just a question of interpretation. I can see how *you* might jump to the conclusions you've drawn, but to someone else . . . it could mean something completely different.'

I squirm further into the sofa.

'Such as?'

'Well,' says Jill, placing a cushion behind my back, 'it could mean that Amy is safe and happy in heaven with Jesus.'

'But he's got his . . . thing out!'

Jill grimaces.

'Maybe that's not what *that* represents,' she says. Her eyes dart around the room, as if looking for another feasible explanation. 'It could just be the light of Jesus showing the way out of darkness.' She pats my hand. 'So the fact that the light switch is in the "off" position could be a good thing. An invitation to reach for the light of faith and take comfort from it – even if it does look . . . unfortunate. It's all a matter of interpretation. Of seeing what you want to see.'

I lean my head against the back of the sofa. Snippets of the last few days explode in my head; shrapnel digs in. Smoulders.

'Best not to take things at face value,' Jill says. 'Help yourself and try to see the other side.'

'*You* don't do that when it comes to psychics.' There's an involuntarily curl in my lip.

'Well, there's only so much an old lady like me can believe in. Who knows, maybe I'll see the other side of the "other side" once I've passed on.' She smiles. 'Now, how about that tea? It's half eleven and I'm missing my second fix of the morning.'

I sit up quickly.

'Half eleven?' I say. 'I've got to go. Can you give me a lift?'

'Of course, but wouldn't you be better off staying in and resting?'

I stand up, push my hair back from my face.

'You're the one who's always telling me to get out and go places and meet people.'

'And that's what you're doing?' Jill says.

'I'm not going to track down a vicar and accuse him of all sorts, if that's what you mean.'

'No?' Her eyebrows rise in accusation.

'No, Jill. I've arranged to meet a friend of mine – Libby.'

'I've never heard you mention her before.' Jill sounds doubtful. I wonder if she's more uncertain over not hearing me talk about Libby before than she is about what I might really be up to.

'Oh, she did a work placement at Brian's agency,' I say. 'Some time ago now. Then she moved to Manchester. She's brought her daughter down to London for the first time. They want to go on the London Eye. I can't not go, as I don't know when I'll get another chance to see them.'

'Well,' Jill says, getting to her feet, 'if you're sure you're up to it.'

I'm not sure, but I have to go.

Fifteen minutes later, Jill pulls the car into a space just behind the Royal Festival Hall. I'm about to open the door but she tells me to wait and let her finish parking.

'I've still got the disabled badge I used for Arthur,' she says. 'Should have given it back really, but . . .'

'You're not coming with me.' I don't mean it as a question, but that's how she takes it.

'Why ever not? I just want to make sure you find your friends.'

'You want to keep an eye on me, more like. Make sure I don't go wandering off again. I'm not a child, Jill.'

She tugs on the handbrake and turns the engine off.

'No,' she says, 'but you're not yourself either.'

I get out of the car quickly.

'Hold on!' Jill calls out as she locks the door. 'I feel like I'm in a race.'

She is. I have to get there first and warn Libby and Esme not to say or do anything to make Jill suspicious. But there's little I can do to hide Esme's resemblance to Amy. Jill is sure to notice it. And Esme could recognise Jill as the school's lollipop lady. Everything is unravelling too fast, too soon.

I plunge into the crowds swarming around the concert hall, walk briskly along the path to the London Eye. It rears above me, the metal frets like a spider's web, sunlight glinting from the capsules as they move in a slow, ponderous circle. People inside the capsules wave at those on the ground, point cameras in every direction.

'There they are!' I say, waving vaguely in the direction of a couple of strangers. I turn back to Jill. 'It's okay. You can go now. You don't want to get caught with your dodgy parking permit, do you?'

Jill slips her arm through mine. She's a little out of breath, her cheeks flushed.

'No rush,' she says. 'It would be nice to say hello. I've never met any of your friends before. It's always been *me* introducing *you*.'

My panic increases as the strangers I pointed out turn and melt into the crowd.

'Gotcha!'

The hand grabbing the back of my coat makes me jump and turn around.

'Hello, *Esme!*' I say. 'Is that really you? Goodness, how you've grown since I last saw you.' Nerves make me speak too loud and too fast.

Esme frowns, goes to say something. I press her head into my belly, but only briefly. Through the crowd I see Libby walking towards us. She puffs her cheeks out and pushes a strand of hair from her face.

'I thought we were going to miss you,' she says. 'It's crazy down here.'

Libby looks quizzically at Jill, then back at me. I shake my head quickly, clench the muscles in my cheeks.

'This is my friend Jill,' I say. 'She brought me down here but she can't stop. Can you, Jill?'

I feel Esme pull back from me. She looks up at Jill. There's a moment's hesitation. Then a shy, curious smile. Not a trace of recognition. I was stupid to think there would be. Jill looks older now. Her hair is white, her skin more wrinkled. She's not in her lollipop uniform either, all that Amy ever saw her wearing. Maybe all old people look alike to children.

Jill, though, is wide-eyed, her lips slightly parted, her gasp audible above the hubbub all around us.

'This is Esme,' I say.

Jill flinches.

'Esme?' Her voice is no more than a whisper, her eyes fixed and unblinking. 'But . . .'

I imagine it's how I looked when Esme first appeared on my doorstep. We stare at one another, looking for clues in each other's eyes.

'She's so . . .' Jill shakes her head. Fear and fascination flash across her face. 'Such a . . . pretty little girl.'

'We're going up there! Aren't we lucky?' Esme says, pointing to the sky. 'Mum's taking me.' She nestles against me and I edge away as subtly as I can.

'Is she?' Jill says, nodding at Libby. 'You *are* lucky. Luckier than me. I've never been on it.'

Esme jumps up and down.

'Then why don't you come too?' she squeals.

'No!' I say, too loudly. 'Jill's got to get back, haven't you?'

Jill purses her lips.

'No,' she says. 'Not especially.'

I put my hand to my forehead.

'Now that we're here, I really don't think it's a good idea,' I say. 'For any of us. I just don't feel up to it.'

'Beth's not been too well this morning,' Jill says to Libby. 'Had a bit of an upset.'

I smile feebly. Esme slips her hand into mine and gives it a sympathetic squeeze.

'I'm sorry to hear that,' Libby says. 'Anything I can do?'

I tell her that a chance to chat and catch up on things would be just what the doctor ordered. I hope she catches the significance in the glare I give her, the imperative in the tone of my voice. Her eyes narrow with understanding. With questions.

'Maybe we'll leave the Eye for another time,' she says.

Esme looks crestfallen. She takes a camera from her pocket.

'But I wanted to take some photos!' she says.

'Ah,' says Jill, 'it'll be a shame for her to miss out. Why don't I take her? It's about time I finally had a go on it. And it will give you two some time together. On solid ground – which is probably just what Beth needs.'

'I don't know ...' I begin, wary of what Esme might say to Jill during the ride.

'Oh that's really kind of you,' Esme says. 'Please, Mum, can I?' She starts to bounce around once again.

'You can if you promise to be *good*,' Libby says firmly. 'This is a real treat. Make sure you take it all in and take lots of snaps. The views should leave you *speechless* – which will be a first!' She puts a finger to Esme's lips, then looks at Jill. 'She's such a chatterbox it drives you mad, and there'll be no escaping it up there.'

We wait in line with them until it's their turn. Esme skips along the platform and steps carefully into the pod, Jill right behind her.

'I really don't think this is such a good idea,' I say. 'Are you sure Esme won't say anything to her?'

'She understands. Esme's not stupid.'

No, I think. She isn't. She's as bright as Amy was – but Amy wasn't crafty, and I don't know Esme well enough to be sure the same is true of her. But, I realise with a start, I do like the girl. She's been considerate, polite and co-operative, remarkably restrained given the circumstances – just as Amy would have been.

Libby looks at her watch.

'It takes about half an hour to go round,' I say. 'Let's find somewhere to talk.'

Over a cup of coffee in the café at the Festival Hall, I tell Libby about Ian's email. She leans in close to me as I describe the picture of the light switch, pulls away again, her face screwed up in disgust. She's even more appalled when I suggest we might consider showing it to Esme.

'Are you mad?' she says. 'Look what it did to you, for

fuck's sake. Imagine the effect it would have on her.'

'But it might jog her memory about the man who took her!'

'Exactly. So I'm not going to make her do anything,' Libby says. 'It's got to happen naturally. Shit, in many ways I don't really want it to happen at all. I feel sick when I think how traumatic it will be for Esme if she does ever finally remember what happened to her. What mother wouldn't?'

I feel the familiar slap of the press claims about me being an unfit mother. I'm about to defend myself when Libby stands up.

'You promised you wouldn't pressurise her,' she says. 'I don't trust you, Beth. You're too ... unpredictable. Flaky. It's dangerous for Esme. God, I wish I'd never started this. I tell you, as soon as they get off that ride, I'm taking Esme back to Manchester.'

'No! You can't.'

'Watch me.'

I leap to my feet; my head swims in stuffy air dense with the smell of coffee and cooking fat. I run after Libby as fast as I can, bump into people and almost lose my balance. A man catches my arm and helps me to the door, where he fans my face with a booklet he's holding in his hand. I lean against the window, press my head against the cool of the glass.

'Will you be okay?' he says. 'Should I get someone?'

'No, thank you. I just need a moment.'

I take the booklet from him and walk away, fanning

myself. Libby is already waiting at the platform where the passengers disembark, her head tilted back, looking up at the capsules, hands shielding her eyes from the sun. I look up too, and see Jill talking, Esme beside her, listening intently. Then she waves at me, raises her camera and takes a picture.

'Libby!' I shout. 'Wait.'

She turns to me.

'I mean it, Beth,' she says. 'Leave us alone. We need some space. All of us.'

Esme glides by as the capsule draws level with the platform. She jumps off, holds out her hand to help Jill down, then runs down the gangway towards us.

'That was awesome!' she says breathlessly. 'You could see everything. For miles and miles and miles. I wished you'd come on too!' She spots the booklet in my hand and prises it from my fingers. 'What's this? More treats? Is this what we're doing next?'

'No,' Libby says, putting her hand on Esme's shoulder. 'Come on. We're going.'

Esme doesn't move. Not her feet, anyway. Tremors ripple through her body, slowly at first, then gather and intensify until she's shaking so hard her legs collapse beneath her. She looks up from the booklet and lets out an anguished squeal.

'No!' she cries. 'Don't take me there!'

'Esme? What's wrong?' Libby says, dropping to her knees and scooping the girl into her arms. Esme thrashes her way free.

'It's the wolf!' she screams, pointing at the booklet. 'And the duck!'

'What?' Libby takes the booklet from her.

I realise it's a programme for *Peter and the Wolf*. I took Amy to see it at the Royal Albert Hall and it gave her nightmares. She whimpered about the poor duck being swallowed alive, how she could hear it quacking inside the wolf's belly. How Peter's grandfather was mean and grumpy, not how grandfathers were meant to be at all.

Esme curls into a ball and drums her feet against the floor. 'It's the wolf. The wolf. I hate it. *She knows that!*'

'I didn't know it was a programme,' I say. 'For anything. Let alone *Peter and the Wolf*. Honestly. Somebody gave it to me—'

'Save it, Beth,' Libby says, lifting Esme to her feet. 'You just couldn't help yourself, could you? Just wouldn't wait. Now see what you've done.' She throws the programme at me. 'Stay away from us. Got it?'

Neither of them looks back as they walk away. I jump at the touch on my shoulder.

'Beth?' says Jill. She's pale and tight-lipped. 'What the hell was all that about?'

I hold my arms out, a picture of innocence.

'I wish I knew.'

'She seemed to think you did.'

I bend down and pick up the programme. A cartoon wolf, dark and shaggy, licks drool from glistening teeth. I can almost feel Amy's tense and trembling body in my arms, the dampness of her tears on my shirtsleeve.

I look up at Jill.

'What did Esme say to you up there?'

'Nothing, really,' Jill says. 'Nothing that gave any hint she was about to have a hissy fit.'

'I want to go home,' I say. 'I'm so tired I don't know which way is up any more.'

As we walk towards the car, I sense an unease in Jill.

'Esme was quite the tour guide,' she says. 'Knew London rather well for a tourist on her first visit. Pointed out all the major sights.' She draws breath as if about to speak, then changes her mind. A moment later she half turns to me.

'I know I shouldn't say this at all, let alone now, when you've been ... when you still are so ... upset, but ...'

'Go on.'

Jill shudders and hunches her shoulders.

'There were times up there when that girl gave me goosebumps,' she says. 'I can't explain it really ... She didn't say or do anything. She didn't have to.' She shakes her head. 'It's probably just me being silly, but once I'd thought it I just couldn't get it out of my mind.'

'Get what out of your mind?'

'That it was just like having Amy by my side.'

7

L ibby doesn't return my calls. I've left so many messages on her voicemail it won't accept any more.
Without an address, directory enquiries tell me they can't
find her home number and, as I don't know the name of
the hotel she stayed at, I can't ask them if she has actually
checked out or for the address she used when checking in.

There'll be too many questions if I ask the police to
track her down. If I tell the truth, my answers will only
make them laugh. If I lie, say she's a relative who's gone
missing after a row, they'll tell me to wait a bit longer or
that they can't interfere. And even if they did help, I've no
reason to believe they'd be any more successful than they
were in finding Amy.

It's a new chapter in an old nightmare. Amy might
have vanished – again. Snatched away right in front of my
eyes. Once more I am culpable in her disappearance; an
innocent mistake, an oversight. Yet again I am powerless
to change it. Lost.

My only option is to see if Ian can help me, but an email
to him gets no reply. The other side is as silent as it was
before.

For days I mope around the house, blank and anxious.

Then it dawns on me: Libby will have to come back to me even if she doesn't want to. The impulse that first brought her to my door still exists – if anything, it has more momentum now that Esme has met me and knows that I believe her. If her behaviour caused Libby distress before, it will only get worse now. Libby can't hold the fire back for ever. Whether Esme's my girl or not, she will come back to me.

A rush of optimism pushes me into action. I strip the wallpaper in Amy's bedroom, take up the carpet. I trawl the West End, collecting swatches of curtain fabric and browsing furniture and carpets. My experiments with samples of paint make a mosaic of the bedroom walls – pink of every hue, soft blues, yellow, vanilla, off-whites and greens.

I tell myself I'm redecorating the bedroom for my benefit, not Esme's, but I can't deny the fact that my indecision over the colour scheme is because the choice should really be Amy's. It was her room after all. In a way, it might yet be again.

I have the same thought when I find myself shopping for clothes. I hold up jackets and trousers to check the sizes and Amy hangs in the air, the same size as she was – and maybe still is. The clothes are empty but soon they could be filled. Every item brings her closer, makes the possibility of her more real.

I emerge from an overheated Selfridges, blinking at the light and bustle of Oxford Street and shocked at the number of bulging shopping bags in my hand. For a moment I think about turning around and taking all the clothes back, but I can't. I'm tired and need some fresh air. Besides, they will all suit and fit Esme as well as they would Amy.

I drift across Hyde Park and find myself just around the corner from Belgrave Square. The door to the Spiritualist Association is open. Inviting.

The receptionist looks up and smiles.

'Mrs Archer! How nice to see you again,' she says. She narrows her eyes and frowns. 'Have you changed your hair? You look . . . different.' Her eyes drop to the cluster of bags in my hand. 'Making the most of the sales, I see.'

'Yes, that's right . . . It's time for a makeover.'

'You're looking good on it. How can I help?'

'I was just passing and I remembered I still haven't paid Ian for the readings he gave me.' I put my bags down and open my handbag. 'What do I owe you?'

'I'm not sure, actually,' she says, rustling through some papers on her side of the desk. 'I don't know if we have a rate for telephone readings or if it's extra for him working over the holiday. But I can ask him.'

'He's here?'

'Came back yesterday.'

I'd lost all track of time.

'Would you like to see him?' she asks. 'He's got a few minutes before his next reading.'

He looks surprised to see me, sheepish even. The blue of his eyes seems darker, the angle of his off-kilter gaze more acute.

'I'm sorry I didn't get back to you about your friend's

telephone number,' he says. 'Requests for such specific help never really work. But I hope the photo I sent from New York meant something to you.'

'Yes, though I'm not sure what.'

He smiles ruefully.

'That's the way of it sometimes, I'm afraid. Maybe it will be clearer in time.'

'It will be clearer even sooner after a session of past-life regression,' I say hopefully. 'I know you don't do it, but could you recommend someone who does?'

He frowns at me.

'I know a few people,' he says. 'But I'd be happier to put you in touch if I felt you'd really thought it through. It's a ... unique kind of therapy. Not something you should do for fun.'

'It's not for me. I think it might help my ... niece.'

'Even so.' He coughs. 'Does she know what's involved?'

'No. She's only ten.'

'Ten?' He blinks and leans forward. 'Like I say, it's not really my area, but before you go ahead, you really need to give this some serious thought. Is your niece distressed?'

'I'm afraid she is, yes. I wouldn't be doing it otherwise.'

'And you think she could cope? It can be traumatic.'

'No more so than it is now,' I say. 'For *all* of us. Believe me, in her state of mind it would be riskier *not* to do it.'

He looks doubtful.

'If you can't help me,' I say, 'maybe I should ask at reception.'

'They don't do regression therapy here.'

I take out my chequebook and ask him how much I owe him. I rip the cheque from the book and slide it across the table.

'Someone will do it for us,' I say. 'I wish it could be you, as we seem to have some kind of connection. But if you won't help ...'

He takes the cheque.

'It's not a case of won't, Mrs Archer ...' His voice trails off and his eyes begin to dart around the room. Eyelids flutter, cheeks twitch.

'There's a man right behind you,' he says in a flat, faraway voice. 'A big man. Not tall. Fat. In his thirties? Younger possibly. Jet-black hair. I ... I ...' He shakes his head and cocks his ear towards me. 'He's talking ... His lips are moving but I can't hear him. No words are coming out.' He shakes his head once more. 'Ah, he's drawing something now. An ... exclamation mark. *Think.* He's telling you to think, Mrs Archer. Think.' He screws his eyes up. 'There's something else. Oh, I see. He's put the exclamation mark in a triangle. Now he's painting a red line around the edge ... Ah, right. It's like a traffic sign. Caution. Warning. *Beware.*'

His body shudders and his eyes refocus.

'Will you take it?'

I don't know who the man is. None of my family, former friends or colleagues fit the description. And it seems a little convenient that this warning from a spirit I don't recognise should turn up just as Ian is trying to dissuade me from something he considers ill-advised.

I stand up and collect my bags.

'I think maybe we'd better leave it there, Mr Poynton,' I say.

'But you've *got* to take it,' he says. 'You said yourself we had a connection. You can't pick and choose what you want to believe just because it doesn't suit.'

I open the door.

'Be careful, Mrs Archer,' he calls out as I walk down the corridor. 'Beware.'

I don't stop at reception to ask for details of any past-life therapists. I'll find them elsewhere. I don't need Ian. Not any more.

His reading was too timely, too pointed to be credible. His job as a psychic is to facilitate, mediate. He's just crossed the line into blatant interference. Abused his gift and undermined my trust in him.

Maybe I was wrong to believe in him at all. Perhaps his prediction about the little girl being close *was* just a lucky guess. And having seen that he'd scored a bullseye, ambition made him send me the picture of the light switch, hoping to hit the target once more. Hoping to make a name for himself.

Another possibility creeps into my head, one I can't believe I haven't thought of before. Wishful thinking blocked it. Now it rushes at me, an endless wave of logic so cold and powerful it knocks the breath from me.

He could be a friend of Libby's, a lover perhaps. An accomplice in an elaborate plan.

It's easy to see how they might have come up with the

deception. Ian is the new boy at the Spiritual Association. The other psychics could have told him about the desperate mother who comes back repeatedly in the hope of talking to her daughter. They might have too much integrity to fool me into thinking they've contacted Amy, but maybe Ian isn't so principled. Maybe he's more ambitious.

Libby saw an even bigger picture. Ian could soften me up with his prediction and she'd move in for the kill with her daughter, who just happens to bear a more than passing resemblance to mine.

They could do some research and drill whatever facts they could find into Esme's head. Esme would be rehearsed until her performance was perfect and natural. Believable enough to convince a sad, suggestible middle-aged woman with a valuable home, large divorce settlement and no one to leave it to.

Then there's the reward. Brian sold some of his shares in the agency to raise the one hundred thousand pounds for information leading to Amy's return or the conviction of her killer. The money is still unclaimed.

I see it all so clearly I stop in the street and start laughing, softly at first, then louder, until my mirthless shrieks degenerate into sobs. The bags in my hands suddenly feel too heavy to carry. Clothes spill on to the pavement; arms reach out towards me, legs run away. There are snide smiles in metal zips, sly winks in buttonholes. A facsimile of Amy's body sprawls in a suit, a silhouette at a crime scene.

I bundle the clothes back into the bags, hold out my

hand to hail a passing cab. I don't know who or what to believe. Everything. Nothing. No one.

'Where to, love?' the cabbie says, setting the meter running as I slam the door behind me.

I need clarity. Once I looked to Ian for that. Now I have to go back to the last place where I thought things made some kind of sense. I can't tell dark from light, the truth from a lie. A lost sheep from a hungry wolf.

I need God to show me the way again. Flick the switch of understanding. *Now* I know what the message in that picture means, even if I don't know who it's from.

'Southwark Cathedral,' I tell the cab driver. 'Hurry.'

The cathedral's main turret looks like an extracted tooth, the spires its redundant roots. A gargoyle over the door-way shows a dragon clinging to the edge with its talons. I know how it feels. The music I hear as I open the doors makes me wobble even further.

It sounds like an oboe, the signature of the duck in *Peter and the Wolf*. I tell myself it's not really there. But it is. And it grows louder as I step into the cathedral.

I'm relieved to see that there's a group of musicians at the front of the church, the gaze of the stone saints above them indifferent to their performance.

A woman near the door puts her finger to her lips and hands me a sheet of paper. *Lunchtime Concert Recital*, it says, featuring a quintet of students from a local music school. It lists the pieces to be performed but all I can hear is music from *Peter and the Wolf*. The cat as the clarinet, cagey and comic. Peter, youthful and playful in the exuberant strings. Grandfather's grumbling bassoon. Worst of all, the anxious, melancholic oboe, prescient of the duck's fate.

Instead of taking a seat in the nave, I hurry down the aisle to the left, towards the Harvard Chapel. But the door is closed. A sign says it will open to the public again once emergency repair work has been completed. I turn the handle anyway and the door opens.

The chapel is dark, the rack for votive candles empty, the window covered by tarpaulin and framed by scaffolding. The funereal gloom makes me shiver.

'What are you doing in here?'

A man appears behind me. He's as grey as his cassock, his body stooped. He points at the door.

'The sign is quite clear,' he whispers.

'But I had to come in. I need to find the truth.'

My eyes fly around the chapel. I can just make out the limp red flag above the door. *Veritas*. And the red panel in the ceiling, its gilding dull and flat. *Veritas*. But the pane in the window below the image of Jesus is masked by the grubby tarpaulin.

'Well I'm sorry,' the man says, placing a hand on my arm. 'You'll have to pray elsewhere.'

'But the window . . .'

'I know. It's very sad. We hope to get the crack repaired soon.'

'Crack?'

'Quite a lot of them, it seems,' he says. 'As you can see, we've got the specialists in, checking for more damage.

We don't want to take any chances, which is why we've shut the chapel to the public. If we *could* lock the door, we would. The sign is enough to keep people out – usually.' He glares at me. 'I'm afraid you're going to have to leave.'

The pressure on my arm becomes more insistent and doesn't let up until I'm standing outside the chapel. The man closes the door, straightens the sign, nods his head at me and walks away.

So much for the truth revealed by the light of God. I'm lost in a murky, maddening twilight. I want Esme to be Amy, but that is not enough. I need to believe it. Just like I believed Ian. Just like I believed God. But I can't trust myself to believe anything, not even myself.

Ian *has* to be a fraud, in league with Libby and Esme. He can't risk a past-life regression as it won't reveal anything about Amy's fate or where her body is. How could it? No one knows. And Esme wouldn't be able to make up details so convincingly if her conscious mind was slumbering under the spell of hypnosis. No wonder he tried to put me off.

But the whole notion of a fraudulent plan is hard to believe too. The scam is elaborate and risky, dependent on a child to succeed. And yet Esme knows things about Amy she couldn't have found out anywhere else.

Through the fog in my head I see Esme listening attentively to Jill as they neared the end of their ride on the London Eye. I remember the hours Jill has spent sitting at my kitchen table or on my sofa. Holding me. Passing tissues. Listening to me talk about Amy. She knows every anecdote, every little detail, as well as I do. Sometimes she even finishes them for me.

She's word-perfect.

Realisation hits me in a hot rush. Jill is the mole who has been leaking details to Libby.

I can't even begin to imagine how they know one another, but I'm sure they do. When they came face to face for the 'first time' at the London Eye, maybe Jill feigned her surprise at Esme's resemblance to Amy.

She could have helped set up the rendezvous and taken me there me to make sure I turned up. Why else would she have had her car with her that day? Jill is a better actress than I ever suspected. Maybe one of the many groups she belongs to is an amateur dramatics society and she's never let on.

I run along the cathedral aisle, chased by the notes from the oboe. The duck laughing, mocking. Seeing everything through the eyes of the wolf.

I bundle myself into a cab and give the driver Jill's address.

When Jill opens her door, she's got a pad and a pen in her hand.

'What's this?' I sneer. 'Making more notes for yet another essay? Instructions?' I push past her and slam the door.

'Essay? Beth, what's—'

'You bitch! How could you do it, Jill? How? After everything I've been through.'

Jill sinks into a chair in the hallway, winded by shock. The pad and pen slip from her hand to the floor.

'Beth,' she says, her voice shaking, 'whatever's the matter? Calm down. Please. You're upset.'

'Upset!' I scream. 'That doesn't even come close. I thought you were my friend, and all the while you've just been collecting information. Grooming Esme.'

'Esme?'

'Or should I say Amy?'

'What?' She rubs her eyes and shakes her head. 'Beth, you're not making any sense.'

'Come on, Jill,' I say. 'You've taken me for a mug long enough. Denying it all now will only make you look as foolish and desperate as I've been.'

'Denying what?' Jill says, her hands stretched out, pleading with me.

'Amy. Reincarnated. As Esme. What is it, Jill? Your way of being cruel to be kind? Jolting me back to life? Like Amy has been – apparently.'

Jill stands up and her legs wobble. She reaches out to the wall for support.

'Let me get this straight,' she says. 'Esme says she's Amy and you think I put her up to it. Is that right?'

'You and Libby and Ian.'

Jill reaches out and takes my hand. I pull it away.

'You can't honestly believe that any of that is true,' Jill says. Her voice wavers and her hands are shaking. 'I'd never clapped eyes on Libby and Esme until the other day at the Eye ... And who's Ian anyway? And reincarnation?

Come on, Beth. It's ridiculous! Almost as ridiculous as you thinking I could possibly come up with such a cruel idea. Even if I *could* do it, why would I want to?'

'You tell me.'

'I can't,' she cries. 'Because I wouldn't. Not to any-body – and certainly not to you.' She pulls a tissue from the sleeve of her cardigan and wipes her eyes. 'It kills me you could even *think* I'd do anything so heartless, let alone accuse me of it.'

'But how else could she know all the things she put in her essay?'

'Beth, I don't know what you're talking about. What essay?'

'The one Esme wrote, of course,' I say. 'You know, the one with all those memories. Details. All the things I've shared with you.'

Jill jabs her finger at me.

'Whatever is in this essay is clearly a pack of lies,' she says, her voice stronger and more composed now. 'And let's not forget, Beth, you shared those memories with Brian, too. First-hand.'

My eyes narrow and skirt around the hall. The blood in my veins is suddenly cold. Frozen by an awful realisation.

'Brian must be involved as well!' I say. 'He's as bored with my grief as you are.'

Jill rolls her eyes.

'Listen to yourself, Beth,' she says. 'It's pitiful. You're tired ... overwrought by the anniversary. I understand that. But you need help. You're deluded. Paranoid. Christ,

142

you could have written that claptrap essay yourself for all I know. It's the Mother's Day cards all over again.'

A card has appeared on the mantelpiece several times over the last few years. I don't remember buying them or writing them. But apparently I did. I can't believe I've done the same thing again. Won't believe it.

My mind replays the moment I first saw the essay on my doormat. I'd been cleaning shortly before. Tidying up my desk. Then I was on the stairs, staring into nothing. Somewhere between the two memories, the envelope appeared.

'I didn't write it,' I say, trying to sound certain. 'Esme put it through my letter box.'

'You saw her do it, did you?'

'No, but . . . She wrote it at school – supposedly. '

'So it's in her handwriting, then?' Jill says.

I shake my head.

'Typed,' I say. 'On a computer.'

Jill snorts with derision.

'So you *could* have written it,' she says. 'I know your psychiatrist told you to write things down, Beth. To get things out. But not like *this*. Not making things up.'

'I didn't!'

I try to remember if Libby or Esme mentioned the essay when we met. I thought they did, but now I stop and really think about it, I realise they didn't. My eyes search the room, looking for something to hang on to, something to stop me going over the edge.

'It's not beyond the realms of possibility, is it, Beth?'

Jill says. 'Only a few days ago you had it in your head that a vicar killed Amy. You can't go around shooting your mouth off, accusing all and sundry. Someone less understanding than I am could tell the press, sue you for slander or defamation of character or something, and God help you then. Do you really want all that on top of everything else? I dread to think what the papers would make of it. They'd probably say you were just trying to shift the blame or attempting to redeem yourself.' She puts her hand on my shoulder. 'You haven't told the police any of this, have you?'

'Not yet, but—'

'Well that's something, I suppose. You can't tell them, Beth. You just can't. You have no proof. Of anything.'

What clarity I had is suddenly fogged by doubt. I sink into the chair.

Jill's right. The police might not believe me, and if it leaks to the press, I'll have reporters on my doorstep once more. Amy's case will be replayed all over again. The public's hate for me will be given extra momentum. *Missing girl's mother loses the plot* is the kindest of the headlines I can see.

Jill picks up her pad from the floor.

'Look,' she says. 'Not instructions or notes. Just a list of addresses I've got to pick up jumble from for the next church bazaar. That *we've* got to pick up.' She gives a little laugh. '*If* you can trust me enough to get into my car and not be whisked away somewhere.'

I feel foolish, weak.

'I think I'd better get you home,' Jill says, her voice kind and concerned once more.

When I get out of the car, I leave my bags on the back seat.

'What about these?' Jill says.

'Keep it for the jumble sale.'

'But it's all brand new!' She starts to rummage through the bags, pulls out a skimpy top and looks up at me quizzically.

'For Amy,' I say. 'All of it.'

'Oh Beth.'

She's just as concerned when she sees Amy's bedroom, stripped bare, dappled with blocks of sample paint colours.

'Maybe I should call Brian,' she says. She's thinking out loud rather than asking my opinion. 'He should know what's been going on.'

'No. Please, Jill. I couldn't face his sarcastic sniggering.'

'You may be divorced, Beth, but I'm sure he still cares about you.'

'I doubt it. Promise me you won't tell him.'

'If that's what you want.' She looks around the room once more. 'I'll give you a hand to get it back into shape, okay? I'm not the world's best decorator, but we'll manage between us.'

Perhaps she just wants to keep an eye on me.

She offers to stay for a bit, but I tell her no. I check to see she's following me as I go down the stairs.

'Where's this essay?' she says.

In the front room, Jill takes the paper from me, pushes

her glasses up her nose and starts to read. She frowns as her eyes move quickly across the page. The muscles in her cheeks twitch.

'Right,' she says, ripping the pages into tiny bits, 'that's taken care of that load of drivel.'

'I wish it was as easy to get it all out of my head. I know it by heart I've read it that many times.'

'I'm sure.'

'I didn't write it, Jill. I swear.'

'Well, it's gone now,' she says decisively. 'And if you've got any sense, you'll send those two jokers packing too. Do yourself a favour. Don't see them. Don't talk to them.'

'I don't have much choice,' I say. 'They've gone to ground and I've no way of finding them.'

'Just as well, all things considered.' She puts her arms around me. She smells of talcum powder and mints.

'Make an appointment with the doctor, Beth. For all our sakes.'

I say I will. But I won't. No doctor can cure me. Only the truth can do that – and I'm no closer to finding that than I am to finding Amy's body.

8

The postcard is lost beneath a drift of leaflets for pizza deliveries and mail shots for credit cards and stationery supplies. The blue envelope from Tesco tells me that 'Every Little Helps'.

The postcard might. It's a picture of a large silver wheel, like the London Eye, only set against a backdrop of unfamiliar office buildings. *The Wheel of Manchester*, it says on the front. I turn it over quickly. My heart is racing, kicking hope skywards.

Dear Mum

I don't like what you did when we were at the London Eye. It wasn't fair. But Mum keeping me away from you isn't fair either. She won't let me ring you or see you. Sometimes I hate her. Sometimes I hate you. I love you both too. More than you know.

Email me. Mum won't find out. She doesn't do computers. It will be our secret. I'm good at keeping secrets. We both are.

iamamy@yahoo.com

Relief that Esme has got in touch vies with consternation. I'm scared of what might follow if I email her, the dark and dangerous road it could take me down, where madness could ambush me at any moment. But the road could lead me back to Amy, put me on the path to redemption.

I read the postcard once more. Her invitation is tantalising and beguiling, but I sense a threat too. What secrets has she been keeping? And what secrets does she think I have? Perhaps she means that she's known all along where Amy's body is and has just been keeping it back. Maybe she's playing with me the way a trickster does a stooge, tempting me further into her web until the sucker punch.

My fingers hover over my computer keyboard, a blank email staring back at me. I start to type, slowly at first, then faster and faster. I don't have to send it, I keep telling myself as I write. The delete key is my escape hatch as much as the send button is a trapdoor into the unknown.

Dear Esme

I can't tell you how much your postcard meant to me. The last few weeks without you have been agony. I didn't know how to find you or whether I would ever see you again. I expected you would never want anything to do with me, seeing as I was so stupid last time we met.

But you have to understand that the *Peter and the Wolf* programme was a genuine mistake. Not a trap. I promise. I wouldn't do anything to hurt or scare you. I hope you believe me. Your postcard gives me hope that you do.

The second chance you've given me is so precious. I'll do

anything to make sure Libby never finds out we're in touch with one another.

Are you sure she won't see this? Libby needs time to trust me again. You must try not to hate her. She only wants what's best for you. Just like I do. Just like I always have.

Beth

I delete my name.

Love, Mum.

I scroll up; the cursor flutters around Esme's name as I dither whether to change that too.

I do. Just to see how it looks. How it feels.

Dear Amy.

The letters flow so easily, without hesitation, just like Esme's stories. Seven letters. Eight keystrokes. It was done in a fraction of a moment, but the thrill of writing her name again, seeing it there, that . . . *that* could last for ever. The cursor pulses next to it. Now you see it. Now you don't.

If I'm signing off as Mum on the email, then I have to call her Amy. But I promised Libby that I wouldn't, and this might still be a test; Libby might be reading over Esme's shoulder. I change it back to Esme but leave my sign-off as Mum; a compromise, halfway to the truth.

The force that makes my finger hit the send button is the same one that's driven me since New Year's Eve: the need to *know*.

The email sits in my outgoing mail folder for an age. The little wheel spins on the screen as the computer thinks about whether to do what it's been told. The bar at the bottom of the screen tracks the email's progress; it's like straining clay through a sieve.

Once it's gone, I sit and wait, willing a message to come in. But it doesn't. I tap the side of the computer and fiddle with the cables, sliding them home firmly in the various slots and making sure everything is switched on.

I read my email again. Maybe I should have waited a day or two before I replied. Perhaps it's better not to look too keen. I wonder if Libby and Esme are sitting somewhere in Manchester reading my message and giggling, planning what Esme should say next.

For a moment I wish it was possible to retract emails. I don't want to be laughed at any more or get more en-tangled up in their games. *If* it is a game.

I check my watch to see how long I've been waiting. It's nearly half past ten. That explains the delay. Esme will be at school. I don't know if she's got her own mobile phone. I can't recall seeing her with one. Surely she's too young for any kind of phone, let alone one with access to email? If she has, then she's umpteen steps ahead of me. Out of reach.

It's unlikely I'll get a reply before four o'clock. And when it does arrive, my computer will inevitably choke. I get up, put on my coat and head for the West End.

*

A new computer will help me track down the truth. It needs to be shiny and contoured, streamlined. The laptop I buy from the Apple store more than fits the bill.

MacBook Air. Its name alone makes me feel energised; light and free. It's primed with software and wi-fi. When I get home I'll be plugged in, switched on. Armed.

My next stop is for a mobile phone. *Ring the Changes*, says a poster in the Orange shop window. I smile and do as I'm told. But I'm as bewildered by the range of phones as I was by the choice of computers. The information on the tickets is just as baffling too. The assistant behind the counter looks up and jerks his chin at me.

'I want to replace this.'

I reach into my handbag and take out a battered black Nokia with a screen no bigger than an inch square. That alone is reason to change it; even with my glasses on I can barely read it.

He raises his eyebrows.

'I'm not surprised you want to change it. Does it still work?' He steps out from behind the counter, walks towards me and takes the phone. 'No camera. No colour. No apps.'

His tone is half sneering, half astonished.

'I have had it a while,' I say sheepishly.

'You're not kidding.'

'I don't really use it that much.'

'No,' he says. 'I wouldn't either.' He drops the phone into my hand as if it's radioactive. 'Pay As You Go?'

'That's right, yes.'

'Thought as much.'

He walks past a rack of sleek and glossy phones with big screens.

'What about these?' I say.

'They're not all available on Pay As You Go,' he says. 'And the ones that are can be expensive without a contract. But you can change plans if you want.'

'Okay,' I say. 'I'll change plans too.'

I pick up each of the phones as I answer his questions.

Yes, it's for personal use. Yes, I'll be using it a lot. For calls, texts, photos, emails and internet. For bringing my long-lost daughter home. Or for hunting down liars and cheats.

When I get home, the computer gleams like a shield. The phone is soon charged and ready, loaded with apps. It's as good as a gun.

There's an email in my inbox. An invitation to be Amy's friend on Facebook. *Amy's* friend. The audacity of it cripples me. The promise of it lifts. I'm so confused. I can't breathe for the lump in my throat.

I've heard of the site on news stories but never looked at it. I've had no need to; the few people I know are pensioners and are no more likely to use it than I am. If I want to know what they're up to, I know where they are and how to find them.

I click on the link and pull my chair closer to the desk. The website loads in a flash, without the constant whir of the fan I've got used to. The cursor winks, encouraging me to enter my first name and open an account. I don't want to but I have to; the site won't let me go any further without one. I type in my name, leaving my profile and location blank. I don't upload a photo, defaulting to an anonymous, ghostly silhouette.

Esme isn't so shy. Just cruel. Or maybe just painfully honest.

The name at the top of her page is Amy Archer. And the picture is *that* photo of Amy, in her school uniform, the one that appeared in the papers and on TV.

She's put up other photos too. There's one of me and Brian at a press conference, and one of Brian on his own. I recognise it from his ad agency's website. The school photo must have been taken from the internet too. The one below it is fuzzy with camera shake and breaking up with zoom; it's me, talking to Libby at the foot of the London Eye.

My eyes drop down the page.

Family: Brian and Beth Archer
Friends: Dana Bishop
Education: East Street Primary
Philosophy: Angel lost in space now back on earth
Music: Spice Girls
Books: *Return from Heaven*; *Children's Past Lives*
Movies: *Spice World*
Television: *Top of the Pops, Live & Kicking, Gladiators*
Games: Juggling, French skipping, being pop stars
Sports: Swimming, rounders, roller-blading

Activities: Tap-dancing, drama, Brownies
Interests: Reincarnation
Other sites I like: www.dailymail.co.uk/
   Our-son-World-War-II-pilot-come-back-to-life

A blue box with Amy's picture inside it pops up on the screen.

> Hello! Email is soooooo boring and soooooooooooo slow. Instant messaging is quicker and fun. Mum won't know we're doing it. No one will as I've fixed the settings so they can't. If you haven't done it before, just write in the box and hit return.

I hesitate, anxious about stepping further into a trap — a high-tech trap, full of unknown protocols and the danger of public exposure.

> Hello Esme.

> Great! This is how I chat to all my friends.

> I hope that means we're friends too.

> You're not my friend! You're my mum!!! I hope you've read the article about that little boy in America. He was just like me. Reincarnated, I mean. Ever since he was two he kept having nightmares about being in a plane shot down by the Japanese in the war. He knew all about it. He even called

his Action Men by the names of three other pilots who died in the same battle. All of the pilots had different-coloured hair so he called each Action Man by the name of the pilot whose hair colour matched the doll. It's a true story, like mine is. You do believe me, don't you?

I pull back from the screen as if she's sitting in front of me and demanding a final, unequivocal answer. She sounds so eager, so excited, like Amy giving me a run-down on a new dance routine or sharing an amazing fact she's learnt in class.

It was hard at first. You can understand why, can't you?

Sure. It must be really tough for you too. I never wanted to upset you but I knew I would. I'm really sorry, Mum. I bet I've made you cry a lot. I've cried loads too, in case you didn't believe who I was. You never liked it when you thought I was lying. The little boy's mum believed him from the start but his dad didn't. Though he did in the end.

Tears spring to my eyes. I dab them away with the tips of my fingers and feel them damp on the keyboard as I type.

I expect your dad would find it hard to believe too.

He doesn't believe in ghosts, does he?

No. But you're not a ghost, are you?

No. I'm Amy. I feel sorry for Mum (Libby) though – she thinks she's losing Esme. My memories with her aren't the same as ours. I love her but I'm not really hers. You get me? She's like the stepmothers in fairy stories – but not wicked and cruel. If she was, I wouldn't have chosen her as my new mum.

The realisation that I'm second best knocks the wind from me. It's illogical to feel betrayed, but I do.

Why didn't you choose me?

I didn't see you.

I was busy doing nothing, I think, not being around when she needed me, just like the press always said.

Would you have come back to me if you'd had the chance?

I'm back now. First chance I got. I've missed you.

I see my hand reaching out to the screen, touching it, as if I were stroking her face.

Why did it take you so long to realise who you were? You said the little boy remembered things from the age of two.

I think it's 'cos he had longer to get used to it. The pilot was dead for sixty years before the boy was born. I came back straight away. I didn't know what was what. I had all this stuff in my head and then there'd be big gaps. It didn't make sense. Bits are still missing.

I know I promised Libby; I know she might even be sitting by Esme's side – but I can't fight the impulse, my need to know.

You can't remember anything about what happened to you?

No. I've got to go. I

I wait for what seems like an age. When nothing appears on the screen, my fingers scramble across the keys.

Hello? Esme? Are you there? Esme?

Maybe Libby was there after all and told Esme not to answer. I panic that I've blown my opportunity. Then I think that Esme could just have run away before I could press her for more details. Details she doesn't have.

I read the article on the reincarnated fighter pilot several times. His parents' confusion about his behaviour echoes Libby's description of her experience with Esme. His father's initial scepticism chimes with mine.

They too put it down to imagination, but were worn down by the boy's unfailing accuracy about details he just couldn't have known. He knew the plane was a Corsair, that it was hit in the engine and exactly whereabouts it went down. He knew that the aircraft carrier it took off from was called the *Natoma*, and that the battle was Iwo Jima. He described his parents' fifth wedding anniversary in Hawaii five weeks before his mother got pregnant, citing it as the moment he chose them to be his parents. And the boy and the pilot were both called James.

The pilot's sister believed the boy's story and so did the pilot's parents. The boy's father researched the story just to prove it was all simply coincidence but instead found himself getting closer and closer to something more fantastical. Eventually he concluded that there are some things that can't be explained. Things that are unknowable.

If I'd read the story when it first appeared in the press I would have dismissed it; uncanny and interesting, yes, but ultimately no more than a story based on coincidence. Now it seems familiar and credible.

The similarities could just be the common characteristics of a reincarnation experience, which would mean that Amy *has* returned. Or maybe Esme has just taken the boy's story as the template for her own, like cribbing answers over somebody's shoulder. But that wouldn't explain the details she knows.

Esme signed off so suddenly, I didn't get the chance to ask if she'd written the essay and put it through my letter box. It could still be the work of my grief-steeped imagination running wild with wishful thinking.

I massage my temples and squint back at the screen. The boy's nightmares ceased by the time he was eight – about the same age as Esme's started. Maybe the pilot's spirit was laid to rest as his story was told. Amy's hasn't been.

I bookmark the web page; it's a stepping stone on the way to the threshold of wholehearted belief.

I can't help wishing that I was her first choice as mother. The pilot didn't have the option of being reborn to his original parents, but according to Esme, Amy did. Not immediately, of course; conceiving – sex – was the last thing Brian and I were thinking of at the time. But surely she could have waited? Picked her moment to make sure she came back to me? I don't dwell on wondering why she didn't, and distract myself by searching Facebook for Esme Lawrence.

She's been less careful with her own page than she was with Amy's. It's open to anyone who wants to look. I move in closer. Esme beams from her home page, her face framed with jazz hands. She looks too innocent to be playing painful and dangerous games like the one she might be playing with me.

There are other pictures too. A yellow hoop arcs above her head like a giant halo as she skips through it down a running track at her school sports day. She smiles from a rickety-looking stage, her silver-foil top hat falling over her face. She drips and shivers on a sunless beach, blows out candles on a chocolate cake.

Her list of friends is long: Lara, Olukemi, Rishna, Poppy, Lola, Josh, Ethan, Henry, Pavel. Her messages are pretty much what I'd expect from a girl on the brink of adolescence.

I soooo love Rhys. He can't leave *Hollyoaks.* He just can't!
    I'll die.
Ugh. Banana flavour anything makes me wanna puke. Love
    bananas tho.
The new boy on *HO* is cute!!! Better than Rhys. ☺
We're doing a Moulin Rouge routine for the end-of-term
    show. Can-can and everything. I want a lacy bra and
    frilly pink knickers but Mum says no. Proper annoying. ☹

Family:	Libby Lawrence
Friends:	Poppy Brewer, Olukemi Sharif, Josh Dobbs, Lara Pryce
Education:	Whythenshawe Junior
Philosophy:	Dance yourself dizzy
Music:	Lady Gaga
Books:	*Skellig, His Dark Materials*
Movies:	*Finding Nemo, The Princess Diaries*
Television:	*X-Factor, Hollyoaks, Glee*
Games:	Angry Birds, Wii
Sports:	Swimming, gymnastics
Activities:	Tap-dancing, singing
Interests:	Having fun, boys

It's easy to get a fix on what she's watching and thinking, who she's talking to, what her plans are. Google Maps lets me track her from Wythenshawe to her school's gates.

She should be more careful. Libby should too. Anyone could cruise the website, befriend her, pry and prey. It's how Amy's killer could have found her if Facebook had existed back then. If it had, I probably wouldn't have let Amy go on it, not at her age. But if she had used it, she'd have been more sensible and I would have been more attentive to what she was saying and doing – despite what the press and the public might say.

Esme's carelessness and the freedom it gives me make me angry. She deserves to be stalked and caught. Goosebumps bristle at the thought.

My search on Facebook throws up lots of Libby and Elizabeth Lawrences, but none of them are the one I'm after. Not from the pictures displayed anyway. I click on each one but most are set to prevent access to everyone other than Friends. If the Libby I'm looking for *is* there, I can't find her. Google can't either.

She's a young woman, probably cut off from an active social life by the demands of being a single mum. The internet would be a source of entertainment, of information, a way of staving off isolation. Either she really doesn't use computers, just like Esme said, or she's gone to great lengths to make herself invisible.

Her obscurity makes me suspicious. I didn't think it was possible to hide so completely on the internet. I only wish it was. I know from long and bitter experience that the finger of accusation can be pointed from news sites and forums, and that bitches with blogs are always ready to speculate and hate.

Then there are the ghoulish sites dedicated to unsolved crimes. I click on one and see a parade of faces, Amy's included.

Some of the other faces are familiar, high-profile cases that dominated the news, just as Amy's did. Some of the photos are black and white, the grainy shots dating the victims as much as their clothes and hairstyles.

I open several of the links to Amy, like Libby might have done to find information for Esme. But they contain none of the details Esme knows – nothing but the basic facts regurgitated by the press at the time, or the voyeuristic ramblings of people who make a hobby of death.

I sit and wait by the computer all night. I try direct messaging her umpteen times, my 'are you there's and 'where are you's like mocking echoes of the shouts I made into the park on the night she disappeared. Calls to a lost girl, lost in the ether.

There is nothing the next day either, or the day after that. I'm back where I started, dangling like a fish on a hook. Waiting. Wanting. Needing to know the truth.

The following day, a ring on the doorbell has me rushing to the hall.

'All set?' says Jill, as I open the door.

I'd forgotten. I'm meant to be taking her in the car to pick up some donations for the next jumble sale.

'Oh, hello,' I say, disappointed that it isn't Esme and Libby. 'I'll be with you in a minute. Come in.'

She follows me into the front room.

'No more from those two jokers?' she says, looking around quickly as if to make sure.

'No,' I say, avoiding her eyes. 'Not a word.'

'Good. That's that nonsense over and done with then.' Jill gives a nod of her head, inviting my agreement.

I smile weakly.

'I'm sorry about ... you know,' I say, shrugging my shoulders.

'Already forgotten, Beth ... My goodness,' Jill says, pointing at the computer. 'Look at this!'

'Yes.' I'm glad of the change of subject and feel my body relax. 'It's my new toy. So much quicker than my old one.'

'Good,' says Jill, edging closer to the computer for a better look. 'So you'll be able to do the poster for the jumble sale in record time.'

'Yes.'

'You couldn't do it now, could you?' she says, raising her eyebrows expectantly. 'I can drop in at the library to get it photocopied once we've finished the collection.'

She's got that jumble-sale tone to her voice – a mix of strict headmistress and bossy Brown Owl. She umms and aahs over my shoulder as I throw a poster together.

'I know you're the design expert,' she says, 'but I'm the queen of the jumble. Let's try putting a full stop after "church hall".'

As usual, we end up with a poster identical in every way to the one for the previous sale – except for the change to the date. She stands over the printer while I get my car keys and coat.

'Come on,' she calls. 'We're late. We may only be volunteers, but that's no reason to be unprofessional.'

In the car, she keeps telling me to watch the traffic,

shouts if I miss a turning. When we get out, she reminds me not to leave the keys in the car and insists I should be more careful with the boxes of crockery.

We pile the bulging bags and boxes at the back of the church hall. I plunge my hand into a black plastic bag spewing clothes. A waft of old sweat, damp and dust creeps around me; Eau de Jumble, as Jill calls it. I should be used to it after so many previous sales, but it still makes me gag.

I untangle a coat with a furry collar from a spangly halterneck top, fold them in half and drop both on the women's-wear table.

'You're going through this lot as quickly as the punters will,' Jill says, as she opens another black plastic bag and releases more fetid air.

'I don't want to be here all day,' I say. 'I've got to get back. I've such a lot of admin to sort out.' It's only a partial lie, but I hide it behind the long drop of a flower-patterned curtain.

When we finish, we stand back to survey the racks of clothes and the tables of tatty bric-a-brac. My hands feel dry and grubby; Eau de Jumble lingers on my sweater.

Jill accepts my offer of a cup of tea, so I walk to the small kitchen at the back of the church hall. Tepid water dribbles over my hands from the immersion heater. The liquid soap has been diluted so much it barely lathers.

Outside in the hall I hear my phone buzzing with a call. I dash to answer it, wiping my hands on my skirt as I go. Jill is standing at the table peering down at the phone. She looks up at me, still squinting from trying to see the screen, but there's something else in her gaze too: curiosity, anger, disappointment.

'You said you'd finished with them,' she sneers.

'With who?'

She waves her hand at the phone.

'Libby's name just came up on the screen,' she says, furious. 'I wasn't prying, just curious about your new gadget. If I'd known how to answer it, I'd have given her a piece of my mind!'

The phone buzzes with a left message. I push past Jill and grab it from the table.

'You're a bloody fool, Beth,' Jill says. 'Your own worst enemy.'

Her footsteps echo around the church hall as she hurries across to the kitchen, muttering to herself.

The message is from Libby. She sounds tired. Stressed. Angry.

'I hope you're satisfied, Beth,' she says. 'Thanks to you, Esme's had one of her worst fits ever. Taken her days to recover. Getting her to go behind my back and sending emails and the rest of it. What were you thinking? She's never lied to me before. Isn't it enough that all this has made a stranger of my daughter already? Back off, Beth. It's not fair on her or me.'

I can hear Jill in the kitchen, know that she can hear me, but I have to call Libby right away. I don't expect her to take my call, but she does.

'How's Esme?' I say, trying not to speak too loudly. 'What happened?'

'You tell me,' Libby says. 'You're the one who's been pressurising her with questions.'

'I didn't say anything, Libby. Not really.'

'Yes you did. You asked her if she could remember what happened to her.' Libby pauses. 'I saw it on the computer.'

'Ah, so you *do* do computers after all!' I don't mean to sound triumphant, but being caught out puts me on the offensive.

'No,' she says. 'I only saw your little *chat* because I found her sprawled on the floor in front of the computer with that . . . Facebook page open.'

'It was her idea, Libby,' I say. 'Really.'

Libby sighs.

'Is she okay now?' I ask.

'She's getting there.'

'Did the fit trigger any memories?' I press the phone closer to my ear. 'Has she said anything?'

'Only something vague about a book,' Libby says dismissively. '*The Man Who Didn't Wash His Dishes*.'

The words wind me as completely as a punch to the stomach.

That book used to fascinate Amy, although I never understood why. It was a simple story, too simple for someone as bright as Amy: a man doesn't do his washing-up for months on end until eventually he can't get into the house for all the dirty dishes. Amy took it out from the mobile library so often the librarian used to call her the Girl Who Didn't Read Anything Else.

Even back then it was an old book. I tried to buy a copy at the time but none of the bookshops could get hold of a copy. Out of print, they said. Unavailable. Never heard of it. Yet Esme has. Because Amy had.

Belief flares in me, flushing my face.

'Is that all she remembered?' I say.

'For now, yes. Other odd snippets might come through later. That's how it normally works.' Libby gives a sad laugh. '*Normally*. I can't even remember normal any more.'

Jill bustles out of the kitchen, tucking her scarf into her coat, jangling a fistful of keys.

'I'd better get back to her,' Libby says.

'Before you go, Libby,' I say, 'I have to ask you something.'

'Go on.'

'Did Esme put an envelope through my letter box on New Year's Eve?'

I clench the phone tight, not daring to think what it might mean if she says she didn't.

'No,' Libby says firmly.

My head swims. I'm sicker than I thought.

'*I* did,' Libby says.

It's as if I've been snatched back from a fire. The searing heat of madness.

'*You* did?'

'Esme asked me to. She wanted you to see her essay.'

'*Her* essay?' I say. I need Libby's confirmation before I can let relief run through me.

'Well it wouldn't be mine, would it?' Libby says

quickly. Then she pauses and her tone becomes suspicious. 'Or are you saying you don't—'

'No, not at all!' I say. 'Of course I believe Esme wrote it.'

Jill shakes her head.

'I've got to go, Libby,' I say. 'Talk later.'

Jill glares at me as I hang up.

'Whatever she said is a lie,' she says. 'And talking to her later – *at all* – is a mistake.'

'But can't you see?' I say, exasperation rising. 'Esme knows something. She *has* to. How else would she know these things? Libby said Esme wrote that essay.'

'She would,' Jill says, shaking her head. 'Look, Beth. We've been over this. I've got better things to do. You should have too.' She jingles the keys at me. 'Come on.'

'But—'

'For God's sake, Beth!' Her face flares with anger. For a moment I think she's going to slap me, and I pull away from her. She pinches the bridge of her nose and breathes out slowly. 'It's just guesswork and gossip.'

'No.'

I get my coat from the kitchen and walk out of the church hall. I don't wait for Jill. Don't look back.

When I get home, I call Libby again. I tell her I have to see Esme, but Libby refuses.

'Please?' I say. 'I need to see her.'

'She's lost enough school because of all this,' Libby says. 'She can't afford to fall behind any more by going down to London again.'

'I could come to you.'

'No, Beth. I can't trust you not to push her.'

'I won't,' I say. 'It's just that I feel so useless down here. I'd like to be able to help.'

'Yeah, help yourself to what you need and bugger the rest of us.'

'No! It's not like that. Really.' I hate the pleading timbre in my voice but I can't control it. 'Esme's the one who got in touch with me. Ask her. She'll tell you. She misses me.'

'Is that meant to make me feel better?' Libby says angrily. 'That she misses you?'

'No,' I say, 'of course not. But it's Esme's welfare we're both concerned about. Why don't you ask her if she wants me to come up to see her in Manchester?'

Libby hesitates.

'She's already said as much.' She sounds deflated, beaten. 'When she first came round after the fit.'

'There you are then,' I say breezily. 'It's better this way. No sneaking around.'

'Maybe,' Libby says. 'But there'd better not be any more tricks or nasty surprises.'

'There haven't been any tricks or surprises at all,' I say. 'Not on my side anyway.'

'Meaning?'

'Nothing,' I say. 'I meant there's just been misunderstandings. Silly, unfortunate misunderstandings. That's all.'

There's a long silence, made longer by the thump of my heart.

'Okay,' Libby says. 'When were you thinking of coming?'

'Tomorrow. I'll get the train tomorrow.'

9

Something in my suitcase rattles as I pull it out of the loft. It's a dove-grey pebble, a souvenir of a week in a Cornish cottage a year after my divorce. I spent the entire time walking along the beach, the scrunch of the pebbles beneath my feet accompanied by the hiss and spray of a churning sea.

I wished the banks of pebbles would suddenly shift and slide, burying me. And when they didn't, I sat down and wriggled into them, beyond the sun-warmed stones on the surface, into the chill and damp beneath. A grave of gravel and stones, with no worms or ants to eat at me, no succulent roots to feed. I wondered what Amy's grave was like. Where it was.

My arms stretched out, my fingers clawing at the pebbles, reaching for her. All I found was a fistful of hard, cold stones. I sobbed and sat up, the drift of pebbles slipping off me like the skin of a snake.

I threw a handful of stones, strafing the sea with splash. One pebble lodged between my fingers. I was about to throw it in but stopped and clenched it in my palm. It was round and warm and smooth. Enduring. Like love.

I brought it back with me, intending to put it next to the

picture of Amy on the beach in Zante, but when I unpacked it back in London, it was just cold, hard and colourless. I dropped it in the suitcase, locked it and buried it in the attic.

It's the first thing I pack for my trip to Manchester. It is my talisman, a way to guide me to the truth, like the pebbles on the path that led Hansel and Gretel back to safety. I pack the laptop too.

Just before I leave, I remember the USB stick Jill was given by the printers used by the Friends of Durning Library. She passed it on to me for back-up copies of the posters and fliers should my computer fail. That won't be a problem any more. Jill has no use for it, but I do.

Whatever I find in Manchester cannot be lost. There might only be one shot to get the truth on record. If Amy breaks through Esme, once and for all, the things she says could be lost for ever; the memories of the little boy who had been a World War II pilot faded away to nothing once his story was told. I cannot take that risk.

If she remembers anything, it won't just be memories – it will be evidence. Perhaps it will identify a culprit, give the police enough to arrest and convict him. It might even lead us to Amy's grave. On the other hand, it might just show Esme to be a fraud with nothing to tell but stories.

The suitcase wheels rumble on the pavement as I head to the tube. I usually walk or take the bus whenever I go anywhere, which isn't often – or wasn't before Libby and Esme turned up. I let my world shrink until it reached no further than Durning Library or Marks and Spencer on the

Walworth Road – Brixton if I was feeling brave. Now it feels bigger.

The underground's musty mix of newspapers, warm dust and coffee breath was once a part of my daily routine, but is now shockingly new. Almost exotic. It's the smell of a past busy with activity and purpose, of a distant land of work and a forgotten world of leisure.

I breathe in the memory of the last tube home on Fridays, of Brian's hand in mine, of laughter, beer and happiness. I remember the trips I took with Amy. How she stood in the Butterfly House at London Zoo, enraptured by the luminous turquoise butterfly that settled on her shoulder. The hiss of lentils as she dropped them into the funnel of a contraption at the Science Museum, and sent them hurtling through plastic tubes with the turn of a handle. The dreams in her eyes as the Sugar Plum Fairy floated across the stage at Sadler's Wells.

I could have all that again, and more. New trips, new experiences, none of them more thrilling than having Amy just a hand and a heartbeat away.

But it could all be snatched away from me too – for the second time.

I am wary. Uncertain. Vulnerable. I am eager. Desperate. Hopeful. I am on the brink of discovering a magical future or reliving the nightmares of the past. Of loving and being loved once more. Of being trapped and fooled. Maybe, I think, the two are not so different after all.

People surge around me on the platform with a frenetic but dead-eyed energy. No one knows or cares who I am or where I'm going. None of them would guess my mission or my mindset. At least I hope they wouldn't.

The train at Euston is busy, the luggage racks stacked with buggies and bags. In front of me, a woman with a dozing toddler on one shoulder struggles to shake the holdall strap from her other shoulder.

'Need a hand?' I say.

The woman passes the boy to me. He stirs but doesn't wake, twists his head into my neck and tickles it with his soft, warm breath.

'He's well away,' I say quietly, brushing his cheek with a finger.

'Let's hope it lasts,' his mother says. She eases the holdall to the floor and puffs out her cheeks. 'No one wants a screaming kid next to them on a train. Least of all me.' She bends down and hauls the holdall on top of the bags in the luggage compartment. 'I don't know which weighs more. That or him.'

'How old is he?'

'Two.'

'Ah, the terrible twos.'

'He saves the terrible bit for me and his dad,' she says wearily. 'His grandma doesn't believe us when we tell her what a demon he can be.' She holds her arms out as I pass the boy back. His eyes open dreamily, then flutter and close. I miss his weight and warmth.

'I believe you.'

'You're a wiser grandma than his is.'

'Mother, not grandma.'

I can feel her surprise. I'm surprised too. The words just slipped out. I don't know if I feel stronger for it, more sure of my belief, or just pathetic and deluded.

'Look after him,' I say as I squeeze past her. I tickle the boy under the chin. 'And you be good. Do as your mummy tells you. You might not always like it, but it's all for the best in the end.'

I walk through to the next carriage, settle into my seat and close my eyes. I catch flashes of days out with Amy at Legoland, Brighton, Hampton Court. I can almost smell her wet woollen coat, liquorice yawns, sun cream and TCP.

A man opposite me tuts when my phone rings. He points to the sign on the window: Quiet Carriage. I get up and take the call by the door.

'Beth. It's Libby. Change of plan.'

'What's happened?' I say. 'It's not Esme again, is it?'

'No, she's fine. It's me. I've got to go to work for a bit. We can't meet you at the station like Esme wanted. Sorry.' She doesn't sound too disappointed. 'I'll pick Esme up from her friend's on the way home from work. We'll be back by the time you get here. I'll text you the address, okay?'

A moment later I have the address and travel directions. *Bus 43, 45, 105 from Piccadilly station.*

I take a cab instead. The driver is incredulous when I tell him I've not been to Manchester before.

'England's second city,' he says. 'And don't let the Brummies tell you otherwise. They've got a rotten accent too. As bad as their football team.'

He points out a few places on the way, his elongated vowels echoing Esme's. The stone of the library is the same grey-white as my pebble. I take it as a good omen. The library's columns and gently curving dome soften the gleaming angled edifice of the nearby Bridgewater Hall.

'Good sound in there, they reckon. Never been in it, mind,' the cabbie says. 'Mozart and violins and what have you, not my bag at all. This place here, on the other hand, is right up my street. Or was, before they knocked it down and turned it into yuppie flats.'

The sign on the door of the red-brick building says The Hacienda.

'Best club in the world,' he says, his voice too wistful for his boast. 'They've all played in there. Stone Roses. Happy Mondays. Even Madonna before she was big. Saw the lot of 'em.'

He looks at me in the rear-view mirror. I guess him to be in his mid-forties, which means he either started clubbing at a very young age, or has fallen victim to nostalgia for a past that was never really his. It strikes me that we may have that in common.

'You've lived here all your life?' I say, shifting in the seat.

'Mancunian born and bred, me,' he says, his back straightening with pride. 'Manc till the day I die.'

'City or United?'

His grey-flecked eyebrows rise in the mirror.

'United! Blood isn't red for nothing.' He gives a snort of derision.

'Don't Liverpool play in red too?' I've assimilated more than I realised from Brian's slavish attention to Sky Sports.

The cabbie sucks in his breath.

'Careful, no swearing in my cab.' He fiddles beneath the dashboard. 'That ejector seat button's around here somewhere.' He winks at me in the mirror. 'It's very tribal round here. In a friendly way. People will always help you out.'

'That must come in handy.'

'Just be careful what you ask,' he says. 'Once a Manc get his gob going, there's no stopping him.'

'Even better,' I say. 'Might make my trip a little easier.'

'Business, is it?'

'Sort of. I'm visiting . . . family. And doing research.'

His forehead rucks with a doubtful frown.

'Can't see there's much to research in Wythenshawe,' he says. 'Except Wythenshawe Hall maybe.'

'What's that?

'A big old house. And a park,' he says. 'Worth a look if you're at a loose end. Wythenshawe's high point. Well, other than its rate of Asbos and its hoodie count.'

'Oh? Is it that bad?'

'Nah, not really,' he says, flashing me a smile in the mirror. 'It's no worse than anywhere else, I suppose. Better than it used to be, apparently. My sister lives there. She loves it. Says she feels part of a real community.' He brakes hard at some traffic lights. A green and silver tram rattles by and gives a forlorn toot. 'Mind you, that backfired on her when she was caught in bed with a sixth-former.

Not much community spirit then. Just plenty of gossip and bitching.'

We pass rows of red-brick terraces interspersed with curry houses, all-night grocers, burger joints and book-makers. Anti-pigeon netting hatches tower-block balconies crowded with satellite dishes, bikes and washing lines sagging with T-shirts and jeans.

It reminds me of the Brandon Estate just down the road from me in Kennington. A lot of single mothers live on that estate apparently, so I'm not surprised that Libby lives somewhere similar.

She hasn't said much about where she lives or her financial circumstances, but I guess her to be struggling to keep her head above water. I can't help thinking that most of the people on this estate are probably in the same boat.

There's the crunch of broken glass as the cab pulls alongside the kerb. The driver gets out and takes my suitcase from the boot. I give him a five-pound tip for his snapshot of a city I know nothing about. For his heads-up on a community I have to dig into and might, just might, become part of.

He slips me one of the taxi firm's cards.

'Just in case you get lost or want to go exploring,' he says. 'Ask for Dave.'

I thank him and put the card in my purse. As I walk to the door of the block, he gives a beep of his horn and drives off.

The door opens before I can press the number on the intercom. Esme flings herself into me.

'You're here! At last!' she squeals. 'I've been looking out for you for ages. Come on.'

Her enthusiasm hits me as much as her resemblance to Amy: the blonde hair, the slightly gangly limbs, the light in her eyes and the smile that packs a punch every bit as potent as it was on New Year's Eve. But there's something else too; I get a sense of her warmth and eagerness, her empathy and desire to please. It's just as beguiling as Amy's used to be.

She takes hold of my suitcase and drags it towards the lift.

'Let me do that,' I say. 'You need to take it easy. After your fit.' It feels wonderful to have a child to mother and fuss over once again.

'I'm fine now,' she says brightly. 'Honest.'

She presses the button for the lift.

'I'm sorry if I said something to trigger it,' I say. 'I really didn't mean to. The last thing I want is to hurt you. I'll be more careful, I promise.'

'It wasn't your fault,' Esme says with a shrug. 'The fits just come out of the blue. You're not to blame.'

'I wish your mother was so forgiving.'

'So do I.'

Esme gives me an odd sideways look, as if she's talking about me and not Libby. The drop in my stomach has nothing to do with the prospect of getting into what looks like an old and unreliable lift.

The doors grate and shudder as they open, releasing the stench of stale cigarette smoke. The No Smoking sign is

179

splattered with what I hope is tomato ketchup, and there's the ghost of old graffiti on the walls.

I get in first and help Esme pull the case in. She presses the button for the second floor and the door slides shut.

'How long have you lived here?' I ask her.

'Nearly two years.'

'You like it?'

She nods her head vigorously.

'Oh yes, it's much better than the B and B we were in before. That was all damp and dirty.' She wrinkles her nose at the memory. 'But at least we had a roof. I feel so sorry for the people who have to sleep in cardboard boxes on the streets. When it's really cold I give them my pocket money for a cup of tea.'

I put my hand on her head and stroke her hair.

'The only good thing about living in the B and B,' Esme says, 'was there weren't any dogs there. The Staffordshire bull terriers around here scare me.'

'They scare me a bit too,' I say, cupping her chin in my hand. 'But apparently they're very good with kids.'

'Good at chasing them.' She looks up, her eyes wide and blue and gorgeous. 'A white one chased me the other week when I was on my roller blades. I dropped my Mars bar and the dog ate it.'

My stomach flips over. I'm not sure if this actually happened or if she's channelling a memory of Amy's, when she too fell over after being chased by a white dog. Only that was a Westie, not a Staffordshire bull terrier, and she dropped an ice cream rather than a chocolate bar. I remember having to buy her another one and soothing her tears as I dabbed TCP on her bloody knees and knuckles.

I can feel her, hear her. Right now. Next to me. Telling me things. Conjuring memories. Mixing them up. Losing the thread, then pulling it and making the colours run until it's hard to tell whether it's Amy's recollections staining Esme's or the other way round.

The door opens on to a lobby with the doors to two flats on each side. The smell of curry mixes with cigarette smoke and bleach. The jingle from an insurance commercial from behind one door collides with the thump of a rap track from another.

The door furthest from the lift is ajar. Esme wheels the case towards it and pushes it open with her foot. 'She's here!'

The sound of running water stops and Libby appears at the end of the corridor, clutching a dishcloth in a rubber-gloved hand. Her auburn hair hangs limp and loose, a few strands clinging to her forehead, which is damp with perspiration. Her T-shirt flaps around her skinny body, making her look younger than I know she is.

'Libby,' I say. 'It's good to see you again. Thank you for putting me up.'

'It's what Esme wanted,' she says. 'There's even been a promise that she'll help with the cooking, although that might not be such a good thing.' She smiles at Esme, who feigns outrage at the criticism of her culinary skills.

'I'd be happy to help in any way I can,' I say. 'Cooking, washing, cleaning.'

'You're good at cleaning!' Esme says, pushing the suit-case against the wall. 'You were always doing it, weren't you?'

I smile ruefully.

'Yes,' I say, 'I'm a bit of an expert.' I try to come across as being amused by my knack for housework, but I'm not. 'I've always got a handy tip or two. Not that I'm saying you need any help,' I add quickly. 'I'm not here to judge.'

Libby's eyebrows rise imperceptibly. I get a whiff of Fairy Liquid as she turns and walks down the hallway.

'Come on,' Esme says, 'I'll give you a tour of the flat.'

It doesn't take long. We follow Libby into a small, square kitchen with basic fitted units and a white lacquer table against one wall. The front room is larger, but not by much; the pine units and recliner sofa look like those I've seen on ad breaks during *How Clean is Your House?* In the bathroom, I have to concentrate to make sure my arm doesn't accidentally sweep the toiletries off the shelf attached to the wall. A limp showerhead drips into a washed-out bath.

Esme points at a closed door.

'That's Mum's room,' she says. 'I'll be sleeping in there too for the next few days.'

'Esme,' Libby calls from the kitchen, 'why don't you take Beth's case to her room?'

'It's my room really,' Esme says, as I follow her. She takes my case from where she left it in the hall. 'But I don't mind you having it. I want you to be comfy. Like a home from home.'

The bedroom is a blizzard of pink and purple. The plastic toys, shiny knick-knacks and glint of the sequinned lampshades make it look shiny and moist. Like an open wound.

The air is stuffy, sweet with the smell of fresh, fabric-conditioned bed linen and sour with sweaty trainers and blow-dried hair. The Spice Girls strut and pout from posters on the walls and Baby Spice grins on the duvet cover and pillow. It's an exact match with the one Amy pestered me for.

Memories rush at me, stealing my breath, hurling me back into Amy's room. Even the layout is the same as hers was: the bed under the window, the dressing table littered with scrunchy hairbands, bracelets and rings, a desk alongside it and mirror panels on the back of the door.

There are a few differences: the CD player that Amy kept on the dressing table has been replaced by a small pink iPod and a speaker. There's a pink laptop on the desk where Amy kept her pads and the Spice Girls have been joined on the wall by Lady Gaga and the cast of *Glee*.

'I hope you like it,' Esme says.

'Of course I like it. I always did.' I help her lift the case on to the bed. 'But it's tidier now than it used to be.'

Esme grins.

'I've tidied up specially,' she says. 'You don't want to look in the cupboards.'

I do and I will. I'm glad of the warning that they're full to bursting and hope I remember to open them carefully.

It's wrong of me to pry and probe. Children have a right to privacy as much as adults do. I wasn't one to go snooping for Amy's diary or rooting through her drawers. I didn't have to. She'd never keep anything from me. But I have to rummage around this time. I'm sure she'd understand — *if* she knew.

'I hope Libby won't mind me bringing one of your toys from London to add to that collection,' I say, pointing at the menagerie of dogs, pandas, penguins and gonks on her pillow. 'It's in my bag.'

Her eyes are wide with expectation. I pull Bagpuss from my bag. She takes the cat and rubs her nose against his.

'Thank you. That's really kind. I've missed him so much.'

She gives him pride of place on her pillow.

Libby calls from the kitchen that tea is ready.

'Hope you like spag bol,' says Esme.

'Lovely,' I say. 'One of my favourites.'

'It's only Asda's own brand,' Libby mutters.

Esme snuggles up to me.

'I'm so glad you're here,' she says.

'Me too.'

'We've got a lot of catching up to do,' she says.

'That's right.' I grip her shoulder. 'Especially me.'

I give the bedroom a quick look as I close the door behind me. It's like the lights going out on a film set. Fantasy or horror? I think. Either way, it's a true story. All that's missing is the truth.

Esme insists I sit next to her. Libby flinches. The conversation between Libby and myself is an effort, but Esme's babble masks the lulls effectively, like Amy's used

to during the tense meals I endured with Brian. Once
we've finished, it's a relief to escape to the bathroom for a
long soak, after which I say I'm exhausted by the journey
and need an early night.

Esme gives me a hug.

'Nighty-night,' she says.

It's what Amy used to say at bedtime too. I'd respond
with a kiss blown from the end of my fingertip and she'd
catch it in her palm.

'Good night,' I say, turning away.

Esme has her left arm held up over her head, hand up-
turned. I can't tell if she's stretching or ready to catch my
kiss. I practically run down the hall to my bedroom.

The room is too full of ghosts for me to sleep. The Spice
Girls smile from the walls like airbrushed zombies and the
dent in the too-thin mattress is the same shape and size as
Amy. It's like lying in her grave.

The flat is quiet and dark. I heard Libby and Esme go to
bed hours ago. Now all I can hear is the groan of the lift
and the faint drone of traffic. I turn on the bedside light,
wait for my eyes to adjust to its sickly pink glow and slip
from under the duvet.

I open the wardrobe door, ready to catch whatever
might fall out. But nothing does. The clothes on the shelves
are folded into neat piles and those on the rack are pressed
and arranged by colour. Amy was neat too; she was like
me in so many ways.

I slide my hand between the jumpers and T-shirts,

inside the shoes on the floor and the pink wicker linen basket, delve into the pockets of cardigans and coats. I'm not sure what I'm hoping to find – anything will do – but I find nothing.

The books on a shelf are arranged in height order, then alphabetised by title, from *The Amber Spyglass* to the *X-Factor Annual*.

Return from Heaven and *Children's Past Lives* have been left lying across the top of the others. Useful background reading to get me up to speed, or clumsy, pointed stage props? I can't be sure. I take them from the shelf and place them on the bedside table, use one of them as a bookmark in the other.

The desk is as tidy as the wardrobe. Beneath a box of pencils and crayons is a sketchbook warped and crispy with dried poster paint. The pictures are crude, the lines wonky and the detail fuzzy. Yellow splodges for flowers in a bulbous vase. Out-of-proportion horses in a flat green field. A triangular mountain, dripping with grubby white snow.

Further on in the book, the pictures become more accomplished. Angels trailing streaks of glitter fall through a jet-black space splattered with planets. At the bottom, two women hold out their hands, catching shooting stars. The picture is repeated and refined on subsequent pages, the sequence ending in a matt-black void. In its centre is a small white cross. Amy's grave perhaps. Or the light of God, showing the way in the darkness. Towards the truth. Revelations. I slam the book shut and put it back in the desk quickly.

There are no notebooks or pads or diaries. If Esme has written anything at all, it will be on the laptop she did her homework on in the front room earlier.

I open the bedroom door slightly, peer through the gap for any signs of life, then tiptoe down the corridor. The front room glows in the light from the roads and the surrounding blocks of flats; I can see the laptop on the table where Esme left it.

It will be safer to take it back to my room and boot it up there, but as I lift it from the table, I hear a door open down the corridor. I put the computer back as quickly and quietly as I can and duck into the gap between the sofa and the wall. Even if whoever it is can't see me, I think, they're sure to hear the pounding of my heart.

I hear someone yawn, and peer from behind the sofa. Esme picks up the computer and walks back out of the room, towards Libby's bedroom. The door closes and I squeeze out from my hiding place. There are muffled voices from Libby's room and a thin grey glow beneath the door.

I inch my way back to my own bedroom, heart loud in my ears. I'm relieved when I finally close the door behind me but disappointed that I wasn't able to get hold of the laptop. Curious, too. What did they want with it so late at night? The possibilities keep me guessing until I finally fall asleep.

The next morning, I hear voices, the flick of a switch, a toilet flushing. I wait a few moments, put on my dressing gown and go into the kitchen. Libby is at the sink, taking the lid off a kettle. She jumps when she turns around.

'Sorry,' I say.

Her face is stretched with tiredness, her eyes narrow and watery.

'Oh, it's just me being skittish,' she says. 'I'm not used to having another adult around.' She shakes the kettle, gauging the amount of water inside it. 'Tea?'

'She has coffee for breakfast,' Esme calls from along the hall. 'Black, no sugar.'

She's right again.

Libby holds the kettle under the tap; the flow of water is grudging. She plugs it in, takes a couple of mugs from the draining board and spoons in some coffee. Cereal boxes, bowls and milk appear on the table. Toast pops up in the toaster.

Libby moves quickly through her well-practised routine, then slumps in a chair, her yawn turning into a call to Esme to hurry up, as time is ticking.

'It's always such a rush,' she says. 'It's not natural to start the day at eighty miles an hour.' She sips from her cup and yawns again.

Esme walks into the kitchen and leans against me. I put my arm around her and give her a kiss on the head. Her hair has a just-brushed smoothness and warmth, the smell of apricots. She pulls away from me and twirls around with her arms out.

'Do you like my uniform?'

'Very smart,' I say.

School uniforms aren't what they were. Amy's was a dark green jumper, skirt and tie in the winter, pale green checked dress in the summer. Esme's is ash-grey leggings and a tomato-red sweatshirt branded with the school's name.

She sits down at the table. An avalanche of Sugar Puffs tumbles into a bowl.

'Have you had your grapefruit?' she says to me.

'Grapefruit?'

'You *always* have it.' She takes a grapefruit from a glass bowl on the windowsill. 'I used my pocket money to get this just for you.'

Her thoughtfulness makes me melt a little more. I haven't the heart to tell her I've not eaten grapefruit for years, so spoon the segments into my mouth with feigned relish. It tastes of the resentful, belligerent breakfasts I had with Brian after Amy vanished, the *Today* programme filling the silence until he left for work.

'Do I have to go to school today?' Esme says. 'I want to stay with my two mums.'

Her pride is palpable. Her happiness, too. This, I realise, is the beginning of our future as she sees it. My gaze collides with Libby's, then ricochets away.

'We'll both be here when you get back,' Libby says.

'There's plenty of time for us to be together,' I say.

'There's for ever!' Esme says. Her eyes burn into me. 'Will you take me to school?'

Sirens go off in my head. I can't be trusted with a child on my own. Not yet. Not ever again.

'No, we'll all go.' Libby raises her eyebrows at me, daring me to say otherwise.

'Lovely,' I say.

I'd rather stay and continue my search of the flat, but there'll be time enough for that.

On the way to school, Esme walks in the middle, a hand in mine and Libby's. We join a procession of mums with buggies and babies, the older children racing ahead on scooters. The women call out instructions to hurry up, don't go too far ahead, stop at the kerb, don't scuff your shoes. Like I used to do with Amy. Like I want to do once more.

Some of the mothers milling around the school gates give me curious stares. A few of them pull away from us, shepherding their children with a hand on their heads. I hear whispers, giggles.

A group of girls playing chase in the playground call out to Esme to come and join in. The girls look familiar from the photos on Esme's Facebook page.

'Off you go, love,' Libby says, bending down and kissing Esme on the cheek. I do the same. The girls stare at me, then wave at Esme, urging her to hurry. I wonder which of them is Esme's best friend, which might be a chatterbox or prone to telling tales. Esme runs off through the school gates.

Back at the flat, Libby puts the kettle on and spoons Mellow Bird's coffee into a couple of mugs. It's the first time I've been alone with her since we sat in the café at the Festival Hall. That nearly ended in disaster. I have to be more careful this time. Let her do the talking.

She makes the coffee and puts my mug down on the table.

'Actually, I prefer it black,' I say. 'Would you mind if I made another one?'

She shrugs and takes a sip from her mug. I tip the coffee down the sink and make another.

'No doubt Esme would have reminded me if she'd been here,' Libby says as I sit down opposite her.

'Yes, probably,' I say. 'She knows a lot about me, of course. But there's so much about you I don't know.'

'Oh, I only know the you from ten years ago,' Libby says. 'Before Amy died. Me and Esme are pretty much in the dark about what happened after that.'

I run my finger around the rim of my mug.

'That's still more than I know about you, Libby. And if we're going to make this situation work, it would help to be fully in the picture. We're sort of family now.'

Libby sighs.

'I'm just a single mum,' she says, flatly. 'Battling on, trying to do the best for my kid. And trying to fit in a life of my own along the way.' She gives a little smile. 'I'm not very good at the last part. A job at Manchester airport doesn't exactly pay for the high life. Not quite what my parents had in mind for me. Or what *I* had in mind for me, come to that.'

'Oh?' I say. 'What did you want to do?'

Libby smiles.

'I always fancied being a journalist. Used to do stuff on the school magazine. I was good at English. Good at school full stop. Then I fell for Esme. That was that.'

'You couldn't go back afterwards?' I say. 'I mean, I know it can't be easy juggling school and looking after a baby, but a lot of girls manage it.'

'With help, yes. My parents weren't exactly falling over themselves to babysit.'

'Oh, I see,' I say, genuinely sympathetic. 'They didn't approve of you having Esme, then?'

'Not exactly, no. In fact they wanted me to get rid of the baby. Kept going on about lost opportunities. University. Big career. The whole shebang. Plenty of time for kids later, they said. With a husband to make it easier. But I couldn't have an abortion or give her up for adoption. I just knew from the very first moment that my baby was special.'

'All new mums feel the same way,' I say wistfully.

'Mine didn't,' Libby snaps. 'Before *or* after I was born. Post-natal depression saw to that.' She puts her mug on the table. 'She didn't have an ounce of maternal instinct in her. I think that's why she was so set on me having an abortion.'

'How do you get on now?' I say.

Her eyes are sad and distant, her mouth tight.

'She's dead. Dad found her in the bath with the curling tongs and an electric fan heater. The coroner found a litre of gin and a couple of hundred paracetamol in her system too.' Another weak smile. 'She was always very thorough, my mum. In most things, anyway. Love just wasn't one of them.'

'What about your father?'

'He emigrated to Australia after Mum died,' Libby says. 'When he looked at me and Esme, all he saw was a granddaughter he never wanted, from a daughter who'd thrown her life away. We were no replacement for his wife. He doesn't even send Christmas cards.' She sighs and leans forward. 'Are Amy's grandparents still alive?'

'I haven't had any contact with Brian's parents since before the divorce,' I say, 'but they're still alive as far as I know.'

'And Granny Jam's still around?'

I try to swallow my surprise at hearing Amy's nickname for my mother.

'Still around, yes!' I say. 'Still making endless jars of jams and pickles. She forgets there's only me to eat it now . . . I end up putting a lot of it in for raffle prizes at the church bazaar. Dad's doing well too.'

I make it sound as though I see them often, which isn't exactly true. Their visits from their home in Hampshire have gradually tapered off since Amy disappeared. For the first few weeks they were by my side, Mum ready with sympathy and assurances that everything would be fine, my father's support quieter and less tangible.

I sensed in him a reluctance, a trace of the media's suspicions about my negligence. He never said anything to me directly, but I could feel a certain detachment where I needed solid support.

I couldn't broach it with him or with my mother; we just didn't do that sort of thing. Dad was a former civil servant, Mum a briskly efficient secretary. They were comfortable, accomplished, respectable – stalwarts of the local yacht club. We tackled problems like a boat around a buoy – with a wide berth and the risk of capsizing. Confrontation was bad form. Boats were for sailing, not rocking.

The waters have been choppy ever since. No wonder the jams and pickles from their harvest of berries and vegetables tend to be delivered by the postman rather than in person.

Libby drains her mug and waggles it at me.

'Another one?' she says. 'I always need a couple to get me going properly.'

I shake my head and she stands up to fill the kettle.

'What about you, Libby? No boyfriends?'

She laughs.

'Esme's got more suitors than I have! Single mums aren't exactly man magnets.' She flicks the kettle on and leans against the draining board as she waits for the water to boil. 'It would be tricky with Esme, anyway.'

'I would have thought she'd like having a man around,' I say. 'A dad.'

'She's got one.'

I frown, then realise she means Brian. I can't help wondering how all this will work if Esme really is Amy. She and Libby would become part of my family, of Brian's. Of Brian's *step*-family. We'd be a mongrel assortment of bastards and ghosts and surrogates, the parts of our family tree making nothing but a blighted whole.

Libby pours water and milk into her mug and sits back down at the table.

'Do you mind it when Esme calls me Mum?' I say.

She crosses her arms.

'I'm getting used to it,' she says sadly. 'But that doesn't stop it hurting.'

'I know. I feel the same.'

Libby looks at her watch.

'I'd better get a move on or I'll be late,' she says. 'It's not exactly my dream job, but it's a job and I don't want to lose it.'

When she leaves, I watch her from the window until she turns the corner by Fags'n'Mags. I wait for a few minutes more, just in case she comes back. It wouldn't surprise me if she did. She must know I'm going to search the flat. She's either as gullible as she thinks I am, or she's made sure there's nothing to find. And maybe there isn't.

Esme's computer is back on the table. It's even older and heavier than my old one. Some of the letters are almost worn away and the screen is streaky with scratches. It clicks and whirs for ages before the screen asks for a password.

'Shit!'

For any other girl it would be easy to guess. If Amy had had a computer of her own she probably wouldn't have had a password at all. She had no secrets from me, nothing to hide, and couldn't have done so even if she wanted to. I knew her inside out because she was so like me.

But if she did have a password she'd have chosen something guessable. Amy Spice, or Tinkerbell. Something girly, fluffy and pink. Esme might be craftier. She's too clever for it to be Amy or Esme or Libby, but that doesn't stop me trying them.

I've seen reports on television preaching about how people are careless with their passwords, choosing ones that are too obvious. Mix it up, they advise. Numbers and letters but not house numbers, postcodes or birthdays. But when I try them, they don't work either.

I shut the lid firmly, wipe it with my sleeve. I put it back on the table in the same position I found it. The opportunity will come for me to get into her computer. In the meantime, I have to look elsewhere.

The top drawer of a black lacquered cabinet is a jumble of extension cables, rubber doorstops, Allen keys and instruction manuals for electrical appliances. The drawer below is stacked with pads and paperwork – utility bills mostly, a pile each for gas, water, electricity and phone, held firmly at the top by a bulldog clip. Beneath them is a Thomson local directory and the Yellow Pages, takeaway menus for Chinese and Indian restaurants, Sellotape, stapler and loose biros. The third drawer has piles of place mats and coasters, blue glass tea-light holders scabby with wax and half-empty boxes of matches.

I'm not surprised at finding nothing. I'd be more suspicious if I *had* found something. But I can't mistake the feeling gnawing at me – not that I've been duped, but that I've overlooked something. I open the top drawer once more, slow my breathing, tell myself to concentrate. My hand hovers over the contents, waiting for instinct to guide me like a divining rod. It reminds me of playing with Amy, when she'd hide something and tell me I was getting close to finding it by saying cold, warm or red hot.

Cold.

I open the second drawer.

Warmer.

I pick up the pads and flick through the jumble of doodles, dates and telephone numbers.

Colder.

I pick up the bundle of bills to see if there's anything underneath or in between the pages.

Red hot.

At first I see nothing but a blizzard of numbers – account details, dates and amounts. There is nothing alarming about the size of the bills and all of them seem to have been paid.

My eyes become accustomed to the uniform layout of the various bills, the length of the name and address at the top of the page, the utility company logos, the boxes with account reference numbers. I dismiss my so-called instinct as wishful thinking and start to put them back.

Then I notice something different.

The name of the account holder on one of the gas bills is Henry Campbell Black. It's dated eighteen months ago and the following bill in the sequence is in Libby's name.

His name appears on the electricity, phone and water bills too, and is replaced by Libby's at around the same time.

The latest council tax bills show Libby's discount for single adult occupancy, but there is no such discount on the older bills, which name two adults: Libby and Henry Campbell Black.

I put the bills back quickly but neatly. I don't know what it is I've found, only that I've discovered a lie. Libby hasn't always been on her own like she told me.

Whoever he is, whatever happened to him could be completely irrelevant. The details are less important than the *fact* of him. He is proof that Libby has lied to me at least once. Proof too that she can be careless. Or that she thinks she has nothing to hide.

I take my laptop from the suitcase and search online for Henry Campbell Black. The only one I can find on Facebook is a long-dead American lawyer. The book he wrote, some kind of legal dictionary, takes up pages and pages on Google, to the exclusion of everyone else. It's as if he's the only person with that name who ever lived.

It would have been less frustrating if there were hundreds of Henry Campbell Blacks. At least I'd know the size of the task in hand and could begin working my way through them, however hit-and-miss the process might be, however time-consuming.

But since the only Henry Campbell Black to leave a digital footprint has been dead for nearly ninety years, what I thought might be a critical clue is cold within just a few hours.

If I ask Libby about him she'll know I've been snooping around and put up her guard even further. Fob me off with another lie. If I ask the neighbours, it might get back to

Libby. I can't risk losing whatever trust they have in me and being told to get out of the flat.

The buzz of my phone makes me jump.

'Hello?' I say.

'Mrs Archer? It's Ian Poynton.'

Maybe *he* is Henry Campbell Black.

'How did you get my number?' I say, my voice sharp with suspicion.

'You gave it to me in your email,' he says. 'Remember? You asked if I could help find your friends in Manchester.'

'Oh, yes,' I say sheepishly. 'That's right . . . What is it? Did my cheque bounce or something?'

'No. Nothing like that,' he says. He sounds hesitant and vague. 'To be honest, Mrs Archer, I'm not sure what this is all about. All I know is I saw something earlier today. Something to do with you. I just know it. I felt the same connection I had with that picture of Jesus.'

'What did you see?' I'm on my guard but can't deny my curiosity.

'Plates,' he says.

The Man Who Didn't Wash His Dishes. I should have seen that coming.

'Plates?' I say. 'Like the plates in a book?'

He doesn't catch the sneer in my voice.

'No. Dinner plates. Different-coloured dinner plates.'

'*Black* ones?' I'm making it easy for him to fake a link between the plates and Henry Campbell-Black, but he tries to outwit me.

'Every colour *but* black,' he says.

'Oh, really?' I toss my head dismissively. Does he think I'm *that* stupid to be thrown off the scent by his bluff?

'But then they fell to the ground,' he says, 'and smashed into bits. That's when I realised they weren't plates as such, but plates of meat.'

'Meat?' It almost makes me laugh.

'As in rhyming slang,' he says, his tone slightly patronising. 'You know, feet. There were footsteps. Multicoloured footsteps. Big ones. Like a clown's shoes would make.'

Maybe I'm the clown.

'Will you take it?' he says.

I hang up, get Esme's laptop from the front room and type *Henry* in the password box. The error message blinks and invites me to try again.

Henry4Libby123.

Libby-Henry-Esme.

Henry Campbell Black.

I try permutation after permutation.

Nothing.

10

The lasagne is glutinous and chewy, full of salt; I can taste the plastic tray it was cooked in during its four-minute spin in the microwave. We eat it, with chips instead of salad, in the company of *The Simpsons*, Esme slurping a glass of Coke and jiggling her legs.

After we've finished, Esme turns the volume up, ready for *Hollyoaks*.

'Have you got homework?' Libby says.

Esme nods, distracted by a parade of pretty boys and pouting girls on the opening credits.

'I'll do it after this, okay?' she says.

She's as good as her word. At the end of the programme she switches the television off with no prompting or argument, and gets out her laptop.

I watch her fingers closely as she types in her password, but she's too quick, her fingers a blur. It's all I can do to count the number of keystrokes. Nine, I think, possibly ten, but I can't be sure.

All I'm certain of is that she didn't touch any of the numbers. It's progress of a kind, but it's still impossible to guess the password even if it does contain only letters.

Software logos pop out like acne over the screensaver

photo of Baby Spice. I take in as much of the detail as I can. Esme sends the cursor darting around the screen like a frantic ant.

'You make it look so easy,' I say.

'It *is* easy.'

'Not to me it isn't.'

'Or me,' Libby says. She's sprawled on the sofa, yawning. 'Facebook. Twitter. It's all gibberish to me.'

Esme shakes her head.

'She doesn't even know how to use iPlayer,' she says to me. I try not to look lost, but Esme sees through me.

'It's the thing that lets you watch TV programmes on the internet,' she explains, slowly. 'I have to get it working for her.'

Libby nods sheepishly.

'Yeah, she does,' she says. 'Dead handy, though. I like to watch it when I'm in bed and can't get to sleep.'

Perhaps that's what they were doing last night. It's feasible, and that leaves me feeling disappointed.

'Other than iPlayer,' Libby says, 'the only thing I know how to do is turn it off. And I only learnt that because I had to. She'd be on it all day otherwise.'

'You don't worry about what she's up to on it?' I say, turning back to the computer.

'I don't know enough about it to stop her,' Libby says. 'Some of the other parents say they've tried to lock certain sites, but the kids always find a way into them. It's not a battle I can win.'

'But aren't you concerned about what she might see?' I say, hoping I don't sound too shocked or judgemental.

'Porn, you mean?' Libby says, yawning again.

I flinch, feel a blush run to my cheeks. Esme looks up from the screen and giggles.

'Porn makes me sick,' she says.

She's so matter-of-fact, she makes me feel old and prudish. I look to Libby, baffled. It seems to me that she's enjoying my embarrassment.

'We looked at it together and talked it through,' she says. 'Making a fuss about it would only make her more inquisitive, more determined to see it. This way I've snuffed out any interest before it starts.'

I can understand her argument, but I don't want her to see that I don't really agree with it. She's been doing what she thinks is right for her daughter; it's just not what I would do with mine. Not that Amy would have looked at porn, let alone been so blasé about it.

If Esme *is* Amy, then I'll take the mantle of mother – and all its responsibilities – without hesitation. But I've too many doubts, too many questions, to rush in. And the longer it takes, the more I questions I have, the greater my doubts.

If Esme can't prove that she is Amy, it's up to me to prove that she's not.

'It's a different world nowadays, isn't it?' I say, trying to sound casual. 'Kids grow up quicker because they're exposed to so many different things much earlier. It's a good thing in some ways, of course, but . . .'

'What?' Libby says.

'Well, it's not all one-way, is it?' I say. 'The internet, I mean. Esme can go exploring, but what about people — strangers — who are interested in *her*?'

Esme turns from the computer. There's an odd, blank look in her eyes, unseeing, as if hypnotised. Her head twitches, begins to shake.

'Esme?' I say, putting my hand out towards her. 'What is it?'

The tremors creep through her body until she slumps from the chair to the floor.

'Esme!'

'Shit!' says Libby, jumping up from the sofa. 'Not again!'

She kneels beside Esme, cradling her head in her hands. I grab the cushion in the crook of my back and pass it to her. She slides it under Esme's head, dabs at the saliva bubbling in her mouth with a tissue. Gradually the convulsions abate, draining away like an ebbing tide.

If she's acting, it's an astonishing performance. I've seen the photos of her on stage. I've heard her talk about becoming a famous singer and actress. But this is too good for a child, however gifted or crafty. To pull this off when I'm so close to her, right in her face, would take more talent than she could possibly have. Wouldn't it?

If so, then Esme has a serious medical condition that has nothing to do with channelling Amy, but which could offer a glimpse behind the curtain of her consciousness and show me how she knows what she knows.

As I shake her, gently, I don't know if I'm trying to

rouse her from the seizure or push her deeper into it.

'Shall I call the doctor?' I say.

'No point,' Libby replies. 'There's nothing they can do. Help me get her up on to the sofa.'

Libby's tone strikes me. It's abrupt and cool – too matter-of-fact to be caring. Esme's slack, drooling mouth suddenly seems to be smirking.

The water I fetch from the kitchen splashes on Esme's face. She opens her mouth, the glass clattering against her teeth as she drinks. She tries to say something, but only air comes out of her mouth.

'It's okay, love,' Libby says, stroking her hair. 'You've had another one of your turns. All over now.'

Esme shakes her head.

'No,' she says, her voice dry and raspy. 'What about the man who didn't wash his dishes?'

'It's only a book,' Libby says. 'Don't worry.'

'No,' she says. 'It's more than just a book.'

Libby's hand strokes Esme's cheeks, as if trying to coax the information from her like a genie from a lamp.

'He's real,' Esme says, sitting up quickly. 'Really real.'

My head races with confusion once more. Is this a genuine memory of Amy's or another of Esme's sick jokes?

'Can you tell me what he looked like?' Libby says.

Esme's face creases with concentration.

'He's old,' she says.

'How old?'

'I don't know,' Esme says.

'Older than me?' Libby says.

Esme nods.

'Older than Beth?'

Esme screws her eyes up and nods her head, slowly.

'Maybe a bit.'

'What else?' I say in a rush. 'What else did you see?'

Even I can't tell if I'm playing along with a performance or witnessing a genuine breakthrough for Amy. My hands grip Esme's shoulders and shake her so hard she bounces up and down on the sofa.

'Beth! Stop it!' Libby says, pulling my hands away.

'He has . . .' Esme squirms around on the sofa. 'He has a funny mouth. His lips are sewn up.'

Libby looks up at me, baffled.

'Mean anything to you, Beth?' she says.

I shake my head, although I could tell her it's probably the same man Ian pretended to contact. He couldn't speak either. I'm no closer to understanding who he is, but at least the story is consistent.

'No,' I say. 'Nothing. Nothing at all.'

'Okay, poppet,' Libby says to Esme. 'Let's get you into bed.' She slips her arms around her. 'She needs to be in her own bed, Beth. You'll have to take the sofa tonight.'

I nod, and help her carry Esme to the bedroom and lay her down on the bed. Esme is suddenly asleep, deeply asleep, the sound and rhythm of her breathing almost imperceptible. She looks like a corpse.

Amy's corpse.

A ball of bile burns in my stomach. I run to the toilet and puke it out in a hot and bitter stream.

The next morning, Esme is the first one up and dressed.

'I know what you're after,' Libby says when Esme makes her a cup of tea.

'What?' Esme says, coyly.

'It's Saturday. You're angling to go to the rehearsal.'

'Can I?' Esme pleads. 'Mrs Frobisher will be angry. She says we're behind with the show anyway. I don't want to let everyone down.'

Libby presses her hand to Esme's forehead.

'How are you feeling?' she says.

'Fine. Really I am.'

Libby looks at me.

'What do you think, Beth?'

It's nice to be consulted.

'Rehearsal for what?' I ask.

'Her drama and dance group do a show a couple of times a year,' Libby says.

'We're doing *Moulin Rouge*! I get to do the can-can,' Esme says, bouncing up and down, bringing one knee up to her waist and twirling her leg.

I've seen the film. Nicole Kidman's character faints and coughs convincingly from tuberculosis. A perfect role model for Esme's little show last night, maybe. Or perhaps it's just a coincidence.

'She seems well enough,' I say, 'given how ill she was.'

'It took her a couple of days to recover from her last fit,' Libby says, 'but this one wasn't anywhere near as bad.'

'I can't imagine what that was like then,' I say. 'This was scary enough.'

There's a hint of pride in Esme's smile.

'So I can go?' she asks.

'As long as you promise to stop if you don't feel right,' Libby says.

'I promise!'

'We can stay and watch the rehearsal too if you want,' Libby says. 'We'll have to sit at the back and keep quiet. And we *will* – Mrs Frobisher will make sure of that! God, anyone would think she's Andrew Lloyd Webber, the way she carries on.'

It's a chance for me to talk to some of the other mothers, see what they know about Henry Campbell Black.

'Why don't you let me take Esme?' I say. 'You put your feet up for a bit. Have a nice bath or something.'

Libby stretches and yawns.

'That does sound tempting,' she says. 'I didn't get much sleep last night. Are you sure you don't mind?'

'Not at all.' I put my coffee mug on the table. 'Right, better get a move on. I don't want Mrs Frobisher on my case, do I?'

Esme dashes out of the kitchen to pack her bag and put her coat on. Libby leans towards me across the table.

'Don't go asking her questions about last night, Beth, just because I'm not around. I don't want you hassling her – ever – but especially not so soon after a fit. I'm trusting you here. Don't screw it up.'

'I won't say a thing,' I say. 'Just keep it light. Besides, she'll be on the stage most of the time.'

We're out of the door ten minutes later, the windows of the flat misting up with the steam from Libby's bath.

We pass a muddy scrap of grass where a handful of older lads sit on the back of a broken bench. One of them, a boy of about twelve, stares at us – at me in particular. I'm conscious that I stand out. The people I've seen on the estate have been dressed in jeans or tracksuit bottoms, their faces pinched and pallid. They either shuffle about, as if weighed down by countless troubles, or swagger by, daring anyone to get in their way. My woollen coat has a smooth, deep nap, my shoes have heels and polish and my back is straight, my hair well groomed.

The boy mutters something to the rest of them, and they start sniggering.

'Where you going, Esme?' the gang leader shouts.

'I've got a rehearsal,' she snaps back.

'Royal Command Performance, is it?' he says, looking at me.

'It *is* for charity,' Esme said. 'For people with learning difficulties. It's on the posters we've put up. But I suppose you have to be able to *read* to understand them.'

'Don't have to read to know what shit looks like,' the boy shouts. 'No one's gonna come to your crappy show.'

'How would you know what it's like?' Esme says.

'My mum told me,' he says. 'She used to be a dancer.'

'Pole dancing's not proper dancing,' Esme says with a shake of her head.

'Your mum's not a proper mum.'

She sticks two fingers up at him. He laughs, then bows at me. I'm relieved when we turn the corner.

'Who was that?' I say.

'Only Billy Gibson. He's thick. Always in trouble. His dad's been in prison. And his mum. The whole family have been banned from Lidl because they've robbed so much off the shelves.'

'What did he mean about your mum not being a real mum?' I say.

Esme shrugs.

'Because she doesn't let me smoke and makes me go to school, probably. His makes him go shoplifting.'

The school hall is a shabby one-storey building, its concrete walls scarred by rust from the drainpipes and faded graffiti. It smells of disinfectant and custard, its floor tiles scuffed by shoes and chair legs. On the raised platform at the far end, a woman pores over some notes on the clipboard in her hand as a chorus line of girls fail to kick their legs out in unison.

'That's it, girls,' the woman says, without looking up from her notes. 'Nice straight legs. Pointy toes. Smile.'

She sounds tired, as if she's said the words a thousand times.

'Sorry I'm late, miss,' Esme says, dashing up on to the stage and quickly stripping off to her leotard.

She takes her place in the chorus line and gives me a wave. Mrs Frobisher turns around.

'Can I help?' she says.

'I just brought Esme along. I wondered if it was okay to stay and watch.'

'*Watch?*'

'I was told I could.'

She looks surprised.

'Well, yes, you can, if you want,' she says uncertainly. 'It's just that people generally don't.' She flicks the pages on her clipboard. 'I like to think I'm creating something here, but most of the time I'm just a glorified babysitter.'

I look around the hall. I'm the only other adult there.

'It'll be nice to have an audience for a change, won't it, girls?'

The chorus line nods. There are whispers to Esme, curious smiles. I walk to the row of orange plastic seats along the back of the hall.

'Right, here we go, girls,' Mrs Frobisher says. 'This time with music. Remember your timing.'

The girls kick out a can-can to music so loud it's distorted and makes the speakers throb. Esme flashes me a quick smile. My smile back is weak, clouded by memories of Amy performing in her school assemblies, bobbing up and down to each note on the piano. Dana, next to her, doing the same, but out of time.

Esme has Amy's rhythm and flair, but she doesn't have her star quality. The thought grows like a bruise. The more I look at her, the less I see of Amy. They *look* alike but are not alike – in the same way Amy was completely different from Dana, despite the so-called physical similarities.

Their teachers struggled to tell them apart. I couldn't see why. They had the same colour hair, but Dana was shorter than Amy, her features pinched, her body clumsy. Amy was the natural choice for Baby Spice. Dana was more

Ginger. She forgot her gym bag every week, hit bum notes on the recorder and read by following the words with her fingers and moving her lips. Not like Amy at all.

The only time I saw any kind of similarity between them was when she stood in for Amy in the reconstruction for *Crimewatch*. My heart broke a thousand times when Dana appeared in copies of the clothes I'd last seen Amy wearing. They looked so ordinary then, not the stuff of enduring memories. Of living nightmares.

As Dana played on the swings, joyless and blank, I wished for someone to grab her instead. That's not something I like to admit to myself, but it's true. I prayed that when the cameras stopped rolling, it would be Amy's face that appeared from under her hood. When it didn't, Dana was a very poor swap.

Esme is too. Yes, she's kind and bright, quick and considerate, polite, sincere and pretty. But it feels to me like she's making an effort, that she has all the facts and details of Amy's life off pat, but has left out the core of the girl.

I realise now that I've had no true *sense* of Amy ever since Esme turned up. I've been blind to the deficiency. Swept up in wishful thinking, confusion, hope, grief – fear. Too busy with hard facts, details and painful memories to feel the soft insinuations of instinct.

Esme is just a shell protecting the truth, and even the hardest shells can be broken. I won't go at her with a hammer blow. I'll do it carefully, so she won't notice. Like pricking an egg with a pin and slowly sucking out the yolk.

At the end of the rehearsal most of the girls drift away

together. A couple of mums turn up but just stand at the door, trailing cigarette smoke. They're gone before I get the chance to talk to them, and Mrs Frobisher is too pre-occupied with turning off lights and locking up.

'Did you like it?' Esme says, her forehead damp with sweat.

'You were wonderful,' I say, giving her a tissue to wipe her face. 'I can't wait to see the whole thing. Are you feel-ing okay?'

'Yes thanks. Except I'm starving. I hope Mum's doing something yummy for lunch.'

'Maybe we could get some crisps on the way home,' I say.

As soon as we turn the corner, I regret taking the detour to the sweetshop. Billy Gibson is smoking outside with a couple of other boys. He nudges them and they laugh.

'Here they are,' he says through a haze of smoke. 'Lady Gaga and Lady La-Di-Da.'

'Piss off.'

'Esme! Please,' I say. 'Just ignore him.'

Billy roars with laughter.

'Oh, I say, Esme, please,' he mimics, his voice posh and high-pitched.

'You're such a prick, Billy Gibson,' Esme yells.

'Esme!' I put my hand on her shoulder, but she pulls away.

'You're not exactly an expert on pricks, are you, Esme?' Billy sneers as I open the shop door.

I tell Esme to take her time choosing what she wants,

hoping the boys will be gone by the time we leave. But when we come out, they're still there.

Esme pushes past them. Billy Gibson sniggers and waggles his tongue at us, as if licking an invisible lolly.

'La la la Lady Gaga and la la la Lady La-Di-Da. La la la Lesme.'

I put my hand on Esme's shoulder and steer her on before she can think of going back. There's a flush of pink in her cheeks and her fists are coiled. She flicks a finger at him. He laughs.

'What's that?' he says. 'Practice?' His fingers flutter and poke at the air. 'Oi! Lady La-Di-Da!'

I keep on walking, not daring to look around to see if they are following us. But as we turn the corner, I glance up.

Billy Gibson flaps a pink wet tongue at me. He shouts something, but the cheers from the betting shop door and the blast of a car's faulty exhaust drown him out.

I can't be sure, but the last word he says sounds like *Henry*.

I slip out on Sunday morning to get a newspaper. At least that's what I tell Libby. She doesn't usually bother, she says, they're just a waste of money. Either gloom and doom or so-called celebrity gossip. It's the gossip I'm hoping to find – only not in the papers.

Billy Gibson is in the same spot I saw him yesterday, only this time he's on his own, smoking. He sneers as I approach, blows a funnel of smoke at me.

I take a twenty-pound note from my pocket. His eyes widen.

'I ain't no rent boy. Even if I was, I wouldn't do crusty old grannies.'

'I don't want you either,' I say. 'I just want some information.'

His eyes narrow with suspicion.

'About what?'

'Henry Campbell Black.'

He walks towards me, hand out.

'You from the social or something? Police?'

'Of course not.'

He grabs my arm, snatches the money from my hand and jumps away.

'I wouldn't tell you nothing,' he snarls. 'Fucking Lady La-Di-Da, slumming it, flashing her cash.' He waves the money at me. 'Ta for this, though. Easiest money I've ever made. No biggie that they call it *mugging.* '

He flicks his cigarette butt at me, laughs as I flap it away, and runs off.

It's not worth reporting him to the police; they'd only say it was my fault. I should have known better, been more careful.

I walk towards an old man shuffling in the direction of the newsagent. The threadbare Jack Russell at his side growls as I get closer.

'Henry Campbell Black?' he says, holding the dog back. 'Don't ring any bells. People come and go all the time around here now. Not like it used to be.' He nods towards the newsagent. 'Try in there.'

The Asian woman behind the counter is so engrossed in her magazine I have to repeat my question twice. She shakes her head.

'No.'

'Could you check the names on your paper round?'

'We don't deliver papers. None of the kids want to work.'

She raises her eyebrows when I buy an *Observer* and drops the change into my hand as if I'm infectious.

The greasy-looking man in the Spar next door says he's only just taken over the shop so doesn't know many people by name yet. He suggests I try the bookmaker.

I walk to the corner, but Ladbrokes is shut, the pavement dappled with ground-out cigarettes. The metal doors of the Beaten Path pub are locked and the streets are empty. Curtains are drawn tight across windows. I feel trapped, shut out. The grapevine the cab driver promised is withered and broken.

The cab driver.

I take out my purse for the card he gave me.

'Cab.' The woman's tone is clipped and bored. 'Where to?'

'Manchester city centre.'

'Picking up at?'

'The Beaten Path,' I say, checking the name of the pub. 'Wythenshawe.'

'Yup. What name?'

'Beth. Is Dave working today?' I cross my fingers.

'Which one?' the woman says. 'We've got three.'

'Oh, I don't know his surname. He's about fortyish, short black greying hair. Red car.'

'Ah, that's Dave Hadfield. Aka Mr Manchester!'

'That's the one.'

'You sure you want him? He never shuts up.'

'That's why I want him.'

She chuckles.

'Suits me,' she says. 'Keeps him out of the cab office bending my ear.' There's the rustle of paper. 'He's on an airport run right now, so he's not far from you. Just a tick.'

I hear her talking in the background, the hiss of radio static.

'Okay,' she says. 'He'll be with you in ten minutes.'

It's a long ten minutes. I feel conspicuous, stranded. As bleak as the maisonettes and tower blocks around me.

Dave gives a toot on his horn as he pulls up to the kerb.

'Hello again,' he says through the open window. 'Are you waiting for the pub to open, or have they just tipped you out after last night?'

The car is warm; the smell of the citrus air freshener doesn't quite mask the trace of pastry. Dave brushes some crumbs from his lap into his palm and throws them out of the window.

'Cornish pasties,' he says. 'Food of the gods. And a godsend to busy cabbies.'

'Even if they are from Cornwall?'

'Manchester can't take the credit for everything.' He wipes his lips. 'Whereabouts in the city centre do you want?'

I puff my cheeks out.

'I'm not really sure.'

I hadn't intended going anywhere; it was his time and knowledge I wanted. But now he's here I feel relaxed. Safe. It's good to have a conversation where I don't have to scrutinise every comment or be on my guard. And it makes a change to hear a man's voice. His has a soothing timbre and the accent is rhythmic and rounded.

'Another mystery mission, is it?' he says.

'Yes. Surprise me.'

He nods.

'Right. King Street will do you, I think,' he says. 'Plenty of things to keep you occupied down there.'

'Such as?'

'Posh frocks and jewellers. Kendall's is just across the road and then it's straight up Deansgate for the Barton Arcade and Selfridges. Credit card beware.'

The car pulls away from the kerb. I text Libby that I've gone for a walk to give her some time alone with Esme, and sink into the seat.

'I didn't even know Manchester had a Selfridges,' I say.

'We've got two actually. Which is, let's see ...' he raises his eyes as if counting, 'one more than you've got in London.' The wink in the mirror makes me smile. 'We've got a Harvey Nichols too.'

'Ah, *designer* cloth caps and clogs.'

He laughs and accelerates to get through an amber light.

'They're all out of clichés, I think.'

We drive pass brown brick warehouse apartments,

the large windows fretted by metallic blinds. Glass office buildings scratch at the sky. Dave sighs as the traffic in front of us crawls to a halt. He lifts a hand from the steering wheel to cover a yawn.

'I'll call it a day once I've dropped you off, I think,' he says. 'Been at it since midnight, me. Need some kip before the match this afternoon.'

'Who are you playing?'

'We're not. It's City v Spurs at home. I want Spurs to thrash them. Then there'll be lots of happy cockneys in a generous mood looking for a cab to Piccadilly station.' He yawns again. 'If I can keep awake, that is. I need coffee.'

'Me too,' I say. 'You're the native. Where's good for coffee? On me.'

He looks at me quizzically in the rear-view mirror.

'For real?'

'Absolutely. I don't want any chain-store muck, though. I can get that anywhere. I want Manchester's finest brew.'

We end up in a café just off a large square dominated by the white ferris wheel I saw on Esme's postcard.

'Not quite as impressive as the London Eye,' I say, as I sip my coffee.

'Ah, but all you can see from the London Eye is London.'

'And up there you can see the Pyramids and Niagara Falls, I suppose?'

'I've no idea. I'm no good with heights, me.'

The whole area was redeveloped, he tells me, after an IRA bomb exploded in 1996.

'Fifteenth of June,' he says with a shudder. 'Worst day of my life.'

'You were injured?'

'No, thank God. Not physically, anyway. I was in town that day, though. I was just coming out of the electricity showroom when . . . boom.' His throws his hands up. 'If that shop's windows had blown out I'd have been cut to ribbons.' He shakes his head. 'It was a beautiful day, too. Blue sky and sunshine. Manchester don't get many of those, so having one ruined by the IRA was a good enough reason to hate them. But what they did to my city? Bastards. All them people cut and bruised and shocked. All them shops and businesses shut – a lot of them have gone for ever.'

'It must have been awful.'

'Do you know the thing I remember the most?' he says. I shake my head.

'The whole sky turning grey,' he says. 'Just for a moment.'

'Yes, I can imagine. All that dust and smoke.'

'No. Not smoke,' he says. 'Pigeons. Thousands of them, all taking off at once. Like a big silver wave crashing over the city.' He lifts his cup to his mouth and blows on his coffee. 'That were an omen, that.'

'Of what?'

'All this.'

He points to the buildings outside. The gleaming glass and metal of new buildings contrasts with the white and grey stonework of Victorian edifices.

'Regeneration. All the cash that poured into the city. All the jobs.' He laughs. 'Funny, eh? That something meant to ruin the city actually brought it back to life.'

I think of Amy and Esme, of transformation, regeneration, rebirth. Explosions, dirt and blood.

'Don't get me wrong,' he says, twirling a teaspoon in his fingers. 'It gutted me at the time. Really shook me up. I'd never felt unsafe in my own city up till then. It was like it had turned on me. Me sister felt the same. She used to live in a housing association flat not far from here – nice place, too. But would she go back after the bomb? Would she heck as like. That's how she ended up in Wythenshawe.'

I'd forgotten about his sister.

'And she feels safer there?' I ask.

'Yeah. No one's going to bomb Wythenshawe! Mind you, there are some who think it would be a good thing.'

'I wouldn't go that far, but . . .'

'Not exactly for tourists, eh?' he says with a laugh.

'Some of the locals are . . . colourful. Billy Gibson's practically wildlife.'

He snorts.

'So I've heard,' he says.

'You know him?'

'Only from what my sister's told me. The whole family's a nightmare by the sound of it.'

I wriggle forward on my chair.

'Has your sister ever said anything about Henry Campbell Black?'

He looks away and screws his face up.

'Don't ring any bells,' he says. 'Sounds a bit posh for Wythenshawe. The only double barrels you'll find around there are on a rifle.' He leans forward. 'Why? Is he giving you problems?'

'Only that I can't find him.'

'Ah, so *that's* what you're doing up here,' he says with a wink. 'What's he done?'

'He's a friend of the woman I'm staying with. He's just disappeared and we're trying to track him down for child support.'

He grimaces.

'I hate it when men knock women up and do a runner,' he says. 'Bloody cowards. Happened to me sister before she met her husband. She'd have kept the baby if the bloke had hung around.' He takes out his phone, dials a number and puts it to his ear. 'Henry Campbell Black, was it?'

I nod and put my elbows on the table, chin cupped in my hands. Dave curls his lip and shakes his head.

'No answer,' he says. 'I'll try again a bit later. Give me your number and I'll let you know if I have any joy with her.'

He smiles as he punches my number into his phone.

'Let's hope me wife don't get nosy.'

That afternoon, I keep my phone beside me during a game of Monopoly with Esme and Libby. Esme chooses to be the top hat, as she's seen them used in black and white musicals on TV. Libby goes for the sack of money. I opt for the howitzer.

Esme has a knack of avoiding properties that don't belong to her and throwing doubles to get out of jail free. Her side of the board bulges with cash from the fines she collects, and she constantly rearranges it to make sure it's still there.

When I land on Bond Street she doesn't even need to look at the card to see how much the fine is. She knows the penalties for all her other properties too, regardless of the number of houses or hotels.

'You'd make a slippery landlord, Esme,' I say. 'I'm being fleeced in my own city.'

'I'm good at the Manchester version too,' Esme says, greedily tucking the cash into her pile. 'But I prefer the London one. It's more glamorous.'

'There's nothing glamorous about Pentonville Road! Or the Elephant and Castle.'

Esme picks up the dice and jiggles them in her hand.

'The subway tunnel ramps at Elephant were good for skating down,' she says. She throws the dice and moves the top hat along the board. 'But the tramps and winos at the bottom were scary.'

Libby shoots me a significant glance.

The ringtone on my phone makes me jump. The screen says *Dave*.

'Ah, it's my friend Jill,' I say. 'I'd better take it in the bedroom. It'll only be about the church jumble sale.'

I close the bedroom door, check that no one is outside and answer the phone.

'Any luck?' I say.

'Yeah. Spurs are two nil up,' Dave says. 'It's looking good for tips at full time.'

'Good, but I meant your sister.'

'I know. Sorry.'

'She couldn't help?'

'I don't really know if what she said helps at all,' he says. He sounds hesitant. 'I can't believe there's one Henry Campbell Black in the whole of Greater Manchester, let alone two in Wythenshawe.'

'Two?'

'Seems so.'

'Your sister knows them?'

'One of them,' he says firmly. 'She worked at the nursery where my nephew used to go.'

'Your sister did?'

'No, this Henry character.' He sucks in his breath. 'She's a woman.'

'Oh. Right.' My heart sinks. Frustration boils. 'Bugger! Look, did your sister say anything else?'

'She was good with the kids, apparently,' he says. 'Even if she was a muff-muncher.'

'Sorry?'

'A lesbian,' he says. 'Bit of a porker, going by the photo my sister sent me.'

'And your sister doesn't know where this woman is now?'

'No idea,' he says. 'She just didn't turn up at the nursery one day. Not been seen since. So that's that then.'

I'm not so sure.

My head rushes with images and echoes with words.

The sly looks from the mothers at the school gates, the sensation of being left out of a joke. The sudden and recent obliteration of Henry Campbell Black from the household bills. The lewd pink wriggle of Billy Gibson's tongue.

Didn't he say something about Libby not being a proper mother? And what I thought was just a slip of his runaway tongue when chanting Esme's name could actually have been what he meant to say: *Les*me.

'Beth?' says Dave. 'You still there?'

I catch my breath. I grip the phone harder.

'You mentioned a photo,' I say, my eyes narrowing.

'That's right. This Henry playing with my nephew in a paddling pool. Taken about a month before she did a flit, apparently.'

'Can you send it to me?'

'I don't think my sister would mind,' he says. 'Hang on.' I hear voices in the background, the clump of car doors shutting. 'Gotta go, Beth. Duty calls.'

A few moments later my phone buzzes with an incoming message.

Here you go. Hope it helps. You know where I am when you're ready to go back to Piccadilly station.

My hand shakes as I open the attachment.

A toddler stands in a paddling pool, eyes shut, mouth open, thrilled at the torrent of water splashing over his head. The woman tipping it from a bucket has meaty hands and thick arms; the rest of her body is lost beneath a baggy beige shirt and grey tracksuit bottoms.

I look closer. The mop of black hair and chubby cheeks make it hard to see her face properly, but I guess her to be in her late twenties, maybe a little older. I zoom in. The picture dissolves into a pixelated blur. But even as she fractures and dissolves, I sense a heaviness about her, a cowering, as if buckling under pressure. There is no joy in her game with the boy, no pleasure in making him squeal.

That night, with the others asleep, I lie on my bed, trying to fit things together. In my head I run through Esme's essay for the umpteenth time, especially the part about her life in Manchester with Libby. There are secrets in it, I'm sure — as sure as I was with the overlooked clue in Libby's paperwork. But I can't see where. Everything flies by, like a speeded-up film.

I pause, flick back and replay the entry about the film again.

Things were easier with Mrs Doubtfire around.
She was funny and kind and made everything all
right. Made a family of three happy and whole.
    Even though it's a bit of a silly film, it
made me cry. Mum too. I told her everything
would be fine. But there are no more Mrs
Doubtfires. Lightning doesn't strike twice.

I've seen the film too, some time ago, but in my memory the family in it comprise a husband, a wife and three children. A family *of five*. Mended by a mannish nanny. Like Henry Campbell Black.

Esme wasn't talking about the film. It wasn't the happy ending that made both her and Libby cry. It was losing Henry Campbell Black.

I get up, tiptoe down the corridor. I take Esme's laptop

from the living room table and carry it back to my room.

My head thumps as I type in the password box.

Mrs Doubtfire.

Bingo. The screen yawns open and I dig around the folders and files with the cursor like an archaeologist with a trowel.

'Spice World' is nothing but photos of the Spice Girls, song lyrics and links to videos on YouTube. Lady Gaga's work is collected in 'Gaga4Gaga'. I'm more hopeful of 'Homework etc.' but it's only bits of poetry, a chapter of a story about a meerkat and a list of Esme's teachers, rated in preferential order. 'Xmas' has her wish lists for the past few Christmases and a shopping list for the next one. I'm touched to see my name on it and feel a pang of guilt for mistrusting her.

But that is the only reference I can find to me or to her previous life. Even her essay isn't on the computer. I expected folders full of research on Amy's case, with links to news sites, information about reincarnation, Kennington, unsolved murders and people who've gone missing.

It's all I can do to stop myself throwing the computer at the wall. Instead I take the USB stick from my bag and copy over all of the files I've found. I can't risk Esme going into the front room and finding her laptop missing. But I need more time than I've got to scrutinise the files.

Even when I've copied them, I still feel cheated. I've not got what I wanted but somehow, yet again, I know I'm close. I shut my eyes and take a deep breath. I try and put myself in Esme's head.

She's crafty and clever. She'd cover every eventuality. She'd expect me to try and look on her computer. If I managed to get past her password, she wouldn't make it easy for me to find incriminating information. She'd hide it as best she could. Bury it in the hard drive, in the last place I'd look.

I move the cursor to the trash can. Open it up.

She's been as careless as her mother was with the household bills, but in a different way. She's tried to be *too* clever. Being overly cryptic has given her away.

All the files in the trash can have self-explanatory labels. All except one.

HCBLegDict.WMA.

I recognise the initials HCB. But I don't recognise the suffix after the full stop or the little logo on the file icon. It's nothing I've ever worked with. Not a Word document, jpg or gif. I copy the file on to the USB stick, close the laptop down and return it quietly to its place on the front room table.

Back in my room, I copy the files to my own laptop. I'm about to click on the file with Henry Campbell Black's initials, then stop.

I remember the light I saw under the door when Esme and Libby were using their laptop. There's no reason why I shouldn't be using mine – I could say *I* was watching something on iPlayer – but I'd rather not make them suspicious.

I swing my legs into bed and pull the duvet over me; I'm caught in a hot little space lit by a forensic glow that makes my shadow sharp.

I click on the file. A small grey dashboard appears on the screen. There are buttons with arrows on it, like on a CD player. Fast forward. Rewind. *Play.*

The inbuilt speaker hisses. It's loud, too loud. I scrabble for the volume button. I don't know what I'm listening to; it could be nothing. But if Libby and Esme hear it too, there will be awkward questions to answer, whether it contains anything revealing or not. Yet again I'm on the brink of being thrown out. Thrown off the scent of the truth.

It could be something perfectly innocent and mundane; a recording of a pop song, or some music track down-loaded from the internet. But then there's a clunk, as if the laptop had been moved and the microphone tested. It goes quiet. I lean in towards the laptop, straining to hear. Like someone at a seance. Is there anybody there?

There is.

I hear someone cough and clear their throat. The sound is muffled but the cough is too deep for a child. Not deep enough for a man.

My mouth is dry and my heart thumping.

There's another cough, a rustle of clothing. Then, suddenly, a voice. A rush of words tumbling out at me so quickly I can barely catch them. All I know is I don't recognise the voice, but the accent has a London twang.

I stop the player, press the back arrow, begin again at the start.

I I

I hope you can hear this. I ain't sure if this recorder thing is working as I've never used one before. It's not mine; I borrowed it from someone at work who lent it to me 'cos I told her I was learning French and had to listen to meself to make sure I'd got it right. She believed me too. Like *I'd* be learning French …

All these computers and gadgets and all that does my head in but I reckon I might just about have got the hang of this now so I can tell you what I need to and you can understand what all this is about.

I *can't* write it, you see. I mean, don't get me wrong, I *can* write, despite what some people used to think, it's just I don't do it good enough or quick enough. And I ain't got too much time as I've gotta catch a train in about an hour. I've got things to do. Well, *some*thing, anyway.

But I've gotta get all this out too. It's like when you wanna be sick or got a cold and your head's full of snot, you know, when it's all inside you and wants to come out? But you don't wanna puke in front of people so you run to the bog or the bushes and do it there? And then you feel all clean? All better?

Well this is me. Puking up the past, gobbing off about it and clearing it all out. *Every bloody bit.*

Like I say, I ain't big on words and books and stuff, especially stories and all that made-up crap, but I like books of spells and star signs and angels and books that tell you what your dreams are supposed to mean. That's my bag.

I've read so many of the bloody things I should be one of them experts you get on the telly, you know, telling everyone how they can be rich and have flashy flats in London and New York and big houses in the country and villas in Barbados. Living the dream with lots of top mates and a decent bloke who loves you to bits and kids that do as you say and bring you tea in the morning – just like the books say.

But I ain't got none of those things. It's not the books' fault. It's all down to me not understanding and getting it wrong like I usually do.

There *was* one book, mind, that made a right big difference to me life. The bloke who wrote it got right under me skin and turned things around, for a little while at least.

It weren't even mine. I found it on the counter of the Little Chef on the A435 when two posh students left it there while they faffed over paying their bill. Instead of just going halves like friends are meant to, they worked out what each of them owed, down to the last penny. Whatever they were meant to be studying it weren't maths, as it took 'em ages.

Anyway, as I was waiting for them to cough up, I spotted this book, on the counter, like I said. I only picked it up because I got the title wrong.

Black Law Dictionary.

I thought it was a guide to black magic, you know, spells and voodoo and recipes for potions to keep evil away and keep me safe. The words in the book were in columns, all lined up, black and neat, like bullets in a box ready for shooting.

Turned out it weren't spells at all. It weren't Black Law but *Black's* Law. Black – with an s on the end. All it was was jargon, you know, definitions and explanations and all that. The sort of things that posh boys and clever people understand. Not for the likes of me.

'A Law Dictionary' it said on the inside page. 'Definitions of the terms and phrases of American and English Jurisprudence, Ancient and Modern. By Henry Campbell Black, MA.'

It was all head-fuck nonsense, like the alphabet at school.

We had an alphabet chart on my classroom wall, see. Scared the shit out of me, that thing. It had little pictures on it ... you know, ball, clock and whatever to the bloody zebra at the end ... all meant to make the alphabet look like a game and make it easy, but that chart was just a trap, like the Child Catcher's wagon in *Chitty Chitty Bang Bang*, all covered with sweets and ribbons so it looked like fun when really it was just a paddy wagon taking kids off to the nick.

Even I knew what the pictures on the wall chart were, but the letters ... they was just shapes, all lines and angles and sticks with knobs on. Meant fuck-all to me. The shiny green apple at the beginning was like a big boulder. Keep out. No entry. Piss off.

But Miss Clapton let me in. She said she could help. I stayed behind after school, like I'd been naughty, and had separate lessons as if the others would catch something from me. I did rhymes and exercises, learnt patterns and shapes until me head hurt so much I wanted to kick the kicking k's back.

I got there in the end, though. I untangled the letters bit by bit until I could put 'em together to make words and write 'em down in the right order. Some of 'em, like 'friend', were easy but others, like 'love', always tripped me up.

I don't use words like that no more, mind, even if I can spell 'em and know what they mean. Now it's words like 'revenge', 'justice' and 'death' on the tip of me tongue.

I ain't got a Scooby about how Black's Law Dictionary began but I ain't never gonna forget my alphabet. It's mine for ever. I've got the same letters, in the same order ... only now they're telling different stories ... ones that belong in a court, not a classroom.

That's why A ain't for apple. It's for Amy.

Hearing my daughter's name spoken by an unfamiliar dis-embodied voice hits me like a fist, winding me. I stop the player once again and throw the duvet back, catching at breath. But I remember to shield the screen of the laptop, shutting out its light; whatever is on this recording, who ever made it, must have the answers I've been desperate to hear for the last ten years. I will not lose them now.

I pull the duvet back over my head, watch the shadow of my shaking hand as I click play once more.

… It's no wonder her name began with an A. It's the first letter of the alphabet, the first letter of the *word* alphabet too … It's used to being first. It's a right show-off, look-at-me letter. It's for A-list celebrities and the best grade teachers dish out … only not to me, of course. They all went to Amy.

She was a double A. Amy Archer. Blessed twice.

My parents didn't get the power of A; no surprise really, as they didn't know much about nothing to be honest. They believed things never changed and said it was pointless hoping they would, so nothing *did* change. Hope was hope-less. Deal with what you got and what you get and just suck it up with no whingeing or bellyaching.

No big surprise then that *I* didn't get a name beginning with an A. I got a D instead.

Dana.

I come up for air again. *Dana.* I reach for my phone on the bedside table. The screen still shows the picture of Henry playing with the toddler at the nursery. *The picture of Dana.*

I try to make out the features of the girl I knew in the heavy, joyless figure in the photo, but she's hard to find. Perhaps in the shape of the eyes and the line of the nose, but they are blurred by fat and the poor picture quality, so it's hard to be certain. She looks older than she actually is. I guessed her to be in her late twenties, when really she's only twenty, the same age as Amy. The same age Amy would have been, rather. I could have walked past Dana on the street and not recognised her.

I take the phone back under the duvet, rewind the recording a little way and press play.

... I got a D instead.

Dana.

The little shits at school soon turned that into Dunno. Then Dumbo. In Spanish lessons, a speccy bitch with braces and plaits spotted that my name was an anagram of *nada*. Nothing. My life in a name ...

I didn't have a bloody chance ... not with my genes. Dad was a postman. He never read nothing except envelopes, and even that was a stretch.

It's funny in a sad sort of way ... he was the one pushing letters into letter boxes but really it was them who pushed *him* around. The letters in his bag controlled where he went and when, as he couldn't go home until he got rid of 'em all.

If dogs growled as he shoved the post through the door, he'd stand there and growl back. Woof, woof. Dozy bastard ... And those red rubber bands they use to keep the post together? Other postmen just chuck them on the floor, but my dad, he brought 'em home, made 'em into balls and dropped 'em from the window of our tenth-floor flat. The balls shot around like the ones in a pinball machine. I'd laugh but he just stared, like he wished he could fly away too.

Mum worked part-time in a crappy shoe shop on Walworth Road. She didn't like it much and only put up with it for the staff discount. Just as well really ... if it weren't for her twenty per cent off, I'd have gone to school in me socks and given the kids something else to laugh at.

'You gotta be more careful,' she'd say to me. 'Look after your shoes. Money don't grow on trees.'

I used to cover up the scuffs with black crayon.

The shoe shop was just around the corner from East Street market, so it was dead handy for end-of-day bargains. We never had cabbage, as Mum said she got enough of sweaty feet at work, but she always got some strawberries in. She smothered 'em with sugar and ate 'em like a Roman eating grapes. She'd sit there with a silly look on her face, all greedy and naughty and smiling. Then she'd pull a face as she bit into the stalk and spat it out. I didn't get why she wouldn't cut the stalks off first, until she told me.

'It's how I first had strawberries,' she said. 'We used to rob them out of some old boy's window box. Had to get them in our gobs pronto. Got caught once. He scared the shit out of me.'

Really she just liked spitting . . .

Dad's mum was different apparently, but she croaked it before I was born, probably 'cos she wanted to avoid meeting me. The story goes she was standing on a chair putting up clean net curtains in the kitchen, then wallop, out of the blue, a brain haemorrhage. The people in the flat below heard the thump as she fell but they thought she was just moving furniture. Grandad found her when he came back from work.

'She was all tangled up in manky netting,' he always said.

236

'Icy cold. It was just like me wedding day all over again, only better.'

They'd only got married because he'd knocked her up. She lost the baby a month after the wedding but it was too late to turn back so they just got on with it, like my family always did, like I always do ...

Grandad hid down the pub, where he was top dog of the darts team, or down the bookies', who were always pleased to see him ... their number one customer. Nan escaped to Streatham Palais for Babycham and Teddy boys.

Grandad reckoned he weren't meant to marry ... I don't mean not marry Nan, I mean not marry full stop. He said that's why he'd lost 'alf his wedding ring finger doing National Service. He only had a stub left and he made out it was a sign warning him not to marry, an omen of only 'alf a marriage if he did.

His disability, he called it ... I think he meant the marriage, not the finger. Didn't stop him handling money as a conductor on the number 3 bus, though, or getting one hundred and eighty for the darts team.

Me dad reckoned it was a miracle they ever had kids, as he says they were never in the same room long enough. They still found time for rows to kick off, mind.

'Thank God for you and your brother,' Grandad would say to me dad. 'If it weren't for yous two, we'd never have got a three-bedroom flat off the council.'

Me uncle legged it as soon as he could and signed up with the army. Mum and Dad tied the knot a year later. They were skint ... always would be, had no chance of stumping up the dosh for their own place … never even thought of it neither. A council flat was the best they could hope for, all they dreamt of really, and true to form, even that dream got buggered up, as there were too many people and not enough flats. Dad blamed the wogs, Mum blamed the Pakis. We all blamed life.

Grandad was pretty chuffed about it, though … he liked the rent Mum and Dad paid him. So did the pubs and the bookies. And he liked having someone to cook and clean and do everything for him too, and made silly jokes about having a slave. Mum never laughed and neither did I …

They phased conductors out on Grandad's route, so he had to get another job. He couldn't become a bus driver, as he was too thick for driving lessons … too thick for any qualifications, come to that … so he ended up at my school as the caretaker. The other kids sneered at me 'cos of him.

'You stink 'cos you wash in the sick he mops up.'

'No one wants to come to your house for tea. All you have is leftovers from the school canteen.'

But Amy liked me. God knows why, I wasn't the sort of playmate for a double-A celebrity like her. She was rich, clever, popular, but *she* liked *me* … Sometimes I thought she only let me play with her 'cos she felt sorry for me and being with a no-mark like me made her look good and got her house points from the teachers for being nice. And she *was*.

She let me copy from her in class … told the others to leave me alone … wouldn't play with them if they didn't ask me too. She even turned down the role of Gabriel in the

238

nativity play just to be a sheep like me. My mum thought it was sweet but Amy's mum weren't happy about it one little bit.

She didn't like me playing with Amy any more than she liked me sitting next to her. She told Amy she shouldn't let me crib her answers and we'd both do better if we sat apart, but Amy took no notice.

My name was top of the list for her parties and no one but me was ever asked for a sleepover. We swapped Skittles and Space Dust in our midnight feasts and got dressed up as the Spice Girls, dancing in front of the mirror. Course, she always got to be Baby Spice, 'cos she was prettier, blonder and the white feather boa belonged to her.

She had more clothes than me full stop ... *and* they came from shops that had names on their plastic bags. Gap. Diesel. Dolce & Gabbana, that sort of thing. Mine came in the plain bags they used on the market stalls ... you know, the right flimsy ones. Either that or there weren't no bag at all, which meant them clothes were knock-off.

I wore some of Amy's clothes, up in her bedroom any-way. I had to take them off when I went home as Mrs Archer would stand by the front door on guard, looking for designer labels under my market-stall tat.

Some people reckoned me and Amy were twins ... pissed Mrs Archer off big-time, that. She'd pull a face every time, say no, of course we weren't, what an idea. We *did* look alike, mind, but I was just a cheap copy, the dodgy fake.

Me and Amy scratched our initials on Mrs Archer's door-step once ... we got a right old slap for that. Real leg-stingers, but I reckon I copped for more of a slagging-off than Amy. It was her doorstep, I suppose. It was as if my initials were worse than the mark of the devil, a bad omen. As it turned out, they were …

I don't think Mrs Archer liked me much before Amy went missing, but afterwards, when I was safe and Amy weren't … If I hadn't been Amy's friend, she would never have been in the playground in the first place. But I *was* Amy's friend, she *was* there and I weren't.

'Where were you?' Mrs Archer kept saying. 'You're sup-posed to be her friend.'

Dad told her to go easy on me. Grandad told her she should know better.

'Dana's in bits,' he said. 'Kept awake by nightmares. She feels guilty enough without you laying into her.'

Grandad was right … but Mrs Archer was too. It *was* my fault. No way could I make it up to her, though I tried. I pretended to be Amy in the reconstruction for *Crimewatch*. I was a dead ringer for her, the coppers said. I bet Mrs Archer hated that. I bet she hated me being the one who could help find her daughter too … And I bet she thought it was the least I could do.

I wanted to do it, but I was scared. I thought the same thing that happened to Amy would happen to me … I reck-oned that if I could play meself, I could rewrite the script and make everything all right, you know. I wouldn't argue with Amy or let her walk off. I'd stay by her side … standing guard … make sure we walked back to my house together with Grandad, like we was meant to …

But the coppers said they didn't need *me*. Amy was playing on her own when she disappeared, and that was the memory they wanted to jog. That was the truth. *I'd* just be in the way. Amy was better off without me ... in the reconstruction and in real life.

In the end, I was dressed up in exact copies of Amy's clothes ... pink tracksuit bottoms, Spice Girls platform trainers, headband and tiger-print fleece. I was like a doll ... an Amy doll.

I spun on the roundabout and sat on the see-saw, Amy's end scraping the ground, my end light and empty ... like I'd been catapulted into space, out of harm's way.

When the coppers gave me the nod, I walked out of the playground, like Amy's ghost. I wondered if the video would just show white noise, and it might as well have done for all the good it did ...

A is for Amy Archer. Who deserved a better friend than me.

B is for ... baby.

You'd think the kids at school would be nice to me when Amy vanished, like they were when George Miller's dog got run over. He got given loads of sweets by his mates and the teachers let him off homework and made him milk monitor two terms running.

But all I got was questions.

'What happened? Where is she? Why don't you know where she is?'

I wouldn't answer them 'cos I *couldn't* answer them ... It didn't take long for them to get nasty.

'It's no surprise you weren't taken! Not even the perverts want you.'

They did a survey. 'Who do you wish had disappeared? Amy or Dana?' For once, I got more marks than Amy.

The empty desk next to mine was like a slap in me face. Every day ... slap, she's not here any more. Slap ... all 'cos of you. No one wants to sit next to you, you're a minger, a curse, evil. Slap. Slap. Slap ...

I missed the touch of Amy's left arm against my right one, the smell of her coconut shampoo, the pop of the press stud on her packet of felt-tip pens. I hid at playtime. Teachers told the other girls to ask me to join in with their games. Course, they didn't want me to play but they had to ask just to keep the teachers happy, but I wouldn't join in anyway. The teachers said I had to try.

'We know it's hard, but you've got to carry on as best you can. When Amy's back, you don't want her being better at skipping than you are, do you?'

I couldn't get the hang of skipping at the best of times, always jumping at the wrong moment and getting caught up in the rope. I was even crappier now because I could hardly get off the floor, and if I did, I felt like I was landing on Amy's grave.

'Don't forget to sing!' the girls shouted.

> I like coffee, I like tea,
> I like Amy to jump with me.

I never skipped again … gave hopscotch, kiss chase and tag a swerve. Even the other kids could see why I wouldn't want to play hide and seek … *That's* why they never stopped asking me to.

I played on me own instead, juggling mainly, just like Amy had taught me. I only got up to two balls, though Amy – of course – could do three. When we juggled the balls against the school walls it sounded like a steam train, but when I did it on me tod it was just like rain … Slow rain.

Me and Amy had this song we liked to sing when we juggled, but when I tried it without her it just made me cry.

> Over the garden wall, I let my baby sister fall.
> My mother came out, she gave me a clout,
> I asked her what all the fuss was about.
> She gave me another to match the other,
> Over the garden wall.

One time, I heard the rhythm of another set of balls against the wall. I turned to look for Amy but … she weren't there and the balls just fell to the ground … like tears, except balls stop rolling eventually and tears don't.

I tried again but chose another song. 'Pokarekare ana'. We'd been taught it by one or our teachers who was a Maori and got us to sing this song when we used these balls on a string … pois, they was called.

> Oh girl return to me,
> I could die of love for you.

I got good at pois. Did it in me bedroom. I kidded meself that each swing would bring Amy back, winding her in like a fish. All I got was empty air ...

Mum and Dad thought a new home and a new school would help. A fresh start, they said, for all of us, where no one knew us and we could get on with our lives. We ended up in Birmingham, of all places. I guess it made sense, as it was a big city in the middle of the country ... plenty of room to get lost in.

Amy came too ...

I vanished at secondary school. I didn't bunk off or anything – in fact I went every day, even when I weren't feeling well – but I just sat in the middle of the class, on me own, doing as I was told. I never answered questions, never got really bad marks, never got really good ones. I was just average, in the middle ... safe.

I was too fat for sports, too flat for the choir. I didn't give or get any Christmas cards ... weren't asked to no parties. Even the bloody teachers didn't know me name. I was famous at the tuck shop and the canteen, mind. Forget sugar and spice, I'm built of sugar and fat, E numbers, additives and salt.

Mum always banged on about eating breakfast, but I didn't have much ... I just wanted to get away from the table and out the house. I was late for school, was meeting me mates, had an essay to hand in ... least that's what I told her.

Mum gave me money for fruit, can you believe? Fruit! Me? What a joke! She got wise in the end and told me to get them wholegrain snack bars, you know the ones, hard as cardboard and sprinkled with shit, but instead I stopped at the Spar near the bus stop for pasties, crisps, chocolate and Coke.

Best part of school for me was lunchtime. I'd go to the canteen late every day, not 'cos I weren't hungry – I was always hungry – but 'cos going late meant more food, as the dinner ladies didn't like waste and dolloped up bigger portions of chips, chicken nuggets, crumble and custard. And I'd get seconds too ... even thirds on a really good day. Food did me good, just not in the way Mum said.

Exams were a bit of a no-brainer for me ... I don't know why the teachers even bothered entering me. Had to, I suppose. Somehow I scraped passes in child care and food technology, got tipped out of school and ended up waitressing at the Little Chef.

At least I got a uniform ... red and white it was, so I didn't stick out, but I never wore me name badge, even though the manager was always on me case about it. He reckoned the badges made it more welcoming for the customers, but I didn't see how. The only thing they needed to know the name of was the food. They weren't ordering me ... I weren't on the menu.

Just as well really, seeing as I hid behind my notepad. I was invisible, even though I got bigger by the day on free staff meals and leftover chips. I got to the stage where I couldn't see me feet, and me hips sent plates flying from tables. Thank God I didn't have to pay for breakages ... or uniforms. I went through three of them, each one larger than the last.

Don't get me wrong, I weren't ashamed of meself ... well, not of me reflection, anyway. I liked the way I looked. But I was glad I couldn't see how I looked ... you know ... inside ...

I lived in a dingy bedsit in the red-light area. All night I'd get the sound of heels clack-clack-clacking up and down outside me window and cars revving their engines. I felt sorry for the women putting themselves in danger like that, but I hated 'em too ... for being available ... not saying no. I hated their punters even more.

One of them had the nerve to ask me how much for a suck and fuck.

'Big girls are better value for money,' he said.

I wanted to spit in his face and punch him, but instead I ran away ... from the bedsit *and* from Birmingham. I ran away from Dana too.

That's when I found me new name, from that book left on the Little Chef counter.

'A Law Dictionary. By Henry Campbell Black, MA.'

I tell you, I was gobsmacked how easy it was to change my name, even for me. There weren't no legal forms or having to ask permission from no one or anything like that. All you have to do is just write a letter claiming your new name and get someone to sign it as a witness and that's it, sorted, job done.

There was this other waitress at the Little Chef ... Cindy, her name was, stank of BO and liked flirting with the lorry drivers, but she was all right I suppose ... well, Cindy didn't get why I wanted to change me name from something 'lovely' like Dana to something 'odd' like Henry. She reckoned if I was gonna change my name I should go for a pretty one ... Tiffany or Fifi, for fuck's sake. As if a pretty name would suit me. And anyway, lots of women have men's names. Terri. Lesley. Jamie. Why not Henry?

Cindy signed the name-change letter for twenty quid and all the day's tips ... I don't think I even said thank you or goodbye but I know I didn't look back as we pulled out of the coach station. Dana Bishop had gone, wiped off the face of the earth, and there weren't no one who would miss her or feel bad about her going, like they had with Amy.

You know that bit in *The Wizard of Oz* when Dorothy and the rest of them see Emerald City for the first time and start legging it down the Yellow Brick Road, instead of just doing that skippy dance down it? They're all excited and out of breath and thinking all their dreams are about to come true ... Well that's how it was for me when I got to Manchester.

I found a bed at a hostel in Ancoats where I used me new name for the very first time when I signed the register. The duty manager didn't even blink.

It was a right shithole, one of those big old Victorian places made out of red brick, although you wouldn't know it what with all the soot and everything. It weren't much cleaner inside neither. The corridors were all flaky paint and smelt of food and damp. There was signs on the walls telling us we couldn't have no visitors or smoke ... couldn't have pets or drugs ... play loud music ...

247

My room was narrow and just about long enough for a single bed. There was a little window which didn't let much light in and a scuzzy sink that glugged whenever anybody in the building was running a tap, which meant it glugged pretty much all the time. It weren't no worse than me bedsit in Birmingham – at least there weren't no prostitutes or punters – but it *felt* different . . .

I hit the Job Centre soon as I'd unpacked, even though they'd always been pretty useless in the past. This time my 'adviser' got me an interview . . . at a nursery of all places. Bottom of the pile, needless to say, just a nursery assistant, but more than I'd ever dared hope for seeing as I'd only just squeaked through my child care exam after all.

I tried not to think of Amy and me own childhood . . . pushed it to the back of me mind. When I showed up for the interview, the playground was noisy and busy with toddlers running around all over the place, wriggling through a red plastic tunnel. *These* kids looked happy, bundles of fun and energy, like all kids should be . . . how I wished I'd been.

I saw me chance to make peace with childhood and put things right over letting Amy down by making sure no other kid came to harm. I belonged there . . . I could help them and they could heal me.

I got the job, but at a price. The nursery manager, Maggie, had to do a criminal record check.

'It's the law,' she said. 'We have to be sure there's nothing in your past to make you unsuitable to work with kids. Don't worry. It's just a formality. I'm sure you've got nothing to hide.'

Shows how much she knew.

Course, I didn't wanna give her my real name, but as there'd be no trace of Henry Campbell Black anywhere and she'd only get suspicious, it was better to tell her the truth.

'It's an unusual name you've chosen,' she said. 'The kids will find it funny.'

I just told them I was a Teletubby ... They took to me right away, probably 'cos I screamed playing chase, jumped at the jack in the box and went mad with paint and Play-Doh. I played every game except one ... In What's the Time, Mr Wolf? I got more nervous waiting for the Wolf to cry 'Dinner time!' than the kids did.

The kids broke my heart every day just by taking my hand ... showing me they trusted me even though they shouldn't – and wouldn't have done if they'd known what I was really like or how I'd let Amy down.

There was one little boy ... Elliot, I think his name was ... he had a big thing about building towers with bricks, you know, the brightly coloured ones with letters and pictures on the side. The nonsense words he made were like the stuff *I* used to write.

Anyway, one day he spelled out 'Amy', and on the row below there was a brick with a picture of a hand. I stuck me foot out and brought the whole lot down, scattering the bricks, like the runes I'd read about in me magic books. It was an omen ... telling me Amy was reaching out to me, not as my friend but to accuse me.

There are ghosts in games, and fainites don't work ... Trust me, I know, I tried.

I got lucky again soon after I started the job, as Maggie had a spare room in her flat in Wythenshawe and wondered if I fancied it. She'd been a foster mum apparently, taking in strays like me. I was the latest but it turns out I weren't the last.

I'd not been there long – two months tops – when Maggie told me her boyfriend had asked her to live with him. I wasn't to worry, she said, I could stay on in the flat. She didn't want to let it go 'cos she needed it as insurance just in case things didn't work out with her boyfriend.

'We'll just put the bills in your name and leave it at that, eh?'

I couldn't believe me luck! First a roof over me head, now a place of me own. I almost hugged her. Then she said I weren't going to be on me own as someone she knew had been dumped in some crappy B and B by the council and she wanted to help her.

'Not the place to bring up kids, as you're all too well aware.'

She must have seen the panic on me face.

'Don't worry,' she said. 'She's only got the one child. She used to come to the nursery but she's about eight now. Bright and bonny little thing, she is. It will be like having a baby sister around. Her mum's only about six years older than you, so you'll have a big sister too. I've got a good feeling about this. I think you're really going to hit it off.'

Well, what could I do? I couldn't say no, that's for sure. Maggie had been kind to me ... generous. I had to be too.

The company would be good for me, she reckoned, and I'd be good for them.

'They need some security. Your brand of TLC.'

A housemate and a ghost moved in.

B is for baby. A new generation.

The air under the duvet is damp and stale and smells of me. I can smell the truth too. Realisation seeps like sweat. Dana and Libby and Esme. Living together. Sharing lives. Sharing stories. Making up tales.

Adrenalin shoots through me. Fury. The need to know it all.

C is for ... cat.

I tell you, Manchester might have looked like the Emerald City that night I first arrived, but I bet it don't rain in the Emerald City like it does here. They don't call this place the rainy city for nothing. It ain't a quiet, misty kind of drizzle ... it just tips it down, hour after hour of fat, cold, steady rain. That's how it was the day Libby and Esme rocked up.

Maggie brought 'em round in her car. I watched from the flat window. The glass was all huffed up by my breath and the raindrops looked like lace, so when I first saw Esme it was like looking through a web ... What I saw was Amy.

When I put me fingers to the window, trying to touch her and check she was really there, I felt the chill of the glass like the skin of a ghost. I told meself it was all in me head, just a trick of the light or wishful thinking, but I knew it was more to do with a guilty conscience.

I've read about déjà vu ... had plenty of them wacky, been-here-before moments, usually in me nightmares. But this time was the worst. Amy was there, close up and real and alive, staring back at me ... through Esme's eyes.

Esme stepped towards me and smiled. *That smile, oh God, that smile.* The one I'd missed for so long, wanted to see again. It was sweet and kind, forgiving ... She cocked her head when Maggie introduced me, like she hadn't heard me name right.

'That's not your real name though, is it?' she said.

Her smile was half playful, half suspicious. It didn't change when I told her it *was* me real name.

Libby might just as well have not been there ... she didn't even register, not right away, but then she pushed into the corner of my eye, all slow, like a tear.

She was pale and pinched and dripping wet, and looked older than she really was but younger in some ways too ... like a large kid – another kid I could help.

I got her a towel for her hair. When she'd rubbed it dry, she looked flushed and giddy, like a toddler after a go on the roundabout.

'We do appreciate this,' she said. 'Don't we, Esme?'

Esme nodded quickly.

'We won't be any trouble, will we?'

Esme smirked and shook her head slowly.

I left them to unpack and went back to Maggie in the corridor. She said I looked ... wired, a bit shocked, like I'd been punched. I told her it was just starting all over again and living with strangers.

'I thought you'd be used to that after all that time in the hostel,' Maggie said. 'It'll be a bit strange at first, but once you've got to know each other, you'll think you've known one another all your lives.'

That was the problem.

Esme caught me looking at her when she was eating a bowl of minestrone soup in the kitchen. She frowned at me.

'What?' she said.

'Nothing.'

The frown vanished and became a smile ... as if she knew what I was thinking. The way Amy always did ... like twins, Miss Clapton used to say, as if we were telepathic.

I didn't want Esme to know she did my head in or that she confused and scared me. I didn't want her to know I believed in ghosts. But I think she knew all that anyway ... That's what scared me the most.

That first night together, I ran Esme a bath, a deep one, chucked in some bath gel and got it all frothy. I left her to it and went and found Libby asleep on the bed. I pulled off her shoes, tucked the duvet around her, picked up their bags of clothes and put them in the washing machine.

Suds splatted against the porthole ... Esme splashed in the bathroom ... rain drummed on the window. I couldn't tell if the flat was washing itself, rinsing off the scum, or whether it was the past washing all around me, trying to get in.

When she got out of the bath, Esme asked me to dry her hair, which is what me and Amy always did on sleepovers. I'd wish my hair was thick and shiny and Baby Spice blonde like hers. I used to think every brush stroke tied us closer, but touching Esme was ... like an electric shock. I pulled back.

'It's okay,' she said. 'You didn't hurt me. It's not that tangled.'

It was for me ...

I ain't touched no one for years, you see, and wouldn't let them touch me. I'd given up good-night kisses years ago, although Mum and Dad weren't that bothered. After that, the only contact I had to put up with was the graze of a hand when I took cash from Little Chef customers. I did me best to steer clear of that too. The touch from the kids at the nursery was different ... more innocent ... so it didn't get under me skin like the rest. It was just part of the job.

Anyway, I rubbed Esme's hair with a towel, all nervous like, then brushed it with long, soft strokes. When I finished, she was all cosy and glossy and relaxed and happy as a cat in the sun ...

Over the next few weeks Libby relaxed too. She was secure and comfy and she liked having someone to help take care of her daughter.

'All I want is to be a better mum to Esme than mine was to me,' she said. 'For us to be a better family.'

She stopped looking all lost and disappointed and didn't keep going on about if only she'd done this or that. She stopped feeling sorry for herself ... got her confidence back, so much so that she began to apply for jobs. And eventually she got one – as a sales assistant at the airport's duty-free shop.

We celebrated with a bottle of the cheapest wine from

Costcutter. Libby and Esme danced to songs on the radio, their hands above their heads, while I watched from the sofa. They wanted me to join in, but I wouldn't. I ain't no good at dancing ... if anything, I'm even worse at dancing than I was at juggling, and that's saying something.

Esme grabbed me wrist and tried to pull me up, but I told her I couldn't, I was too much of a lummox.

'You can't fight it,' she said.

Fingers jabbed into me ribs.

'The rhythm's gonna get you in the end.'

Another jab. And another.

'The rhythm's gonna get you in the end.'

Libby started prodding too.

'The rhythm's gonna get you in the end.'

I struggled and they stumbled and landed on top of me ... I wriggled, and that just made them laugh even more, and all the time their fingers were poke, poke, poking.

'She likes it really!' Esme said.

I begged them to stop and tried to push them off, but they were fitter, slimmer, more bendy. Esme got her arms on me knees and tried to pin me down, but I ... I bucked her off, screaming me head off, and slapped her hard across the face.

Libby yelled at me that it was only a game. I buried me head in the sofa, crying, and kept saying sorry over and over again ...

Esme didn't ask why I hit her, because she knew. She stroked me hand, all understanding like, but her fingers were really just pointing at me ... picking me out ... ready to accuse me.

C is for cats. The games they play with mice.

D is for ... duck.

I never thought I'd have kids as I knew I shouldn't be trusted with them. It was okay at the nursery ... the gates were locked so the kids couldn't get out and no one could get in unless we buzzed them in. And there were other people around ... responsible people to look out for them too, so it weren't all down to me.

It's different for parents, and that's what I became. If that weren't a big enough surprise, an even bigger one was I was good at it ... especially the worrying bit.

Libby's shift work meant she weren't always around to do the school run and I had to stand in when she couldn't. Some days she would take Esme in and I'd pick her up and carry her paintings and wonky pottery back to the flat ... or it'd be the other way round.

I never left the gates until Esme had gone into the school building. When I picked her up, I was always there on the dot ... *before* the dot. I weren't gonna make no mistakes this time. I had me eyes front and back and all points in between, like something out of *Monsters, Inc.*

If I picked Esme up, she had to come back to the nursery with me and wait until I'd finished with the after-hours club for kids with parents who were still at work. Esme didn't mind it, as she didn't like walking on her own on the estate 'cos of all the dogs running loose, you know, thick-necked

Staffies wearing leather collars with spikes and studs. I didn't like them much either, dogs full stop, come to that. I ain't too fussed about cats neither, if I'm honest, but dogs ...

Once, me and Amy got chased around the park by a Westie when we were there on our skates. We'd just got an ice cream from the café. I dunno what the dog wanted more, the ice cream or us, but it ran after us, yapping at our feet. We both fell over and scraped our knees. Mrs Archer put cream on our grazed knees and gave us the money for another ice cream, but I think she thought it was my fault Amy had got hurt as it had been my idea to go out skating.

Esme was way older than the other children in the nursery, but she enjoyed playing with them ... handing out beakers of juice ... sitting cross-legged on the floor for fairy-story time ...

The versions I told were the fluffy Disney and Barbie ones. They had to be ... I ain't never read the books. I've only seen the films, and they don't max out on the gore like I've been told the books do.

Anyway, Esme hunched up during the scary bits, clapped when the hero escaped and groaned when the story finished. I told her I was surprised she weren't bored with them, as she'd heard them enough times.

'I just play along for the others,' she said. 'I'm not into the stories that much. The *real* ones are much better.'

She dragged me into the poky old library on the estate. The books on the shelves were yellowed ... didn't look like no one had ever read any of 'em. She took down a book of *Grimm's Fairy Tales*.

'I know these off by heart,' she said, 'but they'll be brand new if you read them to me. With all the voices and actions. Like you do at the nursery.'

It's like she was challenging me ... daring me to read. To see if I *could*. Testing to see if I was who she thought I was ...

I read her the stories all right, sitting on her bed with me arm around her. I weren't quite word perfect, but good enough to throw her off me scent. What made me stumble weren't the words, but the actual stories. Gory or what? It was like they was written in blood, with heads and arms chopped off and people left for the wolves ...

Every time I looked up from the book, Esme's lips would be miming the words, her eyes fixed on me.

'Families can be so nasty to each other, can't they?' she said. 'Especially the stepmothers. They're *always* evil.'

I looked away. I was as bad as the woodcutter's wife who insisted Hansel and Gretel was left in the forest ... and Esme knew it.

I lost count of the number of times she took that book out ... over and over again, like Amy with *The Man Who Didn't Wash His Dishes*. I only read that because she did, and I only read it once too, as it was a silly book, even for a numpty like me.

Amy kept telling me to read them big thick books by Philip Pullman, but they were too long and there weren't no pictures. But it was one of them books Esme wanted me to read to her next.

And she changed something else too ... Instead of sitting

next to her like I usually did, she made me sit on a chair at the end of the bed. When I asked her what difference it made, she just shrugged.

'Dunno. Just because ...'

I reckon she just wanted a better view, so she could see my reactions to the story. She said she'd not read it before, but she knew it off by heart and was way ahead of every little twist and turn, even getting the spooky sciency bits without me having to explain. Not that I could have, even if she'd asked. To her, Lyra flitting between parallel worlds was real, the sort of thing that happened every day.

The bits about experiments on kidnapped children freaked me out ... I couldn't read on.

'Please,' she said. 'I'm scared too but I want to know what happens.'

She weren't scared, she was playing ... the cat with her mouse. But I carried on reading, from me seat at the end of the bed.

We got through that book ... and the next in the series. That's when Lyra's friend Will gets given a knife that can cut windows between different worlds. Esme nodded, 'yes'. When Lyra got kidnapped, Esme was pleased to see me trembling. At the end of the book, Lyra was still missing.

'It's not a happy ending, is it?' Esme said.

That ain't the ending, I told her, there's still another book to go. So she wanted me to read that to her as well, to see if it all came right in the end.

Course, it didn't. Will and Lyra fess up to loving one

another but are forced to live apart, in different worlds.

'I knew it wouldn't be a happy ending,' Esme said. 'Didn't you?' Her voice sounded all hard and her eyes were like drills.

It ain't *un*happy either, I told her. 'They get to meet up again, after all.'

'But we're not told if that's a good thing or not,' Esme said. 'That bit of the story hasn't been written. Yet.'

That was that as far as me reading to Esme went. She didn't ask me again but sat on her own on the bed, reading to herself. She weren't reading stories either, as she'd moved on to my books instead.

You Can Heal Your Life.

The Element Encyclopaedia of 5,000 Spells.

Working with Guides and Angels.

The Celestine Prophecy.

The Gilded Tarot.

Libby reckoned it was all a load of old crap, but Esme loved it, especially the tarot cards. She laid them out on the floor and asked Libby to pick one. Libby sighed and plonked a finger on the nearest card.

'Ten of Cups.' Esme flicked through the book for the card's meaning. 'A happy family life. True friendships.'

Libby smiled.

'That's nice.'

Esme looked at the card, then back at the book.

'Oh no, wait a minute. Your card's upside down. That means the loss of a friendship. Children may turn against their parents.'

Libby laughed and said that meant things would be staying exactly as they were. Esme mixed the cards up again and said it was my turn. I tapped one with my toe. The Ten of Wands ... I didn't need her to tell me what it meant, as that one always came up for me.

'An oppressive load,' Esme said. 'Pain. All plans ruined.' She was gloating, chuffed to bits ... I tell you, the prophecy in the cards never felt more real than it did that time.

When Esme took her turn, she got the Wheel of Fortune.

'Destiny, an unusual loss, end of a problem, unexpected events,' she said. She pulled her legs up towards her and perched her chin on her knees. 'Ooh, I wonder what they could be?' She stared straight at me. 'Let's hope it's something nice.'

She didn't say it like she was daydreaming ... She said it like a threat.

'It is something nice,' Libby said. 'Esme, get your coat. We're gonna get some fresh air. Blow the evil spirits away.' She chased Esme into the hallway with her arms above her head, like the ghosts in *Scooby-Doo*.

I said I'd stay at home, get the ironing done, but Libby really wanted me to go. We ended up at Wythenshawe Park.

I ain't been to a park for donkey's years. The big bits of grass they've got mean you can see what's what ... who's about and what have you ... but there's nowhere to hide – for the nutters *or* for me. Bushes are dodgy too, as you can't see who's in them, and if you have to run, the roots will trip you over and you'll sprain your ankle so you can't run no more.

Playgrounds are the worst, mind ... Swings and climbing frames ain't for fun or to make you giddy, they're just ... traps. See-saws make you a sitting duck ... and the round-about ... oh God, the roundabout ... It ain't the spinning that makes me belly lurch, it's the memories. Like g-force ...

I kept telling meself to keep calm, everything was fine, nothing could hurt me ... Even so, I could've hugged Esme as she pulled us in the opposite direction to the playground, away from the danger and towards the safety of the community farm.

'She's never been big on swings and stuff, have you, Es?' Libby said.

Esme shook her head.

'They make me sick,' she said. She squeezed my hand so tight it hurt.

I should've known better to think the farm would be okay ... There's shit on every type of farm, city farms *or* pukka ones. Even if I didn't remember that, Esme had.

She fussed over the piglets sucking at their mum ... smiled for her photo feeding a lamb with a bottle ... cast a spell to make the mare give birth to its foal right there, right then.

It was all sweetness and light ... like the nursery rhyme, Old MacDonald with his cow, pig and horse, ee-i-ee-i-o.

Yeah, right ...

And on that farm he had a ... duck.

Ee-i-ee-i-NO.

There they were, above the noise of greedy pigs and hooves in mud. Ducks, squabbling, with a quack quack here and a quack quack there.

The lump in me throat was as big as a boulder ...

Here a quack. There a quack.

Everywhere a crack ... crack.

I closed me eyes and was back in Amy's bedroom during a sleepover. She'd woken up screaming ... screaming the whole bloody house down. Her mum came running in and told her it was only a dream, a really bad dream. She held Amy tight and rubbed her back.

'Was it the duck again?' she asked her.

Amy nodded and buried her head.

'From *Peter and the Wolf*,' Mrs Archer said to me. 'It's a piece of classical music.'

She kept telling Amy it was only a story, only a duck ... that it would make more sense if she was scared of the wolf, but Amy said she was scared of him too.

'He ate the duck, but the poor thing's alive,' she said. 'It's trapped and its friends can't help it.'

I was as scared as Amy and slept in her bed for the rest of the night. Amy didn't wake up again ... I didn't go back to sleep. I had to keep me eyes open ... looking out for the wolf.

Libby wanted to go to the duck pond but I said I needed the loo. Esme said she did too, so Libby said she'd catch up with us in a bit at the café.

'Mum loves the noise ducks make,' Esme said as we walked away. 'She thinks they're all laughing at a really good joke.' Her hand slipped into mine. 'But I don't think they've got much to laugh about, do you?'

'Oh, I dunno,' I said. 'They can swim and they can fly. That ain't bad going.'

'Yeah, but they're not safe anywhere, are they?' Esme said. 'Pike get them in the water. Guns get them in the air. And foxes get them on the land. It's no wonder they sound sad and panicky!'

She squeezed me hand and told me that someone at school reckoned that a duck's quack had no echo.

'I don't believe that,' she said. 'Do you?'

I stared ahead ... didn't answer.

'*I* don't,' Esme said. 'I don't believe that at all. Everything has an echo. *Everything.*'

D is for duck. Sitting ones and dead ones. Ducks that won't shut the fuck up.

E is for ... egg.

I dunno what sort of trick Amy had pulled off by coming back, but it must have been magic ... the sort of things I'd read about in me books. It weren't white magic neither ... not the good stuff. This was black and dirty, the stuff you ain't never gonna shift with bits of crystal or joss sticks.

Some of them books went on about natural law ... you know, about the universe arranging things to be just like they was meant to be. Crappy things happening was tough but there weren't no stopping them.

That's what happened with Esme ... with *Amy*, I mean ... I thought I'd got away and found a new life, but that just weren't what the universe wanted. You can run but you can't hide. Fate's fate, good or bad … *The rhythm's gonna get you in the end* …

I think I knew all that from the word go, really. It's pretty much what my parents believed too, it's just they didn't have poncy words for it … Sod's law they would have called it, not universal law.

Amy had always been good at tricks and I was always the stooge, falling for 'em every time. Pick a card, any card, she'd say, and I'd try to be clever and pick one that didn't stick out from the pack and weren't in the middle or right at the end. But she always got my card, first time, every time. She made money disappear from her hand too … just a quick click of her fingers and ta dah! It turned up in her coat pocket.

I wanted her to show me how to do it but she wouldn't. Magic was the only thing she never let me in on. Everything else, no problem – clothes, felt-tip pens, sweets, fill your boots – but magic? Uh-uh …Universal law, you see. I just weren't special enough to know things. I believed *she* had magic and that *I* didn't.

Until that day at school when, for once, *I* got to be the big I am. *I* was the one with mysterious magic powers and *she* was the one left scratching her head … Sort of, anyway.

I ain't got a clue what Miss Clapton thought she was teaching us that day in science, but I bet it weren't what I actually learnt, which was give me the upper hand over Amy and bingo! Everything's fucked up. Universal law will make sure of it.

Miss Clapton got me and Amy up at the front of the

classroom and then she gave me an egg and told me to squeeze it hard over a bowl. Even I knew it would break, everyone did, but I still jumped when it went crunch. I had yolk all over me fingers.

Then I was told to take another egg and squeeze it at the top and the bottom, instead of from both sides. Just as I was about to start squeezing, Miss Clapton stopped me.

'Do it over Amy's head,' she said. 'I dare you.'

My classmates gasped. Amy blinked and got all nervous as I held the egg above her head.

'I don't want to get messy, miss,' she said. 'I washed my hair last night. And my mum's always on at me about keeping my uniform clean.'

But Miss Clapton told me to get on with it. Amy screwed her eyes up.

I squeezed and squeezed as hard as I could, but the egg just wouldn't break. Everyone thought it was magic, and that *I* was magic too ... Everyone except Amy, that is.

'Do it again!' they shouted.

I waggled the egg in front of Amy's face.

'Abracadabra.'

'It's *not* magic,' Amy said. 'It's science. *Isn't it*, miss?'

The egg exploded and Amy got splattered with slime, all over her hair and face. She screamed at me, saying over and over that I'd done it on purpose.

I always was clumsy ... got me fingers tied up in cat's cradle and dropped catches at rounders – I even dropped Amy's guinea pig, Moon, although that was a good thing, or she'd never have found out it weren't a girl like she thought, but a boy.

I couldn't be trusted with nothing, especially precious or fragile things ... like magic ... or Amy. It was no use wanting it to be different so there weren't no point in trying. If I did, I deserved everything I got ... and the harder I got it, the better.

E is for egg. They're easier to break than universal law.

F is for ... fairy.

Like I say, some things just can't be changed, and people don't like change much anyway. Take the other mums at Esme's school.

I knew some of 'em, the ones who'd got kids at the nursery anyway. They'd drop their toddlers off, then dash up the road to the junior school with the older ones. We weren't mates or anything like that ... just said a quick hello and caught up on what the kids had been up to, if they'd been upset or ill ... that sort of thing.

But they knew I didn't have kids of me own, so their eyes was on stalks when I showed up at the school with Esme. It weren't really any of their business, but I had to say something. I didn't want 'em thinking I'd kidnapped her or got her off the internet.

There weren't no point in lying, so I just told them Esme's mum lived with me. That gave the gossips something to chew on, I can tell you. I said me and Libby were just friends and they were all nice about it – to me face – saying of course we were friends ... it weren't none of their business anyway. And it weren't.

But them tongues got wagging behind me back soon enough and it weren't long before their kids were suddenly too busy to come round to play with Esme. It was me and Mrs Archer all over again ... See what I mean about not changing things? Same old same old. If you think diamonds are for ever, try crap. That just keeps on coming.

I used to go round Amy's house a lot ... at first, anyway. If Mrs Archer opened the door, she always looked surprised, like she didn't know who I was even though she saw me every day outside the school.

I never felt really comfortable there. I mean, Mrs Archer never did nothing to put me off, but I could tell I weren't welcome, even though she gave me glasses of Coke and crumpets with jam.

'Amy's Granny Jam made it,' she would say.

I always made a big show of saying please and thank you and did me best when we did painting or crafts or baking. Everything Amy did was wonderful ... *of course* she was better at things than me. Why wouldn't she be? She got packed off to extra lessons and activities all the time ... piano and horse-riding, Sunday school, one-to-one maths and French, trips to Stonehenge and York.

Amy said her mum reckoned it was every mother's job to give their kids all the opportunities going. But I reckon it was just Mrs Archer's way of splitting me and Amy up, as my mum and dad didn't have spare cash for days out and private lessons and wouldn't have seen the point of them even if they had. Mum said she didn't know why Mrs Archer had bothered having kids.

'She never sees her! Always farming her out to somebody else. Poor kid must feel like she ain't wanted or has done something wrong – always being made to jump through hoops.'

I told her Amy didn't enjoy most of the things she had to do and she'd like it more if I went too.

'Well we can't do much about that,' Mum said. 'But why don't you ask Amy round for a sleepover?'

I didn't … but I made out I had … came up with loads of excuses for her, like she had gymnastics class, or extra maths … her grandparents were visiting or she was grounded for too much back chat.

But Mum didn't give up, and eventually she asked Amy herself when we were at the school gates. Amy was dead chuffed but Mrs Archer made excuses … Amy was tired, had a dentist appointment … her guinea pig needed cleaning out.

'Maybe next time,' she said, but I knew she didn't want it to happen any more than I did.

Amy kept banging on about it.

'But my flat's too small to run around in,' I told her. '*And* we ain't got a garden. Grandad don't like lots of noise.'

'We'll play Cluedo then,' she said. 'Or cards. You've got dolls, haven't you?'

'The lift ain't working,' I said. 'We're on the tenth floor so you'll have to climb lots of stairs.'

'Tenth! We'll be able to see everything.'

'Can't we go to the park instead?'

'We can do that any time.'

She got sulky and said I didn't want to be friends any more ... so I had to give in. I told meself it would be okay ... there'd be safety in numbers.

But I knew as soon as we got home that I was wrong. Grandad gave us a bag of sweets each and put *Spice World* on the video. Amy said it was her favourite film and that she knew it word for word. Grandad said he liked it too. When the Spice Girls sang 'My Boy Lollipop', he jigged his legs and tried to get me to sing along too.

Amy wanted to show off one of our Spice Girl routines but I said no. Mum said Amy was my guest and I had to do what she wanted, it was rude if I didn't. She told us to go and get into our costumes.

We couldn't both be Baby Spice. I didn't have enough clothes to go round, so I let Amy put on my floaty white dress with fluff on the hem. I had to make do with a clapped-out fairy costume. It was way too small for me and the wings were torn and the wand all bent.

I hated the way Grandad looked at us ... stroking his shaggy beard, his smile slippery with spit. He clapped loudly and shouted for more. That's when Amy spotted his bad finger and asked him what happened to it. Grandad held out his hand to her and said he'd had an accident, years ago.

Amy asked him if it hurt and he said no ... which was a lie 'cos it did.

Mum and Dad went out afterwards, down the Canterbury Arms for the karaoke competition. I didn't want 'em to go, but Mum said they had to as there was fifty quid up for grabs and the red leccy bill had just come in.

'Don't worry,' she said. 'Grandad's here. And Amy.'

Grandad gave Mum and Dad long enough to get out of the flat ... then he came into the bedroom, singing.

'My *boy* lollipop!'

Amy giggled. He picked the fairy wand up from the floor ... waved it over our heads ... asked how many wishes a fairy granted.

'Three,' Amy said. 'Everybody knows that.'

Shut up, shut up, I wanted to say ... close your eyes, pretend he's not here.

He sat on the bed ... asked her how many wishes a fairy *got*.

Amy shrugged her shoulders. Grandad slipped off his shoes ... wriggled along the bed.

'As many as they like,' he said.

He brushed some hair from Amy's face.

'My first wish is that nothing ever stops Dana and her parents from living in *my* warm and comfy flat.

'My second wish is that your teachers don't expel you for speaking out of turn and being a liar.

'My third wish is that you do everything I say, like your parents expect you to.

'My fourth wish is that you're just as nice to my friends as you are to me.

'My fifth wish is that you keep our little secret.

'And my sixth wish? Well, that ain't really a wish at all.

It's a promise ... If you don't grant all me other wishes, I'll hurt you.'

All of his wishes came true.

F is for fairies. Their endless spells and wishes.

G ... G is for grandfather clock. That dangly bit hanging down, swinging. Oh God ... oh God ...

H ... H ... H is for ... help me. For ho ... Dirty ho. Dirty, *easy* ho.

I ... I ... is for ... I don't want ... I will ... I have to.

J is for joke. The joke's on me. Ha ha ha. A joke of a girl.

Kicking K. Kicking K. K is for KID! *A little kid.*

L is for lava. Erupting. Erupting like lava. For laughter. Erupting.

M ... M is for ... mask. Happy face. Sad face. Smiling. Masking.

N is for nothing. *Nada.* Nothing.

O ... O is for ouch. And ow. And ... oh God ... For over and over again ...

The room is suddenly lighter, the air cooler. I realise I've been squirming so much the duvet has slipped from the bed and the laptop is precariously close to the edge. My eyes are hot and wet and waves of nausea rush over me.

I turn the player off, curl into a ball and rock myself. Sobbing. Just like Amy must have done that night. Every night it happened. Dana too. *Dana too.* Bile rises in my throat. I hurry from the bed and puke bitter mouthfuls into the pink waste-paper bin.

I turn back to the bed. The laptop's stare is blank and impassive. The player's control panel shows tells me Dana still has more to say. I don't want to hear it, but I have to.

I sit on the edge of the bed and press play.

P ... P is for padlock.

Padlocks are for locking things in.

I turn the player off again. I can't do it. I can't listen. Not yet. Not now. Not ever. But Dana's words burn into me. *P is for padlock. Padlocks are for locking things in.* This has been her secret for a long time. *Their* secret. A living hell. Dana has finally found the strength to let the horrors out. The least I can do is listen.

Q is for ... quiet.

Sporty Spice would've kicked 'em in the bollocks ... they'd have been too scared to touch Scary Spice once, let alone again and again. Things like that don't happen to Posh girls, and Ginger would have mouthed off, screamed it from the rooftops ... but Baby Spice ... she was the quiet one, easy meat, just like me and Amy was.

It ripped me up that it was all 'cos of me that Grandad and his friends got Amy. I tried to keep her away, I really, really tried, but what could I do? What?

And you know something else ... something really, really disgusting? I was actually glad it was happening to Amy too ... *glad.* Shit, what kind of a friend would feel like that? Not the sort of friend Amy deserved, that's for sure.

But I was relieved I didn't have to go through it all alone any more. Having Amy there was like having someone to do detention with or to help me with my homework … bloody selfish of me, I know, and I ain't proud of it, any of it, but Amy didn't mind helping me out with my homework and in a way this weren't no different to that.

Amy was good at keeping secrets too. Like when she broke one of her mum's ornaments. Mrs Archer had this absolutely minging china figure of a little boy her old man had bought her for Christmas. If I'd been given it I'd have been quite happy for it to get broke, which is precisely what happened when Amy and her dad were playing chase. Mrs Archer was always telling us not to play rough games in the house and she'd have a go at Mr Archer about it too, so they had to dash off sharpish to get a new one.

It looked exactly the same – just as ugly as before – but it weren't. Amy showed me where it had a bit of colour missing, on the boy's heel. She said her mum wouldn't notice it as she didn't really like it and didn't even look at it any more so there was no way she would spot the flaw.

'It's like a secret,' she said. 'There, but not there. Right under her nose.'

Like me and Amy and Grandad …

But Amy wanted to tell this time. She said we had to. It hurt and it was horrible and Grandad should be stopped.

'We can't,' I told her. 'No one will believe us. It'll be like those little girls in the old days who made everyone think they had fairies at the bottom of their garden when really they'd just made it all up.'

But she said they would, they'd have to. She kept going on about what the teachers had said in assembly about stranger danger.

'But Grandad ain't a stranger!' I told her. 'And he told us the teachers already know! My dad says there are good secrets and bad secrets. Like him dumping junk mail in the bin instead of delivering it. He reckons what people don't know can't hurt them so sometimes it's okay to not tell the truth as long as it's for the right reasons.'

'But it's not for the right reasons, is it?' Amy said.

'Grandad said you tell anyone and we'll both get hurt,' I reminded her. 'And he'll kick me and Mum and Dad out of his flat. I'll have nowhere to live. I might have to move, change schools. We won't be best mates any more. Please, Amy. You can't say anything. Promise me you won't.'

She promised ... we both did. We crossed our hearts and hoped to die ... *Hoped to die* ...

Our secret made us really tight, even tighter than before. 'Say You'll Be There' became our theme tune. Our code.

We used a code name for Grandad too. The Grey Wolf, we called him. It was Amy's idea. Her dad had a nickname for her mum, two names actually ... sometimes he called her Pookie and sometimes he called her Dabs, although they didn't really suit her, not like Grandad's name did.

He had silvery black hair all over him, even on his back. It was horrible and scratchy, rough ... like a Brillo pad. He had long yellow teeth and he moved quietly and he was always hungry ... Wolf suited him down to the ground.

He was always on our tails. No one batted an eye when

he turned up at the park to take us home. Why would they? They'd seen me with him when he took me to school if Mum couldn't. He was a responsible adult, doing right by his granddaughter, making sure we got home safely and promising us sweets on the way.

Me and Amy tried going to other parks, but Paisley Park was tiny and the playground was crappy and rusty and Burgess Park had loads of old tramps and winos who sat on benches swearing and shouting then got up and fiddled with their zips to piss on the pathways with their cocks flopping out.

The only place we were safe was at school. I couldn't wait to get out of our front door in the morning ... I hated it so much when the holidays came round that Mum and Dad joked about me becoming a right old swot, trying to keep up with Amy and be teacher's pet.

They were so made up when me marks got better and I got a good report that they gave me extra pocket money. But I didn't buy sweets or comics or necklaces with it ... it weren't right to be quids in for looking like I was good when I weren't. I shoved the money in a collection box outside the sweetshop ... Postman Pat it was, like Dad, only *he* didn't have a slot in his satchel collecting for the NSPCC.

Turned out school weren't safe for long ... the Grey Wolf found us there too. We were learning all about Edward Jenner one day, about his injections for smallpox or what-ever, and there he was, the Grey Wolf, coming out the school reception. Turned out he'd gone and got the job as school caretaker.

I can still hear him, clattering around with his bucket and jangling keys. The rattle of his toolbox kept us in line. He used to show up when we were in the hall doing PE with our T-shirts tucked in our knickers, stretching and rolling and bending over ...

He always had an excuse to come in the hall ... fixing a dodgy electric socket ... swapping a light bulb. When he cleaned the windows his breath got them all steamy, the wolf huffing and puffing to get in ... reminding us he was there and that we should be good.

He even came into our classroom, saying he had to bleed the radiators, which meant kneeling on the floor by our desk and looking up our skirts. It made us fidget ... Miss Clapton told us to ignore him. We should let him get on with his job.

We did as we were told ... in silence.

I kept me gob shut when Amy vanished, too. A police-woman sat next to me on the sofa, asking questions and telling me to think, really think, and take me time before I answered. Mum, Dad, the copper – they were all too busy looking at me to notice Grandad at the door, ready to pounce. They didn't see him zip his lips with a finger and thumb.

Me and Amy had had an argument about silly things, I told them, like whose turn it was to choose what film to watch first that night and if All Saints were taking over from the Spice Girls. She'd walked off in a huff and left me on the swings in the playground on me own.

I'd told her she'd better stay as Grandad was coming to get us, but she said she never wanted to come to my house ever again. So I went home ... told Grandad Amy weren't coming.

They asked if I'd seen anyone hanging around in the park, close to the playground, anyone suspicious or scary, and I told them the truth.

'No.'

Mum said she wished she'd never let me go out. Dad said he knew that last drink at the pub was a mistake. Grandad said he felt guilty now 'cos he'd been pleased he didn't have to come and pick us up as it meant he could go down the South Bank and soak up the atmosphere of all the people getting ready for the fireworks.

The copper told us not to blame ourselves ... Shows what *she* knew. She wouldn't swallow my story even if I did tell her. My own grandad? In my own home? With my parents under the same roof? *Grandad's roof.*

It was all down to me ... I was a bad, stupid, dirty girl just like Grandad said ... like life said. It was natural law ... I deserved everything I got. I'd get the same as Amy if I grassed on Grandad, but if I kept shtum, he might let her go.

I slept in Mum and Dad's bed that night. Dad said he'd get some of my favourite toys and bring them in, and Mum went off and made me a hot banana Nesquik. Grandad stuck his head round the door.

'I don't know nothing about this, okay? Nothing,' he said. 'Nor do you. Get it? Keep your trap shut and I'll leave you alone.'

Somehow I knew ... I knew I'd never see Amy again.

I cried my eyes raw and shivered all night long, but next morning I finally saw a way out.

I couldn't do nothing to bring Amy back ... it was too late to save her but I *could* save meself, not by running away or being a smartarse or telling tales. No ... All I had to do was what I always did ... Fuck all.

It was bad enough I let Amy down in the first place at the playground, but then, true to form, I go and do it again ... by doing a deal with the Grey Wolf ... keeping me gob shut so I can stay safe.

He never touched me again, but Amy, she never let go.

Q is for quiet. Silence without peace.

My fists pummel the mattress. How could she do it? Betray her friend to save herself? Keeping secrets. Keeping quiet – at least until she met Libby and Esme, when all the stories and anecdotes came tumbling out in a torrent. *The Man Who Didn't Wash His Dishes*. The flawed figurine. My nicknames. Granny Jam. All of it, laid out on a plate and picked over, memorised and exploited for a revolting, brutal ruse.

I can see it all now – except I don't know where Dana is and I still don't know what her grandfather did to Amy or what he did with her body.

Dana can tell me herself.

R is for ... roller coaster.

No need to tell you I got it all wrong again ... Yet another fuck-up. Sure, the Grey Wolf didn't touch me ... but he didn't have to. I got attacked by guilt and nightmares instead, and not just when I was asleep neither.

It was all up there, on the bedroom wall, like shadow puppets.

There was bubbles getting burst with a bite of sharp teeth ... two girls who jumped off swings, only one always landed on a squidgy bed and the other went down a hole in the ground.

And all the time I could hear the quack of a duck. I couldn't get it out of me head. When we ran around the school hall, it weren't plimsolls I heard squeaking. In the park all I heard was kids squealing and the shriek of bike brakes. At home the lift made a grating noise as it went up and down. That noise was everywhere. I tell you, Amy kept quiet when she was alive but she never shut up once she died.

Esme was her echo.

There was no point in running, as you'll never outrun your fate, never. Esme was my fate, sent back to get me ... one way or the other.

I holed up in me bedroom with the lights out and the curtains drawn but the shadows still found a way in. Esme would knock on me door. Did I wanna play draughts? Could I dry her hair? No ... She said I didn't love her any more but I told her I did, I always had ... always would.

'No matter what?' she said.

'No matter what.'

Libby reckoned a change of scene would sort me out. She'd got lucky on a lottery scratch card and had some money back after a cock-up with her tax code. Right pleased with herself she was, like it was all her doing. She weren't a millionaire or nothing, we're not talking Disney in Florida or a cruise round the Med. We're talking Blackpool.

I weren't gonna go but Libby kept banging on at me. I suppose she must have had a word with Maggie, as *she* chimed in too, even bunging me twenty quid.

'You've not had a proper holiday since you've been here,' Maggie said. 'You deserve it.'

As if.

But, seeing the way it turned out, I guess I *did* deserve it ...

I ain't big on funfairs. I don't get the fun in being scared shitless on roller coasters or spinning round and round till you chuck up or get chucked up on ... Like there ain't enough in the world to be scared of or enough shit flying around already.

Anyway, all the fun of the fair begins before we even gets through the gates. There was a fucking clown sitting in a glass booth. Not a real clown, obviously ... that would have been bad enough. This ... this ... thing was much worse. It was like a big toy, a mechanical toy ... with shaggy silver hair and mad dark eyes, a painted-on smile and loads of yellow teeth.

And he moved, oh God, he moved ... rocking backwards and forwards, rolling about with uncontrollable laughter, like a madman. He had a child clown on his knee and it got tossed about as the big clown jerked around, laughing, laughing, laughing. The little clown had a painted-on smile too ... a really unhappy smile ... and its mouth was open but silent. No laughing, no words, nothing.

Libby wanted a picture of it so I ended up sandwiched between Esme and the clown. Demons behind me, ghosts in front. The air from the generator was like hot breath and made Esme shudder as much as I did.

The clown's laughter followed me around the fairground ... even when I couldn't hear him, I could see and hear Esme ... and the duck – the fucking duck was there too, in the siren at the start of the dodgem car ride.

Soon as it sounded, Esme was after me. Her dodgem hit me again and again and again, the shunts forcing the breath from me and making my neck whiplash. Esme laughed all the while ... laughed and laughed and laughed.

She laughed on the roller coaster too. She got in the car right at the front with Libby, which meant I had to go in the one behind, all on me own, or so I thought, until this nervous, nerdy-looking man gets in and squeezes up to me ... I tried to get out but the safety harness was locked tight.

We chugged up the tracks to the top, way above the ground, and the car sat there for a moment, like it was scared and weren't gonna go no further. Then it tipped over the other side. I screamed. Esme laughed and held her arms above her head as we zoomed around the track.

'That one next!' she said when we got off. It was a tall tower with seats around each side, like a skirt. The seats shot up to the top in one go then hopped back to earth, bit by bit. I couldn't face it and told them I'd watch, but that was almost as bad as being on it meself.

When the safety harness clamped Esme in, all I saw was Amy trapped in the arms of the Grey Wolf. I heard him snorting in the whoosh of air that shot her to the top. It was Esme's mouth that opened wide but it was Amy who screamed out ... over and over and over ...

I ran away and left her dangling at the top of the ride. I had to get out but the clown at the gate wouldn't let me ... He was rolling around, laughing like he was gonna burst, and each time he rocked forward I thought he was gonna reach out and grab me.

I held me breath, waited for a hen party to go by, then slipped out under cover of kiss-me-quick hats and tinsel angel wings.

R is for roller coaster. A gut-wrenching ride where there ain't no way out.

S is for ... sandcastle.

They might call it the Golden Mile, but I tell you, Blackpool Prom weren't shining that day. Nor was the sun neither. The wind had blown over the buckets of plastic windmills outside the shops and the ice-cream counters was closed. Some of the shops had pink sticks of cock-shaped rock in the window ... I ran as fast as I could and ended up on the beach.

The tide was so far out there was nothing for miles but wet sand and scummy puddles. Me legs got tired from running but I could still hear the clown laughing so I kept going. Only I couldn't outrun it ... it was in me head ...

In the end I had to stop ... I was knackered. I crashed out

next to a breaker to catch me breath. Libby called me a few moments later, wondering where I'd got to. She said Esme thought I'd gone off for a go on the giant teacups. Like hell she did. She knew what she was doing all right ... what she was putting me through.

But it turned out it had all got to her too.

'Esme's feeling a bit spaced out after that last ride,' Libby said. 'We're gonna have a sit-down on a bench on the prom for a bit. We'll come and find you later.'

I told 'em to take their time.

There was a knackered old spade half buried in the sand, right beside me ... like someone had left it there just to give me something to do while I waited. I picked it up.

I weren't really thinking what I was doing, just wiggling the spade into the sand, but before I knew it, I'd made a fucking big hole ... big enough for Amy's body but nowhere near big enough for mine. I filled it in, burying her again, just to be sure ...

I chucked the spade away and ran down the beach a bit. I was too scared to stop and too out of breath to keep going, but I just couldn't run no more. So I started walking, straight on at first ... at least I thought I was, but I was just going round in circles, smaller and smaller circles, getting tighter and tighter till I ended up like a bullseye in a target.

Me legs gave out and I went down on me knees ... not to pray ... there weren't no point in that ... no one was gonna listen or help, especially not God.

For once I was glad I had big hands. They was as good as spades and in no time I'd built a wall around me and a moat. I sat there for ages ... didn't budge even when the tide turned and the water got closer and closer.

That's where Libby and Esme found me, all cold and wet and on me knees.

S is for sandcastle, which ain't no place to hide.

T is for ... time.

Amy had everything ... looks, brains, clothes, you name it, she was at the front of the queue. She was dead patient too, had to be with me around her all the time and needing her to show me how to do this and that and everything.

So Esme weren't in no rush to get me. She was having too much fun playing games ... asking me to take her out places ... help with her homework ... go over her lines for the school play. But when I said no and stayed in me bedroom, she got all stroppy.

'What have I done?' she said, all innocent like.

'Nothing,' I said. 'It's just me being silly. Not your fault at all. '

She said her teacher had told her that just because something ain't your fault don't mean it can't be your responsibility.

'Not for causing it, but for sorting it out.'

She weren't offering to help or call off the chase ... She was threatening me.

As time went on, Esme got stroppier ... kept saying I weren't really her friend no more and that Libby weren't her real mum. The flat got smaller and darker ... the shadows on me bedroom wall got bigger and blacker.

After Esme's ninth birthday, the shadows were every-where. She'd be ten next, the same age me and Amy was when she died. Amy never made it to secondary school, whereas I just wished I hadn't.

When Esme's teachers said she had a shot at a scholar-ship at Manchester High School for Girls, Libby was made up and went on and on about it being a real opportunity.

'They don't come around very often,' she said. 'You don't throw them away when they do. Like I did.'

But Esme weren't really bothered. She said even if she passed the entry exam she didn't think she'd actually go there.

'Something will stop me,' she kept saying. 'I can just tell.'

Libby thought she meant the scholarship wouldn't come off or the school would be full, but I knew she meant some-thing random ... something bad ... Me and Esme both knew who was right.

Esme got into the school all right. Passed the exam, got the money, no problem.

'What did I tell you!' Libby said to her. 'Little Miss Pessimist. Saying it would all come to nothing.'

But Esme said it didn't mean anything ... it would still all go wrong. That made Libby wonder if she didn't really wanna go there. Esme said she was upset about leaving all her mates behind.

I knew that feeling ... At the end of junior school, I knew I'd be going off to a pit of a comprehensive on the Old Kent Road with the other no-hopers. I didn't have to wait to be told that by the council. And Mrs Archer didn't have to wait to be told that Amy wouldn't be going there neither. That weren't where girls like Amy went. She was a double-A girl with minted parents. She'd be going to a school that looked more like a big posh house with hockey fields, where the girls had to wear kilts.

The uniform at Esme's new school weren't poncy like Amy's was, but it weren't cheap, so Libby had to save up for it and buy it one bit at a time, way in advance, with plenty of room for growth. She got the lot ... black coat, black skirt, black jumper, black shoes, black socks ...

It freaked me out big time the first time Esme put it all on ... All I could see was Amy, ready for the funeral she never had and ready ... waiting for mine.

'Don't you look smart?' Libby said.

'No. It looks like somebody died,' Esme said. 'Doesn't it, Henry?'

T is for time. Time to die.

U is for ... unicorn.

'The writing's on the wall.' That's how the saying goes, don't it, when something can't be stopped? Well, they're wrong ...

It weren't writing that did it for me, which is no biggie where I'm concerned, I suppose. The message had to be kept simple so even a thick-as-pig-shit waster like me got it, which meant words wouldn't hack it, no matter where they were written or how big.

I needed a picture, and it turned up on me bedroom wall, in the shadows I saw there every night. It was a long, sharp unicorn horn, ramming into the limbs of the puppets and filing down their teeth.

Miss Clapton had told us the unicorn was a symbol of purity and grace, and that its horn had magic so powerful it could heal sickness and cure poison.

This time I just knew magic would work for me ... it was what natural law wanted so I ... so I could put things right.

U is for unicorn. The writing on the wall.

V is for ... *vamos*.

Shit, I'd forgotten I even knew that word. Before, the only bit of Spanish I remembered from school was *nada* – nothing – but it ain't no accident it's come back to me now.

Vamos. That's what I should have said to Amy in the playground, only I didn't.

Vamos, Dana. Let's go. There's *nada* for you here.

W is for ... wave.

Not like a wave in the sea ... I mean a wave goodbye. To Manchester ... Amy ... To me.

A wave of the white flag. I surrender ...

I surrender.

X ...

X marks the spot. Somewhere I won't make a mess for someone else to clean up for a change.

The sea ... I never was much good at swimming ... I never was much good at anything.

Y is for ...

Y is ... because it's the law ... because I ain't allowed to beat Amy ... because I can't take no more ... because this will make us quits.

Z is for ... zip.

The zip on the body bag they put me in – *if* they ever find me. They never found Amy after all ... She found me.

12

Now I know.

My daughter was raped.

Repeatedly.

Right under my nose.

And I never had a clue.

Poor Dana is dead.

Libby and Esme are exploiting her as much as they are exploiting me.

I know who killed my daughter.

Snapping the truth into bits doesn't make it easier to swallow. It sticks in my throat. The rip of it. The scorching guilt. The choke of hatred. For Dana's grandfather. For Libby and Esme. For myself.

Questions flood my head, fight for answers I may not ever get.

How long did Amy and Dana's abuse go on for? Weeks? Months? *Years?*

Who else was part of the Grey Wolf's pack?

How did Amy die? Did she fight? Did she suffer?

Where is her body?

How did this happen? Where was I? Where was Brian?

What does this make us?

I could have prevented it. I was her mother, for God's sake. *Her mother.* What kind of woman am I? What kind of mother? Not soft and supportive, caring and kind. The sort kisses are given to as freely as secrets are shared. Who wants only the best for her child and does all she can to make sure it happens. The sort I thought I was.

With me for a mother, Amy was lost long before she vanished.

The darkness of that truth spreads slowly at first, bit by bit, like insinuating rings of ink in a jar of water. Then shadowy fingers curl, snatch away the light. Snuff out any hope of redemption.

I'd feel a twisted sort of absolution if it had just been a lone paedophile who'd taken Amy. I couldn't be blamed for something random. Couldn't guard against it. No way could it be my fault, despite what the press might say.

Just a lone paedophile? Just? Only a monster could think that. No proper mother ever would. But *I* have. I'm as bad as the perverts who killed her. Shame scalds.

Amy, forgive me. For everything. For letting you think I was loving and trustworthy. That I knew what was best for you. For not being the mother you thought you had. Not being the mother you needed – not even now.

I close my eyes.

I feel their rough hands touching me. Their fetid, panting breath. I twist beneath them, shudder with the pain. I hear their grunts of satisfaction, their exhortations to be good. To be quiet. To make sure it stays that way.

I scramble through my memories, looking for telltale

signs and listening for hints. But I don't hear Amy crying wolf. There are no sentences left half finished by an awkward shrug or a blush. No anxiety or recognition when I took her through the birds and the bees. No clues upon her body.

Those cuts and abrasions on her limbs were just badges from the rough-and-tumble games of an active child. I'd have been more suspicious if she *hadn't* had them. She didn't try and hide her body and would have worn her leotard all day, every day if I'd let her. The skin exposed by her bikini on Zante showed only the touch of the sun.

I thought she loved taking baths because of the nostril-stinging fizz of her bubble-gum-scented bath bombs, the fluffy comfort of her bathrobe. When all the while she was scrubbing at the filth she felt but couldn't reach. It stayed inside her, indelible, for ever.

There were no black marks on her school report, no mention of moodiness, tantrums or bullying. Her grades gave nothing away. Dana's grades actually got better.

I remember her mother beaming as Dana pulled away from the bottom of the class. I put it down to Amy letting Dana copy her and told her not to do it as she wasn't helping her, not really. Not in the long run. She'd do better to learn it for herself.

But they *were* helping each other. Matching equations. Their two times table quick on their tongues. Best friends eager to give teacher the answer — but not as quick to tell tales.

Best friends.

Their names appeared together on the bottom of a picture of a snail made out of bits of gravel and pebbles and glossy with varnish. They won the three-legged race at sports day, Dana's free elbow spinning like a blade on the wheels of a Roman chariot. They whispered and giggled, swapped sweets and lunchboxes, went down with chickenpox and colds in tandem.

Dana was always there. Except the moment Amy needed her the most. When a friend by her side would have ruled Amy out as a target and an extra pair of eyes would have been alert to any danger, Dana was nowhere to be found.

Logic makes me want to blame her, but instinct kicks in and won't let me. It would be easy – understandable even – to damn her for leading my daughter to a pervert's lair. For leaving Amy to her fate in the playground. Buying her own safety with silence. Granting her grandfather the freedom to harm who knows how many other children.

But Dana was a child, *just a child*. Just like my little girl. Two innocents, too scared to stand up and speak out. I understand why.

Dana and her parents were beholden to him at home. Amy and Dana were in his kingdom at school. The teachers ruled the classrooms but the school itself was his. It couldn't open without the keys in his pocket. He kept it warm and light. He magicked away splats of vomit, mopped up pools of pee. He was a hero. A one-man A-team. Trusted and respected. Beyond reach. Above suspicion. Safe.

And I can't shake the thought that Dana endured the abuse longer than Amy did. However long Amy was his victim — and the fact that I will never know is both a comfort and a torment — Dana suffered longer.

Amy's life was taken; Dana's was blighted by a wound that could never heal. She lived under the crippling weight of what she saw as her betrayal, haunted by Amy every moment of every day. Memories of Amy warped her thinking and clouded her sight. When Esme turned up, remorse, paranoia and guilt pushed Dana over the edge. I understand all that too.

I see now that Ian, instead of being an accomplice, might really be psychic after all. It must have been Dana who came through to him and tried to warn me off. A big man, he said, with short dark hair whose lips were moving without saying anything out loud. It was Dana showing him the traffic signal for caution, think, beware. Dana alerting me to danger, not from Amy, but from Libby and Esme. Maybe the Jesus picture was a clue to her as well. Dana *Bishop*. It might even have been a hint about Bishop himself.

The guilt I have lived with for the last ten years is suddenly heavier, laden with a new nuance. The added weight of another lost girl.

If I'd had my eyes open, been there, doing what I should have been doing instead of God knows what, then, *then* I could have saved Dana too.

How many times did I moan about her to Brian? Countless. I went on about how she was holding Amy back, pushed Brian to let me put her in another school. A better school. Only he wouldn't. He said he wanted Amy to be a real kid with friends from all walks of life, not a conveyor-belt boffin with a limited view.

I said he was more concerned that having a daughter in private school would jeopardise his agency's grip on the Labour Party account. He had no right to risk his daughter's future. He claimed I was doing the same thing by wanting to choose her friends. I was a fool to even try, he said; interfering would only force them closer together.

I know now that he was right. And I understand why none of the other girls in Amy's class ever made the grade. Dana would have been left on her own. Their secret bound them tight.

And Brian and I forced them together. Our rows were there right from the start. Even before Amy was born, our happiest times had an undercurrent. Nothing obvious or definable. Nothing we could point at and try to put right.

But there was a hint of trouble, a thin, unbroken line of gunpowder, just waiting for a spark. The big bang never came. Just cluster bombs detonating in muffled slow motion. Instead of a home that invited communication and confidences, Amy endured smouldering silences and spiteful, snarky quarrels that made her prefer being at Dana's to being at home. The blast has only just hit.

Our mouths may have said that love was a wonderful, invisible force for good, that Mummy and Daddy loved each other really, but our hearts — *our example* — showed her that love was hard and painful. Something to be got through and put up with.

Amy's concept of love had landed somewhere in the

middle, a murky no-man's-land where right was so confused with wrong that she could tolerate abuse because she believed it was for the best.

So much for nurturing and instilling positive values and doing everything we could for our daughter. My rounded, engaged and happy child – fortified by all those lessons, activities, trips and experiences – was left defenceless by our legacy of love. I was a poor role model – misshapen, mutant. Warped.

Our daughter couldn't have wished for a better friend. Only better parents. That's a slap that won't ever stop stinging.

And what of Dana's parents?

I used to envy them. For still being together – all of them – like a family should be. For keeping their daughter safe. I can't say I never wished my anguish on any other parent, because I did. If I'd been able to change places I'd have done it in an instant.

I wouldn't do it now, though. Both our girls are dead. The grief and heartache I've endured for the last ten years hasn't even begun for them. And at least my family is blameless. Up to a point, anyway; we never harboured any perverts.

I try to picture Dana's grandfather but can only just make him out against the school's drab brickwork and colourless playground. He's camouflaged by a smear of khaki-brown overalls and a smudge of ashy grey hair, lank as a washed-out mop.

Away from the school he's just a cheery wave with the *Sun* in the queue at the post office, a smoky hello as I skirt by William Hill. A shape. A movement. A wolf in the woods.

Amy never mentioned him unless he'd bought her some sweets on the way back from the playground or praised their new dance routine. The ordinary things grandparents are expected to do. Things Brian and I did too.

She didn't mention his mutilated finger either. If I'd noticed it myself I might have thought her silence strange. Grisly details like that are the stuff of childish tales. How he'd lost it in the mouth of a shark or had it cut off in a fight. How the mutilated stump was kept in the caretaker's shed to wag at naughty children.

And if Amy *had* said something, my political correctness would have kicked in. It's rude to stare, I would have told her; people come in all shapes and sizes. Bodies and minds aren't always whole. Just because people look different doesn't mean there's anything to be scared of. Despair stabs at my ribs.

That man killed my daughter. I don't know his name. I can't recall his face. After all these years, I still have nothing to claw and scream at. No target for my spit or kicks. But I will.

I want my pound of flesh and nothing will stand in my way — unless God has already snatched him to safety in heaven so He can punish me once more.

My eyes drift from the laptop to the picture of Dana on my phone. My finger strokes her bloated face.

'I'll get him for you. I promise. I won't rest until I do. I'll get him for you both.'

A need for vengeance and justice rips through me, forcing me out of the bed and into my clothes. I just want to get out of the flat as quickly as I can, before Libby and Esme find out I'm wise to their scam.

I shut the laptop down, put it back in my suitcase and slip the USB stick into my coat pocket. The door clicks behind me as I let myself out.

I don't wait for the cab driver to give me my change. I'm not even aware if I'm due any. I thought about calling Dave once I got out of the flat and down to the street, but he's done enough already and might not even be working. Besides, he'd have too many questions, too much chat, and my head's full to bursting as it is.

I didn't know which way to go and there was no one around to ask except a group of rowdy clubbers, too incoherent to give me accurate directions. I found my way to the main road and started to walk. Maybe I should have called 999; the police would probably have been at the flat by now. But I didn't think I'd be able to tell the operator the story over the phone. This wasn't murder, rape or deception – it was a cocktail of all three, with reincarnation and psychic intervention thrown in for extra kick. They'd have dismissed me as a crank caller. I had to report it in person.

The road was busy for three twenty in the morning, but none of the vehicles were taxis. Not until I'd walked for fifteen minutes, when a black cab finally went by; it seemed appropriate that I'd been walking in the wrong direction.

The driver's thanks and good night barely register with me; I slam the cab door and stand on the pavement. The sign outside the police station transfixes me. *Police.* It looks so solid, so reliable, but I know that's not the case. Yet I have no choice but to put my trust in them once more.

I open the door and am hit by a blast of hot air. The lights inside are too bright, the walls teem with garish posters and the air reeks of old sweat, stale cigarette smoke, boozy breath and despair. Perhaps all police stations smell the same way; the warm, rancid air reminds me of every police room I sat in ten years ago.

I can't believe they want to make me wait. With a ticket in my hand. Like it's a raffle. The only prize I want is justice, and I've waited too long for that. This is my time and nothing will stand in my way. Not the acne-pocked hoodie or the two drunken drivers. Not even the little lost boy. My girl has been missing longer. The head of the queue starts with me; the rest can get in line.

But the woman behind the desk tries to fob me off with a ticket and a promise that they won't be long. I screw the ticket up and turn it in my hand.

'You've been too long already,' I say. 'Ten years too long.'

'I'm sorry?'

'You should be. We all should. Especially me.'

She sighs and twiddles with her pen.

'Like I say, madam, if you'll just take a seat. We'll come to you as soon as we can.'

'No. Now. I want to report a murder.'

Instead of waiting outside in the lobby with the winos and tarts, they make me wait inside, all on my own, except for the bobby on the door. It's not a cell. I'm not under arrest. I'm not even sure they believe me yet – but they will. They have to.

The clock on the wall has chewed off another quarter since I last looked. Voices and hurried footsteps slip by to next door or beyond. Tending to somebody else's troubles. A case the police consider more of a priority than a murder. Missing what's right under their noses. *Again.* They've been as useless at detecting crime as I was at being a mother. We cannot fail once more.

I hear footsteps outside. Slow and sloppy. The door opens. A man in his twenties steps in and gives me a weak smile.

'Mrs Archer? I'm Detective Sergeant Earnshaw.' He sits opposite me and puts his hands on the table. 'I understand you want to report a murder.' His voice is flat, bored, and his eyes are dull and sleepy.

He's too young, too dozy to get me justice. Esme will run rings round him. But he's all I've got for now.

'Yes, that's right,' I say, pulling my chair closer to the table. 'Murder. Incest. Child abuse. Fraud. Withholding evidence.' I jab my finger at him on every word, just to make sure he doesn't miss one.

His eyes widen. I take the USB stick from my pocket and slide it across the table.

'It's all here,' I say.

He takes the stick and turns it in his palm.

'Let me get this right.' He coughs. 'This is your confession? To murder?'

He's closer to the truth than he knows.

'Of course not!' I cry. 'Are you in charge here? I need a detective, not a clown.'

'Mrs Archer, I—'

I slam my hand on the table.

'Help me! Please. You've got to.'

'I can't help you until you tell me what this is all about.'

I sob through gritted teeth.

'It's about two ten-year-old girls being raped. Over and over again. It's about the murder of my daughter, Amy. Remember her? Amy Archer? No. Because you're too bloody young to know anything, let alone forget it. I want to speak to someone who knows what they're doing. About Amy coming back from the dead. About the police letting murderers walk free.' I stand up quickly. My chair falls and clatters noisily on the floor. 'Do something!'

The door opens.

'Everything all right in here?'

He's older, grizzled, his eyes darkened by late shift rings. Earnshaw shrugs and stands up.

'This is Mrs Archer, guv,' he says. 'As in Amy Archer. You know, the little girl who—'

'You don't need to tell me who she is, Earnshaw.'

I'm reassured by the burly authority in the older man's voice. He steps into the room and closes the door. When he walks behind me to pick up my chair, I smell cigarettes and chip fat. He gestures towards the chair, then sits down next to Earnshaw.

'I'm Detective Inspector Harding, Mrs Archer. How can I help?'

I sit down again, take a deep breath.

I'm encouraged by his familiarity with Amy's case, the jolt of surprise when I run through Libby's ruse, Ian Poynton's predictions and Esme's performance.

'A star-spangled Spice Girl, bounced backwards and forwards between heaven and earth?' I say. 'Who sees into the past through a series of seizures with the voice of my angel in her ears? She must think I'm fucking stupid. Or mad. Or hoping to drive me mad. Like she did Dana. I wasn't born yesterday, detective. And I don't believe you were either.'

'It's a new one on me, I admit,' Harding says, puffing out his cheeks.

'It's a tricky one to pull off, too,' says Earnshaw. 'For anyone, let alone a ten-year-old girl.'

'Oh, she's good, I'll give her that. Delivered her lines on cue and with feeling. And her fit was a work of art. She's been paying attention at her drama class all right. Like a born-to-it pro. With a pushy stage mum behind her, feeding her lines.'

'Maybe Dana put them up to it?' Earnshaw says.

I remember how Dana's clumsy hands sent the marbles tumbling in Kerplunk!, kicked off the spring in Buckaroo. She was too slow for snap, hadn't the logic for Cluedo, couldn't plan a move ahead in draughts.

'No.'

'You can't be sure,' Earnshaw says. 'Clearly it's too complicated a plan for a child to dream up.'

'Once you've listened to Dana's story yourself, you'll realise she wasn't involved in any scam. Besides, you didn't know Dana. This is too complex for her. Way beyond the likes of Dana Bishop.'

'Then Libby would need a good reason to go to all this trouble,' Harding says.

'She's got a hundred thousand of them.'

'Sorry?'

'The reward,' I say emphatically. 'Not much for my daughter's life, but more than we could afford. Enough for Libby to live it up a bit and keep Esme in private school, that's for sure. Then there's the matter of my will. She would have looked at me and seen a relatively wealthy woman with no husband and no kids – not even a dog as a substitute. Rich pickings for a single mum getting by on part-time wages and handouts, wouldn't you say?'

Harding nods his head and leans forward.

'And if Dana believed that Esme was Amy,' he says, 'there was a good chance you'd believe it too.'

'Exactly. Let's face it, I was easy prey. Old before my time, mad with grief, crawling to psychics for any crumb of comfort. I was soft. Suggestible. I thought for a while Ian Poynton might have been genuine, and maybe he is, but . . . if he's not, he wouldn't need second sight to know I'd be easy to break. The only voice he heard was Dana's – not from the other side, but from *in*side Esme's computer.'

I point at the USB stick.

'Dana's A to Z just became an instruction manual to work me,' I say. 'Instead of bringing it to you, they all kept quiet and hatched a plan. Kept a murderer and a paedophile gang from justice.'

Harding picks up the stick.

'We need to listen to this,' he says. 'Get a transcript done.'

'I'll wait.'

He nods and stands up. Earnshaw follows him to the door.

'I'll have some tea brought in for you,' Earnshaw says.

'I'm fine. Thank you.'

The door closes and their footsteps retreat. I can't make out their words in the low murmurs from the corridor, but I don't think they're laughing at me or my story. I'm satisfied I made my case as well as I could, but as I run through all that I've told them, I realise there is one charge I didn't make against Libby and Esme.

There is no specific law against it, but breaking my heart is their biggest crime of all. It's an invisible crime, like embezzlement, robbing my soul blind. I have been plundered, assaulted and mugged of my memories. It's a sentence without reprieve or release. I'm a lifer. Condemned till the day I die.

Harding and Earnshaw can do nothing about that, but they *can* set the wheels of justice moving. It's their chance to be stars. To grab the glory. Shine as Amy's redeemer. Their chance to be my heroes.

For although Dana has told me what the Grey Wolf did to Amy, I still don't know what he did with her body. My heart has been her grave for the last ten years. She deserves to be somewhere better.

Somewhere less remote and forbidding.

They have to find her. They have to let me lay my girl to rest and put the past to sleep.

They have to.

Harding's expression is inscrutable when he comes back into the room. Earnshaw looks puzzled.

'Well?' I say.

They sit down and put the USB stick and a folder on the desk.

'It's very credible evidence,' Harding says, 'as long as it is genuine. We've passed a copy of the transcript on to the Met to see what they make of it.'

'But you've got enough to get Bishop, surely?' I say, impatiently.

'Let's not get ahead of ourselves,' Earnshaw says. 'We have a suspect, that's all.'

'That's more than you've had in the last ten years! And you've got it there,' I say, pointing to the folder, 'in black and white.'

'We need to verify things before we can go accusing people, Mrs Archer.' Earnshaw opens the folder. 'We had to check you are who you say you are too.'

He holds up a picture taken at one of the press conferences. I am pale and pinched, weepy-eyed. Like I am now.

'What are you investigating me for? I've not done anything wrong.'

'No, but we have to check details,' Harding says. 'Like
making sure everybody's who they claim to be. You'd
understand that better than most, given the circumstances,
surely?'

I drop my chin and concede his point.

'So have you found anything else?'

'Not much. Yet,' Earnshaw says. 'We're waiting to
see if the sex offenders register comes up with anything.
There can't be too many people on there with half a finger
missing.'

The quick look between Earnshaw and Harding un-
nerves me. Like there's a joke I can't see, let alone laugh
along with.

'There *is* one thing that's come up, though,' Harding
says, turning a page in his folder. 'About the reward.'

'What about it?'

'One hundred thousand pounds, you said.'

'That's right. My ex-husband sold some of his shares in
his business to raise it.'

'Ah,' Harding says, quietly. 'That might explain it.'

'Explain what?'

'There isn't a reward, Mrs Archer,' Earnshaw says.
'Not any more. I noticed it on the case details on the
computer.'

'Don't be ridiculous! I was there when it was announced. Yet another bloody press conference.' I wring
my hands. 'And the money's certainly not been paid out.'

'No, but it has been withdrawn,' Earnshaw says with a little shrug.

'Withdrawn?'

'That's right,' Earnshaw says. 'About five years ago.'

'On whose say-so?'

'It could only have been your husband, Mrs Archer.' Harding coughs. 'Your *ex*-husband.'

I can't believe Brian could do that without telling me. That he could do it at all. He wanted Amy found as much as I did, and got rid of the shares for less than they were worth just for a quick sale. It doesn't make sense.

Unless he knew something I didn't. Something he wanted to hide. That disgusting picture of Jesus flashes into my mind.

HONOR THY *FATHER* AND MOTHER.

Our Father, who art in Heaven. *Her* father, in her bed.

An awful dread creeps through me, sucking out what's left of my soul and snapping every sinew of trust and hope, of my faith in anything good. I can scarcely believe I'm even thinking that Brian was one of the pack. It's revolting. Horrific. Ridiculous. The man I loved, capable of that?

Instinct flutters, tells me it's not true – but I'm no longer sure my instincts can be trusted, not now. They have proved so faulty, so unreliable and misguided. Now that the idea of Brian being involved has taken hold, it's shaking me and won't let go.

Dana didn't mention him in her A to Z, but then she didn't name any of the pack, other than her grandfather. And Brian certainly had the opportunity, given that he spent more time with Amy and Dana than I did.

Trips to Dulwich Park on Sunday mornings while I lay in bed with the papers. Matinees at the Brixton Ritzy followed by a Pizza Hut tea. He even bought Dana's roller blades. And he suggested getting her a guinea pig that she could keep alongside Amy's, ensuring that Dana was often in our garden. He was always quick to defend her too.

I tell Harding I need some air. He says to take as long as I like.

'There's not much more you can help us with just yet. Best if you take it easy, although it's probably better that you don't go back to the flat.'

'Are Libby and Esme still there?'

'We're going to get them in a while,' Earnshaw says.

'I'll come with you,' I say, standing up.

'That's not possible, I'm afraid.'

'I just want to get my things,' I say. 'That's all. I'll stay out of the way.'

Harding looks doubtful.

'Look,' I say, 'there's nothing I'd like more than to rip them to bits. But I don't want to give them any way to wriggle out of this. Like me assaulting them and gifting them a sob story to run out for the judge. Trust me. I don't even want to see them.'

We go in separate cars, the sirens silent. The woman driving me is under instructions to wait around the corner until Earnshaw and Harding have picked up Esme and Libby. I'm under instructions only to take the stuff I brought along for my trip – and nothing else.

I'm not after souvenirs. I could have left everything there really. It was only clothes, toiletries and make-up. Nothing I wouldn't miss or couldn't replace – other than my talismanic stone that led me to the truth.

I ask the driver to stop at a parade of shops.

'There's something I have to do.'

'No problem,' she says. 'It's not a bad idea to be a few minutes behind the others. It'll make sure your paths don't cross.'

I walk to a mini-market and take the last bunch of daffodils from a bucket outside. They are merely green stalks, slightly thicker at one end, shot through with a bolt of yellow. Like pencils in need of sharpening.

They aren't my favourite flowers and wouldn't have been my first choice. But as I place them at the foot of Libby's block, they seem exactly right. They are the first burst of spring after a long, colourless winter. And on one occasion when Jill used them in an arrangement in the church, she told me that daffodils are the symbol of friendship.

Friends. Solid and true. Like Amy and Dana. Unlike Dana and me. I lay the flowers on the ground and bow my head to Dana's memory.

The flat smells of toast and toothpaste. Libby's mug is on the table, half full with still steaming tea. A spoon is marooned in Esme's bowl of soggy Coco Pops. I get a whiff of Libby's deodorant as I grab my make-up from the bathroom window.

The policewoman follows me around the flat as I collect

my belongings. Esme's laptop, I notice, isn't in the front room where I left it. The stone is still in my suitcase. The rattle it gives as I open the case is an echo of the thrill inside me – the clatter of hope, of a rolling stone with an unstoppable, vengeful momentum.

I slip the stone into my coat pocket. As we drive away, my fingers flex and curl around it, like petals opening around a bud.

13

I bend my head beneath hot, hard jets of water and reach for the tap to turn the heat up even further. Steam smothers me. Citrus-scented suds froth around my feet.

None of it makes me feel any cleaner. Just raw. I wrap a fluffy white towelling gown around me and slump on to the bed. My skin feels so thin my pulse could puncture it.

The hotel is a good one, Harding told me. The choice of delegates and pop stars at the conferences and concerts in the nearby G-Mex Centre, and divas and conductors from the Bridgewater Hall. More importantly, it's only a short tram ride from the police station.

The clock on the DVD player says half past twelve. Libby's been in custody now for over four hours. Time enough for her to come clean and for the Met to bring in the Grey Wolf. The noose is tightening; Amy's body will soon be found. It has to be.

I pick up my phone from the bedside table. Brian's number isn't in my contacts, of course, so I take it from the ad agency's website. The digits themselves are unfamiliar but the tune they make as I dial is etched into my mind.

The rhythm is the tempo of dependence, the sequence

of notes the order of need. A code from the past I've tried so hard to forget. Now it's a clarion for truth.

The phone is answered after three rings by his PA, her voice briskly cheerful. Brian's out, she tells me, in meetings all day, could she take a message.

'No, you can't,' I say. 'Just get him out of his bloody meeting and on to the phone.'

'I'm afraid I can't—'

'Yes you can. Tell him it's about his daughter.'

'Oh God, no. Is she okay?'

'Dead.'

Her gasp rasps down the line.

'I'll get him to call you back right away.'

'No. Just get him. I'll hold.'

My mouth is sour and dry, my lips tacky. Moments later I hear hurried footsteps on the other end of the line.

'Hello! Who is this? What's happened?' His voice is choked with fear. 'Tell me my girls are okay.'

'They're not your girls. Not really. Amy was, though. You didn't even *think* it might be about *her*, did you?'

'What? Beth? Is that you?' His voice becomes a growl. 'What the fuck are you playing at? Have you any idea what you just put me through?'

'I've an inkling, yes. I lost a daughter too, remember.'

'Oh shit, Beth, give it up, will you! You're sick. You need help.'

'The police don't think so,' I say, tossing my head triumphantly.

'What?'

'The police. They believe me. You're going to have to as well.'

I tell him about Ian's prediction, Libby and Esme turning up, the claims they made.

'But it's ridiculous, Beth,' he says. 'Why on earth would they make up a . . . daft, vicious story like that?'

'Money, maybe?' My tone is solicitous. Perhaps now he'll tell me the truth about the reward.

'Money?'

'Yes, you know. The reward?'

Brian catches his breath.

'You're a spineless little shit, Brian!' I yell. 'Even now you haven't got the guts to tell me about withdrawing it.'

He goes to say something but stops. The aborted words come out in a rush of empty air. I wait.

'Look, Beth, no one had come forward after five years. No one was likely to. It was time to let go . . . for both of us. So I did – quietly.'

'You should have told me!' I scream. 'No, fuck that. You should have *asked* me!'

'You'd never have agreed to it.'

'Too right,' I say, nodding vigorously. '*You* gave up too soon. You always did.'

I can't hold back the gloat in my voice.

'I'm . . . I'm sorry, Beth,' he says. 'I thought it was for the best.'

'You thought wrong.'

'And the police think you're right, do they?' His voice rises with indignation. 'What the hell are they doing taking this reincarnation lark seriously anyway? It's beyond farcical.'

'Esme knew things, Brian. Little things. Important things. Things she just couldn't have known.'

'Such as?'

'Like Amy being stung in Zante by the jellyfish and you peeing on it to make it better. Like her roller-blading down the subways at Elephant and Castle. She even knew I take my coffee black and used to eat grapefruit for breakfast. It was uncanny. But I found out how she knew. It was Dana.'

'Dana?'

I like his silence as I explain everything. In the past that silence meant he was tapping on his computer or checking emails as my voice bled into the phone cradled on his shoulder. Now, though, he's so close to the phone I can hear him breathing, the tick at the back of his throat as he goes to say something but decides instead to listen, my voice answering his questions before they've left his mouth.

When I finish, there's a pause, a muffled sob.

'God ... Beth ... I don't ... after all this time.' His tears echo mine. 'Poor Amy. How did we miss all that ... right under our noses?' He sniffs loudly and his tone changes. 'Why the hell didn't you tell me about these two freaks before now?'

'Oh, and you'd have listened, would you? I don't think so. It's just as well I took them seriously or we wouldn't be where we are now.'

His whimpers do not move me.

'We ... let Amy down, Beth.'

'We let them *both* down.'

'Dana's parents did too.' He sounds defensive. 'How could they not have known what was going on?'

'*We* didn't.' I dab at my face with the sleeve of the dressing gown.

'We didn't have a child molester in the house!'

I'm so tense I can't breathe.

'Didn't we?'

There's a pause; the line crackles.

'Jesus,' he says, his voice barely a whisper. 'You think *I* was involved in this?'

I go to speak but no words come out. I swallow and try again.

'I don't know about anything any more, Brian.'

I can almost see him rocking back on his heels, blank with disbelief.

'Jesus!' he says eventually. 'I can't ... I can't believe you'd even think that.'

'I never would have done — if you hadn't pulled the re-ward. That makes it look like you didn't want Amy found. That you knew there was no point looking.'

'But I put the cash up in the first place!'

'Put up a smokescreen more like.'

'You're not serious?' He pauses. 'Is this ... is this what you've told the police? That I offered the reward to cover my tracks?'

'They'll draw their own conclusions.'

'I swear, Beth ... I had nothing to do with this ... You've got to believe me.'

I do – even if I can't forgive him about withdrawing the reward.

'I'm coming up there, Beth,' he says. 'Right away. I'll get the next flight.'

'There's nothing either of us can do. Except wait. *You're* not very good at that.'

'I'll be better at it if I'm with you.'

He goes to hang up.

'Beth? Tell the police I'm on my way, won't you? I don't want them thinking I've done a runner.'

I'm glad he's coming. I need someone to cling to even if it is only Brian. Already I'm aching to be in his arms. I pick up my phone and call Jill.

'Beth! Oh, I'm so glad you called,' she says. 'I would have rung you but ... well, I'm a silly old woman who should be beyond having stroppy sulks by now. And I always was stubborn. You know that better than most.'

'That doesn't matter now,' I say, shaking my head. 'Not any more.'

'I was only trying to protect you. You understand that, don't you?'

'I know. But you were wrong.'

'To want to protect you?'

'About Libby and Esme. Because of them, I know now what happened to Amy.'

The line is so quiet as I tell Jill the whole story that I have to keep asking if she's still there. Each time she gives a breathy 'yes' and tells me to go on.

'Oh Beth ... this is so ... too, too awful. I'm so sorry,'

she says when I finish. 'I can't even begin to imagine how you must feel.'

'I'm better for knowing the truth, however much it rips me up.' I put my hand over my heart and hold it there.

'Really? I'm not sure *I* would be.'

'You haven't lived in limbo for the last ten years.'

'No, of course.' She sniffs. 'Dan Bishop. Who'd have thought it?'

Dan Bishop. I have his name now. And I can see where Dana got hers. She was branded as his from birth.

'Of course!' I say. 'You knew him.'

'Clearly I didn't. None of us did ... not really.'

'But you saw him every day at the school!'

'He was inside most of the time,' she says. 'I was at the crossing – and then only for a couple of hours a day.'

'You never found him creepy?' I squirm on the bed. 'Did he ever say anything ... about the kids?'

Jill pauses.

'I'm not sure we ever spoke to each other,' she says vaguely, 'apart from saying good morning or something inane ... We were both just there ... doing our jobs. Oh God, it makes you wonder who else was involved.'

'Like the vicar, perhaps? See. I wasn't so far from the truth, was I? That picture Ian sent me was a clue. It might have been a reference to Bishop, but it could easily have been pointing at the vicar too.'

I hear Jill suck in her breath.

'Is that what the police think as well?' she says quickly.

'They'll have to look into it.' I cradle the phone between

317

my ear and shoulder and tighten the belt of the dressing gown.

'No . . . I just can't believe that . . . that a vicar would be part of this.'

'Why not? Because he's a man of God?' I say indignantly. 'Look at what went on in the Catholic church for all those years.'

'The vicar isn't Catholic.'

'Oh, and Anglicans wouldn't abuse kids, I suppose?'

'That's not what I meant,' she says firmly. 'It's just that they don't have . . . you know, the same . . . reputation.'

'That doesn't mean they're innocent. Just better at not being caught.' My upper lip lifts in contempt. I wriggle further down the bed, fighting back tears.

'There was one teacher,' Jill says, 'I can't remember his name – Sanders? Anderson? He was a bit . . . odd. Oily. You know, the *type* you'd expect. If you'd told me it was him, it wouldn't have been such a surprise.'

'Dana didn't identify any of the others,' I say, wiping my eyes, 'but the police will get the names from Dan Bishop.'

'So they haven't found him yet?'

'It can't be long before they do. They're just going over things with Libby first. They'll probably want to talk to you too.'

'Me?' She sounds flustered. 'But . . . I can't tell them any more than I've just told you.'

'Even so. I'll give them your name,' I say. I sit up slowly. 'Better still, why don't you come up here? I need you.'

'Oh Beth, I only wish I could. But I'm going to look

after my sister in Essex. She's just come out of hospital after a fall.'

'Isn't there someone else who can take over?'

'No, I'm afraid not,' Jill says. 'She's on her own, you see, since her husband died. I'm sorry. I'm literally on my way out now. I thought your call was the cab company saying the driver was outside.'

'How long are you going for?'

'Not sure yet. I'll have to see how we go.' I can picture Jill at the other end of the phone, hand on her forehead, like she does when trying to make arrangements with reluctant jumble-sale volunteers. 'But if I can get away early,' she says, 'I will. I promise.'

'Maybe the police here can call you?'

'Of course – but reception's not great in my sister's neck of the woods. It's a bit of a backwater, but ... they can give it a go.'

'What's the landline number there?' I look around the room for a pen.

'My sister doesn't have one,' Jill says. 'She's quite an odd fish. Thinks mod cons are just that – a con. She doesn't even have central heating. Or a TV! Gets by with the radio. So my mobile is the best bet.'

There's a rustling noise at the other end of the line.

'Sorry,' Jill says, 'I've got to go, Beth. I can see my cab outside.'

'One more thing, Jill.'

'Yes?'

'Please don't mention this to anyone. Not even your sister.'

'Of course not. I won't breathe a word.'

It's as if the last ten years haven't happened. Brian sits beside me on a blue plastic chair in a cramped, stuffy room with bars on the window and a view of the squad cars outside. Every so often car doors slam, sirens wail, tyres screech. The urgency is always elsewhere.

Meanwhile, we wait. Minutes are dragged around by the hands of the clock above the door.

I remember how we held one another when Amy first went missing. How we whispered encouragement through the tears and kisses, stroked each other's hands, taking it in turns to pretend to be strong.

I remember how the words became harder to find, until a suffocating silence was easier. That too became unbearable. I remember the stench of cadged cigarettes, the darkening shadow of stubble around Brian's jaw, the heavy eyelids, the pulse of the dots in his digital watch.

I remember the way the door opening could make my heart stop still, make my head turn to see who was there and whether I could read their expression. I remember that a single shake of the head suddenly had different meanings.

No, there is no news, but that still gives us reason to hope.

We've found her. No. I'm sorry. I promise we'll get whoever did this.

No. No news, no body, no leads. No more time. No

more detectives. No more inquiries, posters or appeals. No hope. No future. No end.

The mushroom-coloured coffee in the plastic cups is lukewarm and tastes of yesterday, but that doesn't stop Brian drinking it. He runs his hands through his hair. It's thinner than it was back then, greyer. I thought I saw it grow lighter with every minute he spent listening to Dana's testimony. He ended up on the bed in my hotel room, curled in a ball, hugging the computer to him and sobbing into the duvet.

Every word Dana spoke ripped him apart, but he insisted on listening to the recording several times over, because, he said, if he hadn't been too wrapped up in himself ten years ago, Dana and Amy might still be alive.

He takes his cup from the table, swirls the coffee around and tips it into his mouth.

'I'll get another one,' he says. 'You want anything?'

I shake my head. He's just got to his feet when the door opens.

Harding's expression is too blank to read. Earnshaw's is almost bored and detached. They sit down at the table. Harding takes his jacket off and hangs it on the back of his chair. Earnshaw places his elbows on the table and puts his hands together in front of his face, as if in prayer.

'Well?' Brian's voice is tight. 'You've found Bishop?'

Harding nods.

'Alive?' I say.

Harding nods again.

'Bishop has been arrested.'

The hunt is over. I've got Amy's killer. Now I can lay her to rest.

I stare at Harding, senseless not with the news he has delivered, but with my reaction to it. I have dreamt of this moment for the last ten years. An end to the wait, if not the agony. The satisfying smack of justice. The chance to move on.

But now it is here, I feel nothing. Just empty. And the look on Harding's face makes me anxious.

'Has he confessed?' I say in a whisper.

'To rape, yes,' Earnshaw says. 'Not to Amy's murder.'

'Well he wouldn't, would he?' I say impatiently.

Earnshaw coughs.

'I'm not so sure,' he says.

'You can't possibly think he's innocent?' I screw my face up, baffled and angry that they're not pressing Bishop harder.

'He's guilty of rape – at the very least. But murder?' Harding says, shoulders hunched. 'That's not so cut and dried.'

'But—'

'Bishop has been quite forthcoming, Mrs Archer,' Harding says. 'Remarkably so, seeing as the only testimony against him is from someone who's dead. Even perverts can have a conscience, it seems.' He doesn't sound entirely convinced. 'Bishop's an old, not particularly well man, chewed up by guilt. He almost seems pleased that we've caught up with him and given him the chance to make peace with himself. I think if he'd killed Amy he would have told us.'

'But what about Dana's evidence?' I say. 'Bishop told her he did it. You've got it right in front of you.' I look around at them all, blank and mystified.

'Ah.' Harding drops his head. 'Actually, he didn't.'

He slides a printout of Dana's A to Z across the table. The pages are covered in handwritten notes, underlinings and question marks. Harding runs his finger along a couple of sentences.

```
'I don't know nothing about this,
okay? Nothing,' he said. 'Nor do you.
Get it? Keep your trap shut and I'll
leave you alone.'
```

'But that's not him saying he *didn't* kill her!' I shout.

'No, but it's not Dana telling us he owned up to it either,' Harding says, pushing his chair back and standing up. 'The reverse in fact.'

'This is ridiculous.' My hands curl and clench in frustration. 'That's just him telling her to keep quiet.'

'That's how we see it. Hopefully a jury will too,' Earnshaw says. 'But it's vague enough to give his lawyers some wriggle room.'

'So who does he say *did* kill Amy?' Brian asks, taking my hand.

'Simon Palmer,' Earnshaw says.

He looks at me as if it's a name I should recognise, but I don't.

'He used to run the mobile library,' Harding says. 'Amy's school was on his route.'

I remember him doling out the books from his cramped little van. Small but wiry, dirty blond grey hair and glasses that fell so far forward on his nose he had to squint over them. He was the one who christened Amy the Girl Who Never Read Anything Else. We joked together about Amy always taking out the same book and I joined in when he tried to interest her in something else.

I understand now that all Amy wanted was to get out of the van and away from Palmer; it was quicker to just renew the same book. And the story itself was a clue I'd missed too; the Man Didn't Wash His Dishes had to live with his own dirt until the pile of dishes grew so large it trapped him for ever.

I bury my head in my hands. How did I miss all of that? How could he have killed my little girl? Could that quiet and helpful man with the easy rapport with children really have done it? I shudder at the man behind the mask, the real man. The pervert. The killer. The man I joked with every fortnight when Amy renewed her book.

I feel humiliated and foolish. Vengeful. I look up at Harding.

'He must be put away for this,' I say, tears streaming down my cheeks. 'For ever. Promise me you won't let him get off.'

'We won't,' Harding says. 'Once we've found him.'

Brian stands up.

'You haven't got him?' he shouts. 'What the bloody hell are you waiting for? An invitation?'

'We're going full out on that, I can assure you,' Harding

says. 'Bishop doesn't know where he is. Hasn't had any contact with him since the Bishops moved to Birmingham.'

I sob with frustration. He can't get away again.

'Did Bishop tell you what happened to Amy?' I say. I want to know for my own peace of mind, but there'll be no real peace in the knowledge. Just a different kind of hell. Another shade of black.

'He says he wasn't there.' Earnshaw gives a little shrug, as if there's nothing he can do about Bishop's explanation.

'What about Amy's body?' I say, my voice barely a whisper. 'Where is she? I want my little girl.'

Earnshaw sighs.

'I'm sorry, Mrs Archer,' he says. 'Bishop says he doesn't know. *How can I if I wasn't even there?* But we'll track Palmer down and get it from him. I promise.'

I imagine Palmer gloating like a dog over a buried bone, just enjoying knowing it's there. His prize and his alone.

'You have to find her,' I say, my voice fading away into nothing. 'You have to. I need to say goodbye.'

'We'll find your daughter, Mrs Archer,' Harding says, crouching down and resting a reassuring hand on my shoulder. 'One way or the other. You can count on that.'

Brian pushes the glass towards me. Melted ice cubes bob like spit. He sits down opposite me, taking quick sips of his iceless whisky, his second in fifteen minutes. The room smells of the smoke blown back in through the hotel window as he stuck his head out to evade the hotel's detectors.

He gave up years ago – we both did – but so far I haven't

succumbed. Not like I did when Amy first vanished. The stench lingers, as pervasive as despair, only despair can't be washed out or masked with a dose of Comfort.

The last Marlboro Gold pokes from the packet. I bite my lip and look away quickly. When Harding rings, asking us to go into the station, Brian takes the last cigarette from the packet. By the time we get back, I've got a packet of my own.

Palmer still hasn't been found. He's still getting away with murder.

Bishop is hiding behind his plea of guilty to rape and his policy of cooperation with the police.

Libby, Esme and Ian have been allowed to walk free. Insufficient evidence, apparently. The police have failed me once more.

Fuck off, *detective,* for believing Libby's lies. For not trusting what you can see with your own eyes. It seems that having a file on her computer isn't proof she knew it was there, tucked away in the bowels of a machine she didn't know how to use.

Can't you see she was acting when asked to switch it on and log in? Befuddled, blinking and hapless? I bet she was. Ignorant of the password and a stranger to email, the web and the mysteries of voice files? Of course.

And the tears she cried on hearing about Dana's recording! Well, that's how it goes when you're caught in a lie. She didn't listen to it on the computer, naturally – she wasn't daft enough to fall for that. Defeated by the mouse and the cursor, she asked for a printout instead. Good old-fashioned paper. It's easier to handle and amplifies the splats of tears. An ocean of them, apparently, a bottomless well. Too numerous and snotty to be anything but real.

Even the police shrink was convinced. Enough said, then. Who can doubt the double whammy of psychological insight and investigative guile? Not me. Not Brian. However much we tried.

Withholding evidence? Not proven. Case dismissed.

Fuck off, *detective*, for being as oblivious to Libby's greed as she was ignorant of the reward. Apparently. Wide-eyed and speechless at the news of the cash? You don't say. In your considered opinion, no provable knowledge of the reward and no attempt to claim it makes for a case that *could* be argued in court – but not won.

Case dismissed.

Fuck off, *detective,* for still not finding Amy's grave. For breaking my heart and my hope once more.

And damn you, *detective,* for not being able to crack a ten-year-old girl. Who stonewalled you and the shrink with her simple, unswerving defence: 'I don't need an instruction manual. I didn't even realise it was there. I know what I know because I'm Amy.'

No court in the land would prosecute her for childish fantasies, however unpleasant or bizarre. She's only young, she doesn't know what she's doing. It's just her version of an imaginary friend, a phase she'll grow out of eventually – sooner without all this attention.

Case dismissed.

I light a cigarette and open the hotel window. Smoke

streams from my nostrils like ectoplasm. Brian nestles in beside me, sparks a match.

'I can hardly believe I'm saying this,' he mutters, 'but maybe it's better this way.'

I shrug his hand away from my arm.

'I can't see how.'

'God knows I want those two cows punished as much as you do, Beth,' he says, putting his hand back on my arm, 'but Harding's right. It just won't hold up in court.'

'We should still try.'

Brian frowns.

'A private prosecution, you mean?' he says.

'Why not?'

He exhales slowly. The smoke is whipped away by the wind.

'I don't think we'd fare any better,' he says. 'It's going to be hard enough when Bishop comes to trial. And his lawyers are going to love it if we're taking separate legal action against key prosecution witnesses. Let's quit while we're ahead.'

'We're ahead?' My laugh is brittle. 'It doesn't feel like that to me.'

'We know what happened to Amy,' he says. 'We've got one of the men responsible. We *might* still get the other. And that's all down to Libby and Esme.'

I loathe his measured, reasonable tone.

'Forgive me, but I'm finding it hard to be grateful.' I suck in the last mouthful of smoke. 'We still don't know where Amy is.'

'There's still time,' Brian says. 'Harding could get it out of Bishop or Palmer.'

I flick my cigarette stub from the window.

'Harding couldn't get a prayer from a nun.'

I'm not even going to get the satisfaction of seeing Bishop in court. Not yet. Harding has ensured that the hearing to remand him in custody is kept from the press so that Palmer doesn't go to ground.

The tactic works. Two days later, Palmer is in custody too, picked up from a flat in Ipswich. He's been working in the city as a librarian and spending his spare time coaching youngsters at a local swimming club. On his computer's hard drive are thousands of pornographic images of young girls and pages of his own lurid fantasies.

But he's been less expansive with the police.

'He hasn't said a word about Amy,' Harding says. 'Doesn't admit it. Doesn't deny it. Just blanks us – smirking in a sly, supercilious way that's getting right up my nose. It's all I can do to stop myself hitting him.'

'If you don't, I will!' Brian says.

'No,' I say. 'We've got to break his spirit, not his bones.'

'Your wife's right, of course, Mr Archer,' Harding says. 'We can't give his defence team any leeway. Give us time. We'll crack him.'

But they don't. His smug silence taunts and exasperates Harding and makes me hate Palmer more than I already did. Harding switches tack and spends more time questioning Bishop, who is more than willing to supply as much damning detail as he can.

'Not enough to get a conviction for murder, or even accessory to murder, I'm afraid,' Harding tells us, 'but we'll put him away for rape, sexual assault and procuring children, no question of that.'

'So . . .' I say, wringing my hands, 'he's got away with it.' My head drops. 'And I still don't know where Amy's body is.'

'I understand that you're frustrated, Mrs Archer.' Harding looks sheepish.

'You don't understand anything.'

'In my experience,' he says firmly, 'once they've been banged up, they can't see the point of staying silent. They think it might help get their sentence reduced if they cough up information they've previously withheld. So we *could* still find Amy . . . at some stage.' He coughs. 'With any luck.'

I'm demolished and defeated, too worn out to say any more. Palmer has had the last word. I go to stand up, then stop and turn to Harding.

'What about Dana?' I say.

He holds his hands out and tips his head. He looks as beaten as I feel.

'We've got people checking databases of unidentified drowning fatalities, coastguards and so on,' he says. 'But so far they've not come up with anyone who matches Dana's description. She only said she was going to drown herself, but not where she was going to do it. Only the sea. That's not much for us to go on.' He sighs. 'All we can do is wait. The sea still might offer her body up. But with heavy shipping traffic, currents . . . perhaps we'll never find her.'

I swallow back my tears. Dana's parents have no body to bury either. I hope they find some comfort in knowing their daughter's fate. I hope Dana is finally at peace.

'Take me home,' I say to Brian.

He stands up and takes my arm.

I need to get home, safely barricaded behind my own front door, before news of the arrests breaks.

'Are you sure about this?' Brian says on the way back to the hotel. 'You'll have the press at your door day and night. Why don't you go to your parents'? Or come to my place?'

'No.'

My home has been my refuge for the last ten years. I am safe there. I pack my case, put my talismanic stone in my coat pocket. Brian carries the case to the lift and says he'll get the concierge to find us a taxi.

'No need,' I say.

But Dave's phone is switched to voicemail and we end up taking a black cab to the airport. I try him again on the way. He still doesn't answer, but this time I leave a message.

'Dave, it's Beth. I'm heading for the airport. Sorry you missed the fare. But I'll make it up to you.

'On our travels you boasted about Manchester being the city where Jack met Vera, where Engels met Marx, where Rolls met Royce ... Well, it's also where I met you ... and you made it possible for me to meet Henry Campbell Black ... I can't tell you now why that's important, but you'll find out soon enough.

'Remember you had me down as a secret millionaire? Here to do a good turn for someone? Well, I wasn't . . . not in the way you mean. But that's how it's turned out anyway. Keep your eyes open for an envelope addressed to you at the cab office. Bye. And thank you.'

Brian tilts his head at me.

'What was all that about?' he says.

'That's about you settling the reward by sending a cheque to the only person who deserves it.'

14

Brian startles me as I come down the stairs. He's standing in front of the fireplace with his back to me, gazing at Amy's photo on the mantelpiece.

It's odd to see him here again – reassuring, but at the same time unsettling. The comfort of company in the present, haunted by the memories of our past. Of the legacy we left for Amy.

As I enter the front room, he turns to face me and I half expect him to leave the room or make some spiteful comment. But he smiles, a broken kind of smile with a quivering lower lip.

'Okay?' he says.

I nod and walk towards him. I blow some dust from the mantelpiece and place the talismanic stone in front of Amy's picture.

'What's that?'

'A sort of good-luck charm, I suppose,' I say with a sigh. 'An eternal flame for Amy, set in stone.'

He picks it up and turns it in his hand.

'I always loved this picture,' he says, tipping his head at Amy's photo. 'I've got a copy of it on my living room windowsill.'

'Really? I didn't know.'

'I've never stopped loving her, Beth. Never forgotten her. Despite what you think.'

'I know. I'm sorry.'

He kisses the stone and puts it back on the mantelpiece, but to the left of the picture instead of dead centre. When I move it, it is warm.

Brian's arm slips around my shoulders. I bite my lip.

'God,' I say, 'I'm dreading the trial.'

'We'll manage,' he says, pulling me closer to him. 'We've got this far.'

'Only just.' I lay my head on his chest. 'And we've not exactly done it together, have we?'

'I'm sorry, Beth. I should have been more patient. More understanding.'

'Yes ... but I didn't make it easy for you. I was ... obsessed. Mad with it.'

His grip around me tightens.

'You were right,' he says. 'You'll never know how it feels to have let Amy down while she was alive and then given up on her once she disappeared.'

'I was on the point of giving up too. If it hadn't been for that last trip to the psychic ... It's ironic, isn't it? We wouldn't have found the truth if it hadn't been for Libby and Esme's lies.'

I miss the warmth and reassurance of his arms as he turns and sits down in an armchair.

He checks his watch.

'You should be going,' I say. 'Fiona will be expecting you.'

'Actually, she isn't,' he says brightly. 'I called her while you were showering. I'm going to stay for a few days ... if that's okay?'

'Fiona doesn't mind?'

'Not at all. She practically insisted I stay. She's lived with this as much as we have. The girls too. They're being kept off school for a while.' He coughs. 'She said it's been on the news. About the press conference being called, I mean.' He checks his watch again. 'Not long now. The press will be camped on the doorstep within the hour, you watch.'

We sit in silence and watch the clock on the DVD counting down to the next part of the nightmare. At one o'clock, Brian stands up and turns on the television.

The drums bang home the headlines from the BBC: a landmine kills four soldiers in Afghanistan; two men are charged in relation to the disappearance of Amy Archer ten years ago.

We both recoil from the photo of Amy flashed on to the screen. The one of her in her school uniform given to the police to help in the search. The one I saw in the ghoulish galleries of missing people on websites about unsolved murders.

It's on the notice board behind Harding at the press conference too. He blinks at the flash of press cameras as he reads through a statement, occasionally looking up to give his words extra emphasis.

My heart flies to my mouth when Bishop's picture appears. There he is. The man who raped my daughter. The Grey Wolf. The hair is thin but messy, mostly white, but flecked with silver at the sides. His eyes are hard and hungry, dark as bullets. I can almost hear a growl from his slightly open mouth, feel his breath. The gappy teeth still have a bite.

Palmer's face is thinner than I remember, his hair receding. But it's his expression that strikes me the most: insouciant, defiant. Unrepentant. I still see him when the picture's no longer on the screen. I know I always will. Whenever I look at my own reflection, he'll be there, mocking me.

Brian stands up and turns the TV off. He looks out of the window.

'Christ,' he says. 'They're here already. Bloody parasites.'

The doorbell rings.

'Ignore it, Brian,' I say quickly. 'Close the curtains.'

He is strobed by camera flash as he pulls the curtains. The room falls into the murky twilight we endured for weeks when Amy first went missing. Neither a life-giving light nor a mournful dark. Just an endless grubby grey.

The doorbell rings again. Then the phone in the hallway. I unplug it from the wall. My mobile chimes in too. Jill's name flashes up on the screen.

The line is so crackly I can barely make out what she's saying. When the hissing abates for a second, her voice is distorted by echo, as if she's talking through a funnel. Then the line goes dead.

A woman's voice calls from the other side of the front door.

'Mrs Archer? Are you there?'

The doorbell rings once more. My head swarms with memories of Libby's insistence at my door on New Year's Eve. The ghosts and vultures I let in.

'Go away!' I yell from the hallway. 'Leave us alone. We've nothing to say.'

'Mrs Archer? I'm Lois Shaughnessy. Family liaison officer.' A hand flaps a badge through the letter box. 'Can I come in?'

'What do you want?'

'I'm here to help.'

Brian opens the door. Camera shutters whir. Journalists jostle, push microphones forward. The woman steps in quickly and closes the door.

She's about thirty, short, dumpy even, her head lost somewhere between her neck and a blob of curly reddish hair.

'Sorry about that lot,' she says. 'We'll get them moved back.' She puts her hand out. 'I'm Lois. DI Harding sent me down from Manchester to help you through this.'

Brian shakes her hand. I do too, reluctantly.

'Can we sit down?' she says. 'Have a chat?'

She follows Brian into the front room. I go in behind her. She has a hole in her tights just above the heel.

'Harding didn't say you were coming,' Brian says as he waves her towards one of the armchairs.

'Didn't he?' She grimaces. 'I'm sorry. He really should have done. Ideally, you and I should have met before you left Manchester, but ... well, things have moved very quickly.' She undoes her coat buttons and smiles. 'I suppose I'd better start by telling you why I'm here.'

Brian nods.

'I'm part of the investigative team,' she says, 'but my main role is as a more informal line of communication between you and the police. You know, to smooth the way as much as possible. Keep you up to date with any developments, talk to the press on your behalf, explain what will happen between now and getting to court – that sort of thing. Anything really. Anything that helps.'

'We didn't get one of you when Amy first went missing,' I say. I feel defensive and I don't know why. Perhaps she's here to keep an eye on us.

She nods her head.

'Ah, well, the job didn't exist then, you see,' she says. 'It was created after the inquiry into the murder of Stephen Lawrence. I'm sure you remember that? Awful case. The only good thing to come out of it was the creation of family liaison officers. I'm sure you'll find it useful if—'

My mobile interrupts her.

'Beth? Can you hear me? It's Jill.'

'Just about,' I say, putting one finger into my ear to hear her better. 'It's a dreadful line. Shall I call you back?'

'Won't make any difference,' Jill says. 'It's always like this here. I've just heard the news on the radio and wanted to tell you I'm thinking of you. And Brian. It's just dreadful. I only wish I could be there to help. I don't like the idea of you being on your own.'

'Oh, we're not. The police have sent us a . . . sort of go-between.'

'Oh, you mean Lois! I spoke to her earlier. She sounded very nice. I don't think I was able to tell her anything useful . . . but she seemed glad that I'd called.'

'You rang her?' I say, puzzled.

'I rang the police in Manchester. You said they might want to talk to me, but I knew they'd have trouble getting hold of me so I called them as soon as I got a signal. Didn't last long, needless to say, but long enough to say what little I had to tell them.'

'Right.'

The line begins to crackle. I twist around on the seat, trying to boost the phone's signal.

'Looks like my luck is about to run out,' Jill says. 'If you want to talk, text me and I'll find a proper phone. I'll be back as soon as I can. Keep me posted.'

'I will,' I say. 'Hope your sister feels bet—'

The phone hums with an empty line.

Lois tuts.

'I had the same problem when I spoke to Mrs Redfern,' she says. 'It's mad that there are still so many mobile black spots, isn't it? Still, it was useful to talk to her. She gave us the names of some other people to talk to.'

'Like who?' Brian says.

'Some of the teachers at Amy's school. A few of her contacts in the local community. We haven't spoken to them all yet, but we will. People are keen to help.' She coughs. 'I am too, Mrs Archer. I know you're angry and frustrated, but you've got to remember, I'm on your side.'

We swap smiles. Hers is sympathetic, mine circumspect.

'So,' I say, 'what happens next?'

'We build our case. Meticulously. We lean on Palmer. Relentlessly. And we wait. Patiently. It could be quite some time before this gets to court. But it will be worth it. We'll get a result.'

God has other ideas, though; He decides to punish me once more. Three weeks after Bishop and Palmer are remanded in custody, God, disguised as a prisoner with a life sentence and skilled with a knife, steals Palmer away. Snatching Amy's body from me for ever, blessing Palmer with celestial rest and condemning me to eternal torment.

Lois and Harding can barely look me in the eye.

'He was meant to be in isolation!' I sob. 'Out of harm's way!'

'He was,' Harding says, shaking his head. 'But they couldn't keep him locked up twenty-four hours a day, every day. And the prison officers don't have eyes in the back of their heads. I can't express how deeply we regret this, Mrs Archer. The prison authorities *are* investigating.'

I slump on the sofa, sobbing into my hands. Brian sits beside me. There is no comfort in the arm around my shoulder. Instead of my daughter's body, the best I can hope for is some bureaucratic inquiry that will find no one at fault and move on.

'The bastard got away with it,' I say. 'And he'll get a funeral too. Where's the justice in that? It's so bloody unfair. What have I done to be punished like this? Haven't I suffered enough?'

Lois squeezes next to me. She smells of coffee and cigarettes.

'I promise we'll do anything we can to help you through this,' she says. 'We won't just walk away and leave you to it. We can arrange for you to have some counselling, for as long as you need it. We've got some very good people.'

'I've done all that,' I say, clenching my fists. 'It doesn't work. Nothing does.'

Brian stands up.

'I think it might be better if you leave us alone for a bit,' he says.

Out in the hallway I hear Lois tell him that she's only a phone call away if we change our minds.

'Just one more thing,' she says. 'Dana's parents would like to meet you. When you're ready.'

'I don't know,' Brian says. 'We'll see.'

The door opens to journalists' questions and camera flashes, then shuts them out. Brian coughs and comes back into the front room.

'I don't want to see Dana's parents,' I say as he sits down.

'They've lost their daughter too.'

'I know.' I sigh heavily. 'I can see how meeting and talking might help us — all of us. But not just yet, eh? I can't face having to handle their grief as well as mine.'

'What about your family?' Brian says. 'They'll be in touch now the news is out.'

'Maybe. Mum anyway. Some of my so-called friends

too, perhaps.' I can't help my snide smile. 'I don't want to deal with any of them right now, okay? If they call or turn up . . .'

Brian nods.

'If that's what you want.'

For the next few days we drift around the house, barely talking. I spend most of the time in Amy's bedroom, my back to the mirror to block out the memories I might catch there. The slabs of colour from my experiments with paint samples now look like tombstones.

Brian offers to redecorate, but I tell him to leave it.

'You got rid of every trace of her last time,' I say. 'There's nothing you can do.'

'It's more about removing any trace of Esme and Libby,' he says, pointing at the walls.

'They're in here,' I say, jabbing at my temple with a finger. 'There's no escape from them now either. They've taken every part of me. Christ, even Bagpuss has gone.'

I left him behind at Libby's flat in my rush to collect my things. Lois could get him back if I asked her to, but I never want to see him again. He has been sullied by Esme's duplicitous kisses. He's the Grey Wolf in another disguise.

I shut the door when Brian talks to Fiona on the phone downstairs, but I still catch the odd sentence.

'Beth's resting . . . I miss you too . . . I'll be home soon . . . Give my love to the girls.'

I tell him he should go back to his family, but he says he can't until he knows I'll be okay.

'Then you'll be here for ever,' I say flatly. 'You might as well go now.'

'I don't want to leave you on your own. How about spending some time at your parents'?'

'Maybe later.'

I want to be here for the moment, alone once more with the memories the house holds. The regrets. Maybe I'll move. Perhaps there'll be a 'For Sale' sign outside my house after all. Just like Ian had said.

'Your parents could come here,' Brian says.

My mother would fuss and fidget, boil kettles constantly, polish and vacuum and cook. Dad would sit in a chair, stoic and silent, uncomfortable with my tears, still doubtful of my innocence.

Brian is on the point of calling them when Jill steps in to save me.

'My sister's on the mend,' she says on the phone, 'and the hospital have finally got their act together and managed to get the home help in place. I'll be back tomorrow.'

Brian doesn't leave me until she arrives.

'It's good of you to come, Jill,' he says as he opens the door.

'I'm only sorry I couldn't get here earlier. Where's Beth?'

I sit up from the sofa as they come in. Jill looks pale and tired but finds a smile.

'Don't get up, Beth,' she says.

I collapse into her arms as she sits beside me. Her

embrace is a fortress, strong and impregnable. It's the safest I've felt in weeks.

'I wish I could wave a wand and make this go away,' she says. 'It's so unbelievably cruel.'

Brian makes some tea for us, then sits down. He seems agitated.

'If you want to go, it's fine,' I tell him. 'Jill's here now.'

'No, it wasn't that,' Brian says thoughtfully. 'It's just ... I've been thinking. What Jill said about waving a wand to make it all go away.' He rubs his eyes with the hub of his palms. 'I can't believe I'm going to say this, but ... would it be worth asking that psychic to see if he knows where Amy's body is?'

'What?' I say, sitting up.

'Brian, you can't possibly be serious?' Jill puts her hand on my arm and leans towards him. 'Don't you think they've done enough harm already?'

'Over the years, yes,' he says. 'But this one ... He seems to have got a lot of things right. He might be able to help.'

'*Seems to*,' Jill says, shaking her head. 'That's not nearly enough ... particularly for something like this. He could send you off on a wild goose chase, and Beth's been chasing shadows for too long already ... If you'd seen the state she was in after that horrible picture of Jesus, after all that false hope of the last ten years, you wouldn't even contemplate such a ridiculous, *dangerous* idea ... And you still don't *know* that he wasn't involved with Libby and Esme.'

'The police can't find any link,' Brian says.

'Maybe they should ask a psychic to help.' Jill sniffs and

takes a sip of her tea. 'I'm sorry. I shouldn't be so flippant. Shouldn't have said anything, really. It's not my place. It's your decision.'

'Beth?' Brian says, tilting his head towards me.

'I don't know,' I say.

'But the picture. Dana. The thing about the book,' Brian says. 'Even Esme turning up. It's all too . . .'

'Premeditated? Convenient?' Jill mutters.

'Accurate.'

'You've changed your tune,' I say, leaning back. I want the sofa to swallow me up.

'Everything's changed, Beth,' Brian says. 'Look, I'm not saying I believe, wholeheartedly, one hundred per cent, but . . . there's a doubt in my head now. A crack. Maybe it's worth a try? It might be our only hope of ever finding Amy.'

'He couldn't help me when I asked him to find Libby's telephone number.'

'Oh come on,' he says. 'That's not exactly the same thing, is it?'

'Isn't it?' Jill says, putting her cup down. 'Needles and haystacks come to mind.'

'He couldn't help then because it was a specific request about a particular detail,' I say, closing my eyes. 'I'm not sure this is any different.'

'It's not treating the "other side" like directory enquiries.' Brian's voice has the sneer he once used to dismiss psychics.

'No, more like a missing persons bureau,' Jill says. 'And

they haven't come up with anything in the last ten years, have they? If Ian *is* genuine, his "gift" would have told you where Amy was buried before now, and spared you all this heartache. Why prolong it? I hate to be so brutal, but it's time to face facts. We'll probably never know where she is.'

'Bishop might tell us — eventually.' Even I don't believe that's true.

'That seems as likely as this Ian doing so,' Jill says. 'But I'd take Bishop's word over his any day.'

I remember what Ian said the last time I saw him, about not choosing which of his predictions to believe or ignore.

If we did ask him and he gave us a location, what then? We'd have to convince the police and get them to excavate the site, with the press prying and speculating from the sidelines. And if Ian was wrong and told us to look elsewhere, then somewhere else, how long would the police cooperate? How would we cope with the stress, the anguish of dashed hope? It would be like Millennium Eve all over again, a scab that just won't heal.

Ian has been wrong before; his 'connection' with the picture of Jesus sent me running around the streets, a madwoman making wild accusations. Unsubstantiated ones — there is no evidence that any vicar was involved with Amy's abuse. Not so far. I can't see how there ever will be. But then maybe the error was mine in interpreting the picture as a lead to a vicar, rather than a clue to Bishop, or to Dana.

What Ian might say could be read in so many ways and

take us down blind alleys. Further into despair. I'm too tired to go on.

'Let's wait for Bishop's conscience to get the better of him,' I say, my shoulders slumping.

'But he says he doesn't know!' Brian throws his hands out towards me.

'He could be lying,' I say.

'And Ian will be lying if he says he *does* know.' Jill takes my hand. 'For what it's worth, I think you've made the right decision.'

'Me too,' I say.

Brian falls back into his chair and sighs heavily.

'If you're sure, Beth?' he says.

'Quite sure,' I say. 'You won't see or get in touch with Ian, will you? Go behind my back, like you did with the reward?'

'No. I swear.'

He looks at his watch and stands up.

'Before you go,' Jill says, 'I've had an idea that you might want to think about. I've interfered enough already and if you want to tell me to take a running jump then I'll understand.'

'What is it, Jill?'

'I went to St Anselm's on my way here, you know, to say a prayer for you and Amy, and I wondered ... well, if you'd thought about having a memorial service?'

Brian suggested one a year after Amy vanished, but it was too final to me, too much of a full stop. She might still be alive. And although that hope faded bit by bit over the years, I just couldn't face shutting the door on her completely.

If we were ever to have a service for her, it would be a funeral, with a body in a coffin carried in a procession to a grave with a headstone adorned with flowers I could replace each week. The chance of that has been snuffed out for good now; a memorial service is the best I can hope for.

'I did think about a service myself,' Brian says. 'But I thought I'd give Beth some time before I suggested it.'

'I'm sorry,' Jill says. 'You're quite right. I should have kept my mouth shut.'

'No, it's fine,' I say. 'I'm touched you thought of it.' I look up at Brian. 'You want to do this?'

He nods.

'Do you?'

I am wary of a church service. God has played a long, cruel and vindictive game with me, let me believe that there is always hope, a chance to start again and lead a good and meaningful life.

I regret that I ever believed it.

All the alternative venues for some kind of service seem wrong too. The park is too public and too painful. Nothing could exorcise the ghosts there. I cannot even think of walking into Amy's school, and the hall where she went to Brownies and did her dance class is too functional, its memories too frivolous.

'Maybe we should have a word with the vicar,' I say, shuddering at my suspicions about the local clergymen.

'I spoke to Philip when I was there,' Jill says. 'He said he'd be happy to offer guidance on the service. He suggested you might want to consider a memorial plaque too.'

It's a consolation prize for plucky contenders who haven't quite made the grade.

I felt the same years ago when I considered planting a tree in Amy's memory. It would bear her name and be a living monument, an ornament to the park. Somewhere for me to sit. Something for me to care for.

But I couldn't escape the thought that the other bereaved families who planted trees in the park also had graves to visit, or places made sacred by their loved ones' ashes. The tree was an add-on, a supplementary flourish.

I'm ambivalent about the plaque being in the church, too. It wouldn't just concede my defeat at the hands of God, it would write it on the walls for all to see. A scoreboard and a trophy cabinet. But I am cheating Amy once more if I turn down the offer of the plaque. It may only be a facsimile of a grave, but it's the best she'll get.

We agree a date in early April. Maundy Thursday. The day of the Last Supper, when Jesus anticipated his betrayal and crucifixion. Entirely appropriate for my final farewell to Amy.

Brian stands back from organising the service. Not because he doesn't care, he says, but because he thinks doing it will help me heal. But nothing ever will.

I choose pop songs over hymns, poems over prayers and dither over the type of plaque. Stainless steel is too cold

349

and corporate, marble too fancy and formal. Sandstone is warmer but drab, and wood not special enough. I choose a silvery slate for its elegant glow, for being halfway between light and dark.

The inscription is harder to decide. The list supplied by the plaque company is generic and bland. Amy's epitaph isn't going to be off the peg or shared by countless others. Some of them resonate in ways they don't intend.

Step softly. A dream lies buried here. This isn't Amy's headstone. She isn't buried here.

Called by the one who loves her dearly. It's as good as a summons from the Grey Wolf.

Our littlest angel who went back to heaven. And then returned again as Esme.

'There,' I say to Jill. 'That's what I want.'

She pushes her glasses back on her nose and squints at my writing on the notepad.

Amy Elizabeth Archer
1989–1999
Let Love Lead the Way

'It's a Spice Girls song,' I say.

'Ah, I see. Perfect.'

The day of the service is bright with spring but the warm sunshine fails to breach the church walls. The pink roses in the vases all around the church have no scent and the photo of Amy on the altar jumps in the stuttering flames of the candles. The music from the speakers is underscored by an incessant hiss and the poems are deadened by dull acoustics.

When we file outside to unveil the plaque, the sun goes in. God turning his back on me one more time. I hear a titter in the wind in the trees.

15

Jill holds on to my arm as we catch our breath climbing the hill to the Royal Observatory. Sunlight glints from the offices at Canary Wharf on the other side of the Thames.

Jill sighs.

'You can just feel summer coming, can't you?' she says.

I can't, but I nod anyway. I don't think I will ever feel warm again. Parakeets squawk from the trees overhanging the path.

'It's funny how they survive here. You'd think it would be too cold for them,' Jill says. 'Did you know we've even got them in Kennington Park now?'

I shake my head.

'They've adapted. Found a way to survive.' She snuggles into me. 'Just like you have.'

'They're making a better job of it than I am.'

'You're getting there, Beth.' She takes a deep breath and leans into the hill. 'Shall we?'

We walk on, the incline growing steeper. Two boys on bikes whoop as they fly down the hill, spraying stones behind them. They bounce and flex, absorbing bumps and swerving to avoid potholes. Amy used to love riding down hills. I'd watch her, envious of the full-pelt thrill of her descent but worried by her precarious rush.

'They're not even wearing helmets!' I say.

'I think that's wonderful.'

'They'll know all about it if they fall off.'

'But it's their confidence I like,' Jill says. 'They're not expecting to fall.'

'*Every* child falls,' I say, shuddering. 'Mothers should be more careful.'

As we approach the Greenwich Observatory, a red ball slides up a spindle protruding from one of the turrets, stopping halfway.

'It must be almost one o'clock,' Jill says, pushing back her sleeve to check her watch.

A few moments later, the ball slides right to the top, waits for a minute or two, then falls in one smooth drop. I think of Esme being catapulted into the air on the Ice Blast ride at Blackpool, then falling back to earth, loaded with lies.

The police may have warned them not to get in touch with me, but there's nothing I can do to stop them intruding into my thoughts, even though I fight it. If they have tried to contact me, I wouldn't know it. I haven't logged on to the computer since I returned from Manchester, and my mobile has been switched off. But they infiltrate every memory of Amy like weeds in a crack. When I try and picture her, Esme gets in the way, sly and precocious. Alive.

The Meridian stretches out in front of us, like a solitary

tramline. A sign says that it divides east and west, and marks the point from which the whole world takes its time. The official starting point of the new millennium. My stomach knots.

Two Japanese tourists ask me to take their picture, both of them with one foot either side of the line, straddling time. One of them stands behind the other and peers over her friend's shoulder.

Two become one.

The picture is blurry with camera shake but the tourists smile and thank me. As I walk on, I hear them ask somebody else to take the picture again.

'Come on,' says Jill, 'let's step over it.'

I take her hand and cross the line. As my foot touches the ground on the other side, I try and convince myself that I've stepped out of the darkness of the past. Moved into the dazzling light of a new world and time.

But the silver line is hard, horizontal. Capable of being crossed, but not bent or altered. Like the truth. Amy is missing on both sides of the line and I am a disgraced mother.

'I want to go home,' I say. 'I'm tired.'

There's a police car parked outside my house when we arrive. The door opens and Lois climbs out. She looks flushed and flustered.

'Thank God you're back,' she says quickly. 'We've been trying to get hold of you for hours.'

'My phone's switched off,' I say, frowning. 'Why? Oh God . . . it's Bishop, isn't it? The other prisoners have got to him too. Or he's had a heart attack or something. This can't be happening. It can't! He's got to be convicted!'

Lois steps towards me and takes my hand.

'It's not Bishop, Beth,' she says. 'The trial is still on course ... But there have been ... developments. She squeezes my hand. 'We think we've found Amy's body.'

I have waited so long to hear those words that I can only blink at her. Realisation seeps through me, like water into sand.

'What?'

'We've found a body,' Lois says, trying to be calm. 'We can't confirm that it's Amy's yet, but we're confident it is, seeing where we found it.'

'Where?' I wail. 'Where is she?'

'A body was discovered earlier ... under a classroom block at Amy's school.'

I let go of Lois's hand, push away Jill's outstretched arm, ignore their calls for me to go into the house. My steps are slow and uncertain, then quickly gather pace until I'm running as fast as I can down the road in the direction of the school.

'Beth!' Lois calls behind me.

I keep running. A stitch stabs at my ribs. As I turn the corner, there's a small group of people milling around the school gates, trying to peer through them.

'Oi! Do you mind?' one of them says as I barge by. 'We were here first.'

I shrug off the hand at my shoulder and pull at the gates. The two policemen on the other side shake their heads.

'There's nothing to see,' one of them says. 'You should all go home.'

'It's my daughter that's buried under there! You've got to let me in.'

The people behind me gasp and whisper, press in for a closer view. The gates clang and squeak as they strain against their hinges.

'Beth!'

I turn to see Lois getting out of the police car. She pushes through the crowd and tells the policemen to unlock the gates. When they step aside, I see the school behind them.

It hasn't changed much. It looks smaller, a little shabby, the paintwork flaking. The windows bloom with paintings of gaudy daffodils, giant eggs and malformed chicks. Shaky, mismatched letters spell out 'Happy Easter!' Alongside the words, a wide-eyed Jesus shoots up to heaven trailed by patchy glitter.

The single-storey classroom block is tucked away in a corner of the playground. Its windows are blanked out and a tarpaulin tunnel runs from the door to the police vans parked outside. I start to run towards it but Lois pulls me back.

'We can't go in there, Beth,' she says. 'It's a crime scene.' She takes my arm and steers me towards the school's main building. 'We can wait in the headmaster's office.'

'Is Brian there?'

'He was in Oxford for a meeting. But he's on his way back now.' She looks at her watch. 'Should be here pretty soon. Let's go in and wait, shall we?'

I stare at the classroom block, willing myself to see through the walls but scared of what I might witness if I could. I imagine men in white protective suits and face masks carefully sifting layers of rubble, the pop of flash bulbs recording every stage.

I remember receiving a letter from the headmistress explaining that the classroom had to be built to relieve overcrowding. She regretted that it meant the loss of a small part of the playground but was sure that parents would understand the need for it, and reassured us that the benefits would be felt by everyone at the school.

Amy was excited about it as it was going to be her form room. She never even saw it completed. When they broke up for the Christmas holiday, the block was nothing more than muddy trenches surrounded by wire fencing, hazard signs and cement mixers. A ready-made grave.

I sink to the ground.

'Oh God! Look!'

My hand shakes as I point at the trail of large multi-coloured footprints painted on the ground for children to hop on. They weave across the playground, doubling back on themselves before disappearing under the classroom block.

'Just like he said,' I cry.

'Who?' Lois looks around, confused.

'Ian Poynton,' I say. 'He saw coloured footprints. Plates of meat, he said. Feet.' I turn to her, frantic with confusion. 'Could ... could he have been right all along after all? Or ... maybe he was one of Bishop's pack too?

'I can't say anything about him being psychic but it's very unlikely he was part of the gang, Beth. He would only have been around fifteen at the time. Besides, he didn't grow up around here. He's from Weston-super-Mare, I believe.'

'Another victim then. It's the only explanation. How else would he have known where Amy was buried?'

My body freezes. Over Lois's shoulder I see Amy's ghost appear beside the plastic tunnel. She stands there, pale, insubstantial, motionless as mist. Her spirit free now that her body has been released from its grave. My gaze fractures with tears. She rocks backwards and forwards with her thumb in her mouth and a hunted look in her eyes.

There's a shape behind Amy's ghost. A woman. And a man. I blink and wipe the tears away. I see Libby and Harding. I look again. It isn't Amy's ghost. It's Esme, living and breathing. Real.

'I . . . I don't understand,' I sob. 'What are they doing here?'

The three of them are ashen and silent, their eyes fixed on the ground. Harding looks up and sees me. He says something to Libby and Esme, and ushers them back into the plastic tunnel, then gestures to Lois that she should take me into the school's main entrance.

Lois grips my arm.

'It wasn't Ian who told us to look here,' she says quietly. 'It was Esme.'

I turn to her, stupefied.

'No . . . I . . . don't . . . She can't . . . '

*

Helped by a policeman, Lois half carries, half pushes me towards the school's reception. I'm numb as they guide me along a corridor and lower me on to a sofa in the head-master's office. The seat sags beneath me. I feel as if I will never stop, that I'll keep on sinking to the floor, into the earth, a grave of my own.

The policeman pours me a glass of water from the bottle on the head's desk and tries to put it in my hand. I'm shaking so much I can't grip it. When I finally take it, the water spills to the floor. I lean back and rub my eyes.

'I don't understand,' I say. 'How did she know?'

Lois sits beside me; the seat sags further.

'Esme had one of her fits earlier,' she says. 'Her worst yet, apparently. When she came round, she kept scream-ing at Libby to get her out. Libby thought she meant out of the flat and tried taking her for a walk, but Esme kicked off again, screaming about not being able to breathe, telling her to dig. *Under the classroom.* Libby told Harding. He told the Met. They gave the order to start digging.'

'But—'

'DI Harding was quite shaken by it,' Lois says. 'Not her fit – he didn't see that – but Esme's insistence. He said it was so overwhelming . . . the details she gave so . . . compelling, so specific, he couldn't ignore it.' She rubs her eyes as if she's been dazzled. 'And the details were bang on too.'

'Such as?'

'What part of the site to dig up. The colour of the carpet the body was found in. That it was buried face down.'

My hand flies to my mouth.

'Oh God! Amy.'

Lois pulls me towards her; my sobs soak into her shoulder.

'I'm sorry,' she says, 'but you always said you wanted to know.'

'It's all I've wanted for the last ten years. Now that little monster has robbed me of even this tiny crumb of comfort.' My fingers clench into a fist.

'We'd never have found Amy's body without Esme.'

'That's what I mean,' I say, pummelling the sofa. 'Instead of ... the relief of finally finding Amy, I'm just bloody angry at Esme for keeping up this cruel pretence. Can't she see how much it hurts? Why didn't she just tell us this before? Why won't she tell us how she knew?'

'As far as she's concerned, she has.' Lois shakes her head. 'We're looking into every possible alternative angle. But right now we're so stumped, reincarnation is looking like the most straightforward explanation.' She sighs. 'God, I never thought I'd hear myself say that.'

I push her away.

'No. It's ridiculous that you're even thinking it,' I say, fury making my voice sound unfamiliar. 'There's an explanation right under your nose. You've got to find it.'

A police car edges through the school gates and pulls up outside the main entrance. Brian climbs out of the back. His face is haggard, his shoulders stooped, as if the core of him is being sucked out bit by bit. A policeman escorts him into the school. A few moments later Brian is in my arms, whatever he's saying lost in anguished tears.

I hear him gasp and pull away. I look up. He's seen Esme and Libby as they walk across the playground. He moves to the window, slowly, as if under a spell. There's a desperate tenderness to the clawing of his fingers at the glass.

'Amy,' he says. 'Oh God, it's Amy.'

He didn't see Esme in Manchester, didn't want to in case he lashed out at her. The full impact of her resemblance to Amy rocks him on his heels. She looks up at the window. Her eyes widen and her mouth drops open.

'Daddy!' she squeals, and runs towards the school's entrance.

Brian backs away from the window and turns to me, trembling. Footsteps slap in the corridor outside. The door bursts open and Esme throws herself at Brian.

'Daddy! I missed you!' she cries.

His hand slowly reaches down to touch Esme's head.

'Amy,' he says, then pulls the girl closer.

Libby stands at the door, sobbing.

'She's gone,' she moans. 'My baby's gone.'

I take a fistful of Esme's hair and pull her away from Brian.

'How did you know where my daughter was buried? No more tricks, you sick little bitch. I want the truth!'

Esme screams and kicks at me.

'Beth! Let her go!' Libby yells. 'You're hurting her.'

'*I'm* hurting *her*?'

Lois prises my hand from Esme's hair and pulls me away. Esme runs back into Brian's arms. Libby stands in front of her, shielding her from me. The three of them walk slowly towards the door.

'You're not going anywhere!' I scream. 'Either of you. Not until I get some answers. Lois, don't let them get away.'

But she lets them go, closing the door behind them. My screams give chase.

'How did you know? How did you know?'

The door opens again and I fly towards it, crashing into Harding. He steers me back to the seat.

'You can't let them get away with this!' I cry. 'You can't. They've got the answers to all of this. I need to know.'

'Of course,' he says, his voice and calm and considered. 'We all do. But I think I know how we might sort this out, so we can get to the truth once and for all.'

The interview room at the police station is hot and stuffy. Light from windows with reinforced glass is trapped behind grey slatted blinds. Beyond them I can hear voices, footsteps, the clunk of car doors, sirens. They didn't use sirens when they brought us here from the school, but they made sure we travelled in separate cars. Libby and Esme weren't made to wear handcuffs, though, despite my insistence that they should.

Libby is thin-lipped as she listens to Harding. When he finishes, she blinks.

'Past-life regression therapy?' she says.

'That's right. It's where people are sort of hypnotised so they can access memories of previous lives.'

She laughs.

'You think I don't know what it is?' she says. 'After everything I've been through with Esme?'

'Oh, your research into reincarnation, you mean?' I say. 'The details you've picked up along the way to give your story some meat?'

'Not exactly,' Libby says tersely. 'I saw references to it when I was trying to get my head round the idea of Esme being the reincarnation of somebody else. But I didn't want to put her through it. I still don't.'

'I'll bet,' I say through gritted teeth.

'Meaning?'

'Meaning that we'll throw open the doors of her ugly little mind and, guess what? The cupboard will be bare. Nothing of Amy whatsoever.'

'If you feel like that, why are you set on doing it?' Libby says. 'You said you wanted to know how Esme knows the things she does.'

'I do.'

'Well, if you're so sure Amy's not inside her, why put her through it?' Libby stands with her hands on her hips, daring me to answer.

'Because,' I say, 'it's time this ridiculous ruse was scuppered for good. There'll be nowhere else for Esme to hide and she'll be exposed as the liar she is. Like you will be. With any luck you'll be put away for a long, long time and she'll go into care. Then you'll have some idea of what it's like to have your daughter snatched away from you.'

'Beth, please,' Brian says. 'This isn't helping.'

'Like you'd know anything about helping,' I say angrily.

He glares at me from across the room. Its grey walls are scuffed, the orange plastic chairs around the table the only colour.

'Let's try and keep this civil,' Harding says calmly, as he paces slowly around the room. 'This is a difficult situation. Best not to make it any worse than it needs to be.'

'Could it get any worse?' My laugh is hard and hollow.

'Oh, it could,' Libby says, nodding her head. 'And it *will*. So I won't give consent for Esme to have the therapy.'

'You can't do that!' I tell her.

'And *you* can't make Esme do it. She's *my* daughter. No surgeon would be allowed to operate on her without my say-so. This is no different.'

'It's completely different.' I turn to Harding. 'Isn't it, Inspector?'

Harding sighs.

'Libby, if your daughter needed an operation to save her life and you refused it,' he says, his tone level and reasonable, 'a surgeon could go to court to overturn your decision . . . I'm prepared to do the same.'

'You'd be a laughing stock,' Libby sneered.

'It's not unknown for the police to act on tip-offs from psychics. This is slightly different, but . . . there is a precedent.'

'That's ridiculous.' Libby's eyes are raw and angry. 'And anyway, Esme isn't dying!'

'No,' Harding agrees, 'but this might be the only way of solving this. What's more, it's the only way of finding out if Bishop was involved in Amy's murder or not. Justice is at stake here.'

'That's not as important as my daughter's welfare,' Libby argues defiantly, jabbing her finger into the air.

'It is to me,' I say. 'More so.'

Libby starts to weep.

'Don't make her do it, Beth. Please,' she cries. 'You said yourself how heartbreaking it is to have your daughter taken away. If Esme does this . . . she'll be gone for good. I just know it . . . My little girl will be lost.'

I try to shut her words out, but they burn into me.

Harding looks at me and then at Libby.

'Why don't we let Esme decide? I'll get the therapist to explain it to her thoroughly, answer any questions she might have . . .'

'You're not using Ian Poynton, are you?' I ask. 'He's not exactly impartial.'

'No, although we've still found nothing to link him with Libby or Esme or to prove he's a fraud.'

'Of course you haven't.' Libby throws her hands up. 'Because we don't who he is.'

'He can't do it anyway,' Harding continues. 'He's not trained. But I've found someone who is. Ingrid Williams. She's a very experienced qualified psychotherapist and hypnotist. Highly respected. Esme will be in safe hands.'

'Does this Ingrid know what all this is about?' I say, shifting in my seat. 'I don't want her influencing Esme, leading her on.'

'She knows the basics,' Harding explains. 'No names or specific details but she understands the sensitivity of the case and has agreed to proceed on one condition.'

Libby and I both cock our heads.

'That neither of you are in the room at the time ... Apparently it's normal practice for one of the parents to sit in with the child. It seems the child's past life experiences are somehow tied up with the parents' issues in the here and now. I told her that could get in the way this time, given the circumstances. So she agreed it should just be Esme and herself.'

'Where will this happen?' Libby asks. 'I'm not doing it at Beth's.'

'Here at the station, in the suite we use for rape victims. There's a special room for kids with props like soft toys and murals to help them relax and tell us what we need to know. There's a two-way mirror so we can see what's going on. I'll watch from behind there with Libby. Beth, Brian and Lois will watch in a different room via cameras. Agreed?'

'Yes,' I say without hesitation.

Harding and I look at Libby. She's got her arms folded and her eyes narrowed.

'Libby?' Harding's eyebrows arch.

'Agreed,' she says reluctantly. 'If Esme says she's okay with it.'

'I'm sure she will.' Harding gives a reassuring nod of his head. 'She seems keen to sort this out once and for all. Ingrid will have a chat with Esme on her own to put her at her ease. If she's still okay with it, we'll go from there.'

16

She's a tall, large woman. Not fat. Just big-boned. She fills the shorter stretch of the L-shaped sofa in the interrogation room, her oatmeal suit and russet blouse complementing the orange sofa cover. Wide brown eyes peer from behind large round glasses, her broad face made broader by mousy hair pulled back into a thick bun speared with a silver pin.

She's a mix of wise and watchful tawny owl, and sturdy, no-nonsense brick wall. Esme will never get past her.

Esme sits on the longer stretch of the sofa, smiling and cooperative, seemingly oblivious to the danger she's in. I pull my chair closer to the screen. Brian does the same. The hand he puts in mine is hot and sweaty. He's like an earnest student, eager to please. Ready to suck everything in. To become a stronger believer. I let go of his hand.

'Ready, Esme?' Ingrid says.

Esme nods.

'Good girl. Okay. Make yourself comfy.'

Esme lies stretched out on the sofa and pulls a cushion under her head. Ingrid clears her throat and shuffles closer to her.

'I want you to imagine you're on a giant leaf on a lily

pond. Like a big frog, sitting in the middle of the water, nice and dry, nice and safe . . . Feel the sunshine warm on your back . . . Hear the water lapping around you . . . See the little flashes of sunlight on the water.

'Now, let the flashes merge together to become one great dazzling blaze of light. And as they do, you feel your-self drifting away . . . very slowly. You're moving closer to the light . . . nice and slowly.

'You're surrounded by the light. It's warm and bright – so strong you feel you could walk upon it . . . I want you to stand up and step off the lily pad and on to the light. You feel safe and happy. You're walking slowly . . . into the past. And when you get to somewhere you want to stay, sit down and rest, breathing gently . . . gently . . .

'Now . . . tell me what you see . . . what you feel and hear.'

I'm sitting on a swing in the playground – but I'm not swinging. Just using my feet to rock backwards and for-wards. Dana's on the swing next to me, getting higher and higher.

She says she likes All Saints more than the Spice Girls and reckons they're better and prettier. As if.

'You're only saying that because you're jealous of me for being more like Baby Spice than you are,' I tell her. 'You're too ugly and clumsy to be in *any* girl group, let alone my one!'

I shouldn't have said that, I know. She's my friend. My best friend. I just wish she didn't have a grandad. But that's mean, as I have a grandad so why shouldn't she? Mine doesn't do what hers does, though. He's not a Grey Wolf.

It's not Dana's fault. Or mine. Dana says it's just the way it is. The way it has to be. I suppose she's right but I really wish she wasn't.

I've been on at her again about telling someone about the Grey Wolf. He's coming to pick us up a bit later on so I can have a sleepover at Dana's. We're going to stay up late and watch the fireworks on the telly. We might even see them from her balcony as her flat is on the tenth floor! And we'll get pizza and Coke and sweets. All that'll be great . . . It's what happens after that I don't like. It's . . . horrible and . . . and it hurts.

I don't want to go there . . . I want to tell someone to make it stop. It's Millennium Eve and Miss Clapton said that whatever you're doing on Millennium Eve sets the tone for the rest of the year. If I don't tell someone about the Grey Wolf *tonight*, I'll be doing what he wants for the whole year. For the next thousand years.

Dana jumps off the swing. She says she's going to start her own girl group and it will be better than mine. *She'll* be on *Top of the Pops*, she reckons, and *I'll* just be watching on telly.

She couldn't get a group together. Not enough people like her.

'People only play with you because you're with me.' I shouldn't have said that either, but it's true. 'And even if you *did* get a group together, it wouldn't be as good as my group because *I* won't be in it.'

She says that's *why* hers will be better and that she never wants to see me again.

'Suits me!' I say. I jump off the swing and start walking out of the playground.

Dana calls out after me.

'Amy, where are you going? Stop! We've got to wait here for Grandad.'

'I'm going home,' I shout. 'I'm not coming to yours tonight.'

'But you have to! It's all been arranged. Your mum and dad are going out.'

She's right. But if I tell them about the Grey Wolf they won't go to the party and will stay in with me instead. Maybe they'll tell the police about Dana's grandad and have him taken away.

'I'm never coming to your house again. Ever!'

I hear Dana laugh.

'Yes you will. Tonight. You'll have to. Your mum and dad will make you.'

I turn back to look at her. She gets back on the swing again and sways gently.

'See you in about five minutes, Amy,' she says in a sing-songy way. 'I'll wait here. Don't be long. You know Grandad doesn't like waiting.'

I stomp off home. I take the short cut through the railings instead of going all the way to the gates closest to my house. The lights are on at home even though it's not dark yet, so Mum must be doing her cleaning. She likes to see she's got every little bit of dirt up. I fumble in my pocket for my front door key, then remember I didn't take it with me. No need. Mum and Dad would be in tomorrow when I got back from Dana's.

I ring the bell and wait . . . Maybe Mum's got the radio on. I ring again. Longer. I put my head against the door and listen. I can't hear the Hoover. Or a radio. I lean on the doorbell. One long ring then five short ones. I peer through the letter box and call out to Mum. I see her coming down the stairs. She's got her dressing gown on and her hair wrapped up in a towel.

When she opens the door her skin is glistening and there are wet footprints on the carpet. She looks surprised. She asks me if I've left something behind, says she thought she put everything I needed in the overnight bag she gave to Dana's mum earlier.

'I'm not going to Dana's,' I say.

I brush past her, head for the kitchen. Tell her I need a drink. I open the fridge and ask if I can have a Coke and something to eat.

Mum stands in the hallway, halfway between the kitchen and the front door. She pulls her dressing gown around her, does up the belt.

'What do you mean, you're not going?' she says. 'Are Dana's parents ill or something?'

No, I want to say, her parents aren't ill but her grandad is sick. The sickest man in the world. But I can't tell her. I'm not brave enough. She just won't believe me. She won't.

'We had a row,' I say. 'I don't want to be anywhere near her.'

She asks what we rowed about and laughs when I tell her. It's not a proper laugh though. It's the same sort of laugh she has when I tell her I'm too tired to help do the dishes or go to Tesco. Like a snort. A bit angry.

She walks down the hall and comes into the kitchen. She takes a can of Coke from the fridge, hands it to me and closes the fridge door.

'You're eating at Dana's tonight. Her mum's got everything in. And me and your dad are going out.'

I open the can of Coke.

'I'll be okay here. I'll be good. I'll just watch the telly.'

She tells me I can't stay here on my own.

'I'm ten years old!' I say.

'Exactly.'

She puts her hand on my shoulder.

'Off you go, love,' she says. 'Hurry up back to the playground or you'll miss Dana.' She looks out of the window. 'It's not dark yet, so you'll be fine. I'd take you over there myself but by the time I get dressed, Dana's grandad will have gone.'

'Good,' I say.

She tries to steer me towards the front door. I push back against her.

'Amy, come on!' she says. 'I don't have time for this. My bath's getting cold and I've still got stacks to do around here, including getting your dad's dinner, wherever *he* is . . .'

'No, don't make me go. Please.'

She says I have to. I can't go mucking people about. All

the plans have been made. Dana's mum has bought food especially. The cab to the party is booked and they can't not go as it's too important to Dad's business. And how often does she get to go out anywhere these days?

'You could find someone to sit with me,' I say.

'Oh, I *see*,' she says. 'You expect people to drop every-thing at the last minute on the biggest party night of the year? Of the century? And all because you've had a tiff over the Spice Girls? I don't think so, Amy. I didn't bring you up to be selfish.'

She's about to open the front door. I put my foot against it . . . Tell her I don't want to go. She says I'm going, like it or not. Tantrums don't cut it with her. I'm old enough to know better.

Her mouth is all tight and her cheeks are twitchy. If I tell her about the Grey Wolf now she'll feel sorry for me and be angry with him instead. I won't have to go to Dana's.

'But he touches me,' I say in a whisper. 'The wolf. Her grandad.'

She steps away from me. Quickly. Like I've hit her.

Suddenly she doesn't look like my mum any more. Her face is all long and stretched and her mouth is just a big 'O', like the winners on *Stars in Their Eyes* when they can't believe they've won.

When they can't believe it.

'What did you say?' Mum says. Her voice is shaking as much as her hands. I've never seen her so upset. 'No. This . . . this can't be happening.' She puts her hand to her forehead. Looks at me. She's dazed and blinking, like she's just woken up. 'It . . . just can't. Not again. That's . . . not fair. What have I done to . . . Why me?'

Maybe the Grey Wolf has been touching her too. Or maybe she just means why has a good mum like her ended up with such a nasty, naughty girl like me, who'd upset her so much just so she can get her own way.

'I didn't mean anything, Mum! Really,' I say. 'I just made it up! To get out of going to Dana's.'

Mum turns away from me mechanically and walks quickly up the stairs. I hear the bathroom door slam, the click of the lock.

She's always got mad at me for lying, but never quite this bad. I feel stupid for telling her. Why *would* she believe me? It sounded so silly when I said it. It sounded like a lie.

I'm standing at the bottom of the stairs. I don't know what to do – go to the park or go up to her and say sorry for lying and making her angry. I tiptoe up the stairs and stop on the landing.

I hear a crunch in the bathroom. Like a glass or something breaking. I hear her crying and muttering something about lies and not being a good girl.

'I hate you,' Mum says, over and over again.

There's a tinkle of broken glass. It can't be the toothbrush mug, as there's only one in the bathroom and I've already heard that break. It has to be the mirror.

I'm too upset to cry. My mum hates me. I shouldn't be here . . . she doesn't want me to be. I don't want to be either . . . not if she doesn't love me any more.

I go back down the stairs. Mum's words get louder. Her tears get louder too, so it's hard to make out everything she's saying. But I catch bits of it. There's something about Sunday school, the love of God being painful and wrong. About history going round and round. About vicious circles.

I open the front door. I remember the way Mum's face looked as we stood on this exact spot just a few moments before. It wasn't like the winner of *Stars in Their Eyes* . . . It was more . . . more like she'd seen a ghost.

I run across the road, slip through the gap in the park railings and leg it as fast as I can to the playground.

Dana isn't there. No one is. It's just me.

I don't want to go to Dana's. I can't go home. If I'd been clever I would have grabbed my key from the table in the hall and let myself in once Mum and Dad had gone to the party. Too late now. Maybe I'll go back later and see if they've left a window open or something. You never know.

I sit on the swings for a bit, thinking about Mum. She was so angry with me. Her and Dad have rows sometimes but she never looks like she did just now. Mum and Dad never seem to really make up when they argue. I hope me and Mum can. And I hope she doesn't tell Dad about me lying about Dana's grandad, or he'll kick off at me too. There's enough arguing in our house as it is, usually Mum and Dad rowing about me.

Sometimes I wonder what they were like before they got married. I know they worked together making up adverts. Mum did the drawings and Dad the words. Like the people who wrote the picture books I read when I was younger. If they'd written a book, Mum would have drawn a princess in a fairy castle looking out for a prince. And Dad would write a story where they fell in love for ever and ever and had a wedding with white horses and a glass carriage.

Once, Mum showed me where she lived before she married Dad. It was a flat above a launderette in Finsbury Park. I didn't like it much. It was grey and dingy. Mum said all she could smell when she lived there was soap and steam but that didn't mean she felt clean.

We used to pass Dad's old flat on the way to the cinema in Brixton. It was really cool. It was a fire station before it became flats, and it had big windows and glossy red drainpipes. Dad told me he had a blue flashing light in the front room and a doorbell that sounded like sirens. Mum called it a lad's pad. Dad looked sad whenever we went past it.

He looks sad a lot – most of the time actually. When we play draughts or watch television or when Mum goes on about me changing schools and how they have to push me harder.

Even if I do well she seems disappointed. No wonder she went mad just now. Me lying to her, on top of everything else, like *only* getting seventy-nine per cent in my end-of-term maths test. *Only.* I was top of the class! She always wants more. It's the same with her cleaning the house – there's no pleasing her. Things can always be whiter or shinier.

She makes me go to every class and activity going. They're meant to be fun but sometimes I reckon she just doesn't want me around. It's like a different kind of detention. She says she wants me to be exposed to as many influences as possible. Broadening my horizons, she calls it. She says that her job as a mother is to make me the best I can be. Which doesn't include making up lies about my best friend's grandad so I can get out of doing something I don't fancy doing and mucking up everybody else's plans while I'm at it.

I shouldn't have said anything. Dana was right.

I get off the swings and climb up the slide. My feet make the metal squeak.

There's a dog!

It dashes out of the bushes and runs towards me. It's a black and white bull terrier and it's wagging its tail but not in a happy way. I can see its teeth as it barks. They look sharp and shiny.

I sit at the top of the slide and growl back at the dog. That makes it angrier and it tries to climb the slide. I look around for the owner but no one's around. It's just me and the dog. It sits at the bottom of the slide. I shoo it away but that just makes it bark again. I can't outrun it. I have to wait.

It's getting darker. I'm getting cold and scared. I can see car headlights through the tall hedge along Camberwell New Road. And a number 36 bus. Its windows are all misted up. I wonder if the people on the top deck can see me even though I can't see them. I wave, and that makes the dog start barking again.

If Dana hadn't been so horrible . . . if I hadn't tried to be clever and tell Mum . . . if she'd believed me . . . I wouldn't be here now. Trapped and alone. On New Year's Eve. On *Millennium Eve*. This is how it's going to be for the rest of my life.

There's someone in the alley leading to the One O'Clock Club, but it's dark and I can't tell who it is. They move into the glow from a lamp post and stop. It's a man. He's got a woolly hat on and he's eating chips from a Kentucky Fried Chicken bag. The dog looks up and sniffs.

'Help me!'

He walks towards the slide and smiles. He's got greasy lips.

'Hello, Amy,' he says. 'Looks like you've found a new friend there.' He points at the dog and walks closer. 'Looks like you need the help of an old one.'

He takes his hat off. It's Mr Palmer from the mobile library, one of the Grey Wolf's friends. He's the one who likes me dressed in a tutu but with no tights or knickers on.

'I'll get the dog away from you,' he says. 'My car is just around the corner.'

It's too cold to wait for the dog to move, and even if it wanders off it might come back. Mr Palmer can save me. Save me from a year – a thousand years – of being alone and angry.

The dog growls as he gets closer. Mr Palmer waves a piece of chicken, then throws it to the far end of the playground. The dog chases after it and Mr Palmer walks to the slide. He puts his arms out.

I lean towards him, but he drops his arms and turns his back to me. He tells me to get on his shoulders and wrap my legs around his neck. Quickly! The dog's nearly finished the chicken, he says. I mustn't scream or shout or I'll only get the dog excited again.

I do as he says, like I always have. It's better that I do.

He tells me to grip my thighs tight around his neck and takes my wrists. I look back to make sure the dog isn't following us. It's still snuffling around, looking for more chicken.

He carries me out of the playground, through the alleyway, towards a green car. He unlocks the doors, puts me in the back seat and gets in beside me.

He says his little damsel in distress is safe and sound now. He's the prince rescuing Rapunzel and he deserves a reward.

His hand slides towards me, but then he stops and sighs and sits back in his seat. He says that everyone's doing something special to celebrate Millennium Eve, something different. We should too. He drums his fingers on my knee. This time he wants it to be different. This time he wants me to fight him. He puts a hand around my neck.

'I want to feel you squirm.'

He gets out of the car and locks the door behind him. He takes something out of the boot. When he gets back in, there's a length of rope in his hands. There's something else too . . . some stretchy straps, like the ones Dad uses to hold things on the bike rack. I wriggle and kick as he ties my hands behind my back.

'That's a good girl,' he says, and wraps the straps around my ankles.

He chuckles when I scream.

I'm bundled to the floor of the car . . . trapped between the back and front seats. He stuffs a dry chamois leather in my mouth . . . squeezes through to the front seat. He starts the car.

I scream, choke . . . fight for air.

I can't breathe . . .

I try to spit the cloth from my mouth but choke even more. I taste oil and dirt. The cloth clogs my throat.

I . . . can't . . . breathe!

Can't breathe!

My heartbeat is hard . . . loud. My eyes feel like they're bursting out of my head . . . Puke spurts from my nose. I can feel it in my throat. It's hot and thick and I can't swallow it but I can't spit it out. It keeps on coming . . . thicker . . . blocking me up. Drowning . . . drowning my breath.

Street lamps whiz by. They're all hazy . . . hazy and flickering. Fading. Fading . . . away.

It's dark and quiet . . .

I'm cold . . .

I'm going up in the air . . . Slowly. Like a balloon at a party. Now I'm shooting up, like a rocket. Whoosh! Right up into the sky. It's getting even darker . . . even colder.

I can feel something soft and light falling around me. It's see-through too, a bit like a veil.

When I look down, I can see the earth, way, way below me. It looks so tiny. Now it's getting bigger and bigger. I'm zooming in. Fast. I can see London, like at the start of *Mary Poppins*. I'm getting closer and closer.

There's Mr Palmer.

He takes my body from the back seat and puts it in the boot of his car. He has to bend my knees to make me fit, and covers me up with a tartan rug. He weighs the rug down with a toolbox at one end and a shovel at the other.

He drives for a while, then stops outside a lock-up garage. He unlocks the door, pulls the car into the garage, closes the door and walks away.

He's back. He's wrapping me up in a roll of red carpet. Now he's gone again. I'm left there. On my own.

Now he's driving, to . . . to the council depot. He puts me in the back of his mobile library van. Someone asks about the carpet and he says it's to stop the kids getting the van messy with their muddy feet like they do every winter. And to stop them slipping. He says he needs it even more this year as one of the schools on his route is a bit of a building site.

We're driving along a road . . . the road to school. The school gates are open even though term hasn't started so the builders can get in. I can't see any police, though . . . Maybe they only look for good girls.

The Grey Wolf's there! He walks across the playground and I think he's coming to help Mr Palmer, but he goes into the school reception instead. They don't even say hello.

There are teachers in the staffroom. They're drinking coffee and flipping through notes. Planning lessons and trips I won't get to do. But they look so serious, I know they're talking about me too.

'So much for a happy new year, eh?' Mr Palmer says to a couple of them when they come out for a cigarette. He climbs out of the van. 'Any news?' He sighs and shakes his head when they say no. 'Fingers crossed they find her safe and soon, eh?'

He goes into the school and comes out half an hour later with Mr Slater, the head of English. Mr Palmer has a sheet of paper in his hand. He tells Mr Slater he'll have all the books he's asked for this term.

He pretends to do paperwork in the van and shuffles books about. The first one he takes off the shelf and puts into a box is *The Man Who Didn't Wash His Dishes*. He's still there as the teachers leave the school. I try and call to them but no words come out.

The school playground is dark now. He pulls me out of the back of the van and into a trench where the new classroom will go. He picks up a builder's spade . . . digs a hole in the trench . . . He's putting me into it. Face down.

No! . . . No!

Soil and stones falls on top of me. It pitter-patters on the carpet . . . I feel really heavy.

Let me out! Let me out!

He's gone. It's quiet again. Dark and damp.

Now it's the morning after he buried me. There's a builder wearing a dayglo yellow waistcoat and a white plastic helmet. He pours in concrete – all over me. I can't see anything any more but I feel like I'm inside something. It's all around me. I don't mean the earth and concrete. Whatever it is, it's warm and wet and it's beating like . . . like being in a heart . . .

Esme wraps her arms around herself, shivering. Ingrid looks over to the mirror on the opposite wall. She's pale, shocked – but there's a glint of pride in her eyes too.

'Okay, Esme. I want you to imagine a great big smiley, happy orange sun in the distance, getting bigger and bigger as it comes closer . . . warmer and warmer. Smile getting brighter . . . and happier. Feel its warmth. Reach out to-wards it.'

Esme's hand reaches out.

'Feel it on your hands, your legs,' Ingrid says. 'Feel the way your muscles relax.'

Esme wriggles on the sofa.

'You're warm. Comfortable . . . safe. Drifting, down . . . down, gently, gently . . . Feel the sofa all around you, supporting you, holding you . . . Safe.'

Esme opens her eyes and stretches. She sits up and squints at the mirror. Yawns. Smiles.

'Well done, Esme,' Ingrid says. 'I think we'll leave it there for the moment.'

Lois seems to move in slow motion as she switches the camera off and shuts down the TV monitor. The room is silent. I stare at nothing, unblinking, feel myself grow faint and force myself to breathe. Short gasps of air collide with quiet sobs.

Brian cries into his hands, wipes his nose on the cuff of his shirt. Lois passes him a tissue from a box on the table, then takes one out for me.

She thinks I'm crying because I believe what Esme has said, but I'm not. I'm crying because something *like this* did happen to Amy. Because Esme is still making things up – about the way my daughter died. About me.

I want Brian to reach out and touch me, to hold me, but I'm scared that if he does, I'll shatter into a thousand tiny pieces. The look he gives me has the same effect.

'She came back,' he whispers. 'Amy came back. To tell you . . . about that . . . And you . . . you . . . told her to go back to the playground . . . to him.'

I jump as he thumps the table then falls across it, sobbing.

'What were you thinking?' he bawls. 'How could you do it? Turn her away when she was asking for help?'

I reach to put my arm around him.

'Brian, I . . .'

He leaps away from me, staggers and falls to the floor.

'Keep away from me, you . . . monster!'

He crawls to a corner of the room and sits there, hunched up, rocking himself.

'Brian, please. How can you even begin to believe this is true?' I cry. I try to stand up but my legs give way and I slump back into the chair. '*Any* of it? Let alone that she came back and I ignored those . . . those things she supposedly said. It's all lies! Every last word of it. Why can't you see that?'

I look across the table at Lois. She looks shaken, circumspect; she's scraped the polish from all of her fingernails and the skin around them is raw and bleeding.

'Oh God,' I groan, my fists tightening. 'You believe her too, don't you?'

'Well,' she says quietly, without looking into my eyes, 'some of the details are bang on.'

'Oh, you've got proof Amy came back, have you?' I cry. 'Eye witnesses? CCTV footage?'

'No, although if she came back through the gap in the railings like she says—'

'Like *Esme* says!'

Lois nods.

'Like Esme says, then she wouldn't have shown up on the cameras by the gates on the main road anyway.'

'Oh God. I can't believe this is happening.' I thrust my arms out to her, my palms up, pleading.

Lois tilts her head to one side. 'Esme's right about a few other things too.'

'Such as?' I ask, defiantly.

'Palmer did have a green car. It's something we checked when we were trying to put a case together.'

'A coincidence,' I say. 'Or a lucky guess.'

'Then there's the way she says Amy died.' Lois thumbs her pages of notes. 'We're still awaiting formal confirmation of cause of death – not easy to work out after such a long time – but the initial findings haven't identified any signs of injury or attack. So choking is as likely as anything else.'

'Or being strangled.'

There's a pause.

'Or being strangled,' Lois says, eventually. 'I have to say, it makes a kind of sense in some ways, but in others . . .' She screws her eyes up and shakes her head.

'It's simple really,' I say, glaring at her. 'Any *real* detective would be able to work it out. Dana knew more than she said in her memoir and told Esme about it. Mystery solved.'

Lois raises her eyebrows and sighs.

'I have considered that,' she says. 'It's possible, of course, but . . .'

'But what?'

'Dana was scared of Esme, of who she thought she was,' Lois says. 'Too scared to confront her directly and make her talk about things she wanted to forget.'

'As far as we know.' I sit back in my chair, arms folded, daring her to challenge me.

'As far as we know,' Lois says reluctantly.

Brian stops rocking and looks up. His eyes are red and raw.

'But . . . but what about the things Esme told Beth that aren't actually included in Dana's testimony?'

I turn to him, dumbfounded.

'Like what?'

'Well,' he says, 'Dana doesn't say anything about Amy being stung by the jellyfish on Zante and me peeing on her foot to neutralise the sting, does she? Or about roller-blading down the tunnels at Elephant and Castle. And what about all that stuff about where we lived before we were married? And the broken bathroom mirror . . . I remember that . . . You said you'd done it when you were cleaning.'

'I *did*! It was an accident!'

My mind is racing.

I think of the other discrepancies that Brian mentioned. I've read Dana's A to Z a thousand times but I overlooked those missing details. There are other gaps too, I realise. Like Esme knowing that I drink my coffee black and used to eat grapefruit for breakfast. Like Amy wanting to have stripes like Bagpuss instead of chickenpox spots. I didn't notice before that they were missing. I was blinded by anger, grief and confusion.

'It doesn't mean what you think it does,' I say. 'That Esme is Amy. In fact it proves my point that Dana *did* talk to Esme about Amy. So she must have known what happened to Amy all along. Which means Esme did too!'

'And that would make Dana's testimony just a pack of lies,' Lois says slowly, scribbling on her notes. 'I wasn't aware of these discrepancies. You should have told us this earlier, Brian.'

He shakes his head.

'I didn't know I knew,' he says. 'It's only just dawned on me, now that we're looking for things that *aren't* there, rather than the things that *are*.'

Lois clears her throat and draws circles around the notes she's just made.

'Actually, I'm not so sure Dana *was* lying,' she says. 'Think about it. Why would she include so much detail about every aspect of her life, her friendship with Amy, their abuse and so on, but miss out really critical bits? She actually said she was going to tell all that she knew. *Every bloody bit*, she says at the start of her recording . . . I think she did tell us. She was at the end of her rope, wanting to make amends to Amy. If she knew *all* the details she'd have come clean. It was her last chance to be forgiven for keeping quiet about everything.'

'That's just guesswork,' I snap.

'No, it's *detective* work,' Lois responds. 'And besides, Dana must have hated her grandfather. She'd have given every single detail she had to incriminate him. If there was no truth in what she said, Bishop wouldn't have confessed at all, let alone so readily.'

Brian nods.

'So we're back where we started. The only explanation for Esme's account of what happened to Amy is that she *is* who she says she is.' He looks at me, his eyes alight with hate. 'So we have to believe what she says about coming home and you just running away from it and hiding in the bathroom. How could you? You're her mother! I can't believe it . . . The papers had it right all along: you're to blame for Amy's death.'

'No!'

'Yes!' The finger he points at me is like a dagger. 'All those years of playing the martyr. The heartbroken mother, grieving and wringing her hands. All just to hide your own guilt.'

He stops and catches his breath. Then his mouth freezes, open wide. Appalled. Realisation creeps across his face.

'You,' he whispers. 'It happened to you too, didn't it?'

'What did?'

'What Bishop was doing to Amy.'

My head no longer feels part of me and shakes of its own volition, only subtly at first, then faster, more furiously. I slam my hand on the table and jump to my feet.

'Don't be so bloody ridiculous, Brian!' My eyes dart around the room, trying to find something firm to hook on, something to hold me back from the edge. 'Do you think I'd have let Bishop touch me?'

'Not Bishop,' Brian sobs. 'Someone *like* Bishop. When *you* were a girl.' His voice grows stronger, more certain. 'That's what you meant when you said to Amy "not again" ... You didn't ask "why Amy?" You said "why me?"'

'No!' I thump the table again. 'I didn't say *any* of that. Esme made it all up, for Christ's sake!' I bury my head in my hands and scream, pace around the room. 'Why can't you see that this is all part of her game?'

'Because it's the truth.'

I snap my head up, wipe snotty tears from my cheeks.

'Oh, it's the truth, is it, Brian? Don't you think if I'd been abused as a kid I might have said something about it before now? To you, my husband and confidant? My one-time best friend who knew everything there was to know about me? Who used to love me for it? Or to the psychiatrist you were so insistent I went to see?'

'*Amy* didn't say anything!'

'She was a child.' I'm so exasperated I can barely muster the energy to argue any more. But I have to.

'Dana didn't say anything either,' Brian says. 'Not even when she was an adult.'

I can feel Lois staring at me, her eyes probing.

'It's not at all unusual for people who were abused as children to remain silent into adulthood.' Her voice is softer than it has been, more sympathetic, as if inviting my confidence. 'Some never speak up about it.'

'Oh God!' I stand in front of the wall, rest my head against it. 'I have nothing to speak up about.'

'It would explain a lot,' Brian says thoughtfully.

I turn around. He's nodding to himself, like some bloody TV detective on the scent of a crucial clue.

'She always was a bit——'

'She? You mean me? I am still here, Brian.'

'You . . . you were . . . I don't know . . . switched off.' He shudders. 'Cold.'

'You were always saying I was *too* emotional!'

'I meant in bed.'

My body recoils as if from a punch.

'Fantastic! This just gets better and better.' I bite my lip so hard I taste blood. 'Jesus, how is this happening to me? Ten years ago I went through every parent's worst nightmare. My child was taken from me. Vanished. Presumed dead . . . For ten years I've endured a living hell I wouldn't wish on anyone.'

I walk around the room, looking at Brian and Lois in turn, like a lawyer arguing a case in court.

'Then Esme turns up to really twist the knife. Ripping apart my memories of Amy one by one . . . *raping them* . . . destroying me. And when we finally learn the truth – due to my own efforts, I might add, seeing as the police have been no bloody use at all – the real perpetrator gets away and I'm the one who ends up in the dock. All on the say-so of some spiteful, evil girl with an eye on the main chance.'

I point at Lois.

'Esme's the one you should be locking up, not me. But, oh no, the dozy police, who couldn't find a fuck in a brothel, swallow her ludicrous story even though they've got no definite, unshakeable proof. Or have you? Go on; I'm all ears.'

Lois fiddles with the pen in her hand.

'Like I said, we're not saying there's a case to be answered here.'

'So I can walk out right now, can I?'

'Yes.'

'No!' Brian says. He pulls himself up and stands in front of the door with his arms folded. 'She's to blame. You've got to charge her.'

'I am *not* to blame,' I say, just inches from his face. I hold his gaze. 'And even if I was, I don't see what I could be charged with. Blame isn't a criminal offence, as far as I know. Besides, there is nothing to build a case on.' I step back from him and put on my coat. 'In some ways I wish there was,' I say. 'I can just imagine the press interest in a test case for reincarnation. Like proving the existence of Santa Claus. Good luck with that.'

'You're not going to let her go, are you?' Brian implores, leaning against the door.

'She's not under arrest,' Lois says simply.

'No,' I say, 'just under suspicion. And God knows that's nothing new for me.'

'But you can't let her go.' Brian clutches his head. 'You heard what Esme said!'

'That's the problem,' Lois says. 'It's what *Esme* said. Not Amy.'

'So *you* don't think Esme is Amy?' I say, with a nod of satisfaction.

Lois stares into me. I hold her gaze. She blinks.

'It's not a matter of what I think.' She puts her pen down. 'It's a matter of what I can prove.'

I walk towards the door.

'Stand aside, Brian,' Lois says.

Brian's eyes are hard with hatred.

'I never really knew you, did I, Beth? All those years and you ... What kind of a woman are you?'

I chew my bottom lip, hold back the tears.

'Clearly,' I say, 'I'm the kind of woman who'd marry a man foolish enough to believe this crap ... the kind who was so devoted to her child that she never gave up on her ... even though you, *her father*, had.

'The kind of woman who ... who, when she found out the truth, took your indifference as a sign of guilt and, in a moment of ... madness, accused you of being involved. Who knew in her heart that such a thing was absolutely ridiculous ... who didn't really need your denial to know she was wrong. The kind whose heart you have broken a thousand times over … but never more completely so than now.'

Lois gets up from the table and leads Brian away from the door.

As the door swings to behind me I walk along the corridor, out of the police station.

Seeing Esme and Libby in the car park stops me dead. They're about to climb into a police car when they see me too. Esme's mouth twitches, as if she's holding back tears or words. Or she might be suppressing a smile.

I shiver.

Libby's hand is shaking as she puts it on Esme's shoulder.

'Come on, Esme,' she says. 'Let's go.'

The girl stares at me a moment longer, then turns to get into the car.

'My name's Amy,' she growls. 'Get it? *Amy*.'

I walk on and don't look back. I blink at the bright sunshine and take the long route home, past Amy's school. Hazard tape criss-crosses the closed gates and there are still police cars in the playground.

I lean against the gates, grip the railings tight. A policeman on the other side walks towards me.

'Can I help you?' he says.

'Help?' I start to laugh. Hysterically. 'Of course you can't. You never could. No one can help me.'

He frowns and checks the padlock on the gate.

P is for padlock. Padlocks are for locking things in.

'I think you'd best be on your way,' the policeman says. 'There's nothing to see here.'

'No. That's right,' I say. 'There is nothing to see here.'

I let go of the railings and walk away. Nothing to see. Least of all the truth.

There are hordes of journalists outside my house. They rush at me as I approach. I'm buffeted by questions, blinded by camera flash, jostled and chased right up to my front door. I slam it shut behind me, breathing deeply, then run to the front room and close the curtains.

I am glad of the refuge of darkness, but the clamour outside filters through. The reporters keep calling my name and shout out questions about Amy and Esme.

Mrs Archer. Amy. Esme. Amy. Mrs Archer.

Esme.

Amy.

I feel like I'm going to explode, and put my hands to my head, holding it, keeping myself together.

I walk slowly towards the fireplace. Amy stares back at me from the photo on the mantelpiece. My reflection hovers in the mirror above. Above Amy. I'm like her ghost. An echo. Or she is like mine.

I grab the mantelpiece for support, feel something move beneath my hand. My stone. My talismanic stone. A symbol of love and hope and truth. I hold it in my palm. It used to be round and smooth, but now it feels jagged, as rough as pumice.

Mrs Archer.

Amy.

Mrs Archer.

The stone ricochets from the mirror. Cracks ripple.

Acknowledgements

Thanks to the many people who helped get me to the end of my rainbow.

Oli Munson at A.M. Heath, who set me on the Yellow Brick Road and helped me skip without tripping. Thanks also to all at Blake Friedmann.

Jemima Forrester at Orion – for waving your wand and making the world spin. Your insights made the editorial process magical – and the book so much better. And cheers to everyone at Emerald City (aka Orion) especially Kate Mills, Gaby Young, Louisa Macpherson, Jon Wood, Jane Selley and Laura Brett.

Marietta Crichton Stuart, Jean Dobson, Rebecca Howe, Suzanne & Betty Jansen, Gordon & Jill Johnston, Diane, Graham & Aiden May, Ant Parker, Kathryn Penn-Simkins, Mark Rogers, Marnie Searchwell, Dave Sellers, Claire Dissington & Albert, Chloe Thomas, Ginny Tym, Helen de Vane and Judith Weir – for making Kennington less like Kansas and more like Oz.

Jadzia Kopiel, life coach extraordinaire, who helped make sense of the tornadoes. Mark Russell and Richard Vessey for seeing off the lions and tigers and bears.

Everyone at NIBS writing group for their wicked

critical support. Sarah Evans whose endless readings and telling feedback pointed the way. Claire Collison and Sarah Waters for proving it could be done.

Polly Beale, Candy Bowman, Judith Buck, Jacques Christen, Len Dickter, Kerrie Finch, Lynne Foster, Rick Gem, Jo Hadfield, Paul Kitcatt, Maureen Landahl, Lorna, Patrick, Oscar & Maddie Mills, Jane, Laura & Elen Morgan, Consalvo Pellecchia, Nigel Rees, Andy Tough & Cathy Brear, Carolyn Yates – and all the other fully paid up members of the Lollipop Guild.

Bella, my fluffy outsized Toto.

My mum Joan, sister Sue and niece Eléna. There's no place like home.

My dad Jim – my Tin Man, Scarecrow and Lion all rolled into one. I miss you.

Boosie. Because, because, because, because, because . . . because of the wonderful things he does.

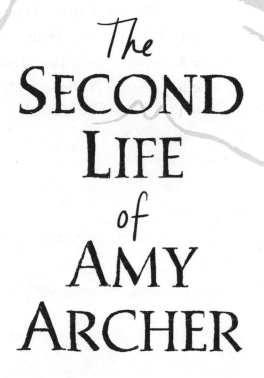

The
SECOND
LIFE
of
AMY
ARCHER

Reading Group Notes

A Note from the Author

The Second Life of Amy Archer took around a year to write but its DNA can be traced back to a story that featured on television around twenty years ago. It might have been *Crimewatch* but I can't be sure.

The story showed preparations for a reconstruction of a missing girl's last known movements. They didn't just show the 'missing girl' in the place where she'd last been seen; they went behind the scenes too, something I'd never seen before or since.

I watched a young girl – an actress with a resemblance to the missing girl and dressed in identical clothes – being briefed by police, who told her where to stand, what to do and so on, as if they were directing a film and telling a story. Which they were of course. Or part of a story anyway.

The image struck me. It was blurring the lines between fact and fiction; the reconstruction was simultaneously real and fake. The police were after information, so they could only show what they knew to be the facts; this girl, in those clothes, in that place at that time.

What happened after that was a mystery; a matter of conjecture. Any hunches the police might have had couldn't be portrayed for fear of polluting the memories they were hoping to jog.

It got me thinking about memory and perception. About how the actress might feel tracing the steps of someone who looked just like her, who'd been in that exact spot, in those exact clothes, and never been seen again.

I wondered how that might affect her. Would she grow up haunted by her missing twin? Perhaps she'd be anxious about being the 'type' who fell prey to paedophiles. If she had kids of her own when she grew up, would her doppelgänger experience make her more anxious about stranger danger? Then again, maybe she'd just forget about it all and go back to her friends at drama class. The acting experience might even end up on her CV.

And I wondered how it might affect the parents of the missing girl. The heartbreak of seeing 'their daughter' again. The tease of it. The hope.

Like a lot of writers, I kept a notebook where I jotted down thoughts, observations, phrases and the like, for use in the books I never seemed to get around to writing. I scribbled in my notebook: 'Police reconstruction. Fall out for lookalike/parents?'

But I took it no further.

The idea sat in the notebook for the best part of twenty years. I can't say I forgot about it completely as it sprang to mind every time I saw a police reconstruction on television or heard press reports of another missing child.

When I began taking my writing ambitions a little more seriously, I knew this was the idea that I wanted to run with. Here was the essence of a novel that would eventually become *The Second Life of Amy Archer*.

I knew when I started that this book would be about second chances, about loss and hope, memory and illusion, doubt and belief.

My story emerged from the gaps in between.

R.S. Pateman

In conversation with
R. S. Pateman

Beth's is a very strong, authentic female voice, and as a reader you are constantly in her head, living the nightmare right alongside her. Why did you choose to write a novel with a central female narrator?

I'm not much of a planner when I write. I tend to just jump off and see what happens and where I land. It makes for a chaotic – but interesting – writing process.

I knew the basic premise of the book, but didn't have much idea about the plot *or* how it would be told. However, writing in the first person has always felt right to me, so when I sat down to write the book, that's what came out.

Only it wasn't Beth's voice at first, but Libby's. And it was past tense, not present. I suppose the biggest surprise was that it wasn't Dana's voice that came to me. It was wondering about the effects of being a reconstruction double, like

Dana, which had sown the seed for the story after all.

Somewhere along the line though, I'd made a (unconscious) decision not to tell it from her point of view. And I don't know how or why Libby became the narrator. As Esme's mother she wasn't the obvious choice, which is probably why the first few thousand words didn't feel 'right'. So I tried doing a chapter in Beth's voice. That was better. I had a sense of Beth right away. When I tried the chapter in the present tense she became even clearer.

I jumped ship; the real drama was in Beth's head as Amy's grieving mother, rather than Libby's, the (possibly?) scheming fraudster. Seeing events through Beth's eyes made the action and its emotional fallout more immediate, intimate and intense. There was more scope – and greater ambiguity – in Beth's view of things.

There was never any doubt that in *this* novel my narrator would be a woman. That may well have its roots in my childhood. I grew up in a children's home run by my mum. We 'lived in', and as the residents and staff were all female, I was immersed in a world of female sensibilities for the first twenty-two years of my life.

What are the challenges and rewards of writing an unreliable narrator?

Again, my chaotic writing process meant I didn't know I was writing an unreliable narrator until I was two-thirds of the way through the first draft. I knew 'something' was missing and, after running through the story with a friend of mine, I changed the ending to give it more emotional punch. The new ending meant that Beth would have to become an unreliable narrator.

The challenge was in giving clues throughout the book so that the 'reveal' at the end wasn't completely out of synch with Beth's character. The clues had to be subtle but discernible, but not enough to be damning and irrefutable. There had to be scope for doubt and uncertainty.

The reward was pulling the rug out from under the readers' feet and, hopefully, surprising them and making them reappraise their perceptions of events and characters – just like Beth had to do in the light of Esme's claims.

'Faith makes fools of us all.' Does clinging to psychics help or hinder Beth?

Both. Faith can be a strength, but if it becomes so entrenched that it clouds judgement, then it can be a liability too. It's a matter of balance – not one of Beth's strong points perhaps!

What made you choose to leave the ending so deliberately ambiguous? How do you think readers will interpret it?

All the way through, I couldn't make up my mind if Esme was who she said she was or if she was making things up. I hoped it would become clear as the book went on. It didn't.

I wanted Esme to be Amy – but if she was, that would make Beth guilty. And if Esme *wasn't* Amy, that would make her a vicious little girl. I couldn't bring myself to point the finger at either of them, so left it open.

What's more, siding with Beth or Esme would also mean coming down one way or the other on the possibility of reincarnation. And that's another can of worms entirely.

The different ways readers have interpreted the ending are really interesting – and just as inconclusive! So far, the split is fifty–fifty on Beth being guilty. Or not.

Have you ever had any experiences in your past that informed your writing about psychics and the possibility of reincarnation?

I've been to see psychics umpteen times with varying degrees of 'success'. Some of the things I've been told were incredibly accurate – others were way off the mark. And while some of the things they've predicted have come true, others haven't. Yet.

I've had one or two 'spooky' things happen to me as well. Not ghosts, but odd occurences, sensations and déjà vu moments. Enough to leave me undecided on the possibility of certain phenomena like reincarnation.

As Jill says, it's all a matter of interpretation.

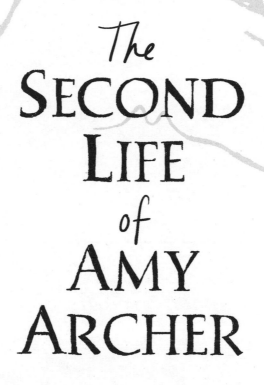

The Landscape of

The
SECOND
LIFE
of
AMY
ARCHER

There's very little in the novel that could be called autobiographical, but the location is one major exception. All of the four and a half novels I've written and stashed in my desk are set in Kennington, south-east London (and so is the desk).

Kennington has played a big part in my life – and my family's. My grandparents were from the area and lived there or thereabouts for most of their lives. In 1954 they moved into a new block of flats by the park. Four years later, my parents married and lived in the flat with my grandparents for a while. I live in the same flat now.

Sitting on my sofa seven floors up, all I can see is sky – and the top of a beautiful tree in Kennington Park. I've 'wasted' many hours looking at it, especially once its intricate architecture has been exposed by autumn gales.

I think of it as my family tree as it has been admired by three generations of my family (four, counting my niece Elena). It's a constant. I love that. It anchors me.

And when – purely by chance – the Art team

at Orion came up with the cover of the book, it seemed so right (and a bit spooky) that it should feature bare trees.

Kennington Park was south London's first public park. Like most parks, it suffered from years of maintenance and infrastructure cutbacks, vandalism and crime.

I used to walk my dog Bella here, and kept thinking someone should do something about improving and repairing the park. It turned out that someone was me; in 2002, I co-founded the Friends of Kennington Park. In 2011, after a lot of hard work by a lot of people, the park was awarded a Green Flag for excellence in a public open space.

Voluntary work with the Friends was rewarding – but it gave me the perfect excuse for not writing. A new playground for local kids? Or another chapter? No contest for a writer looking to procrastinate.

That changed when I saw two very successful local authors in separate TV interviews – both filmed in the park. They'd got on with their writing. It was time I did the same. And I did – but I had to leave Kennington to do it. The novel was written at a friend's house in the middle of nowhere in the Cotswolds, an experience and location which inspired my next book.

But I don't resent the time I spent on the park. Apart from helping to restore a great public space, I see it as a kind of prep for my writing career – it has given me ideas, experience of public speaking, developed research skills and nurtured the dogged determination any writer who wants to be published needs.

*S*ometimes *I see her in the roundabout's blur. Hear a giggle in the squeak of the slide. But she's not really there, of course. Nor are the slide or the swings. I have been robbed of the last place Amy was ever seen.*

One of the biggest changes brought about by the Friends is the new playground. It opened on the site of a derelict tennis court in 2005.

But it's not the playground Amy went missing from. *That* was the playground once found on the park's border with Camberwell New Road. My sister and I used to play there very happily when we visited our grandparents.

Fast forward forty-odd years and the site was considered too small, too detached from the rest of the park and too close to the road. It was a sad, neglected space and felt unsafe – not right for a playground but ideal for a crime scene.

So, after years trying to change people's perceptions and experience of the park, it turns up as a crime scene in my book. I hope the other Friends will forgive me!

The park's Arts and Crafts style café was opened in 1871, making it one of the earliest refreshment houses of its kind still in use today.

My granddad used to take my sister and me to the café for an ice cream after we'd been in the playground or watched the Punch & Judy shows that were put on regularly in the park in the 1960s. I've never liked Punch & Judy but I've always liked ice cream.

The café was closed for many years but

re-opened, quite by chance, at the same time the Friends group started. Moving the playground next to the café put children and parents at the heart of the park and changed its atmosphere for ever.

Beth's boycott of the café has everything to do with its location and nothing to do with its coffee! The squeals and laughter of children are too much for her to cope with over a cappuccino.

I'm not especially religious but I do like churches. Southwark Cathedral is not too far from home and has a lovely human scale – it doesn't overpower or intimidate but it still impresses. I never feel I *have to* whisper when I'm there – only that I *want to*.

I've found the peace of the cathedral's Harvard Chapel useful for mulling things over, like life, love – and writing. So when Beth needed somewhere to think, the Harvard Chapel was the only possible place for her to go.

As in the book, the word *veritas* (truth) appears three times in the Chapel – in the stained glass window, on a flag and in a stone on the ceiling. When I've been trying to untangle knots of plot (in my fiction and my life) those words have proved rather useful.

Maybe I just noticed them when I'd floated the idea I most wanted to pursue. Or maybe someone was trying to tell me something after all. Veritas? Who knows.

Designed by Sidney R J Smith, who was also responsible for the Tate Britain art gallery, the Durning library is one of the prettiest buildings in Kennington.

Like libraries all over the country, it is more than just somewhere to borrow books from. It's a vital part of the community – a source of (among other things) training, information and internet access.

Most of the people involved in the various community groups have some kind of link with the library. If the park is Kennington's lungs, the

Durning is its heart. No wonder it is defended so vigorously whenever cutbacks loom - or that two of the novel's characters are Friends of the Durning Library.

It has played its part in the Friends of Kennington Park too, hosting umpteen public meetings and launch events for the five booklets I've written on the park's history. So it was a no brainer when it came to choosing the venue for the launch of my novel.

Questions for Discussion

1. Do you think Beth is guilty or has Esme been manipulating her from the start?

2. Do you think readers who have children will respond differently to this novel than those who have not? In what ways do you think their responses will differ?

3. Beth and Brian dealt with their grief over the loss of Amy in very different ways. Beth never gave up hope of one day finding out the truth, while Brian tried to move on and rebuild his life with a new family. What do you think of their separate coping mechanisms?

4. The bond between a mother and daughter is incredibly strong. Do you think it's natural that a mother would find it harder to move on with her life in this situation?

5. To what extent do you think Beth is a victim of her own wishful thinking?

6. Do you need to have a belief in reincarnation to believe Beth could be guilty?

7. What beliefs do you think the author holds about religion and reincarnation?

8. Do you believe there are genuine psychics? Have you ever had any experience with a psychic?

9. If Esme really is Amy then Beth would have a second chance at happiness. Do you think she ever really believes that she and Esme could connect and live as mother and daughter?

10. 'Now I know. My daughter was raped.' Not knowing the fate of your child is an unimaginable thing, but in this situation, do you think finding out the truth is far worse? Would it have been better for Beth never to have known what happened to her daughter?

Further Reading Suggestions from R. S. Pateman

We Need to Talk About Kevin Lionel Shriver
A mother examines her role in raising a son who carries out a fatal attack on high school students. Was it nature or nurture? The mother's unblinkingly honest, angry narration makes for an uncomfortable, unforgettable read.

Harvey Mary Chase
A whimsical Pulitzer Prize winning play – and one of my favourite films (the original version, with Jimmy Stewart, that is). It plays with perceptions of mental health and attitudes towards it. A man (who likes a drink or two) says his best friend is an invisible 6'3" white rabbit. And who are we to doubt his sobriety or sanity?

Paranormality: Why We See What Isn't There Robert Wiseman
A Professor of Psychology debunks supernatural phenomena and the work of psychics.

Utterly convincing – unless you *want* to believe otherwise...

So Many Ways to Begin Jon McGregor
A tender, poetic account of a man's struggle with the realisation that his whole life – and sense of self – has been built around a lie.

Blacklands Belinda Bauer
A twelve-year old boy corresponds with a paedophile in his quest to find the grave of his older brother. An unusual and compelling psychological suspense/crime/coming-of-age novel.